Wayward Guilt

Heroes of Grant's Crossing
Book 1

H.M.S. Brown

Leaux Cay Press, LLC

Wayward Guilt

Book 1 of Heroes of Grant's Crossing series

Copyright © 2023 H.M.S. Brown

First edition: July 2023

Library of Congress Control Number: Pending

For any inquiries, please direct all correspondence to the publisher, Leaux Cay Press, LLC, at 1391 W 5th Ave, Suite 102 Columbus, OH 43212.

ISBN 978-1-961411-00-5 (eBook)

ISBN 978-1-961411-01-2 (Paperback)

ISBN 979-8-851792-07-6 (Kindle Paperback)

www.hmsbrown.com

Edited by Sagewood Publishing

Cover design by Kylie Sek at Cover Culture

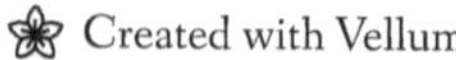 Created with Vellum

Foreword

Wayward Guilt is a work of fiction - Military fiction, small-town fiction. I didn't serve in the military, so I appreciate all those who patiently told me their stories and answered my myriad of questions in preparation for this book. I will be forever grateful to them, for they served in the US Army, some as Rangers, some not. I appreciate all the input the men and women I spoke to provided me. They were all truly generous with both their time and knowledge, and I hope I've done them justice here

Despite my best efforts, I'm sure I've made mistakes in depicting the lives of active-duty men and women in the military. For those, please accept my apologies. Any mistakes made are my own. I can only imagine what living and working in a war zone is like, and in the end, this is a work of fiction. Though it's fiction, I did my best to portray these men and women realistically with the respect and honor they deserve.

The time period of this book runs from approximately 1990 through 2014, with the last couple of chapters and epilogue working their way into 2015. RIP (Ranger Indoctrination Program) is now RASP (Ranger Assessment and Selection Program). DADT (Don't

Ask Don't Tell) has been repealed. Women are now allowed to become Rangers, and gay marriage is legal, though precariously so.

To all of my readers, this has been a labor of love that started during the lockdown in 2020. While I miss having a daily commute to my living room, I am thrilled to finally be able to share this with you.

I'm nervous and anxious and excited all at once. Fine. I'm scared to death but hope you all fall in love with these characters as I did while creating them.

Happy reading and THANK YOU!

- Heather, a.k.a. H.M.S. Brown

Contents

Content Warning ... ix

Prologue ... 1

1. Afghanistan - August 2014 ... 5

2. Grant's Crossing - August 2014 ... 12

3. Grant's Crossing - August 2014 ... 22

4. Grant's Crossing - Late December 2014 Four
months after Joey's funeral ... 32

5. Pittsburgh, Pennsylvania - Spring 1990 ... 41
Joey - 8 years old

6. Grant's Crossing - present day ... 53

7. Grant's Crossing - Spring 1992 ... 60
Joey - 10 years old

8. Grant's Crossing - present day ... 66

9. Grant's Crossing - Summer 1992 ... 72
Joey - 10 years old

10. Grant's Crossing - present day ... 82

11. Grant's Crossing - 1994 ... 88
Joey - 13 years old

12. Grant's Crossing - present day ... 97

13. Grant's Crossing - 1997 ... 100
Joey - 16 years old

14. GRANT'S CROSSING - FALL/WINTER 1997-98 ... 108
Joey - 16 years old

15. Grant's Crossing - present day ... 112

16. Grant's Crossing - January, 1998 ... 114
Joey - 16 years old

17. Grant's Crossing - present day ... 120

18. Grant's Crossing - present day ... 127

19. Grant's Crossing - Spring 2000 ... 132
Joey - 18 years old

20. Grant's Crossing - April 2000   138
Joey - 18 years old

21. Grant's Crossing - Spring 2000   144
Joey - 18 years old

22. Grant's Crossing - present day   153

23. Grant's Crossing - Day after Prom 2000   155
Joey - 18 years old

24. Grant's Crossing - present day   165

25. Grant's Crossing - August 2000   167
Joey - 19 years old

26. Grant's Crossing - present day   174

27. Grant's Crossing - August 2000   177
Joey - 19 years old

28. Grant's Crossing - Present day   185

29. Grant's Crossing - August 2000   188
Joey - 19 years old

30. Grant's Crossing - present day   193

31. Grant's Crossing - September 2001   197
Joey - 20 years old

32. Fort Benning, Georgia - January 2002   204
Joey - 20 years old

33. Grant's Crossing - present day   209

34. Iraq - Autumn 2004   212
Joey - 23 years old

35. Grant's Crossing - present day   218

36. Afghanistan - 2005   221
Joey - 24 years old

37. Grant's Crossing - present day   228

38. Grant's Crossing - July 2010   230
Joey - 28 years old

39. Grant's Crossing - present day   239

40. Afghanistan - January 2011   244
Joey - 29 years old

41. Grant's Crossing - present day   252

42. Delaware, Ohio - Autumn 2012   256
Joey - 31 years old

43. Grant's Crossing - present day   267

44. Grant's Crossing - Autumn 2012   269
    Joey - 31 years old

45. Grant's Crossing - Present day   278

46. Grant's Crossing - August 2014   280

47. Grant's Crossing - present day   283

48. Afghanistan - August 2014   289
    Joey - 33 years old

49. Grant's Crossing - January 2015   298
    Five months after Joey Parker's death

Epilogue   308

Excerpt from Safe Now - Heroes of Grant's
Crossing Book 2   314

Acknowledgments   321
About the Author   323

Content Warning

The book contains situations that may act as triggers for some readers. There is on-page domestic violence, a violent, non-combat death, combat violence, multiple combat deaths, and an on-page attempted suicide.

If you or someone you know is in an abusive relationship, please know that you are not alone and that you have options. The National Domestic Violence Hotline is a 24-hour confidential service for victims, survivors, and all those affected by domestic violence. Help is available 24/7 at 1-800-799- SAFE (7233). Texting is also available. Text "START" to 88788. Online chatting is available via https://www.thehotline.org. All calls are free and confidential. Texting charges may apply.

If you suffer from PTSD and want help, please reach out to https://www.ptsd.va.gov.
   In addition, the Veterans Crisis Line offers 24/7, confidential crisis support for Veterans and their loved ones. You don't have to be enrolled in VA benefits or health care to connect. You can dial 988, then press 1. Or you can text 838255. Texting charges may apply.

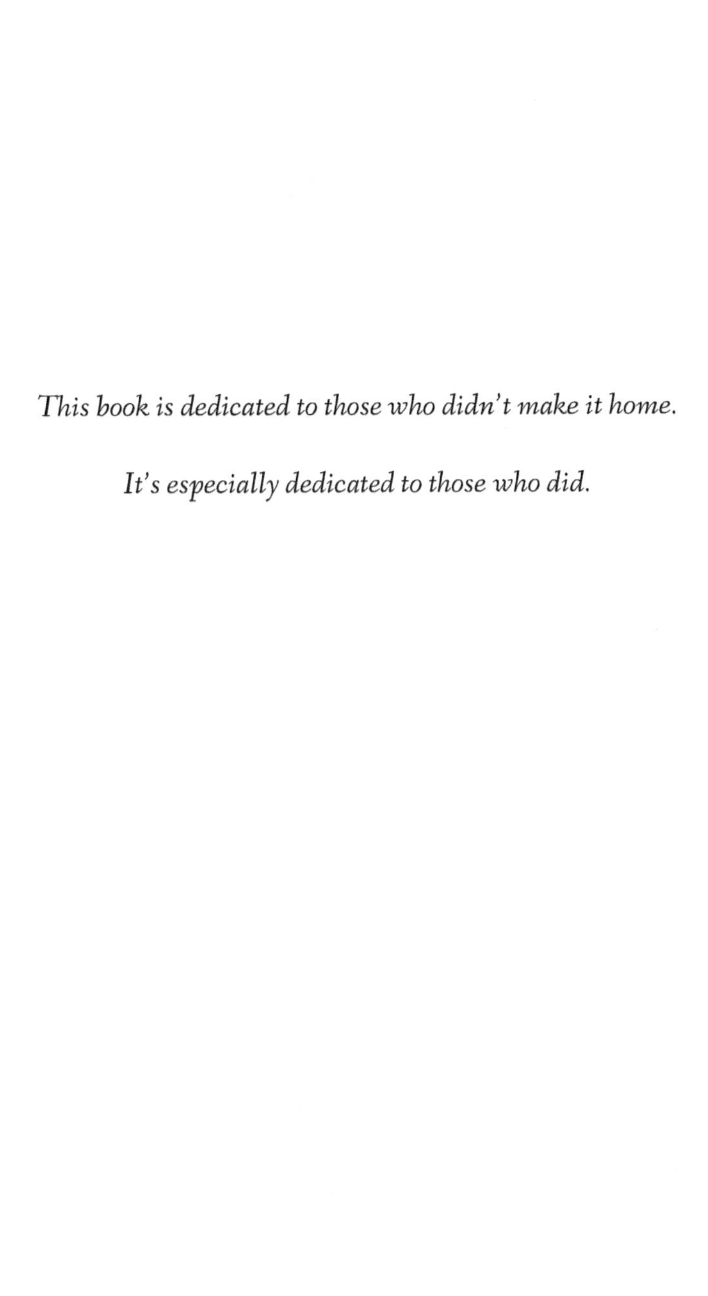

This book is dedicated to those who didn't make it home.

It's especially dedicated to those who did.

Prologue

Grant's Crossing, Ohio - September 15, 2001

WITH HIS DAUGHTER AT HER FRIEND'S HOUSE FOR THE
evening, Abe Mitchell looked forward to a quiet dinner with his son.
Derek, a year out of high school, had been rather quiet since he and
his friends met with the Army recruiter in town today.

They grilled out for dinner, so Abe finished up with the steaks
and veggies on the grill while Derek set the table and fixed drinks.

Smiling as if he'd created a masterpiece, Abe carefully dished
out their food and sat down. Not wanting to rush his son, he talked
of his latest renovation jobs before Derek brought up the meeting
with the recruiter.

"I've decided, Dad," Derek said while stabbing a piece of
zucchini. "I want to enlist."

With a deep breath, Abe set down his fork while he finished
chewing a bite of his steak.

Uncharacteristically nervous, Derek lifted his gaze.

Abe wiped his mouth with a napkin, carefully folded it, and
placed it on the table. "And you're sure this is what you want to do?"

"Yes."

"What would you do?"

"I'd be a combat medic."

"Combat medic," his dad repeated, knowing the title alone implied his son would be in combat zones. Abe's brother-in-law, Mick, was drafted and served in Vietnam just prior to the fall of Saigon. He now walked with a cane and a prosthetic limb as a result. "When would you leave for basic training?"

"Within a month or two. Possibly sooner, depending on how quickly everything checks out."

Abe grunted in response.

So soon.

"What about Joey and Juan?" Derek's best friend, Joey, whom Abe considered a second son, practically lived at their house since Joey's mom worked long hours just to make ends meet. Juan, whom his friends affectionately called Tank, was often there as well.

"They're enlisting, too. We want to be Rangers."

Abe arched his brows but appreciated the confidence in his son's tone when he said the word Rangers.

Derek gestured with his fork while explaining. "They're a more elite kind of soldier. There's extra training, tougher requirements."

"Do Joey and Juan want to be combat medics as well?"

"No. Not sure. The recruiter said they could test for other jobs to see what they'd be good at doing."

"For how long would you serve?"

"Four years."

"Four years, huh?" Abe said, more to himself than Derek, though his son heard him anyway.

"Yes."

"What would you do after?"

Derek paused. "After?"

"Yes. Would you be a doctor or something?"

"Oh." He took a quick sip from his glass. "No. But I could be an EMT. A paramedic."

Abe nodded and took another bite of his dinner. "Are you

looking for my permission? Because you're old enough to do this on your own, son."

"I want to do this, and yes. I know. But," Derek took a deep breath and took a second or two to look his father in the eye. "I'd rather go with your blessing."

"My blessing, huh?"

"Yes. Please."

Abe grabbed his glass and took a drink. Setting it down, he exhaled slowly and nodded. He aimed his brown eyes toward his son and smiled. "You've got it."

"Yeah?" Derek broke into a big grin, audibly exhaling in relief.

"Yes," Abe assured him. "It takes courage to take action after what happened in New York this week. I'm worried that whatever skills you learn as a medic will definitely be put to use."

Derek nodded without answering.

"As you know, I didn't serve. Vietnam ended while I was still in high school, and Desert Storm started when you and Lainee were little and my business was just taking off. So, I admire you for having the guts to serve."

* * *

Late October 2001

Abe pulled into the departure lane at Port Columbus International Airport and flicked on his hazard lights. Putting the truck in park, he stepped out to say his goodbyes to Derek and Joey, who were both heading to Fort Benning, Georgia for their basic training.

They would meet Tank at the gate since his own family was dropping him off.

With no bags, Derek and Joey only had the large, brown envelopes provided to them by their recruiter. They'd get everything else they needed upon arrival at Fort Benning.

Derek gave Lainee a big bear hug. "Better write me, Lainee, ok?"

"I will. I promise!" She gave Joey a hug, too. "Bye, Joey."

After hugging his sister, Derek turned to Abe, who followed up his handshake with a fatherly embrace.

"Thanks, Dad."

"I'm proud of you, son." Abe hugged Joey for a few extra moments as well. "I'm proud of you, too, Joey. Be careful."

Looking at them both, he placed a hand on the shoulder of each young man standing before him. "You two take care of each other, okay?"

"We will, Dad."

"We will, Mr. M."

Derek and Joey looked back toward Abe and Lainee and gave a final wave.

"Bye Dad! Bye Lainee!"

Abe returned their wave. "Bye!"

Derek and Joey exchanged nervous, yet excited glances before disappearing on the other side of the sliding glass doors.

Once they were out of sight, Abe exhaled as he and Lainee climbed back into his truck. Taking a moment to fasten his seatbelt, he glanced back at the closed doors to the terminal and worried about when he'd see his son again.

As if reading Abe's thoughts, Lainee spoke up. "We'll see him at graduation, Dad."

"You're right," Abe smiled her way and pulled away from the curb. "We'll see him then."

Chapter 1

Afghanistan - August 2014

THE LAST GUNSHOTS ECHOED ACROSS THE VALLEY AS FAINT beams of morning light crept through the mountain peaks of Afghanistan. Soldiers rose from their positions of cover, each taking inventory of the dozens of bodies lying on the ground. Most, but not all, were Taliban fighters.

As the smoke lifted, the medic gave chest compressions to a fallen Army Ranger. The rhythm broke the silence. "Come on, Joey! Come back."

"SERGEANT!"

Sergeant First Class Derek Mitchell lifted his gaze; his blood-covered hands rested on the dead man's chest while his grief-stricken eyes stared at the two men closest to him.

"He's gone, Doc."

"No!" Derek's green eyes shifted from soldier to soldier. "He can't. How will I..."

He turned his palms upwards and stared at the still-wet blood that covered them. These hands had saved the lives of so many of his fellow Rangers.

Just not his best friend's life.

Not today.

Derek's gaze drifted sideways to the man he'd known since he was ten years old, to the man who now lay dead on the filthy, callous ground in the middle of nowhere.

Joey's glazed blue eyes stared up at nothing.

Wiping his bloody hands on his pants, Derek closed his eyes and swallowed hard. "Fuck." He made the sign of the cross before gently closing Joey's eyelids.

It wasn't supposed to end this way.

It never once occurred to him that his best friend might not make it back.

The captain motioned with a circular wave of his arm. "Let's move out."

Derek gripped the front handles of the stretcher carrying Joey Parker. Weary from the losses they couldn't prevent, the men not carrying the two fallen men or their gear held their weapons at the ready, remaining somber yet vigilant. One ambush was more than they'd bargained for that morning, and it was time to move before Taliban reinforcements came back for another.

Derek risked a final glance back to where he'd last seen his best friend alive. His gaze followed a trio of snow finches fluttering up from the blood-soaked ground toward the light of the rising sun.

Another Ranger tapped Derek's shoulder, prompting him to get moving.

In the desolate mountains of the Hindu Kush, the cadence of their combat boots hitting the dirt was the only sound breaking the mournful silence.

Bagram Air Base

An Army Ranger, with his arm in a black sling, walked down a long hallway toward a room containing a handful of gurneys, two of which supported the fallen soldiers from their early morning mission, both carefully preserved in cold, black body bags. He winced in pain as he adjusted the strap on his sling supporting his newly-injured shoulder and stepped inside.

His own arm stitched up from the same mission, Derek kept vigil by the table supporting the body of his best friend, newly-promoted Sergeant First Class Joseph Miles Parker. Still sporting smeared blood on his uniform, Derek hadn't left his friend's side since they'd returned to camp that morning.

"Hey, Sarge?" Rass said, his Texas twang singing through.

Derek lifted his bloodshot eyes to reveal the devastation that hardened his face. Since grade school, he and Joey had been inseparable, best friends since they were ten. Like so many young men and women barely out of high school, Derek, Joey, and their friend, Tank, enlisted together right after 9/11.

Thirteen years later, one of them wouldn't make it home.

"Cap'n wants to see you."

Slow to react, Derek nodded and stood up. He placed his hand on Joey's shoulder, separated by a stiff piece of plastic, and let his thoughts wander. "I'm sorry, brother."

"Want me to stay with 'im, Doc?"

"No thanks, Rass." Derek shook his head and walked out the way the other Ranger had just come in. He met his captain just outside the CO's office. "Captain."

"Sergeant Mitchell." The captain beckoned him into a room where a chaplain was waiting. "Upon the death of his mother two years ago, Sergeant Parker named you as one of his two emergency contacts. Were you aware of that?"

"Yes, sir."

"The Army will notify his other emergency contact, Abraham Mitchell, back home."

"Dad?" Derek's head popped up, crushed at the thought of his dad being visited by another Army officer and chaplain.

The captain regarded Derek with sympathy and nodded his

head. "You're being granted emergency leave to escort him back home."

"Yes, sir."

"At Dover, they'll help you work through the details for the honor ceremony and interment. You have thirty days to take care of Parker and get your head back in the game. Then you'll report back to Fort Benning."

"Sir?"

"You're not coming back here, Sergeant. Pack up his personal effects. You leave at 1300."

"Yes, sir." Derek saluted the captain and left.

Muscle memory got him back to the barracks, where he was greeted with near silence. The men exchanged somber glances, saddened by the loss of two men on the overnight mission. A small chorus of "Doc" or "Sarge" called out to Derek as he drifted toward his bunk.

Barely acknowledging them, he sat down across from Parker's bunk.

"Need some help packin'?" Rass sat down on the next bunk over.

"What?" Derek said quietly, blinking his eyes when it registered someone had spoken to him.

"Would you like some help packin' Parker's personal effects, Doc?"

Jonesy sat down next to Rass. "We'll help you, Sarge."

Derek grunted in the affirmative and sat there, staring at the floor, while they started packing Joey's personal effects into a duffle bag.

A notebook slid off the bed onto the floor with a slap. Rass leaned in to pick it up, but stayed his hand when Derek reached it first. A picture slipped out from between the pages.

Derek closed the notebook and stared at the picture of Joey and his long-time boyfriend, Logan. Both men smiled at each other as if they had the rest of their lives together.

Who would tell Logan?

Derek opened the notebook enough to tuck the picture back inside when he caught a few words. Joey always wrote in this notebook as if it were a journal of his innermost thoughts. It was full of letters.

To Logan.

Derek started reading, then snapped it closed. He squeezed his eyes shut, silently berating himself for intruding on his best friend's innermost thoughts.

No. Not yet.

After a few minutes, he went one bunk over to pack his own duffle for the trip home.

Curious, Rass smacked Jonesy with his good arm.

Maintaining a watchful eye Jonesy continued packing Joey's belongings. "Whatcha doin', Sarge?"

Derek stuffed two shirts into his own duffle. "Packing."

"Yeah, but that's your stuff."

"Yeah."

"Where are you going?"

"Home."

"Huh?"

"Joey's my brother. He's family. I'm taking him home."

"Ladies and gentlemen," the captain's voice came over the speaker as the plane taxied from the runway to the terminal at the airport in Columbus, Ohio, "we are pulling up to the jetway now. Our plane is carrying the remains of a deceased soldier returning home from Afghanistan, so we ask that all passengers remain in their seat and wait to retrieve your belongings from the overhead bins until he has been safely removed from the aircraft."

The cabin volume dropped as low voices murmured over the sound of the droning engine. In their seats, passengers turned left and right to catch a glimpse of movement through the windows.

Traveling in his fatigues, Derek's detached expression never changed during the captain's announcement. He'd already arranged to exit the aircraft and meet them on the tarmac. At least now, he wouldn't have to navigate his way through a crowd of people.

A flight attendant wearing a friendly smile approached. "Sir? You're welcome to disembark now. Please follow me."

"Yes, ma'am."

Derek stood up to his full height of just over six feet and shoved the book he never got around to reading into his backpack. He blindly followed the flight attendant to the front of the aircraft, never once caring that all eyes were on him as he strode down the narrow aisle.

Through the windows, the passengers stayed silent while a flag-draped casket moved down the conveyor belt into the waiting hands of the baggage handlers.

Derek crossed through the jetway and then down the outside steps to the tarmac. By the time he walked to the other side of the plane, baggage handlers were already carefully loading Joey's casket into the transport vehicle. Derek grabbed their two duffle bags off the conveyor belt and placed them inside the truck.

He accompanied his best friend's body to an outbuilding where a hearse waited to take him to the funeral home in Grant's Crossing. He caught the first glimpse of his dad's SUV as they slowed to a stop. Without a word to his father, he stepped around to the back of the transport to take care of Joey.

Abe Mitchell, standing nearly as tall as his son and with wavy, salt and pepper hair, walked over but stopped in his tracks as they moved Joey's casket out of the truck for the few short steps to the hearse.

Derek made it a point to avoid making eye contact with anyone. His dad could read him like a book and would know that, despite all his years serving as an Army Ranger, he was barely holding himself together.

The owner of the Frazier Funeral home stepped out of the hearse to offer Derek assurances that he would take good care of Joey, whose remains they had entrusted him to carry home.

Derek stepped away to grab their duffle bags, not paying attention to Jeff Frazier's words to his father.

"I'm so very sorry for your loss, Abe. I'll take good care of Joey and see that he arrives back home safely."

"Thank you, Jeff."

Abe waited for his son as the hearse drove away.

Derek returned and set the duffles on the pavement. He stood up to face his father. "Dad."

"Son."

Derek's chin trembled as he struggled to get words out. When he did, his voice cracked. "I couldn't save him."

Abe nodded and embraced his son for a long minute.

A few moments later, Abe reached down for one of the duffles. "Come on, son. Let's go home."

Chapter 2

Grant's Crossing - August 2014

Abe Mitchell drove the hour-long ride home to Grant's Crossing, Ohio, in silence since Derek had drifted off to sleep by the time they'd entered the freeway. Parking his SUV in the driveway next to his beautifully renovated Victorian home, Abe reached over and put his hand on Derek's shoulder to wake him up. "We're home, son."

Derek jerked awake, taking a few moments to look out the windows and get his bearings. He turned and focused his eyes on his dad.

"You go on. Your Uncle Mick is already inside. I'll get the bags."

Accustomed to following orders, Derek wandered inside, where his maternal uncle, a veteran Marine who left his leg behind in Vietnam, greeted him with an understanding embrace.

Abe followed his son inside. Dropping the duffle bags inside the entryway, he exchanged a look with his brother-in-law, who, like Abe, shared the same concern but wasn't as fazed by Derek's detached state of mind.

"Your bedroom's ready," Abe said to Derek. "I've got beer and pop in the fridge. Plenty of snacks, too. Lainee and Tasha will be over in the morning with Catie. Um, are you hungry?"

"Yes, sir." Derek responded by rote.

Abe didn't think Derek had any idea if he were hungry or not. One look at his son's detached expression and Abe knew eating out was not in the cards for tonight. "I was going to suggest going out, but I can just bring something home instead."

"Yes, sir."

Abe remained silent while Derek's eyes scanned the room as if subconsciously cataloging entrances, exits, anywhere someone could hide or anywhere they could take cover.

His son was trained for combat zones, not the civilian world.

"I'll be back soon." Abe turned his eyes back to his brother-in-law; grateful he'd been able to extend his visit after they'd received notification about Joey's death earlier that week. "Mick?"

"I'll be here, Abe." Mick assured him as he led Derek to a chair at the large kitchen table.

Abe made the short drive to the town square that made up the heart of the small town of Grant's Crossing. He parked in front of Jo's Bar & Grille, a century-old tavern-turned-local sports bar. Walking inside, an enthusiastic crowd greeted him. Many knew Derek was coming home, but they did not yet know about Joey. Having barely gone out since the day the officer and chaplain informed him of Joey's death, the bad news hadn't yet made its way through the town grapevine. He could thank the funeral home director's discretion for that.

As he stepped up to the bar, he couldn't hold back the ghost of a smile when he caught sight of a big *WELCOME HOME DEREK* sign hanging above the bar.

"Hi, Abe." The ever-cheerful owner, Jo Porter, greeted him with an excited grin. "I heard you were heading out to the airport to get Derek. Where are you hiding him? We have the welcome party all planned."

Jo's Bar & Grille was always the go-to place for welcome-home parties whenever the active-duty men and women of Grant's

Crossing came home on leave. It may have been a small town, but it did more than its fair share of service to this country and always ensured those who served were treated well upon their return.

"Hi, Jo. Yes. Derek's at home with Mick right now. May I get three bacon cheeseburgers to go, please?"

Jo tilted her head to the side. "He's not coming in?" she asked.

Abe's eyes scanned the length of the bar where he caught sight of Tank and Kiro, who made no effort to hide their interest in his arrival. "Not tonight," he answered, turning his attention back to Jo. "He needs to rest up a bit."

"Jet lag, huh?"

Spending many years as an active-duty Army wife, Jo smiled in understanding. "I'll get those right out for you."

"Thanks."

Juan "Tank" Palacios and Kiro Marinov exchanged glances, then made their way around the corner of the large, rectangular bar in the center of the restaurant.

"Mr. Mitchell," Tank said.

"Juan." Abe turned to other young man. "Kiro."

In a quiet voice so as not to be overheard, Kiro leaned his elbow against the bar, his brows furrowed. "What's wrong, Abe?" Kiro asked. "I'm not complaining he's home, but don't Derek and Joey have another month or two on their deployment? Why is he back already? Is Joey back, too?"

Abe grunted in response, pressing an imaginary spot on the floor with the toe of his boot.

Tank's war-hardened expression remained unreadable though Abe was certain he already knew something was wrong.

"Abe?" Kiro prompted.

Unsure how to respond, Abe met each of their gazes for a few seconds, then glanced away as someone else passed them by. Confident they wouldn't be overheard, he took a deep breath and leaned closer. "Joey didn't make it."

"What?" Kiro recoiled like he'd taken a kick to the stomach.

Tank's face fell. He set his bottle of beer on the bar. He turned and leaned both hands against the bar, exhaling slowly.

"He's gone, Kiro. Killed in action. They notified us at the house this week."

"Killed?" Kiro's mouth opened, but no other words came out.

"Derek escorted his body home." Abe shook his head. "I don't know more than that at this stage. He looks exhausted. Slept the entire way back from the airport."

"Jesus, Abe. I'm sorry. What do you need? I can come by later...."

"Not tonight. Please." Abe held up his hand. "Tomorrow would be better."

"Yeah. Yeah. Sure."

"Derek's barely said two words since I picked him up. I doubt he's eaten or slept in a while."

Having trouble keeping his emotions in check, Abe stared at the ground for a few moments to collect himself. With a shake of his head, he lifted his eyes. Tank was still leaning against the bar, eyes closed, his head hanging down.

"His heart's been ripped right out of him." Abe squeezed his upheld hand into a fist for emphasis.

"And yours, too," Kiro said.

Abe blinked, stunned by the revelation. Joey had always been like a second son to him, but his grief would have to take a back seat to remain strong for Derek.

"He's just...," Abe exhaled. "I don't know. Still in shock, I guess."

Kiro nodded in understanding. As firefighter paramedics, he and Tank had seen their fair share of families at their worst while dealing with the loss of homes, families, and friends.

"Kiro?" Abe's expression lacked his usual confidence.

"Yes?"

"If you come over tomorrow, would you please come alone?"

"Alone?"

"I don't think he'll be up for crowds for a while, and I don't want to overwhelm him with a houseful of visitors. I don't even know how long he's going to be here."

"Of course. I'll bring lunch." Kiro tilted his head toward Tank. "He won't be able to stay away, you know."

"I know."

Kiro put his hand on Abe's shoulder. "Abe?"

"Hmm."

"Anything you need, ok? I mean it."

Abe nodded, then hesitated, sensing all eyes on him before he continued in a low voice. "Would you mind letting folks know? I don't have it in me. Not... not tonight."

"Yeah. Sure."

"We'll do it," Tank cut in, still staring at the bar.

"Appreciate it."

Jo came back up with the bag, carrying their dinners inside.

He pulled his wallet out to pay. "What do I owe you, Jo?"

She waved her hand dismissively. "It's on me, Abe. Let Derek know we're glad he's back. Can't wait to see him."

Abe forced a smile as he put his wallet back in his pocket. "Thanks." Grabbing the bag, he gave a last nod to Kiro and Tank and walked out.

Inside, everyone had gone quiet as all eyes turned to Kiro and Tank.

Saying nothing, Tank's eyes traveled back around the room and met the gaze of Jo's husband, Mike Porter, who was behind the bar drying off glasses. A retired Army veteran from Desert Storm, his face dropped as he read Tank's expression. He turned his head toward the door through which Abe had just exited, then back to Tank and Kiro.

His grim face mouthed, *"Joey?"*

Tank responded with an almost imperceptible nod.

With a resigned exhale, Mike stopped drying the glass and dropped his chin to his chest.

"Hey Kiro," a voice called out from the crowd as curious eyes turned their attention back to the front of the bar where he was standing. "What's up?"

"Yeah, Tank. What happened?" Another person followed up.

"When's Derek getting here?" Yet another excited voice asked.

Closing his eyes, Kiro dropped his gaze to the floor and took a deep breath or two before facing them. His voice cracked when he opened his mouth in an attempt to speak.

Tank reached his arm around Kiro's shoulders and leaned in. He spoke softly so only Kiro could hear. "It's okay. I've got it."

Kiro's eyes were already watering as he responded with a nod.

Tank enlisted with Derek and Joey after 9/11. He served in Iraq with Joey and in Afghanistan with both of them. Tank's jaw was tight when he lifted his eyes, and a crease had formed between his brows in a futile attempt to school his expression before delivering the heartbreaking news to the rest of the crowd. He clenched his fist, struggling to maintain his composure before speaking.

With his arm still around Kiro's shoulders, whether to support Kiro or himself, he didn't know, he lifted his eyes to face all his friends and family in the room. Everyone there was someone he'd grown up with or had known his entire life.

"I uh... have some bad news." He paused long enough to take a breath. Scanning the room, Tank swallowed hard before continuing. "We lost Joey. He was killed in action."

There was a collective gasp, followed by many people muttering "No!" throughout the room. Several brought their hands to their mouths upon hearing his words. Jo's eyes watered as her husband wrapped his arms around her and pulled her close. Her older brother, Quinn, had been engaged to Joey's mom when she passed away. Joey would have become her nephew.

"He was killed in action and Derek... escorted his body home." He held up a hand as they started calling out questions. "Abe asked us to give them their space."

Many nodded in tacit agreement, the mood of the night clearly turning somber as if a dark cloud now loomed overhead.

Tank threw down some bills and chugged the last of his beer. With one last look at Kiro, he slammed the bottle down and left.

As soon as he walked out, Kiro reached into his back pocket for his wallet. "Jo? Can I settle up, please?"

Jo wiped tears off her face and nodded. "Yeah. Sure."

Kiro paid his tab. "Oh, and Jo?" He pointed up at the far wall. "Do you think you can get rid of the sign?"

"What?"

"D's not here to celebrate."

"Oh. Yeah," she sniffed; having seen firsthand the effect the death of a soldier has on military families. "Of course."

Mike was already ripping the sign off the wall as Kiro walked out.

Abe sat inside his car with the engine running for a few minutes before he could bring himself to go inside his house.

Two years earlier, after his mom died, Joey Parker had no other blood relatives and asked Abe to be his emergency contact, claiming he wanted the Army to notify someone who cared should he ever fall in combat.

He also gave Abe power of attorney for his finances.

Just in case.

Having always considered Joey a second son, Abe never hesitated to sign on the dotted line. Joey explained he made Derek his beneficiary and emergency contact as well, so the Army would, he hoped, grant him emergency leave should the worst ever happen.

Abe now appreciated and hated how prescient yet thoughtful Joey had been.

The Mitchell family had treated Joey like one of their own for as long as they could remember. But tonight, as a parent, Abe had to remain strong for his other son, no matter how broken his own heart was. With a deep breath, Abe scrubbed his beard with his hand and opened the car door. Grabbing the food from where it sat on the passenger seat, he stepped out onto the driveway.

Tank had pulled up while Abe sat in his car. He patiently waited for Abe to exit his vehicle, then approached with a somber expression on his face. "I'm very sorry, Mr. Mitchell."

Abe paused long enough to acknowledge him with a quick nod. "Thank you, Juan."

"How's Doc?" he tilted his head toward the house to indicate he was asking about Derek. "How's he doing?"

Abe breathed out with a shake of his head. "When I picked him up, the only thing he said," his voice caught in his throat, "was that he couldn't save him."

"*Dios mio,*" Tank kicked at the ground. "He was there."

Neither man spoke while they contemplated what had to be going through Derek's head right now.

"You, uh, want to come in?"

"No thanks, Mr. Mitchell. If it's all the same to you, I'll stay out here." Tank sat on the bench outside the front door on the covered porch.

Abe grabbed the doorknob but hesitated. "I'll leave it unlocked."

Tank only nodded as the front door closed. He called his wife to let her know he loved her and why he wouldn't be home that night. He may have been honorably discharged a few years earlier, but it was thanks to Derek he was alive at all.

As if it were his duty to stand guard, he reverted to his Ranger training, eyes scanning the neighborhood from the Mitchells' front porch, ready to fend off any unwelcome visitors, well-intentioned or otherwise.

As Abe entered the house, Mick limped to the front door, relying on his cane more than usual. He intercepted Abe by grabbing his arm and kept his voice low. "He hasn't said a word."

Abe nodded and tilted his head toward the front porch where Tank was keeping vigil. "Juan is out front. He may be there a while."

Mick understood and shuffled back to the kitchen.

Pausing a moment to ready himself, Abe followed Mick and walked in to find Derek sitting at the kitchen table. He'd wrapped his fingers around a bottle of beer that he occasionally brought up to his lips for a swig, eyes locked on nothing in particular.

Abe understood Mick's worried expression when he saw the two empty beer bottles already on the table. Mick's coffee cup sat empty.

Abe pulled the food out of the bag, setting the plastic containers down. He handed one to Derek before handing another to Mick and placing the last in front of his own seat. "Burgers from Jo's. Fries, too. Want some ketchup?"

Derek shook his head as he opened the container of food and ate as if on autopilot. His eyes checked the door from time to time while chewing each bite in slow motion.

With a worried glance, Abe grabbed the ketchup and Cokes out of the fridge for himself and Mick. He dumped some ice in glasses and poured their drinks. Before sitting down, he grabbed the two already-empty beer bottles off the table to drop them in the recycling bin by the back door. Derek took one last pull from his current bottle, his eyes remaining glued to his father, half expecting him to comment on his drinking.

"You're home, son." Abe popped the cap off another bottle and placed it in front of Derek. "And you're safe. That's all that matters now."

Derek gripped the proffered bottle and eased it closer to him as if it were a safety net offering the only security and comfort he could find.

Abe sat down to his own dinner and took a drink, then squeezed some ketchup onto the carryout container. He dug into his burger as the three men ate in silence.

If his son wanted to drown his grief in the bottle tonight, let him at least be at home where he was safe and had people to watch over him.

Couldn't blame a man who wanted to forget.

Chapter 3

Grant's Crossing - August 2014

Sweat dripped down Derek's back under the blistering sun, with temperatures already topping 85 degrees by ten am. Birds sang from atop the branches of trees whose leaves were just beginning to fade in the late summer heat. Beneath the shade of a tall oak tree, a group of mourners assembled near a freshly dug grave.

"Good morning, family and friends," the Army chaplain began to speak, temporarily bringing an end to the quiet whispers. Keeping their heads down so as not to make eye contact with each other, they listened as he offered words of comfort.

"It is our honor to welcome you today, as we gather together to remember the life and service of Sergeant First Class Joseph Miles Parker."

Derek had been in a daze all morning long, barely registering being led around by both his father and Tank, who were both hurting as well. Nothing clicked with Derek as his body merely went through the motions. His brain was in a fog, relying on his friends and family to guide him from one place to another. At least his Army training was drilled into him enough to react properly when addressed by any officers in attendance.

"No plot on this sacred ground can be purchased; each must be earned. And we know that Sergeant First Class Joseph Miles Parker has earned his place among us here today."

Throughout the entire ceremony, Derek's thousand-yard stare never once wavered.

"For our comrade in arms," the chaplain continued, "our nation bestows military honors. In life, he honored the flag, and in death, the flag will honor him."

The chaplain beckoned Derek, his father, and his sister to stand. In full dress uniform, Derek stood, remaining stoic as the lone rifle volleyed three shots, each one echoing in the distance. The only sign it fazed him at all was a rapid blink of his eyes after the first shot, until it sounded again. Another blink.

A third shot.

A third blink.

Derek sat back down in between his sister and his father. Out of character for her, but precisely what he needed, his sister held his hand throughout the entire ceremony. He felt out of place sitting down while in uniform, but Joey had no blood relatives, no next of kin. Joey had designated Abe and Derek as the ones he trusted to take care of everything in case he should ever fall.

Another officer assisting with the ceremony approached and stood in front of Abe. He bent forward. "On behalf of the President of the United States, the United States Army, and a grateful nation, please accept this flag as a symbol of our appreciation for your loved one's honorable and faithful service."

Tank's hand fell to Derek's shoulder as Abe accepted the neatly-folded flag that had just covered Joey's coffin. Tank had been standing steady behind him throughout the ceremony, wearing the same dress uniform and tan beret.

Chaplain Bryant gave a brief benediction. After the service, he said a few additional words of comfort to Derek.

Derek acknowledged the Chaplain, then turned to work his way toward the car with his family. The house would quickly fill up with people and those paying their respects, and the sooner he could get home, the sooner he could pour himself a drink.

All he wanted to do was forget.

Perhaps, he could return to being oblivious to the events of the day within a few hours.

Derek eyed the people there. A good number of his high school friends he hadn't seen since he was last on leave, and their families, all dressed in black in the hot August heat. In the distance, he saw a tall man in a dark suit walking away from the crowd. When the man turned around for one last look, Derek recognized both the anguish and the heartbreak on his face.

Logan Shepherd.

Equally devastated by Joey's death, both men locked gazes for a few seconds before Logan, barely maintaining his own composure, turned and walked away. Derek turned his eyes back to Joey's gravesite just as Quinn Strager dropped flowers by Renee Parker's gravestone. It broke Derek's heart that she and her son were both laid to rest so young.

Life could be so fucking cruel.

Feeling his father's hand on his back to guide him, Derek reverted to nodding at all those offering condolences, making only a few exceptions to actually talk to them.

Derek couldn't carry on the same: "I'm sorry for your loss" or "He's in a better place" conversations for long. Fortunately, his dad and Tank both ran interference and stepped in whenever someone asked whether Derek was with Joey when he died.

Though they probably meant well, he couldn't bring himself to deal with what he felt were nothing more than shallow pleasantries combined with morbid curiosity. A disheartening combination for someone merely wishing to get away from them all.

Mike Porter, the only other mourner in dress uniform, served as one of Joey's pallbearers. Derek concentrated on his captain's bars, shining brightly in the morning sun. Mike took a few moments to offer relatable comfort to Derek afterward. Promising to be at the house later, they parted ways so Derek could rejoin his dad and sister.

Derek sat at the large desk in his father's office and gulped down a glass of whiskey. He was refilling his glass when Tank entered. He held up the bottle as an offer.

When Tank shook his head, Derek set it back on the desk, not bothering to replace the cap.

"Whiskey, huh?"

"Dad's out of beer."

"How many have you had so far?"

"Just a few." He took a sip. "I'm shooting for 68."

Tank let out a humorless chuckle at the 68 Whiskey combat medic reference and sat down in a chair across the desk. "I talked to Marisol's brother out there. Carlos Ramirez was his name, I think?"

"Yeah. I saw him." Derek took a drink, thinking back to when Joey had told him Ramirez had saved his life the night his father died. "I couldn't do what he did."

Tank's lips tightened, knowing full well what Derek was referring to, but he said nothing.

"I'm not going back."

"Hate to break it to you, Doc, but you don't have a choice in the matter."

"To the sandbox, I mean. My orders are to go to Fort Benning when my leave is up. I'll finish out my last few months there and then, if I can, I'll be home by Christmas. I think. Or New Year's."

"You're not going to re-up again?"

"Nope."

Tank gave a slow nod. "Didn't think so."

Derek poured himself another glass of whiskey and downed most of it in one swallow after he set the bottle back down on the desk.

"What are you going to do when you get out?"

"Get a job. Find a place to live. Dad'll let me stay here for a while if I need to."

"You'll come out with your paramedic certifications, right?"

"Yep."

"Well, the lead B-shift paramedic is looking to move back out to California in the new year so he can get back with the Hotshots. That means a spot'll be opening up at GC Fire. You should put your name in for a January start. You'd be working with Kiro. With all your experience...."

Derek took another sip and gave a hard stare. "No *civilian* experience...."

"Something you'll learn, Doc." Tank exhaled in frustration. "Come on. I've seen you at work before. I've seen you save lives."

Derek glanced up from his desk for a moment, thinking back to their last mission together.

"Besides, you've talked about working as an EMT since before we even enlisted. Employers are jumping at the chance to hire veterans. Chief Travis is a good guy to work for. I mean, his humor is for shit," Tank chuckled, "but he's fair. I'm on shift tomorrow and will talk to him for you."

Derek finished his glass of whiskey and nodded, resigned to the fact that he'll eventually have to reenter the civilian world. "Ok. Yeah. Thanks."

"Wouldn't hurt if you came to the station one day while you're home." Tank stood up to leave. "At least you could meet him."

The two men stayed in relative silence for a long minute. Derek poured another drink for himself.

"92%."

Tank's eyes lifted. "Come again?"

"92%." Derek stared at his glass, angling it as if getting a better view of the amber liquid inside before taking a sip. "92% of all soldiers in Iraq and Afghanistan make it home alive. You were part of that. Why wasn't Joey?"

Tank stepped over to the door but turned around with his hand on the doorknob. He had numerous scars on his own body that served as constant reminders of the injuries he sustained that had nearly cost him his life. Were it not for Derek's skills and quick work in the field, he wouldn't be standing here today.

He wouldn't be married to his high school sweetheart, and he wouldn't have his three children.

He owed everything to his friend.

Derek glanced up, his eyes glazing over like he was already well on his way to hitting that 68-glass goal.

"It wasn't your fault, Doc," Tank said, the words hanging in the air. "I heard from Rass. He told me what happened." He took a breath and offered a reassuring glance. "He's worried about you. So's Jonesy."

"Roger that," Derek mumbled into his glass before realizing he'd already emptied it.

Derek poured yet another glass with Tank looking on. His hands were noticeably less steady than they were a couple of glasses earlier.

With a sad exhale, Tank walked out and closed the door behind him. Abe, Mike, and Kiro each lifted their faces up to Tank when he walked into the room. With the funeral over and the house full of food brought in by friends, family, and neighbors, Abe was ready to take it easy for a while and concentrate on Derek.

Tank met his eyes. "Abe, mind if I go up and get him a change of clothes? I hate for him to drink while in uniform."

"Yeah." Abe started to rise, but Kiro's hand on his shoulder stopped him.

"I'll get it." Kiro disappeared up the stairs.

"He's blaming himself." Tank said as he took Kiro's place next to Abe. "I've talked to one guy who was there, and it was bad. But from what he said, Derek did everything he could. I mean, Derek's good, Abe. Really good. I can't even tell you how many lives he's saved, my own included, but he's taking this one personally, like Joey's only gone because he failed in some way."

Abe nodded absently, but his shoulders still sagged.

"He didn't kill Joey, Abe. Help me convince your son it wasn't his fault."

Kiro returned with a pair of jeans and a t-shirt for Derek, going straight into the office.

"Kiro and I are on shift tomorrow, but I'll stop by the day after to check in on him. I'll do that every day if I have to. He just looks...." Tank paused and exhaled.

"Looks what?" Abe asked, raising his eyes to meet Tank's.

"He has that look I've seen from some men who ended up heading down a really dark path."

In the chair to Tank's left, Mike Porter nodded in agreement.

"But they come back, right? After a while?" Abe asked, knowing he was kidding himself but desperate not to lose Derek, too.

Abe thought back to how he'd set the example when he ventured down a similar path after the death of his wife, Derek's mother, once holing himself up in that same office with his own bottle of whiskey. When his wife died, he'd drowned his sorrows with his brother and brother-in-law... for the first few days at least. After that, he had the kids to keep him tethered to real life until he sent them to New Orleans for a summer to be with his in-laws. Once they were gone, he returned to the bottle.

That he still kept his business going was thanks to his brother. That he kept eating and functioning at all was thanks to his wife's best friend, who, along with her husband and son, Kiro, now took the same care of Derek.

Both Abe's brother and brother-in-law currently sat across from him, ready to stand vigil again, this time for their nephew.

"He's grieving." Abe's voice cracked as his daughter, Lainee, walked back down the stairs, sitting on a step about halfway down to listen in on the conversation.

"Yes, he is. You all are. And yes, some come back." Tank answered honestly as he glanced over at Kiro who had returned, listening intently. "But some don't, Abe. I'm worried."

"Combat medics live by three rules, Abe. One is that good soldiers die. Two is that combat medics can't save every one of them."

Abe met Tank's gaze. "And three?"

"Three is that they'll go through hell and high water to change the first two."

Tank stood up again and placed his hand on Abe's shoulders. "Look. You know I'll do whatever I can for him. I know Kiro will, too. I, uh, told him about a paramedic spot that should open up around the new year and invited him to come in and talk to the Chief. I think it would be good for him."

Abe stood up and extended his hand to Tank. "Thanks, Juan." Abe gave him a nod. "Thanks for being there for him."

"Always."

Tank nodded to both Kiro and Mike as he placed his tan beret back on his head. He hesitated at the front door and spoke over his shoulder. "Your son literally saved my life, Abe. I'll be damned if I don't do everything in my power to save his."

As the door closed behind Tank, Abe's stomach sank at his words. Heartbroken, he turned his head and stared at the closed door to the office where his son was currently drinking his way through his grief.

Derek changed into the civilian clothes Kiro brought down for him, then poured another glass of whiskey. He sat down at the desk and started turning the pages of Joey's most recent letter-filled notebook, the one he was still writing in when he died.

Derek closed the notebook and finished off his latest glass of whiskey when a flash of white fell out onto the floor. He blinked a few times and squinted his eyes, taking a moment to register the envelope that landed by his feet. He knitted his brow and leaned down, taking at least three swipes before finally grasping it with his fingers. He slapped them on the desk and pulled himself upright in his chair. His eyes took a few moments to focus, but he eventually recognized his name written in Joey's handwriting. He opened it and started reading.

D,

I plan to burn this when I'm discharged, but if you're reading this and I'm not there, it's because you're going through my things after I'm dead. And if I'm dead, you should know right now I couldn't be saved. I know how good you medics are. Blame the guys who shot me or blew me up, but not yourself. While you're at it, kill a few of those fuckers for me when you go back.

You know I don't have much, but all I have is yours. You're my beneficiary on everything, so whatever payout you get from the military when I'm gone, use it for yourself. Maybe you should buy yourself a new truck because that old car you've had since high school is a piece of shit. Until you get your own place, speaking from personal experience, there's nothing better than a few blankets laid out in the bed of a pickup truck under the night sky with someone you love. Or at least lust after.

Trust me on this.

Oh, and tell your dad I'm really sorry about getting a visit from an officer and a chaplain. I know his first thought would have been that they were there for you. And you can tell him that's ok. He's been your dad a lot longer, but I still can't believe he was willing to treat me as if he were mine, too.

You became my brother, D, at a time when I was a lost kid moving to a new town after my bio-dad died. My mom gave me a loving home, but you, your mom and dad, Lainee - you all gave me a family. Abe's the only real dad I ever had, and he's a damned good one, too. Tell him I hate that we'll never go on another camping trip together. Those trips were my favorite things growing up, but you've gotta promise me you'll keep taking them. Never use me as an excuse not to go. Take K with you. He'd love that.

I'm gonna miss hearing about all your crazy exploits with all the women you sleep with. The guys were right about you buying stock in Trojans since you go through enough. Like you've always been with me, just be honest with everyone. Don't hide who you are, even if that means you're a womanizing, drunk bastard.

"I can do that," Derek said as he emptied another glass of whiskey. He returned to the letter.

You're my best friend in the world, D. Always have been. You guided me when I couldn't find my way. You kept me grounded. Never lose yourself because of me.

Your brother,

Joey

Derek closed his eyes. "No promises, brother."

Chapter 4

Grant's Crossing - Late December 2014
Four months after Joey's funeral

THE DUSTY GLOW OF SNOW-COVERED CHRISTMAS LIGHTS illuminated the trees lining the park inside the square that made up the heart of Grant's Crossing. Pine-tree garland intermingled with white lights wrapped its way up around each of the streetlights connecting to stars, bells, and snowmen.

Excited children played with their new presents, once carefully wrapped and lovingly placed under family Christmas trees, now getting a workout. They took delight in sugar cookies and candy canes. Today, their parents were happy to see them bouncing down the sidewalks wearing their new coats and hats.

As younger kids built snowmen in the park inside the square, older kids carried their new sleds to slide down the hills at nearby Taft Park. Couples walked arm and arm with a hot coffee, grabbing a seat at one of the tables scattered around the old carousel, after which Carousel Square was named.

Inside Jo's Bar & Grille, Derek and Abe Mitchell shrugged off their coats at a booth near the window with a good view of the square. They sat down and placed their food orders for a welcomed meal out before New Year's. Honorably discharged a few days earlier on Christmas Eve, Derek embraced one aspect of civilian life by not shaving. A thickening beard now covered his face.

He scanned the restaurant, noting all the changes since it first became Jo's Bar & Grille a few years back. He was accustomed to coming to this neighborhood sports bar while on leave for welcome home parties, always more interested in flirting with women and grabbing drinks with Joey and Tank than anything else. It was in this space, more than thirteen years ago, that they first discussed enlisting in the Army.

So much has changed since then.

He stared through the fogged-up windows at the snow-covered trees lining the square across Adams Street. He used to love downtown Grant's Crossing in the winter, even on overcast days like this one. This year, it seemed especially cold and uninviting, despite all the lights and holiday decorations that would remain up through early January.

There was a time when he, Joey, and Juan would all go to the park for some of the best snowball fights. His lips curled up in a smile at the memory before it hit him, it was now all in the past.

When a hand tapped his arm, Derek redirected his gaze to his dad. Abe jutted his chin toward the bar. Drew and Quinn Strager headed their way. Drew, now married with three or four kids, Derek couldn't remember exactly, was in his deputy uniform, soon to become the youngest-ever Delaware County sheriff after the new year.

Never married, Drew's older brother, Quinn, wore a suit, still working as a detective with the Delaware, Ohio Police Department. Since the death of his fiancée two years earlier, he poured his heart and soul into his work. The wrinkles he now sported made him look far more hardened, as if life had dealt him a crappy hand.

Both men offered warm smiles as they greeted Derek and Abe at their table. Shaking his hand, Quinn spoke first. "Welcome home, Derek. I heard you were back in town."

"Thanks, Quinn." Derek offered a steady handshake in return. "Got home last week."

Quinn's face lit up. "A nice Christmas present." Quinn extended his hand to Abe and exchanged warm smiles. "Happy New Year, Abe."

"Happy New Year," Abe responded in kind.

"Good to see you, Derek." Drew offered his hand as well, which Derek happily took. "Glad you're home for good now."

"Thanks, Drew." Derek couldn't help but laugh as Drew and his dad shook hands in greeting, "Congratulations on becoming our new sheriff."

"Thank you."

Quinn winked at his younger brother. "He thinks he runs the whole county now. Already bossing the rest of us around. Probably serves us right for all those times we picked on him as a kid."

With a quick shake of his head, Drew changed the subject. "Any plans for New Year's Eve? Jo's going to have quite the party here this weekend. Would be nice if you could make it."

"Gotta support our little sister," Quinn added with a smirk, pointing his thumb back at Jo, serving a customer from behind the bar, the lone girl of the four Strager siblings.

"Speaking of which," Abe held up his hand. "We're having a few friends over tomorrow evening to welcome Derek home and celebrate Joey's life. After the funeral last summer wasn't a good time for either."

Derek pursed his lips and stared into his glass before taking a long pull of beer.

"It'll be low-key. We'd love for you to join us." Abe nodded toward the bar. "Jo and Mike as well, of course. I've already talked to Marisol and Rod."

Once engaged to Joey's mom, Quinn nodded, his expression solemn at the loss of the man that would've become his stepson.

"Derek's even cooking dinner for us."

Derek's face shot up when his dad kicked him under the table. "I think I've talked him into making one of Katherine's old recipes. Haven't had any jambalaya in a while."

Quinn responded first. "That sounds good." He jabbed a good-natured elbow at his brother. "Count me in."

"Me, too. Thank you." Drew turned his attention back to Derek. "I hear you're going to be stationed with GC Fire now. You'll be working with Kiro as our newest paramedic?"

"Yes. I start at the end of January."

"It'll be a huge change from what you're used to," Quinn added.

"Yeah." Derek lifted his beer bottle for another gulp. "Something other than gunshots and IEDs."

Quinn and Drew exchanged looks without flinching but said nothing.

The server returned with their food as Drew and Quinn said their goodbyes, wishing them a Happy New Year.

Abe dropped some cash on the table after they'd finished eating. He waved at Jo as they walked outside into the crisp, late-December air. He pulled his collar closer and unlocked his truck.

"You handled that well."

"What am I supposed to say, Dad?" Derek's eyes darkened in anger as he sat in the front seat. "That I'm thrilled to be back where absolutely everything reminds me of my best friend who didn't make it back? And oh yeah, how about you, Quinn? Hang out at the cemetery lately to spend quality time with your fiancée and her family? Because that's where they all are now."

"I'm just saying ...."

"Saying what?" Derek cut him off, his anger unmistakable. "I watched him die right in front of me, Dad. It was my job to bring him back alive, and I failed. People walk up to me and thank me for my service. They want to shake my hand. But for what? What did I ever do but train for a job that I failed to do? All I could do was hold his hand while he cried out for his dead mother. Do you know what that's like? Because if you don't, I really don't want to hear it."

Abe turned the ignition and revved the engine to get the heat going. He twisted to face Derek and met him with an equal amount of ire. "Do you honestly think I don't know what it's like to hold someone's hand as they lie there dying? When there wasn't a damned thing I could do about it?" Abe smacked his hands on the steering wheel. "What do you think happened when your mother died?"

Derek at least had the good sense to look sheepish. "You weren't trained to help her."

"It was my job to protect her, Derek. It was my job as a husband and father to protect my family, and I failed, too. So don't ever fucking tell me I don't know what that was like, because I do."

Abe took a deep breath and calmed his voice. "You lost your best friend and your brother. I lost a son."

"I know."

"You're not the only one grieving."

"I know, Dad. Shit. You're right. I'm... I'm sorry." Derek stared out the window. "It's just..."

"Just what, son?"

Derek dropped his voice to a whisper. "Everything reminds me of him."

"And everything will. For a long while, it will." Abe glanced over at his son but said nothing else on the short drive home. Abe shut off the engine when he parked in the driveway. He reached out to open the door when Derek spoke again.

"I let him down."

"What?"

"Joey. I let him down." Derek stared through the front windshield for a few seconds, then turned to his father. "And I broke my promise to you."

Abe furrowed his brow. "What promise?"

Derek shifted in his seat to face his father. The cold began to seep into the truck's interior with the engine off, but it didn't seem to faze either of them. "Remember when you dropped us off at the airport on our way to basic training?"

"Yes."

"You told us to take care of each other."

Abe closed his eyes for a second. "Son, you always took care of each other."

"That's just it, Dad," Derek contradicted him. "I didn't. If I did, Joey would be here."

Abe let out a gruff exhale.

Derek pulled the handle of the truck door but didn't yet push it open. Tears welled in his eyes. "How do I live with that?"

Derek opened the door and went inside the house.

After a few seconds, Abe shook his head and followed.

The next afternoon, Derek sat on the floor of an extra bedroom where Joey stored his belongings from the old apartment he'd grown up in with his mom. Derek found several more of Joey's notebooks dating as far back as their basic training.

He turned through page after page of Joey's notebooks. His friend poured his heart and soul into every word throughout their training, deployments, leave, and through the loss of his mother. Each entry read like a love letter, starting with *"Dear L"* and ending with *"Love, J"*, but to a stranger, or fellow soldier, they were all vague enough to sound like they were written to a girlfriend back home.

Knowing better, Derek ran his hand down his face and turned another page. All of Joey's letters to his mother could be mailed. All his letters to Logan had to be encrypted.

Joey wrote about his fears. He wrote about his emotions and

even his most private and dirty thoughts, all to someone he could never publicly acknowledge as the one he loved even after the repeal of Don't Ask, Don't Tell. He wrote about everyday things he wanted to share with Logan but couldn't. The words on the page spelled out his hopes. His aspirations. His dreams for the two of them after he was discharged from the Army.

Derek placed them back inside one box and opened another with nothing but pictures inside. With a deep breath, he crossed the room over to Joey's bed and sat down.

He pulled out some pictures taken when they were kids at Taft Park, a few blocks away on the Scioto River. They spent so much time there growing up. It was a favorite place for young kids to hang out during the hot and humid Ohio summers.

Derek's mind wandered back to the first time he and Joey met when his dad walked into the room. "You ready for tonight?"

"Yeah," Derek shrugged. "All the stuff's downstairs, ready to go for dinner."

"I'm not worried about dinner." Abe's concern showed on his face. "Are you ready to relive everything?"

"I'm sure alcohol will play a role," he said, much to his father's chagrin. "I texted Logan. But I didn't hear back, so I don't know if he'll be here or not."

Derek pulled out a picture of three young boys holding their arms in the air as they yelled over the railing of a playground fort. It was a picture of ten-year-old Derek, Joey, and Tank, or Juan as they still called him then. He passed the picture to his dad, who took it as he sat on the edge of the bed.

"That had to have been the first summer Joey was here."

"I think it was, yeah," Derek agreed, "summer before fifth grade, right?"

"Yes. You and Juan would run in circles every time you were at the park, run up the fort and yell 'I'm the king of the fort,' then disappear down the slide only to run around and do it all over again." They both laughed at the memory. "I remember when Katherine told me how this cute little blond kid ran up and just joined in one day. She didn't even think you knew each other's' names yet when this was taken."

"We probably didn't, but she was always taking pictures." Derek chuckled at the memory. "He just started showing up every day."

"Yet, you were both best friends by the end of the summer."

"That was the best summer," Derek said, his expression dreamy. "Joey kept following us around. Eventually, he told us his mom worked at the diner, and he was mostly on his own during the day. So Mom would take a picnic lunch to the park so he'd eat something other than peanut butter and jelly."

"Well, a fifth-grader's culinary repertoire isn't that extensive."

"Mine sure wasn't."

"Definitely better now."

Derek grunted, but curled one side of his mouth into a momentary smile. He pulled out another picture, this time of his family. They huddled around each other in their backyard. "Joey's mom must have taken this."

Abe leaned in as Derek ran his thumb over their faces. Abe, his mom, Lainee, Joey, and himself.

"Lainee would have been about seven in this if Joey and I were ten."

Abe chuckled. "I didn't have any gray back then."

"There are just three of us now."

"Yeah," Abe agreed. "Hey, remember that first time he came over? He heard me call out to Katherine. I don't know what happened. A branch or something was falling." Abe smiled at the memory. "Anyway, I yelled for her to watch out, and he thought I was yelling at her because I was mad."

"I forgot about that." Derek's brow furrowed. "He started hitting you. I kept yelling at him to stop, but you stopped me."

"He was just defending her. He thought I was going to hurt

her." Abe took the picture and smiled down at it. "All I could do was hold on to him and wait until he grew tired. Until he learned I wasn't going to hurt her."

"I think he was afraid of you for a while."

"But he warmed up to me eventually." Abe cleared his throat. "The next time your mother and I talked to Renee, she explained what had happened to Joey while they were still in Pittsburgh."

Derek sighed. "Yeah. Can't imagine what he went through."

Chapter 5

Pittsburgh, Pennsylvania - Spring 1990

Joey - 8 years old

THE 9-1-1 OPERATOR ANSWERED THE CALL. "WHAT'S THE nature of your emergency?"

An eight-year-old boy cried as he spoke, "HELP! My dad's gonna kill my mom! He's got a gun."

"What's your name?"

"Joey Parker."

"And what's your address, Joey?" the dispatcher calmly asked.

"Uh...2734 Parish Street."

"Ok, Joey. Good. I'm going to send someone out, ok?"

His frightened voice came through between sobs. "Hurry! He's hurting her!"

"Stay on the phone with me until the police arrive. Ok, Joey? Are you inside the house?"

"Yes," he cried.

"And Joey, are you somewhere safe? Can you hide behind a door?"

"I have to close it."

"Ok. Joey." the operator answered. "I'm going to wait while you do that, ok?"

The woman's voice on the other end of the phone was calm and soothing as she spoke to the panicked child. Each time she spoke his name, she connected with him, doing her best to keep him calm and grounded until the police arrived.

Joey gave a frightened look in the direction of the other side of the house, where he could hear his parents arguing.

"What the hell are you thinking?" Renee Parker yelled at her husband. "Bringing a gun into this house? You could have killed us!?"

"You don't like it?" Matt Parker marched around the couch, and without a word, he cold-cocked her with it. She collapsed on the floor with a loud thud, knocking over one of the kitchen chairs as she fell. "Shut up, Renee. It's my gun. It's my house. I'll do what I want."

Joey pulled the phone cord and stretched his arm. His voice was strained. "I...can't...reach the door."

Sirens began to wail in the distance as a loud gunshot sounded, followed immediately by the sound of glass shattering on the floor.

"MOMMY!" He yelled at the top of his lungs.

Joey let go of the phone, the phone cord snapping the receiver back against the wall, causing hard pieces of paint-covered drywall to fall to the floor. He tore out of the room, and his eyes grew wide as soon as he saw his mom on the floor. One of her eyes was already swelling shut, and a small stream of blood dripped down her face and onto her pretty floral t-shirt. He ran to her and held on to her for dear life again as she tried to push him away.

"Go to your room, Joey," Renee Parker said in a whisper as she slowly rose up to her knees and fell back against the cabinets. She grabbed him by the shoulders. "I'm ok, baby. I'm ok."

He wiggled free and flung himself back at her, hugging her tight. She grabbed his arms again and pushed him away, her blood now staining his t-shirt, too.

He looked up at his dad, seething in as much anger an eight-year-old boy could muster. "YOU LEAVE MOMMY ALONE!"

"SHUT UP, YOU FUCKING BRAT," his dad yelled. "GET OUT OF HERE." With a sneer, he waved his gun toward Joey in the hallway, then wiped his mouth with the back of his hand that held the gun. "I never wanted you, anyway."

The rain poured down during one of the first big thunderstorms of the season. The visibility was low, and the bright flashes of lightning timed themselves just as the police officers' eyes adjusted to the darkness.

Officer Martin Cato had been out to this old gray bungalow with its poorly-patched roof before, usually because Matt Parker hit his wife. He had no prior criminal history beyond petty theft just out of high school. He wasn't technically considered a violent offender because every time they came out here, the wife always refused to press charges. She would claim he didn't mean it when he hit her before, but her fear was always undeniable. Prior to tonight, Parker had never brought a weapon into a situation which made this call that much more dangerous.

According to dispatch, the boy sounded terrified. The operator had even heard a shot fired while on the call. Something caused Parker to escalate to a whole new level. They hoped to calm things down before he acted on anything.

Four Pittsburgh police officers surrounded the house. Receiving confirmation the others were in place, Officer Cato pounded on the door. "POLICE! OPEN UP!"

Renee pulled herself up to her feet, more afraid than ever for the safety of her son.

"Joey," she called out weakly as she continued to use the counter for support. "Go to your room."

She winced in pain and brought her hand to her stomach. "Please."

"This is your fucking fault." Matt Parker waved his gun in her direction.

Cato's rookie partner, Carlos Ramirez, sidestepped to the front window and leaned his head down to get a peek inside. The living room and kitchen made one large room giving him a good view of the situation inside.

"Shit." He straightened up to describe the scene to his partner. "Two adults, one child. The man has a gun and is with the woman in the kitchen. The boy is around the corner a few feet away sitting on the floor against the wall."

Cato closed his eyes for a moment and muttered an oath under his breath as Ramirez continued. "Woman has already taken some punches. She and the boy look scared shitless."

Officer Cato nodded, then pounded on the door again. "OPEN UP!"

"Matt." Renee said his name. She could hear Joey crying just around the corner. Her voice was low. Calm. Cautious. "Your gun fired by accident. It broke a window but didn't hurt anyone."

Her breaths grew short, but she remained as calm as she could, her shaky voice betraying the fear she felt as her heart rate soared through the roof. Her hands shook as she slowly followed the L-shaped counter around to place her body between Matt and Joey.

Not quite there, she closed her eyes. She had to lean against the refrigerator to rest and catch her breath as she held her hand to her chest where he'd kicked her.

As soon as she reached her hand around the side of the fridge, Matt yelled. "STOP MOVING!"

Her eyes flew open to find they were staring down the barrel of his gun. His hand shook, but he used the gun to point toward the door. "You did this."

Officer Cato pounded on the door one last time. "OPEN UP!"

Matt's voice sounded from behind the door. "I SAID GO AWAY!"

As soon as Matt yelled, Cato signaled to the two police officers in place behind their cruiser. Then he nodded to his partner. As soon as he did, Ramirez stepped back from the door and kicked it open.

Matt and Renee both jumped as the door slammed against the inside wall. A picture landed on the floor with a loud crash. Ramirez and Cato stormed into the house, accidentally punting a pan out of the way. The rainwater it had been collecting now fell directly onto the old, wooden floor.

"WHAT THE FUCK!" Matt yelled as he yanked Renee by her neck, placing her between him and the two cops who were standing with weapons pointed directly at him.

"Don't. Move." Cato commanded.

Water started forming a puddle on the dark, wooden floor behind the two policemen, their eyes not moving from Matt or the silver gun he held in his right hand.

Renee's hands reflexively clutched his forearm to hold herself up and prevent her from being strangled since her legs were giving out on her. "Joey," she choked.

"Put the gun down." Officer Cato instructed him. His voice was calm but in command.

"Get the fuck out!" Matt's low voice growled. He waved his gun up and then pointed it directly at Renee's head.

"Put...the gun...down!" Cato kept his gun pointed at Matt with one hand while he extended the other to make a downward motion.

"FUCK YOU, YOU PIG!"

"MOMMY!"

"It's ok, baby." Tears streamed down Renee's face as she tried to calm her son.

"We don't want you to do anything you might regret," Cato spoke in a calm voice.

Matt released a nervous laugh. "I've already got plenty of regrets."

The air became thick and stifling. Renee gasped for breath, not because of the gun pointed at her head but from his words. She was never the religious type, but in an instant, she secretly prayed to anything she could think of to keep her son safe.

The tension grew with the standoff between the three armed men inside, each with their fingers on the triggers, poised to shoot.

Outside, two more police officers, Braxton and Cooper, approached the house with caution. Braxton dropped to one knee outside the broken living room window, rain pouring down on top of him as he leveled his weapon directly in line with Matt, eyes focused, ready to make the shot. Cooper circled the house to position himself at the back door if anyone tried to make a run for it. More sirens sounded in the distance indicating their backup was drawing near.

Noticing movement out of the corner of his eye, Cato saw Braxton positioned outside the window. He looked up at Matt and pointed his weapon at the ceiling. "Ok." He showed his left palm as well. His facial expression was serious but in control, as Renee's showed nothing but fear. Her gaze darted back and forth between the cops and in the direction of Joey, who was still crying.

Ramirez glanced at Cato, who gave him a nod without taking his eyes off Matt and his gun.

Ramirez nodded back and started to lower his weapon as well. He pointed his free hand in Joey's direction. "Let me take your boy outside, ok?" He kept his weapon at the ready but slightly lowered as he sidestepped toward Joey.

Renee's tears fell as she nodded gratefully at the officer who wanted to keep Joey safe.

"Don't you dare touch my son," Matt threatened with a voice so angry it shook. His bloodshot eyes widened, not quite focusing on either officer.

Officer Ramirez stopped moving, right index finger poised by the trigger. He was far enough over that, outside the window, Officer Braxton now had a much cleaner shot.

"Matt," Renee said between sobs, "Let him take Joey outside. He'll be ok."

A bead of sweat dripped down the side of Matt's face as his gaze darted from Cato to Ramirez and back. "Shut up, Renee. Let me think."

Outside the back door of the mudroom that led to the kitchen, Officer Cooper carefully turned the handle.

It wasn't locked.

A wall inside the back door extended just far enough inside to give him enough cover to enter the house unseen.

The door creaked as it opened.

"Shit," he winced.

"What was that?" Matt's eyes darted in the direction of the back door. His grip on Renee's neck tightened as he pulled her back against him while he backed up against the counter. "WHAT WAS THAT?"

Lightning flashed outside. A second later, a loud clap of thunder rattled the windows giving Officer Cooper the cover he needed to slip inside unheard.

"MOMMY!"

"Shut up, Joey!" His dad barked at the frightened boy.

Trying to get a full breath, Renee croaked, "It's ok, Joey. Stay where you are, baby." More tears fell as she gave a pleading look to the police officers in the room.

The police officers held steady while a cornered Matt grew more and more frantic.

Officer Ramirez edged his foot over toward Joey. At the same time, Matt rotated himself and Renee in the same direction to keep him in his sights.

"Leave him alone," Matt's voice sounded a bit off as he stared at Ramirez, his eyes still wide after seeing the movement.

Outside, the rain continued to pour. Another clap of thunder masked the creaking sound of the door as Officer Cooper slowly let it close behind him. Peering further inside the house, Cooper had a view of Cato with his palms out and weapon pointed toward the ceiling. To Cato's left, Ramirez edged closer to the young boy.

Cooper made momentary eye contact with Ramirez, whose nearly imperceptible dip of his chin acknowledged his unspoken communication.

They were ready to shoot.

"MOMMY," Joey cried out again.

"It's ok, baby. Just stay still." Her voice cracked with every word she spoke. "We'll be ok," She released another sob, still struggling for air. "We'll be ok."

From the back room, Cooper caught Joey's eye from where he hid in the narrow hallway. Cowered on the floor, the boy was visibly shaking. He lowered his weapon long enough to raise his index finger to his mouth and arch his eyebrows. Then he held out his palm and motioned for Joey to stay there. He mouthed the words to stay there, hoping he would understand. The boy was crying and clearly afraid. He also didn't have a way out. Any exits were blocked by either Cato and Ramirez in the living room or his parents in the kitchen. Best for him to stay put.

"FUCK!" Matt panicked even more.

With his hand still up, palm still facing out, Officer Cato spoke up in a calm, steady voice. "Why don't we all lower our weapons here and talk about this, ok?"

"Why don't you get the fuck out of my house?" Matt hissed.

"You know we can't do that." Cato remained calm.

Matt caught a glimpse out the front window only to see another police car pull up. "Fuck."

Outside, more sirens drew near, including another police car and an ambulance which held back at a safe distance from the active scene but at the ready. The sirens all shut off as they arrived, but their flashing lights continued to light up the street like a patriotic Christmas tree.

Neighborhood porch lights were turned on, and the officers outside worked to establish a perimeter. The curious residents of the nearby houses were all instructed to go back inside.

Not wanting to make the situation more volatile than it already was, Officer Cato continued to talk to Matt, hoping to keep him as calm as he could.

Officer Ramirez took another half step toward Joey, causing Matt to rotate once more with Renee, now giving Cooper a clear shot at Matt from the mud room now that Renee was no longer directly in his line of fire.

Officer Braxton was still poised at the window, as yet unnoticed by Matt. He still had a clear shot and held steady, ready to squeeze the trigger at a moment's notice.

Cato spoke again. "Come on now. Let's talk about this. We know you don't want to hurt your family. Let's get them out."

"GOD DAMMIT! GET THE FUCK OUT OF HERE!"

"MOMMY!"

"SHUT THE FUCK UP, JOEY!"

Matt shoved Renee to the floor.

She landed hard as he rounded the corner and pointed his gun toward Joey, who screamed bloody murder at the sight.

Ramirez instinctively dove down as shots from at least four different guns rang out. He used his body to cover Joey knowing his kevlar vest would provide enough protection in case Matt's aim were any better than his judgment.

"JOEY!" Shots were fired above a screaming Renee as she curled up in a fetal position, covering her head with her arms after feeling the wind caused by the officer diving past her.

Blood splattered all over the cabinets and counters as Matt's arms flailed about like a fish gasping its last breath on dry land. He collapsed onto the kitchen floor. The gun he'd been holding landed on the kitchen floor with a flat thud, having only intentionally fired two shots.

"HOLD YOUR FIRE!" Cato yelled to his fellow officers.

The shooting stopped almost as quickly as it started and silence took hold of the room. Joey wailed, frightened by all the quick movement and loud gunfire. He was engulfed by arms he didn't recognize. Strong arms that allowed for no movement.

Like the water leaking down from the ceiling above, blood seeped out of Matt's body, his lifeless eyes now staring up at nothing, the thick red liquid flowing out as he lay there like a thrown-out rag doll.

To the sound of rain falling outside, the three officers who had fired all kept their weapons pointed at Matt as Cato stepped closer and kicked Matt's gun back toward the living room, away from Matt, Renee, and Joey.

"Get the paramedics in here!" Officer Braxton's voice called out from outside the window.

"JOEY!" A terrified Renee started to crawl toward her son.

"DON'T MOVE!" Cato commanded in a sharp voice that froze her in place. "Ramirez?"

With his back to the kitchen, Ramirez rose to his knees with a grunt. "He's ok." Ramirez tried to catch his breath. His strong arms may have been firmly wrapped around a sobbing boy, but his eyes were fixed on a small hole in the floor mere inches from where they'd ducked. The shiny metal bullet from Matt Parker's gun was embedded in the now-splintered wood.

Cato saw a hole in the back of his partner's jacket. "Jesus, Ramirez. Were you hit?"

Ramirez held the boy tight. He swallowed and let out a grunt. "I'm... ok.'

Officer Cooper pointed his weapon toward the floor as he approached the lifeless man lying on the kitchen floor. He crouched down and switched his weapon from his right to his left hand. Reaching his arm out, he felt Matt's neck for a pulse. He holstered his weapon and turned his attention to Cato. A single shake of his head signaled that Matt Parker was dead.

While still holding Joey, Ramirez lifted his eyes up to Cato, who passed along the communication with a shake of his head. Ramirez grimaced in pain as he released a still-sobbing Joey to his mother, who cried harder as soon as she wrapped him safely in her arms.

"I love you, Joey. I love you so much."

Chapter 6

Grant's Crossing - present day

"He didn't tell me about that for a long time," Derek said to his dad while looking at a picture of Joey and his mom taken shortly after they arrived in Grant's Crossing so many years ago. "Joey once told me the officer who saved his life took a bullet when he dove down to protect him from the crossfire." He shook his head. "How could any dad turn a gun on his own kid?"

Abe rested his hand on his son's shoulder, unable to fathom how a man could try to kill his own son. "I don't know, son. You and Lainee tested your mother's and my patience to no end, but there was never a time we didn't want you."

Derek laughed. "Could you imagine a couple more Dereks and Lainees running around this place while growing up?"

His father didn't hesitate. "Oh yes. Absolutely."

Derek raised an eyebrow at his father's enthusiasm.

His father grinned. "We were the luckiest people in the world, and no matter how hard it ever got, I wouldn't trade you or Lainee for anything." He breathed out a laugh. "Hell. We wanted a few more, but it just wasn't in the cards. With Joey, though, we ended up with three, and Tasha makes four. And now I even have a granddaughter."

Derek smiled at the thought of his niece and his sister's girlfriend, with whom Lainee was already making marriage plans. He grabbed another shoebox of pictures and started rifling through them.

Abe stood up and motioned for Derek to follow. "Why don't you bring those pictures downstairs? We can all look at them together in the living room."

Derek looked forward to seeing everyone, but at the same time, he dreaded seeing everyone. The last thing he wanted to do was spend an evening dredging up old memories of his best friend who should have lived well beyond his thirty-three years on this earth.

He loved Joey like a brother. Lack of common DNA aside, they were brothers. Good times. Bad times. They stuck together. First dates. Losing their moms. Losing their virginity. Serving together on countless missions.

Though it had been four months, Joey's death was a still-fresh wound, and opening that back up was not something he was sure he could handle. He barely made it through his last few months of active duty as it was. He would need a small miracle to make it through the evening.

Like any mission, he was resigned to go through with it regardless of any internal fear he possessed. All he could do was muddle through and do his best to make it out in one piece. If all went well, the evening would be over quickly, and he could move on... or at least go back to escaping reality with a few bottles of beer.

He took a final scan of Joey's room and grabbed the two shoe boxes of pictures to follow his father. He shuffled downstairs and paused in the hallway, not quite ready to face the simmering pain he knew would bubble to the surface throughout the next few hours.

Friends and family were due to arrive within the hour. Dinner wouldn't actually be served until later, but most everything was ready. Gatherings in the Mitchell home inevitably ended up with everyone going back and forth between the living room and kitchen anyway, so it's not as if he'd be alone while chopping vegetables and stirring the jambalaya and gumbo that were on the evening's menu.

For tonight though, escaping the crowd for a few minutes by himself every now and then would most likely be what got him through the evening.

Derek took in a deep breath and released it slowly. Thinking of it as another mission, he squared his shoulders and stepped into the living room.

Outside the kitchen, the living room was the most used room in the large Queen Anne Victorian home he and Lainee grew up in. Derek's parents bought it as a fixer-upper back in the mid-1980s, a few years after they were married. They worked on the turn-of-the-century house room by room, slowly but surely turning it into a gorgeous, loving home. They'd originally planned on having a large family, but his mother's first bout with cancer changed their plans after only two surviving children. Their mother was now buried next to their little sister, who never made it out of the hospital.

Growing up, Derek and Lainee never once felt as if they weren't enough. Their parents' world revolved around them in a home with no shortage of love and support. Their friends were always welcome, thanks to a never-ending "what's one or ten more?" mantra. Sleepovers were always great fun, especially with an extra few bedrooms upstairs, not to mention the attic playroom, which provided nearly limitless space for kids to play.

Derek stood barely a step inside the large living room that was still fully decorated for Christmas. His mother was a firm believer in the twelve days of Christmas and didn't remove any of their Christmas decorations until Epiphany. His mom used to play Christmas music all the way through January 6th despite it driving his father nuts to hear it after the new year. Abe never once complained or asked her to change that tradition in all the years they were together.

On the occasions Uncle Mick visited around the new year, they turned it on just for him, just to keep that memory alive. Derek was happy to play Christmas music through New Year's, and after that, he went back to nothing but country. With his mom's side of the family being originally from New Orleans, he had his fair share of jazz and zydeco, too, but they all loved their country music. He'd been hooked ever since he was a kid.

The room had a seven-foot tall Christmas tree festooned with ornaments they'd made and collected over the years. It stood majestically in front of the large bay window that extended into their wraparound porch.

Family pictures hung on the wall, and candles, the battery-powered kind meant to look like candles, were carefully placed in every window. Greenery laced with white lights ran up the banister and across the mantel.

"Here." Abe stepped away from adding a log to the warm fire and reached out. "Let's set those on the coffee table."

Derek handed the two boxes of pictures to his father and swallowed when he caught sight of how his dad had rearranged the decor atop the mantel. His father had cleared some of the seasonal decorations away to make room for pictures of Joey.

Derek's heart sank upon seeing a folded flag in a triangle taking its solemn place as the centerpiece. Abe had moved it from the office to lovingly center it between pictures of Joey starting as a young boy and teenager through to his late 20s and early 30s.

"I thought folks would want to see pictures of happier times."

"Happier times," Derek whispered to himself. He cleared his throat. "Yeah. Good."

Swallowing hard, Derek willed himself to step closer to the pictures. The pictures showed the age progression of three men starting as young boys in their PJs at one of their many sleepovers. Joey was in the center with Derek and Tank on either side of him, all three smiling their hearts out.

Another picture showed them as teenagers on the shore of a

lake holding up fish they'd caught. Big grins covered their faces despite Joey and Tank holding two to three fish each, while Derek only had one. Derek snickered at that picture. He hadn't even caught the one. Joey had given him one of his to hold up in front of the camera.

A third picture showed the three young men fresh out of basic training with matching close-cropped haircuts. Like most of his adult pictures, Joey was in uniform since they'd enlisted together a year out of high school.

A fourth picture showed them several years later at Bagram Air Base in Afghanistan, looking a bit more battle-hardened in full combat gear. Though still in their 20s, lines had started to form around their eyes and mouths. They still grinned in each other's company, their friendship as apparent as the summer sun was bright.

Derek dug through the first shoebox and pulled out more pictures. One was the family picture of Joey with the Mitchells when he was only ten. Another was a copy of the picture that had slipped out of Joey's notebook back at Bagram, of Joey and Logan together, looking as happy as two people in love could be.

Abe placed them all on the mantel between the other framed pictures, resting them between pieces of pine branches so they would stay upright and on display. Derek's head snapped toward the front door when the doorbell rang.

"I'm going to work on dinner," Derek announced as he retreated to the kitchen, leaving his father to greet the first guests of the evening. From the back of the house, he could hear their voices.

"Come on in," Abe's deep, welcoming voice rang out.

Derek couldn't make out what they were saying, but as they drew nearer, the voice he heard was Quinn's sister-in-law, Marisol, followed by Quinn himself.

"Your home looks so beautiful, all decorated for Christmas," Marisol said in her mild Mexican accent.

"Thank you," Abe answered back. "Lainee, Tasha, and I decorated after Thanksgiving. Even little Catie helped."

"It's so warm and inviting," she gushed.

"Derek's in the kitchen working on dinner, so make yourself at home wherever you'd like."

Derek stirred ingredients into the pot of gumbo while eavesdropping on their conversation.

"Oh my. Look at this picture, Quinn."

Derek peaked around the opening to the kitchen for a glimpse of their family friends in the living room. Quinn joined Marisol at the mantel and reached his hand out to bring the picture of him, Joey, and Joey's mom. Joey was proudly holding keys to a new-to-him car about the time he got his driver's license. "Imagine. That could have been mine." His voice came across as a near whisper, as if trying to keep his sadness at bay.

"It *was* yours, Quinn," she said as it should never have been questioned. "You may not have been married when this was taken, but you were always there for her. From the time you filled her pantry the day she moved in." She pointed to the keys Joey was holding in the picture. "To the time you taught him how to drive."

Quinn's voice dropped too low for Derek to make out his response.

"There are some more pictures on the coffee table." Abe said "Derek and I were looking through them before you arrived."

Quinn reached in and grabbed a picture from on top. It was of a young woman in a sundress with long, curly, brown hair and a young boy of around nine or ten years old. "Look, Marisol. This is how they looked when we first met them."

"Oh, yes." She smiled as she carried the picture into the kitchen and greeted Derek with a warm hug and a kiss on his cheek. "Hello, Derek. Welcome home."

Derek returned the hug. "Thanks, Marisol." Turning to Quinn, he offered his hand. "Hi, Quinn."

"Hi there." He gestured toward the oven. "Smells good. Jambalaya?"

"Not yet," Derek smiled. "You're smelling the gumbo."

"You're cooking this?" Marisol arched her brows with an impressed smile.

He raised one shoulder in a shrug. "Mom's recipe. More or less."

She showed Derek the picture in her hand. "Your father was just showing us some pictures. This is about the time they almost made it to Grant's Crossing." She glanced up at Quinn, "Remember how their car broke down? Carlos warned us they might not make it the whole way."

Derek inwardly cringed at the mention of her brother's name, the police officer, now detective, who saved Joey's life all those years ago.

"I'm grateful she got as close to town as she did." Quinn smiled fondly at the memory. "I think I fell for her the moment I first saw her stranded on the side of the road. All she wanted was to be brave for Joey so he wouldn't be scared."

Chapter 7

Grant's Crossing - Spring 1992

Joey - 10 years old

A HORROR MOVIE FLASHED IN RENEE PARKER'S MIND. "PLEASE don't let there be any children hiding in that corn," she muttered under her breath as she made a 360-degree turn to survey the cornfields that surrounded her broken-down car. It was only June, so the corn wasn't even knee-high, but out in the middle of nowhere Ohio with no buildings in sight, she preferred to hope for the best and fought back every worst-case scenario that was working its way to the forefront of her mind.

A siren sounded from behind their car. She popped her head around the side of the car to see a police vehicle had pulled up behind them.

"Oh, shit!" She stepped to the back of her car then waited as the officer stepped out. A tall, handsome man with short, dark hair and sunglasses put his hat on and approached her, stopping at a safe distance.

"Afternoon, ma'am," he greeted her with a concerned expression. "What seems to be the trouble?"

"My car just died," she sighed, gesturing with both arms toward her car. "It backfired again, then something started rattling. A few minutes later, it quit on me."

The police officer looked inside the car where Joey was sitting in the back seat. "That's my son." She smiled as the officer raised an arm up to wave to him. "We're on our way to Grant's Crossing."

"Grant's Crossing, huh?" He made a show of looking at the Pennsylvania plates on the car. "Is your name Renee Parker, by chance?"

Red flags started flashing in her mind. She took a step back but was abruptly stopped by the rear bumper of her car. "Uh..."

"I'm sorry." He held up his hand and took a slow step back, "Pretty sure you're going to be moving into my brother's place."

"Your brother?"

"Yes. My brother is Rodney Strager."

"He's married to Marisol Ramirez?"

"Yep. That's the one." He extended his hand and stepped back toward her. "I'm Deputy Quinn Strager."

Renee pressed her lips together in amusement after catching him wince upon stating his title.

"It's very nice to meet you."

Schooling her features, she reluctantly extended her hand to shake his. "Uh...nice to meet you, too."

"Tell you what." His confident voice conveyed he had a plan. "Let me give Frankie a call to tow your car to the new place so we can unload it for you. Then he can take it back to the shop to see what needs fixed. Wait right here."

Before she could protest, he stepped into his cruiser for a few minutes before returning.

She stood there wringing her hands until he returned. "Um... I don't have any money to fix my car. I don't even have a job yet."

"Don't worry. I'm pretty sure my sister-in-law already has an idea for that." He offered a warm smile. "In the meantime, Marisol's on her way to take you both to your new home."

"I don't want to put anyone out." Renee willed her worried

heart rate to slow down. This was not a good start to their new life in Ohio.

"Put anyone out?" he chuckled. "We're happy to help. Unless you and your son prefer to walk the last few miles to Grant's Crossing? It's not too hot out today, but between a young boy and all your stuff, I assure you, catching a ride is much easier."

"But…"

"But…" She attempted another protest.

"But nothing." He smiled again. "We've got you covered. Besides, Marisol's brother already told us he'd be surprised if your car actually made it the whole way. He asked us to keep our eyes open for you."

She couldn't believe her ears and coughed out a laugh. "He what?" She pressed her lips together again and turned around to check on Joey before returning to her worries. "I don't have enough money to pay for anything but my first month's rent which, I know, is already discounted, and hopefully a trip to the grocery store. Ugh. This can't be happening." Her palm went up to her forehead, shoving her bangs further up in the air. She closed her eyes and muttered. "Breathe, Renee. Breathe."

"Look, Mrs. Parker. Marisol should be here in a few minutes. We're barely outside of town, so she won't be long."

Renee looked up at the sky, squinting as she blinked a few times to keep tears of frustration from falling. She huffed out an exhale and turned to the side of the car.

"Joey? Do you want to get out of the car and stretch your legs for a few minutes? Officer Carlos' sister is going to give us a ride to our new house. Just stay over here off the road, ok?"

"Ok." Joey stepped outside and looked all around with a worried expression. His knees were pulled together as he bounced a little bit. "Mom? I have to go to the bathroom."

She exhaled and looked around to see a tree with some shrubbery below it. She glanced up at the deputy and then back at the tree. Returning her gaze to the deputy, she caught his eye. "He has to pee. Can he go..." She pointed.

He looked over by the tree and then at the bouncing boy. With a smile, he nodded and walked back to his cruiser.

Renee directed Joey to the other side of the tree. "Stay behind the tree and make it quick, ok? Don't get too close to any bushes. I don't want you getting poison ivy or anything." As soon as she said that, it hit her. Having lived in a city all her life, she wouldn't even recognize poison ivy until after the itching started.

"Ok." Joey was already unzipping his fly as she took a few steps away to give him a little privacy, grateful at the moment she didn't have a little girl with the same problem. A minute later, he was done.

"Zipped up?"

He pulled his shirt up and looked down at his pants. "Yep."

"Ok. Let's go back."

Within ten minutes of Deputy Strager's calls, a tow truck pulled up to their car, followed by an SUV with a woman driving. A young, olive-complexioned tow truck driver with black hair and a mustache stepped out of his truck to introduce himself. He extended a calloused hand in greeting.

"Hello. I'm Francisco Serratos." He rolled his Rs with a pronounced accent. "You can call me Frankie." He noticed Joey and smiled at him. "*Hola.*"

Ready to show off his Spanish skills, Joey walked up to him and stuck out his hand as the woman driving the SUV joined them. "Hola. Me llamo Joey Parker."

"Your name is Joey Parker?" Frankie looked impressed and shook Joey's hand. "Con mucho gusto, Señor Parker." *Very nice to meet you, Mr. Parker.*

Renee's smile had pride written all over it as she listened to her son speak in Spanish. She looked up at the lady she could only assume was Marisol and saw that she was also smiling.

"I know more," Joey added. "I can count to twenty, and I can say '*Ella es una pu...*'"

"Whoa, whoa, whoa..." Frank and the lady both cut him off. "You don't want to say that word, *niño*. The rest of it was really good, though. Maybe we can teach you a few more phrases that you can say," he offered with a laugh.

Not knowing any Spanish, Renee was confused. "What did he say? Joey? What did you say?"

His eyes widened. "I don't know."

"Where did you learn your Spanish?" The lady suppressed a grin as Frankie started hooking Renee's car up to the tow truck.

"Officer Carlos taught me." Joey beamed a proud smile as the lady pursed her lips in disapproval.

The lady leaned closer to him. "Well, my name is Marisol, and Officer Carlos is my brother. The next time I talk to him, I'm going to tell him he shouldn't have taught you that phrase. Think you can promise not to repeat it?"

"Yes, ma'am."

"Good boy."

Joey still looked worried as he turned his face to his mom. "Is Officer Carlos in trouble?"

Renee turned her eyes to Marisol with a knowing smile that was instantly mirrored.

"Maybe a little bit." Marisol's smile broadened. "Hi. You must be Renee Parker." She extended her hand. "I'm Marisol Strager. Welcome to Ohio."

"Thank you, Marisol. It's nice to meet you. I'm so sorry you had to drive out here to get us. I didn't mean to trouble you."

"Not at all." She assured Renee. "You're close." She looked over at her brother-in-law. "Quinn told me you needed a quick ride to get the rest of the way into town, so I'm happy to drive you. I also hope you'll join us for dinner tonight. I figured you wouldn't want to cook right after moving in. We're just grilling cheeseburgers, but we'd love to have you over."

"Are you sure it's no trouble?"

"Promise."

"Then we'd love to. Thank you." She tousled Joey's hair.

He tried to duck away as the adults chuckled. "Mom!"

"Did you hear that, Joey?," Renee asked. "Cheeseburgers for dinner tonight."

His face lit up with a smile that stretched from ear to ear. "Yay!"

Renee smiled over at Marisol. "I think he approves!"

"I think you're right." She looked back over at the deputy, whose gaze wasn't moving from Renee. "Quinn?"

"Yeah?"

"Care to join us? Dinner's at 5:30 tonight."

"I'm on 'til six but can be there right after. Save a spot?"

"Claro que si!" *Of course!* "Drew and Jo will be there, too." Marisol referred to her other in-laws, Quinn's younger brother and sister. "Of course, Drew expects to be fed since he's going to help carry everything into your new home." She held up her hand. "And before you ask, it's no trouble."

Chapter 8

Grant's Crossing - present day

Marisol squeezed Quinn's arm. "You didn't have to work until six. You just wanted them to come home to a full pantry and refrigerator."

Quinn nodded. "No, I did, but after Drew called to say they only had some peanut butter and jelly on top of a few cans of food, I was able to take off a little early and go shopping. I still had the key from when Drew and I painted the place a few days before, so I snuck in a few bags of groceries." Quinn laughed after recounting that first family cookout. "That boy could put away the food, and he was only ten years old."

"And then they became teenagers." Abe said as he left the room to open the door for Tank and his wife, Araceli. "Come on in." Abe took their coats. "Derek's working on dinner."

"Doc!" Tank entered the kitchen with outstretched arms and a big grin. He pulled Derek into an enthusiastic embrace. "Good to see you, man."

"You, too." Derek grinned, returning the embrace.

"They finally let you out, huh?"

"Yeah. Christmas Eve."

Tank laughed again and tousled Derek's still-short hair. "Looking pretty shaggy there."

Derek knocked his friend's arm away with a friendly shove, then immediately ran his fingers through his dark hair, which was beginning to grow out enough to show some waves. "Close to three weeks now since my last cut."

"I see you haven't bothered to shave in a while, either." Tank scratched his own clean-shaven face in reference to Derek's thickening beard.

"I think I like it."

"It suits you."

"Thanks." Derek picked up the large wooden spoon on the counter. "How've you been?"

"I'm doing really good."

"I hear you've been promoted."

"Yeah. I'm a Lieutenant now."

"That's great. I guess I'll have to follow *your* orders now, huh?"

"Nah, man. You don't have to go into the heat yet, but it's a big responsibility to take care of the men who do."

"I'll get my certifications eventually."

"And I'll help make sure you make it out okay. We've got a great group of men there."

"No women yet?"

"Not yet. Speaking of women though," Tank leaned forward, his grin turning mischievous. "Araceli's pregnant again. Can you believe it?"

"Oh, yeah? That's great. I'm happy for you. You've always wanted a big family." Derek gave the pot on the stove another stir.

"Celi told me this is going to be the last one unless I buy her a bigger house."

They both laughed.

"When you do, I'm happy to help you fix it up."

"I could use your help now."

"Tell me when, and I'll be there."

Tank reached out and squeezed Derek's shoulder. "I'm glad you're home for good."

"I'm just glad I'm out." Derek tilted his head to one side and shrugged. He took a quick swig from his beer bottle while stirring the gumbo.

Tank dropped his arm, and they stood in silence for a minute.

"I miss him too, you know."

"I know," Derek said, not looking up from the gumbo. "It's just...."

"Just what?"

Derek stopped stirring and stared back at his friend for a moment, opening his mouth as if to say something, then closing it with a shake of his head.

"What is it?"

He leaned back to rest against the counter. His shoulders sagged. "He should be here."

"We all knew the risks, Doc."

"Yeah. I really miss him."

"I know."

"It's fucked up."

"Yeah. It is."

"Derek Mitchell?" Derek turned his head when Tank's wife sing-songed from the next room. "Where are you?"

Tank patted Derek on the back. "Come on. Let's get you through the evening first, alright?"

Grateful for Tank's understanding, Derek nodded and stood straighter just as Araceli entered the kitchen, her pregnant belly leading the way.

Unlike her husband, she let out a big squeal at the sight of Derek. And, like her husband, she greeted Derek with a big hug.

"It's so good to see you back home. I was just saying the other day how much I missed you." She turned her head to Tank. "Didn't I, Juan?" Her accent only made an appearance when she spoke her husband's given name.

Tank placed his arm around her waist and kissed her cheek. "Yes, you did."

She reached in and gave Derek another hug. "We're so glad you're back."

"Thanks, Celi." Derek couldn't resist smiling at the happiest, most upbeat person in his life. Her optimism was so contagious she could make Ebenezer Scrooge smile. He knew Tank would do anything to make her happy, as would they all since, despite not being related by blood, they were family. "Glad to be back."

Still smiling, Derek gestured toward the large kitchen table. "Have a seat and make yourselves at home. The food's not going to be ready for a while. Dad wanted to make sure we all had time to catch up."

The doorbell rang again, and a familiar voice sounded in the distance. A few moments later, Kiro walked into the kitchen carrying two large bags. As if he lived there, he set them on the table and started unpacking. "Your dad mentioned you were cooking jambalaya, but didn't plan on making pralines, so Mom sent me with dessert." He handed a large container to Tank. "Put this in the fridge."

Tank accepted the heavy container and tilted it from side to side. "What is it?"

"*Soutliash.*"

"What?" Celi asked.

Kiro bobbed his head from side to side, a typically-Bulgarian trait he picked up from his parents. "Rice pudding. More or less."

Tank placed it on a shelf inside the fridge as Kiro instructed.

He handed another big container to Derek. "Here. *Tikvinik.*"

Derek perked up and snatched the container from Kiro's hands.

He opened the lid and peeked inside at the powdered sugar-covered, pumpkin-filled flaky pastries. "Oh, how I've missed you." He popped one in his mouth and placed the rest on top of the refrigerator. "Thanks, K."

Kiro reached back into the bag and pulled out another two containers. "Here's a *meze* platter." He opened the containers, both filled with olives and other Mediterranean delights, all to be eaten as finger food. He handed one last container to Tank. "That's the salad. Put this in the fridge, too."

Tank placed it on an open shelf in the refrigerator. "I thought you said she sent dessert."

Derek nodded in agreement. "You know this wasn't a potluck, right?"

Kiro stopped moving and gave Derek a blank stare. "Have you met my mom?"

Derek held up his hands in surrender as they all laughed. "As long as Anna Marinova is in our lives, we'll never go hungry."

Kiro beamed a proud smile in return. "That's for damn sure." His parents owned Baba's Diner, known for its delicious Bulgarian food on the square down the street from Jo's. His mom always sent food to the fire station while Kiro was on shift. Even when he wasn't on duty, the other firefighters occasionally benefitted from her culinary skills. Kiro wasn't so bad in the kitchen himself, though his mom was known to shoo him out of there regardless. She ruled the roost, something no one ever disputed.

Araceli popped an olive into her mouth with a smile when Tank took his seat beside her and availed himself of some of the finger food Kiro set out.

Kiro turned to shake Derek's hand and pull him into a manly half hug. "Good to see you, D."

"Thanks, K." Derek pulled back and smirked. "Dad said you'd probably bring something."

"Well, he was right."

Abe walked into the kitchen with Quinn and Marisol right behind him. "Look at these pictures from the park, Juan."

Tank accepted the offered pictures. "Oh, man. We couldn't have been older than ten or twelve in these pictures."

Derek leaned over Tank's shoulders. "Sounds about right."

"Are those comic books?" Kiro asked with a laugh.

"Oh yeah," Derek said, grabbing one of the pictures. "Joey and I went through comics like there was no tomorrow."

Chapter 9

Grant's Crossing - Summer 1992
Joey - 10 years old

Having bounced out of the bookshop with his new comic books, Joey was as giddy as a schoolboy, which was true since he was going to start fifth grade in the fall. He and his mom finally arrived at Taft Park, located along the Scioto River just a few blocks from their new home. It had baseball diamonds, soccer fields, a building with a concession stand for when recreational leagues had games, and a few shelter areas of various sizes for small and large gatherings alike. There were walking paths weaving their way in and around beautiful shade trees with leaves that turned a stunning orange, yellow, and red every autumn. Plenty of benches were dotted throughout for folks to rest and relax within the park as well as take in a gorgeous view across the river.

Joey thought the best part was a huge playground where children of all ages could be entertained. It had everything from swing sets for little and bigger kids to a massive wooden fort, complete with rope ladders and a mini-zip line chair a couple of feet above the ground.

Joey ran off to the wooden fort where some other boys about his age were playing. Renee sat down on a bench to watch, all the while entrusted with the safety and protection of her son's new comic books.

The boys started climbing up the ropes to the covered section of the fort before jumping down the covered slide that twisted around once before opening to the ground, all covered with brown pieces of mulch. Joey got in line and started following them.

"Hey Juan! I'm king of the castle!" A skinny white boy with dark, wavy hair called out.

"I'm coming up, Derek. Better be gone by the time I get there," the olive-skinned boy, bigger than Derek and with jet-black hair, yelled while climbing the rope ladder while Derek slid down the slide. Joey ran over to the rope ladder to follow him up.

"I'm king of the castle now." Juan cried out as he thrust his hands in the air. Joey climbed into the fort just as Juan dropped his arms, almost clipping Joey in the nose except for the quick reflexes that had him snapping back as Juan's arm came down.

While his quick reflexes prevented him from taking an elbow to his nose, it didn't prevent Joey from falling backward onto his butt. "Hey!"

Not expecting someone to be there, Juan jumped back in surprise. "Sorry." He reached his hand down to help Joey up, then turned to jump to the ground just as Derek arrived and jumped down right behind him. Joey followed suit and landed in the dirt, catching his fall with his hands. After going around in circles, they would climb up the ladder, stand in the fort, then jump off or slide down the slide. Climb up and slide down. Over and over and over.

When a car horn sounded, Juan waved his goodbye and ran over to the parking lot, and got into a dark blue sedan. Joey turned around and saw Derek run off as well, leaving Joey alone in the fort. He took one last look and jumped off to run after him, but Derek had already disappeared from the playground. Joey looked left and right and didn't see him anywhere. Joey shrugged and then ran to the swings, where he sat down, swinging higher and higher, finally jumping off while on an upward swing to run over to his mom on the bench.

"Ready to go home?" Renee asked. Joey's face was flushed red from playing.

He nodded. "Yep."

Joey played at the park all summer, eventually learning the names of a few of the neighborhood kids who spent a lot of time there, including Juan and Derek, and Derek's sister, Lainee, which Derek said was a nickname from Catrina Alayne. Being a few years younger than they were, Juan and Derek were fiercely protective of her, so Joey felt like he should be, too. She always smiled up at him with her light blonde pigtails and giggled before running away. Joey thought she was weird, but he thought all girls were weird. He played along anyway and always helped her climb when he was in line behind her.

Sometimes, he saw a younger boy named Kiro out there as well. Kiro's mom was a nice lady who worked with Joey's mom at the diner. Kiro had a little sister, too, but she wasn't old enough to play with them yet, so she stayed near her mom.

He was happy when he learned that Juan and Derek were going to be in the same grade he was, all fifth graders, giving him friends before school even started. Juan always had to go home when his mom finished work which was earlier than Joey's mom. Juan always waved goodbye to them before disappearing into her shiny dark blue car after his mom honked from the parking lot.

One day, when Joey's mom was still working at the diner, and Juan had already left with his mom, Joey heard Lainee cry out in the distance, "Stop it!"

He and Derek were doing their usual climbing up the fort only to slide down over and over again when they both perked up.

"Leave me alone!" An indignant Lainee huffed when two boys kept making faces at her and trying to push her off the swing. When she didn't move for them, they would push her sideways, causing her swing to twist and turn.

Derek was already off the slide and running in their direction when Joey slid down to run after him.

"She said, leave her alone," Derek yelled as he was still about twenty feet away from them. One of the boys, older than Lainee, but about the same age as Derek and Joey, turned his head and sneered. His blond hair fell into his eyes. From a distance, Joey saw him bare his crooked teeth and shove Lainee off the swing right in front of Derek.

Derek's sister landed face-first in the wooden mulch. She started crying, but as she started to get up and step away, a red-headed boy pushed her back down. "Get out of here, little brat."

Derek got the first swing in as he ran up and punched the blond kid in the face. Joey's eyes went wide, but he kept running because he had to protect Lainee, too. All he could picture was his mom getting hit by his dad, which made him run faster and faster to catch up. He couldn't let that happen to Derek's little sister.

The red-headed boy who had pushed her down never saw him coming. He wasn't even looking in his direction. Joey surprised him by running behind him and shoving him straight to the ground. "Get away from her." He cried out as he stood over him. The kid landed hard, his arms and legs sprawled out on the ground. But then the boy turned and jumped back up and clobbered Joey in the nose. Joey felt something warm dripping down his face, but he stayed on his feet and punched back, making the rookie mistake of keeping his thumb inside his fingers when he first clenched his fist.

"Ouch!"

Angered at hurting his own thumb, Joey tried again and hit the redheaded kid's jaw with his fist, forcing the boy back while Derek fought the blond-haired boy.

Derek had taken a couple of hits before hitting the blond-haired boy again, this time in the nose, which the boy covered with his hand, leaning forward as blood dripped through his fingers. Derek pulled his fist back to throw another punch when they heard a woman yell out in a pronounced southern drawl. "THAT'S ENOUGH! ALL OF YOU!"

Joey and Derek looked at each other in frozen silence, fists clenched. Joey with his bloody nose, and Derek with the start of a shiner and a busted lip. Lainee was crying in the background.

"DEREK ABRAHAM MITCHELL!"

A wave of silence spread throughout the playground like wildfire. They all knew someone was in big, big trouble as soon as they heard a mother yell out a first, a middle, *and* a last name.

Every single kid in the park froze.

They had to pay attention. It was a real rule all children followed. Middle names only came out in the most dire of situations and only ever as a last, dangerous, spine-tingling resort. But no matter whose mother had yelled, and no matter which kid was full-named, every kid was required to pay attention.

And they did.

Because if they didn't, they all knew the consequences.

Fortunately, the two boys Derek and Joey had fought froze as well. But like the cowardly bullies they were, they darted off in the opposite direction as soon as they realized Derek's name, and not one of theirs, had been called.

Derek dropped his fist. Joey turned and saw Derek's mom, with her straight blonde hair and deep green eyes, wrap her arms around Lainee, holding her close. Lainee's sobs turned to hiccups with an occasional sniff. In a gentle voice, the lady stroked Lainee's hair, "You're ok, *ma cherie.*"

Still frozen in place, Joey's fists loosened as he watched Derek walk over to his sister, hanging his head down. "I'm sorry, Mom." Derek put his hand on Lainee's shoulder, probably not the best of moves since he still had blood from the other boy's nose on his hands, which meant Lainee's shirt now did, too. "Are you ok, Lainee?"

"What were you two thinking?" Derek's mom lowered the volume of her voice, but there was no mistaking how angry she was and who was on the receiving end of it.

And while she didn't call Joey's name, he knew he was in trouble, too. He and Derek were in this together, so he didn't say a word, not that his voice would have worked even if he wanted it to.

"Look at you both." Her angry yet caring eyes shifted from Derek to Joey and back to Derek.

"I'm sorry, Mrs. M," Joey mumbled.

"I'm sorry, Mom," Derek responded, sounding just as dejected as Joey, "but they...."

She cut him off in an instant. "Derek, we're going home. Now."

"Yes, ma'am."

She turned her eyes to Joey, striking fear into his heart as it would any kid on that playground right now. "Joey, I think you should go home, too. You can tell your mother I'll be stopping by later after she's off work."

Joey swallowed hard. "Yes, ma'am."

He didn't bother to look back at Derek. He knew his time was limited, so he turned and walked for about five steps before tearing off at a dead sprint the rest of the way home.

Meanwhile, back at the playground, in an all-encompassing wave, a collective sigh of relief fell across the other children when it was apparent they weren't in trouble. Once they sensed the all-clear, they returned to their regularly scheduled playtime.

The back door clicked. Renee turned the handle and walked into the kitchen, happy to return home after a long day of work. She knew her workday wasn't done the moment she set her purse and keys on the table and glanced over to the counter to see opened jars of peanut butter and grape jelly. With a sigh, she twisted the lid on the grape jelly and put it in the fridge. She covered the peanut butter and wrapped a twist tie around the bag of bread, pushing them both against the back of the counter.

Opening and closing her hands, she washed them and dampened a dishcloth to wipe off the cabinet handle that still held a small glob of grape jelly. "Oh, Joey."

The house was quiet, so she walked up to his loft to find him sound asleep on his beanbag chair.

"What the...?"

She rushed over and dropped to her knees. "Joey? Baby? What happened? Are you ok?" He woke with a start as she cupped his face, looking him up and down. His nose and eyes were swelling and turning purple underneath.

He flinched as she gently pressed her fingers around his nose and eyes. "Ouch!"

Her hands still cupped his face as she leaned back and switched from concern to disappointment. "Joseph Miles Parker."

He tensed up as soon as she full-named him.

"Were you in a fight?"

"Yes?"

"Ok." She sat back and cocked a brow. "What happened? Tell me everything."

Joey recounted the story of what happened. He told her about the boys picking on Lainee and how he and Derek stuck up for her when their bullying turned physical. Just as he was finishing up, there was a knock on the door.

Renee pressed her lips together in a straight line as she exhaled. "I'm going to go get that, ok?"

Joey nodded, then stared back at the floor.

"Hey."

"Yeah, Mom?"

"I love you, ok?"

"More than anything?"

"And no matter what," she added as she walked downstairs.

Still in her work uniform, Renee opened the door to be greeted by a slightly taller woman with a young boy in tow. Looking down at the boy, complete with his own black eye and a cut lip, she could only assume he was Derek.

"Hi."

The woman spoke in a pronounced southern drawl. "I'm Katherine Mitchell. This is my son, Derek. Are you Mrs. Parker?"

Renee smiled. "Yes. Call me Renee. Please come in." She closed the door after they stepped in. "Would you like some tea? It's already sweetened. I hope that's ok."

"Oh, I'm southern. Sweet is the only way to make tea." The woman's smile was genuine. "And please, call me Katherine."

Renee felt instantly comfortable around her. She called up to the loft. "Joey? Would you come down here, please?" Returning her gaze back to Katherine and Derek, she extended her arm. "Let's sit down in the kitchen." She walked in and moved her purse and keys to the counter, grateful she'd done a bit of cleanup when she first got home.

She poured four glasses of sweet tea and set them down on the table. She'd also picked up some cookies the day before, so she placed them on a plate to share. Joey showed up in the kitchen but didn't step inside until Renee caught him hiding behind the wall.

"Come on in and sit down, Joey. It's alright." She beckoned him inside, where he sat down next to her without a word.

Joey and Derek looked at each other's faces, both sharing a proud smirk until both their moms cleared their throats, bringing them back into the real world.

Katherine took one look at Joey. "Looks like you're not immune to a shiner or two either, are you, young man?"

His eyes widened for a moment. "No, ma'am."

"Well. You should both know that the other two boys are going to be punished as well. Their mothers were not happy with what they did to Lainee." She directed her gaze to Joey's mom. "Renee, I am so sorry Joey got involved in this. My son is not the type who gets into fights with other boys. But nor are my children taught to walk away. Lainee stood up for herself as much as she could until the other two boys started physically hurting her, which is when Derek and Joey both made a beeline to stop them."

She looked at both Joey and Derek. "I'll never repeat this, but I'm proud and grateful to both of you for standing up for Lainee, even if that meant resolving it through physical means. Though," she gazed pointedly at Derek, "if you ever tell your father I just said that, I'll recant everything."

Joey knitted his brow. "Recant?" He turned his confused gaze to his mom and then back to Katherine.

Katherine smiled. "It means that I'll take it back and pretend I never said it, so I hope you never have to resort to fighting ever again."

Renee smiled at Joey and rubbed his back. She could tell he and Derek wanted to talk to each other. "Joey, do you want to go upstairs and show Derek your room?" She looked across the table. "Derek, do you like comic books?"

Even his swollen, black eye widened at the thought of looking through comic books. "Yeah!"

Katherine cleared her throat with a sideways glance towards her son.

"I mean, yes, ma'am."

Renee turned her attention to her son, "Joey, want to show him your collection?"

"Yeah...yes, ma'am."

She shook her head, suppressing a smile. She stood up and placed some ice cubes inside two plastic bags, and wrapped them inside a towel. She handed one homemade ice pack each to Joey and Derek. "Go on, boys. Run upstairs."

They took the packs and ran from the room.

"Now." Katherine waited until they'd left the kitchen, then turned back around and picked up a cookie. "It seems our boys have become fast friends. Do you have dinner plans this weekend? Abe and I would love to have you both over for a cookout."

"Sounds great."

Chapter 10

Grant's Crossing - present day

"Pretty sure that fight cemented our friendship." Derek grabbed the box of pictures from the coffee table between two couches next to the fireplace.

"That it did." Abe stood up to toss another log onto the fire." You and Joey could be such troublemakers."

Derek sat down and started sifting through pictures. "The day of the fight, he gave me a grand tour of his comic book collection. It was his pride and joy. I had to learn to enclose them all in plastic bags; otherwise, he wouldn't let me borrow them." Derek took a sip of his drink before continuing. "He had everything: X-Men, Captain America, Iron Man, of course. Once I showed him my collection of Batman, Superman, and Wonder Woman, the DC versus Marvel comics debates began. Eventually, he started coming over to our place after school since his Mom was still at work...."

"...or working two jobs," Tank suggested.

Derek agreed, and then turned his head as Lainee walked through the front door.

"Hello, everyone! Happy New Year!" Lainee greeted everyone, lighting up the room with her bright smile that extended all the way up to her beautiful green eyes, the same color she and Derek both inherited from their mother. She wore her long blonde hair in a braid that hung almost to her waist.

After a big hug, Abe helped her out of her coat while she shifted her young daughter from one arm to the other. "Sorry I'm late, but someone," she kissed her daughter on the cheek, "didn't want to take a nap today!"

"CATIE CAT!" Derek leaned in to kiss his sister on the cheek and take his niece into his arms. He carried her back to the couch, where he set her on his lap, making her giggle while bouncing her on his knee. "Where's Tasha?" He carefully untied and removed Catie's purple knit hat and matching purple coat freeing her out-of-control blonde curls.

"Still on her way up from Cincy."

Kiro made a space for Lainee next to Derek.

"She should be here pretty soon," she added.

"We're talking comic books," Tank said.

Lainee rolled her eyes. "Of course you are."

"And how Joey was always over here after school." Derek made faces at little Catie, who matched him - silly expression for silly expression.

"I think Joey's mom liked it since Mom and Dad always made us do our homework right after school."

"Don't remind me." Derek made another face as Catie broke out into fits of giggles.

"And you both graduated at the top of your classes," a proud Abe reminded the room.

"You guys used to read a lot of graphic novels, too, right?" Lainee asked.

"Oh, yeah. Still do, though now it's more *The Walking Dead* rather than *Batman & Dracula: Red Rain*. That graphic novel became one of his favorites. I swear, it didn't take us long to read everything in each other's collections."

"You're such a nerd."

"Yes, I am. My collection has everything in nearly mint or mint condition thanks to Joey's influence. I'd probably have enough to buy a new truck if I were to sell them all."

"Didn't you read them as well, Tank?"

"Oh no," Derek spoke before Tank had a chance to answer. "He read poetry."

"What?" Lainee couldn't believe what she was hearing. "How did I not know this?"

"That's because somebody's girlfriend," Derek winked while pointing obviously at Araceli, "loved Lorca."

"And Pablo Neruda," Araceli added with a quick shimmy.

Marisol wore a proud expression on her face as she listened to her former students discuss her favorite writers.

"Do you still teach those, or have you moved on to something else?"

"Something else?" Marisol scoffed. "Those are all classics, along with Miguel de Cervantes and Gabriel Garcia Marquez, and Borges, and Allende...." She shrugged. "I studied Spanish lit, and I love sharing that with my students."

"How were you both allowed to take Spanish, anyway?" Derek asked Tank and Araceli. "You grew up speaking it!"

Tank held up his hands. "It was an easy A."

Marisol turned her attention to Derek. "Tell me. How did you and Joey get so many comic books?"

"Shrewd entrepreneurial skills," Abe explained.

"I remember you both raked leaves or shoveled snow to make money. I opted for babysitting." Lainee picked up a picture, made a silly face while showing it to her giggling daughter, then placed it back inside the box to grab another.

On the opposite couch, Tank leaned closer to Araceli as if telling a secret; he spoke at full volume, "They always argued about DC vs. Marvel."

"We *debated*, thank you very much," Derek corrected his

friend.

"Seriously. You and Joey would never shut up." An exasperated Tank held up one hand for each comic book hero. "Batman. No, Iron Man. No, Batman. No, Iron Man."

Laughter filled the room.

"*Dios mío,*" Araceli directed a pleading look at Lainee. "They were always like this, weren't they?"

"Sure were."

"I'm still a DC guy, but Joey loved his Marvel Universe," Derek said, keeping the conversation on the important topic at hand. "He dragged me to every one of those movies. We were going to see *Guardians of the Galaxy* when we got back to Benning." Derek's smile faded as he held Catie still and stared at the fireplace for a few beats. "Now I can't bring myself to watch it."

Trying to keep it light, Tank held up both hands. "You even...," he made air quotes, "...*debated* comics while we went camping."

A smile pulled Derek from his reverie. "Yeah. Those were some great trips."

"Yeah, they were," Tank agreed.

"I loved every minute of those trips." Abe tipped his glass in Tank's direction. "Katherine and I always wanted a lot of kids, so as much work as it was, camping with you three growing boys every summer was the best. I guess I can't really call that work, can I?"

Derek jutted his chin toward his friend. "I think Tank enjoyed being with only two other kids instead of his seventeen siblings."

"Hey! There were only six of us." Tank tried to contain his laughter. "Poor Enrique. I left my little brother home alone with our four sisters. I don't think he's ever forgiven me for that."

"Might be more convincing if you didn't laugh while admitting that," Derek quipped.

"You're working on your own family now," Abe said. "Since Araceli got pregnant again, I don't think you've stopped smiling."

Araceli and Tank both beamed broad smiles, proving Abe right.

"You both always wanted your own family," Derek said. "I wouldn't be surprised if you're already planning your fifth."

"Don't rush us," Araceli said, trying but failing to look upset. "Let us have our fourth baby first!"

"We should go again this summer," Abe said. "It's been a long time, and it might be good to get back to nature."

"That sounds like fun. I haven't been camping in forever." Tank directed his gaze to his wife. "We want to take the kids camping when they're a bit older."

"You should come with us," Derek said while sifting through more pictures.

Tank offered his wife an excited look that she countered with an appeasing smile. "We'll talk about it."

Lainee leaned forward. "I can be in town to help you watch your little ones. It'll be like one long play date for Catie."

"See?" Tank held a hand out. "I can go."

Celi arched her brow.

Tank turned back to Derek. "I'll uh... have to let you know."

Derek pulled a picture out of one of the shoe boxes on the coffee table. "Oh look - this is from the sleepover for Joey's thirteenth birthday. And here are the camping pictures from that year. God, rafting on the Nantahala and Ocoee rivers was so much fun." He held it out of Catie's reach so Tank could see.

"Yeah. It was," Tank said, smiling at the memory. "That's when your dad tried to teach us the constellations, but Joey would always get the names wrong, so he started making up his own."

"He was hilarious. Forever calling them the Big and Little Flippers."

"And don't forget the coat hanger."

"The coat hanger?" Like everyone else, Quinn's furrowed brow gave away his confusion.

"Yeah," Derek said while catching his breath as his laughter died down. Joey's birthday is in August, making him a Leo. The constellation for his sign looks like a coat hanger."

Tank pointed to Derek. "You had the teapot."

Derek shrugged. "Sagittarius," he said to heads nodding in understanding.

"Yeah," Tank shook with laughter. "That turned into a teapot murder bot like the thing in the first *Transformers* movie."

"Sure, but yours was just a tent."

"We Libras are practical. Besides," Tank leaned back and put his arms around Celi's shoulders. "It's a big tent. I like to be inclusive."

Joey's final letter popped into Derek's head. "Hey, K," Derek addressed Kiro over the top of Catie's big curls.

"Yes?"

"You should go with us next summer."

Tank gave Kiro a friendly tap on his arm. "You should."

"I'd like that."

Chapter 11

Grant's Crossing - 1994

Joey - 13 years old

"HEY." JOEY PULLED OUT A NEW COMIC BOOK FROM HIS backpack and dropped it on Derek's bed as he walked in. "Have you seen this Captain America?"

"Not yet." Derek picked it up and took a seat at his desk. "Is this part of *The Fighting Chance* series?"

"Yeah. It's pretty good." Joey plopped down on Derek's bed and leaned against the wall. "I've got 'em all now if you want to read more."

"Have you seen the latest *Batman: Bloodstorm*? Came out last year, but I just got my hands on a copy." He reached to his nightstand for the graphic novel and handed it over to Joey.

"Cool." Joey opened it up and started reading.

Derek's mom knocked on the door, pleased to find both their noses in books. "Hey, boys. Dinner'll be ready in half an hour. Chicken creole. Hope that's okay."

"Yep. Thanks, Mom." Derek returned to the comic book after she closed the door. "I love Mom's chicken creole."

Joey tilted his head. "Have I had that yet?"

"Pretty sure," Derek replied without looking up. "If not, you'll love it. You know Mom's cooking is the best."

"I don't know. My mom makes a pretty great meatloaf."

"Meatloaf?"

"Yeah. I like it."

"If you say so."

A half-hour later, Lainee barged into Derek's room.

"Hey!" Derek cried out.

"Derek? Joey? Mom wants you downstairs," she blurted out before disappearing down the hall.

Derek finished the last page and closed it. "Come on. Let's go."

Joey rushed out of the room first. "Race you downstairs!"

Derek chased him downstairs where they almost missed the turn into the dining room and back to the kitchen.

"Slow down, boys," Abe called out as they whooshed by him.

"I won," Derek exclaimed with his arms triumphantly raised in the air.

"Yeah?" Joey challenged him. "I'm taller than you are."

"No you're not. I'm taller.

"Are not."

"Boys?" Derek's mom spoke up. "Alright. Shoes off. Stand straight. Back to back."

Derek and Joey kicked off their shoes, sending them flying in all different directions, then rushed to stand next to each other to see who was taller.

Derek pushed Joey back. "No tip toes!"

"I'm not!"

"Yes, you are."

"That's enough," Derek's mom spoke. "Heels on the ground. Both of you. Come on."

Derek and Joey calmed down enough to place their feet flat on the floor. Derek's mom placed a hand atop each of their heads. "Hmm. It's pretty close."

"I'm taller," Joey whispered.

"Are not," Derek whispered back.

"Am, too. I'm already taller than my mom."

"Abraham. Would you come here, please?"

"Is everything okay?"

"Yes. I need a second opinion, please."

"Of course." Abe joined them in the kitchen where Katherine addressed him over the top of Joey and Derek's heads.

"Who do you think is taller? This one? Or that one?"

"Did she point at you or me?" Derek asked Joey.

"Don't know," Joey answered. "I couldn't see."

"Joey?"

"Yes, ma'am?"

"How tall is your mama?"

"Five feet six inches, I think."

"Wow. Then you're both taller than she is."

"Yes!" They exclaimed in unison, happy to finally be taller than a lot of the girls in school.

"Now which one of you is taller. Hmm. Abraham? I think it's this one. What do you think?"

Abe rubbed his fingers along his clean-shaven jawline as if deep in thought. "I agree. Definitely that one."

"Well, Mom? Who's taller?"

"Sorry to break the news, but Joey's taller this time."

"Yes!" Joey pumped his fist in victory.

Derek's shoulders slouched in defeat. "I'll never be taller than Dad."

"Sure you will, son. I was barely over five feet tall at your age. Only five feet, four inches tall the start of my sophomore year. I grew another eight inches by the time I started at Tulane." Abe squeezed Derek's shoulder. "You'll get there."

Derek's mom clapped her hands. "Now put your shoes by the back door. Derek, fix the glasses. Joey? Need you to set the table, please. Dinner's almost ready."

They worked at setting out flatware and plates, and even though

Joey wasn't a Mitchell by blood, he was close enough, meaning he shared in the chores around mealtimes. Derek's mom almost always did the cooking, so whichever kid was left got to help Abe with the dishes. Tonight, Lainee had that pleasure. Setting the table was definitely the easier chore, so Joey and Derek were happy tonight, restarting their DC vs. Marvel comics debate they'd been having since they met two years earlier, Derek said, "There's going to be another Batman vs. Predator series this year." He filled the glasses with sweet tea, spilling a little over the sides as he poured.

"Yeah, but not until Christmas." Joey started laying out the flatware. "In the meantime, We have over 300 Iron Man comics to read. Can DC top that?"

"Yeah. Superman."

"That's enough, boys." Katherine smiled as she patted Derek's back. "Abe? Lainee?" She called out from the bottom of the stairs. "Dinner's ready."

Everyone sat down at the table. They bowed their heads while Katherine said grace. They made the sign of the cross, which Joey didn't really understand, but he said *amen* anyway. He wasn't raised in a religious family but had learned from his mom always to respect others' beliefs, especially when he was in their home. Derek never really talked about it, so Joey felt it was either too personal or he did it because his parents made him.

"I hear you're taller, Joey. Ha. Ha. Derek's shorter."

"Don't make fun of your brother, Lainee," Katherine put an end to the teasing.

"Why? Derek makes fun of me all the time."

"I'm your brother. I'm allowed."

"At least Blake doesn't pick up on me anymore."

"He'd better not or Joey and I will have to..."

"Derek!" Abe's stern voice called his name.

"Talk to him, Dad. That's all."

Abe cleared his throat as he ran his napkin across his lips. "Are you ready for our camping trip this year, boys?" Abe asked, effectively changing the subject.

Derek cut a bit of chicken. "Camping then the Aquarium of the Americas."

The boys camped out every summer while Derek's mom and sister got a head start visiting his mom's side of the family in New Orleans. Derek and his dad always joined them after, but it started with a week of getting all muddy, catching their own meals, and living in a non-climate-controlled tent.

"Yeah!" Joey sipped his tea. "I can't wait to go again. Last year was a blast!"

"Don't skip over Joey's birthday, Dad."

"That's right, son! You'll be thirteen on Friday, won't you, Joey?"

"Yes, sir. August 4, 1981!"

Abe shook his head. "Teenagers already. How time flies."

"Goodness, Abraham." Derek's mom gave a mischievous smile. "Let's not rush it." She turned to Joey. "You're planning a sleepover, right? Probably filled with comic books and action flicks?"

"That's right." Joey shared a grin with Derek. "Derek'll be there. And Juan, too. We're going out for pizza first."

"The Three Musketeers."

Lainee rolled her eyes while her brother laughed. "What does that make me? Maid Marian?"

"No, Lainee." Derek turned to his little sister. "That's Robin Hood. You'd be Maid Catrina of Grant's Crossing or something."

"A maid?" She scrunched her face when he used her first name, which she had never used. "Can't I at least be a queen or at least a princess? Can't I be somebody powerful?"

Her mom came to the rescue. "You can be whoever and whatever you want, Lainee."

"Not according to Derek. I just have to be some girl who sits around and waits to be rescued. I'd rather do my own rescuing." She was incensed. "Besides, who rescues them when they need it?"

Joey spoke up when he saw Derek had just taken a bite. "We don't need rescuing, Lainee. We're boys."

Derek arched his eyebrows and nodded in agreement while he chewed.

"Someday, you'll need me to come to your rescue, you know," Lainee insisted, causing both boys to laugh. "Well? You might."

Joey and Derek received a raised eyebrow from Derek's mom as she cleared her throat, putting a quick end to their laughter.

Lainee rolled her eyes again. "Boys have all the fun."

Abe rested a hand on her shoulder. "You're always welcome to come camping with us. It's going to be a great trip this year. We'll go fishing and white water rafting...."

"That sounds fun."

Derek looked panicked. "But, Dad...."

Abe held up a hand that stopped Derek in his tracks. "And you'll have to clean your own fish."

"Ewww..." Lainee made a face. "And spend a week with boys who don't take showers and stick bugs on me?" She shuddered as Derek laughed. "I'd rather go to the Aquarium with Mom and Uncle Mick."

"See?" Abe glanced over in time to see Derek exhale in relief. "Looks like you'll be having some fun, too."

"Wait." Derek stopped laughing. "I thought we were all going to the aquarium after Dad and I get there."

"We are," his mom assured him. "We'll go again when you and your father fly in. Then we'll go for beignets and crawfish."

"Yes!" Derek and Lainee were both happy again.

"Have you tried beignets, Joey?" Derek's mom wondered as she cut herself a bite of chicken.

"No, ma'am." Joey shook his head. "What are they?"

She narrowed her eyes. "Hmm... it's a fried pastry that's covered in powdered sugar. Sometimes it has a fruit filling."

"Like strawberries?"

"Yes. Or raspberries. They're delicious but really filling, too."

"Is it like a funnel cake you get at the fair?"

She made a face. "Not quite, it's got a different texture, and it tastes much better." When Joey looked a little confused, she continued, "Tell you what. I'll make you some for your birthday. How about that?"

Joey perked up. "Yes, please!"

Joey spent the night with the Mitchells the night before they left on their camping trip. He, Derek, and Juan made quick work of the beignets Derek's mom had made the weekend earlier for Joey's birthday, so she made another batch for their trip. Renee planned to drive Lainee and Katherine to the airport the following day so they could fly down to New Orleans to be with Katherine's side of the family.

As for the campers, apparently leaving at six o'clock sharp was way too early for twelve and thirteen-year-old boys because Joey, Derek, and Juan fell asleep the moment they buckled their seatbelts in Abe's SUV and didn't stir again until Abe was well past Cincinnati and coming up on Lexington.

"Are we there yet?" A groggy Derek asked his dad as they pulled off the highway.

Abe laughed. "Almost halfway. I just need a bathroom break and to top off the tank."

Abe shifted the car into park after pulling into the gas station. "Boys? If you need to pee, better do it here. We won't stop again until we get to the campground."

"Huh?" The boys answered in unison, their sleepy lids barely opened when they realized they weren't moving.

"And don't forget, we already have plenty of snacks inside the car," Abe added, figuring they would want one of every snack inside.

He got out to top off the tank on his SUV while they ran inside to use the bathrooms.

A few hours later, they pulled into their designated campsite in the Nantahala National Forest and started setting up their large tent. It slept at least six, which made it perfect for Abe and the three boys, along with a good portion of their stuff. It also had a screened-in section outside the main tent where they slept, so they could be protected from the weather during meals if need be.

Before too long, they'd picked up some live bait and rented a small motorboat from a shop on a nearby lake. They slowly made their way out to a great spot in an inlet away from other boaters. Once Abe killed the engine, they dropped their hooks in the water.

"This is the life." Abe smiled as he cast his line.

"Yeah," Derek agreed as he stuck a worm on his hook. "Don't think Lainee would have wanted to see the worms, much less touch them."

"Oh, I don't know," his dad laughed. "She had no problem taking care of a spider for you that one time."

Joey and Juan snorted.

"That doesn't count." Derek passed the container of worms along with a dirty look.

"Was that last year when you were stuck out in the rain and refused to come in the house?" Joey asked.

Derek exhaled. "I didn't think I told you about that."

"You didn't," Joey smirked. "Lainee did."

"In my defense, my hands were full, and there were two spiders." Any chance of credibility was lost when Derek held his hands wide enough to hold a watermelon. "Really big wolf spiders. And when she opened the door, one dropped right on my forehead. I shook it off, but then another one landed on the doorknob. I only got wet because she had to go in for a container to capture it. She took her time, too," he huffed.

"She just doesn't like to hurt anything," Abe explained. "She really wouldn't hurt a fly."

Derek shuddered as Joey and Juan laughed at the thought of Derek getting totally drenched in the rain while Lainee saved one lone wolf spider.

Back at the campsite, they scaled and cleaned all the fish they caught that afternoon. Supervised by Derek's dad, they cooked them on a skillet over the campfire. The boys always did a little bit more to prepare their dinners than on the previous year's camping trip.

They topped off the day by telling ghost stories and stuffing their faces with s'mores. More than one marshmallow went up in flames and landed in the campfire, though never without the requisite dive-bombing sound effects.

Fortunately, Abe always made sure to pack an extra bag of marshmallows for just this contingency.

Five days passed by with the four men, as Derek, Joey, and Juan were quick to label themselves, doing nothing but living out in nature. Derek loved hiking and fishing the best. Juan loved telling stories around the campfire and picking out constellations. Joey loved being on the water, something they definitely planned to do at least twice next year.

Chapter 12

Grant's Crossing - present day

"Look at this picture." Lainee reached into the box of pictures she now held on her lap and pulled one out of Derek, Joey, and her mom. "Mom was so beautiful."

"Yeah, she was." Abe's eyes were full of sadness and love. "We tried so hard to protect you from the cancer's return, but you were both too smart. You figured it out."

Derek eyed the picture Lainee held up for him to see. "We spent so much time with the Milanovs. I didn't see Joey as much for a while."

Kiro took the offered picture. "Mom still tells stories about how your mom was one of her very first friends here. She helped my parents get settled and find jobs. Heck, your mom even kept the books for a while after Mom and Dad bought the diner. Mom always said that she could never repay her for everything she did for us."

"They became best friends. Since they were both new to Grant's Crossing, I think they decided it was best to join forces." Abe laughed at the memory.

"Mom said she and my grandparents had a lot of help after they first left Bulgaria." Kiro laughed. "Pretty sure she decided to adopt you Mitchells as her way of paying it forward."

Abe shared a grateful look with Kiro. "Your parents have always been good to us. I'm proud to call them friends."

They looked up when the doorbell rang. "That should be Tasha." Lainee ran to answer the door, returning with her girlfriend, as well as two more Strager siblings.

"Hi, Jo. "Quinn leaned in to hug his sister then glanced back at the front door. "Where's Mike tonight?"

"Holding down the fort at the bar," Jo answered of her husband. "I'll be honest. It's nice to escape for a bit."

"I don't doubt it."

"Nice to see you off duty, Quinn." Drew shook his brother's hand, drawing him into a hug.

"You as well."

Drew moved on to kiss his sister-in-law on the cheek. "Rod at the office preparing his case?"

"Yes," Marisol beamed a proud smile for her husband. "He goes to trial next week."

Derek handed his niece to his dad and stood up to check on dinner.

"Smells great, Derek." Drew stepped closer to the stove, where Derek was stirring some food in a huge soup pot. He closed his eyes and waved the delicious aroma closer.

"Thanks. That's the gumbo. Jambalaya will be ready a little later."

"Progressive dinner, huh?"

"It's the best kind."

"I might have to start running again after tonight."

Lainee laughed as she walked past her brother toward the refrigerator to refill everyone's drinks. "Yeah. Dad's happy that at least one of us picked up some of Mom's culinary skills."

"I did learn quite a bit from her," Derek said as he leaned in for a half hug from his sister.

"I miss her so much."

Derek pulled his sister closer. "Me, too."

Chapter 13

Grant's Crossing - 1997

Joey - 16 years old

The Grant's Crossing Fighting Cannons football team was off to a rough start to the season with their opponent keeping them down to a single field goal. Joey sat with Derek's family in the stands since Derek and Juan were both on the field playing their hearts out.

"Dad? Why isn't Derek doing anything?" Lainee called out, extending her arms in frustration at her brother, who couldn't seem to make it past the defensive line each time the quarterback handed him the ball.

"Give him a chance, Lainee." Her dad leaned toward his daughter while keeping an eye on the game. "It's the first game of the season. They're just getting their footing."

"Wouldn't it be easier to get his footing if he actually stayed upright for more than a few steps at a time?"

Joey's shoulders shook in a failed attempt to contain his laughter. She made a good point.

Sitting farthest away from her dad, Joey leaned in so only Lainee could hear. "Good question, Lainee." He shrugged and tapped her arm with his elbow. "If they keep playing like this, it'll be a long season."

Derek ended up being pummeled all night long by the other team. The Fighting Cannons' offensive line, which included Juan and a tall kid named Logan Shepherd, a First Team All-State lineman who was already being scouted by Big Ten and SEC football programs, was not doing well at all. They had the effectiveness of a bunch of kittens trying to tackle the New England Patriots in the Superbowl for all the progress they were making.

Or weren't making.

The fourth quarter started with the Cannons down 7-3. After several minutes of play, the score remained unchanged.

Lainee exhaled and slouched down in her seat, exasperation seething up through her pores. "At least we're in the final quarter. It'll be over soon, right?"

"Yep," Joey agreed, knowing his friends on the field were probably more frustrated than the fans seemed to be in the stands.

The cheerleaders did their best to keep the fans in the game by starting another cheer. Smiles pasted on their faces, they started waving their silver and navy pom poms.

"LET'S - GO - CAN-NONS!"

Clap. Clap. Clap clap clap.

"G - C - CAN-NONS!"

Clap. Clap. Clap clap clap.

Joey and Lainee joined in, but not nearly as enthusiastically as they had in the first half.

Joey offered a glance toward the band on the other side of the stands. He couldn't even remember the last time they'd played anything. Halftime, maybe? During a time-out?

The refs signaled the two-minute warning, adding to the pressure to make a final score.

On the second down, the quarterback handed the ball off to Derek. Out of nowhere, Logan blocked one of the other team's players, giving Derek a small opening to spin around and gain a few yards.

The fans sat up a little straighter for the next play.

Then it happened.

Juan rushed forward like a bat out of hell and made a jaw-droppingly brilliant block to create a massive hole right down the middle of what was left of the other team's defensive line. Derek slipped through and broke into a sprint toward the end zone.

Everyone in the stands jumped up to their feet, yelling and screaming. "RUN, DEREK! RUN!"

"Did you see that block by Palacios?" A parent behind them yelled out. "He rolled them over like a tank out there!"

Derek was still running toward the end zone when another man yelled. "YEA! WAY TO GO, TANK!"

Enough people overheard the Tank comment that more voices started yelling that as well before going all out and cheering for Derek as he ran down the field. Joey and Lainee screamed their heads off the second he cleared their opponent's defensive line and crossed over the 50-yard line. With no more players in front of him, Derek ran another fifty yards to coast right into the end zone.

"GO, DEREK!" Lainee screamed, no longer unimpressed.

Yelling and screaming with Lainee, Joey almost didn't notice Derek's dad surreptitiously helping his wife to stand.

Abe's hand was wrapped around her waist, supporting her as she stood. She was grinning, excitement apparent on her face, but she was otherwise standing still, not bouncing up and down like he, Lainee, and the rest of the fans.

Joey turned his head back to the field in time to see Juan and the team running toward Derek in the end zone. Derek's hands were in the air until he leaned backward and pointed them both toward Juan, his mouth wide open, yelling at the top of his lungs. They chest-bumped the second they reached each other before the team closed around them in the end zone.

After the Cannons scored the extra point and took the lead at 10-7, it took the refs a few minutes and a delay of game penalty to break up the team celebration and get the game going again. With less than half a minute to go, all the Cannons needed was to keep the other team out of field goal range to maintain the lead and win the game.

It was a tense eighteen seconds, but the Cannons' defense managed to hold off their opponents. At the other end of the stands, the tiny school marching band started playing the school fight song, barely able to be heard above the din of the cheering crowd.

With the final whistle, everyone jumped to their feet once again, excited to start the season with a win.

Lainee's loud cheers drew Derek's gaze right to them in the stands. The whole family and Joey waved down to him, sharing in the excitement before the team disappeared into the locker room.

Derek's parents waited for the crowd to thin out a bit before leaving, so Joey stayed with them after the teams left the field. The sounds of shoes clanking against the metal steps echoed out in the nearly silent night. They sat chatting about the game as spectators filed out of the stands, many patting Abe on the shoulder to congratulate him on Derek's touchdown. Joey heard several comments about how proud he and his wife must be. Abe and Katherine were both soaking it up.

Happy about the win, students turned their excitement to the post-game dance, soon starting in the high school gym. Joey would catch up with Derek and Juan there after they cleaned up from the game and the coaches released them. In the meantime, with most of the crowd gone, he talked to Lainee as her parents stood and carefully worked their way down the steps toward the parking lot. He noticed they took their time and wondered if their mom wasn't feeling well tonight but still wanted to see Derek play.

Joey and Derek yelled when they saw each other, greeting each other with handshakes and half hugs. "Hey, Tank," Joey laughed as he called Juan by the new nickname he was given in the stands. "Great game tonight!"

Juan rolled his eyes and shook hands with a half hug. "Thanks, man." Juan put his hand on the shoulder of another player who walked up next to them. "Were it not for Shepherd here, I would never have been able to plow the road for Derek to score the winning touchdown."

Joey looked up at the crooked grin of a just over six-foot tall, dark-haired fellow sophomore and extended his hand. "Great game, Logan."

"Thanks." Logan shook Joey's hand, holding on for what seemed a second longer than normal. His eyes sparkled before Joey looked away. "Hey, there's a party tonight at Hunter's place after the dance. You guys should come."

"Can't," Joey offered in response. "I have a meet tomorrow."

Logan furrowed his brow. "Meet?"

"Cross country. First one of the season."

"Oh yeah? You run track, too, right?"

"Yeah. Distance and relays, mostly."

"We'll be on the team together then. Long jump and triple jump this year. Coach wants me to try running distances, too, but I'm not so sure about that. I like to run, but not for speed."

The sound of girls' laughter nearby drew their gaze. Derek couldn't pull his eyes away from one of the girls as they walked by.

Joey smacked Derek in the arm. "When are you going to ask her out, D?"

"Ask who out?" Logan asked.

"Kaitlyn," Juan and Joey answered in unison.

Juan gave Derek's shoulder a friendly shove to pull him out of his daydream.

Shrugging him off, Derek gave them all a dirty look. "Shut up, Tank."

Juan stared back for a second before laughing. "That's going to stick, isn't it?"

"Tank?" Logan looked confused. "Where did that come from?"

Joey tilted his head in Logan's direction. "Some guy in the stands yelled that he plowed through the other team's defensive line like a tank, and it caught on."

Logan nodded and patted Juan on the back. "Not a bad name. Do that every game, and we'll both end up playing for Ohio State."

Juan laughed as he turned to eye Araceli with her long, black hair pulled back on one side with a barrette leaving behind a few wispy strands hanging down to frame her round face. Still in her cheerleading outfit, her brown eyes sparkled as she smiled in his direction.

"If it helps us win, I'll do it." Juan sounded confident as she walked up to him. His own smile widened when she grabbed his hand and pulled him toward the dance floor.

"In the meantime, I have more important things to do," he called back with a grin. He wrapped his arms around his girlfriend and danced to a slow song by Matchbox 20.

"He's already forgotten about us, hasn't he?" Joey asked.

"Yep." Derek and Logan both agreed.

Derek opened the door the next evening to Joey, Renee, and Quinn. "Hi. Come on in." He held the door open, shaking Joey's hand with a half hug. "Mom and Dad are out back."

Renee gave him a hug before Quinn held out his hand. "Great game last night."

Derek shook his hand and grinned from ear to ear. "Thanks!"

Quinn gave him a playful jab with his elbow and leaned in. "Bet that touchdown in the fourth quarter felt good."

"Oh yeah. Definitely."

Renee and Katherine greeted each other with a hug. Then, they each exchanged quick pecks on the cheek from Abe and Quinn. The two older men shook hands and immediately escaped to the grill so they could bond over cooking over an open flame and its modicum of danger, leaving the women behind to chat.

Joey walked outside and received a warm hug from Derek's mom. "I'm so proud of you. Derek said you beat everyone at the cross country meet this morning."

"Thanks, Mrs. M." He grinned. "Got a PR, too."

Her brow furrowed. "A PR?"

"Personal record," he translated.

Her face lit up with a smile. "Ahh. That's terrific, Joey. Your mom must be so proud, I'm sure."

"As proud as a mama can be," Renee added as she sat at the table on their deck.

"Make yourselves comfortable. Dinner's just about ready. I just need to pull something out of the oven."

Renee started to get back up. "Let me help you."

"I've got it, Mom." Joey turned to follow Derek's mom inside.

"Thanks, baby."

Joey followed Katherine through the back door to help and was put right to work carrying out the food. Once he set the broccoli rice casserole on the table outside, he went back in just as she was transferring a tray of drink glasses to the table where a pitcher of iced tea waited. Her hands were shaking, and started to give way. Joey rushed forward to get his hands underneath the tray to catch it at the last second before it crashed to the floor.

"I've got it, Mrs. M," he said while the tipped-over glass teetered on the edge. His fingers gripped both the tray and her fingers, which no longer supported the tray at all. He adjusted his fingers so she could pull her hands away.

"I've got it." His voice softened as he looked directly at her, trying to offer up as much assurance as a sixteen-year-old kid could. He knew every member of the Mitchell family was strong and independent. And while he did his best not to show it, it surprised him that Derek's mom was anything but that at the moment.

Derek's mom pressed her lips together as she gave Joey a slight nod and withdrew her hold on the tray. She rubbed her hands together as she fought back tears. "I guess I'm a bit clumsy today." She forced a laugh. "Thank you." She turned back around to the counter and tried to look busy as if she were hiding her fear from him.

"It's no problem." Joey turned and set the tray on the kitchen table, righting the tipped glass. He was grateful that nothing had fallen to the floor and shattered. "We all have those days."

Joey kept his voice cheerful as he placed the pitcher of tea on the tray and picked it back up. He glanced outside to see Derek watching through the door with a sad expression on his face.

Joey nodded. "D. Get the door, will ya?" he called out through the screen.

Derek opened the door as Joey stepped out to set the drinks on the table. Derek followed a moment later with a large bowl of tossed salad, his mom close behind.

Abe fixed his wife's plate. When he placed it in front of her, the meat was already pre-cut, and the servings were smaller than what everyone else had. Derek and Lainee helped her as well, even while spending most of their time gabbing with Joey, his mom, and Quinn. Though it seemed a bit off, Katherine's warm smile was still convincing, all things considered.

Chapter 14

Grant's Crossing - Fall/Winter 1997-98

Joey - 16 years old

After dinner, Renee and Quinn relaxed with Abe and Katherine while the kids shared in the cleanup. As soon as they could, Joey and Derek grabbed their jackets and walked the few blocks to Taft Park, where they'd always played as kids. Younger kids, anyway. With the exception of an older couple walking down the path by the river, it was deserted for the night. The sun was long gone, and the stars were out, occasionally obscured by dark clouds drifting by.

Derek was unusually quiet as they wandered to the playground, each sitting on a swing, digging their toes in the ground below. Sure, they were sophomores in high school, but they could still chat on swings for hours like they'd done as children. Joey rocked himself back and forth, but Derek barely moved, his face staring down while he apathetically kicked at the soft pebbles beneath his feet.

"Mom's sick."

Joey stopped swinging. "Sick?"

"Yeah." Derek didn't look up at first. "That's why she almost dropped the glasses tonight." He turned his head enough to look at his friend. "You know she's not clumsy, Joey. She just says that sometimes around other people."

Joey conceded his point with a nod. He clasped a swing chain in the crook of each arm and pushed off with his foot just enough to stay in motion.

"Remember when she was sick a couple of years ago and went through chemotherapy?" Derek's voice cracked as he spoke. "She's going through it again down in Columbus at OSU. The James or something. Anyway, Dad goes with her every time, so Uncle Ben has been taking charge of things at Dad's work. She's trying something different to see if it'll help, but I think it's worse than what they're telling us. Lainee and me... we can tell when she's having a bad day, but they're still trying to hide it from us. Dad runs a lot of interference, so we don't bother her. Probably for Lainee's sake. She's just a kid." Derek forced a laugh when thinking of his twelve-year-old sister. "Though she'd say different."

Derek kicked a bunch of pebbles away from him, creating a divot in the ground. "I'm sorry we haven't been able to hang out as much lately. We've been having some dinners with the Marinovs. And when we aren't with them, Mom's been teaching Lainee and me how to cook. So, I've been making most of the dinners lately. But, I think it's because Mom..." His voice got caught in his throat. "She isn't strong enough to do it herself anymore, but she knows a lot and is a great cook, so learning from her is kind of fun, I guess."

"Well, maybe someday, cooking will help you get dates." Joey's half-hearted attempt at a joke fell flat when Derek only shrugged.

"Lainee usually makes a salad and then runs off to her room. I think she's just scared of what will happen."

The leaves rustled in the breeze, falling to the ground like snow. Joey heard Derek sniff a few times but didn't say anything.

Derek swung back and forth a couple of times, then stopped again. "Joey."

"Yeah?"

Tears streamed down Derek's face. "What if she...?"

Joey forced a lump down his throat. "No, D," He pleaded, his voice barely above a whisper. "Don't say that."

"Dad says I need to watch over Lainee more than usual." Derek pressed his palm to his eyes to wipe the tears. He sniffed again. "Why would he say that if she weren't... if she weren't dying?"

"I don't know."

They rocked back and forth on the swings for a while until Derek abruptly stood up. He wiped his face with his hands and sniffed. "I'm going home now."

"Ok."

Derek took a few steps, then stopped. He turned back to Joey, who was still rocking on his swing, "Thanks for helping Mom tonight."

"She's family, D."

Derek nodded and started walking.

Joey remained on the swing until Derek was out of sight, then turned for home.

The season opener ended up being the only game Derek's mom was able to watch that season. By Halloween, she hardly left the house. After Thanksgiving, she took a turn for the worse. The day after Derek's birthday in early December, Joey came over to help them convert Abe's downstairs office into a bedroom when climbing stairs became too much for her. Her good days over the holidays weren't nearly as good as what they'd considered bad days during the fall, and she barely made it through Christmas. Shortly after the new year, she entered at-home hospice care.

She passed away on a Sunday afternoon.

They held the funeral on a warmer-than-usual day in mid-January. There wasn't even any snow on the ground though it was overcast and gloomy most of the day, typical for an Ohio winter.

With their respective families, Joey and Juan sat behind their friend who, along with his sister, bookended their father as if they were there to keep him upright.

Maybe they were.

The sanctuary of St. Mary's was filled to the brim that day. All the pews were filled with friends, family, and well-wishers from all walks of life there to pay their respects. Even Derek's fellow football players were there, sitting together as the team they were.

Derek's family was up from New Orleans, all speaking with the same southern drawl his mom had. His Uncle Mick walked into the house after the graveside service carrying a bottle of whiskey that he and Abe later shared. From what everyone remembered, there was plenty more whiskey waiting in the wings.

Joey and his mom both helped out at the house afterward. She took charge in the kitchen to keep everyone fed while Derek and Lainee's father and uncles hit the bottle.

Joey bounced from sibling to sibling, making sure Derek and Lainee were both alright. Joey could relate to losing a parent, but even knowing it was coming, it didn't make it easier when it actually happened. Downstairs, Derek sat in the corner with a graphic novel in his hands, just staring into space. Joey never saw him turn a page but figured it was more of a shield to help keep others away.

Derek had been stoic since his mom died, in sharp contrast to his sister, who couldn't close her own floodgates of tears. She remained scarce, sequestering herself in her room. Every time Joey checked in on her, she yelled at him to get out. And every time she yelled, he waited until she stopped, then held her while she cried.

Chapter 15

Grant's Crossing - present day

"Gumbo should be ready soon," Derek said, resting his shoulder against the archway dividing the kitchen and dining room.

"So many came for the funeral," Abe acknowledged before reaching in and grabbing some of the finger food Kiro brought. He paused, staring at nothing in particular. His voice was sad at the memory, but smiled at the thought of how many people had come out to pay their respects to his wife. "People loved her. That's what helped me get through the day, I suppose."

"When Mom died, I couldn't cry."

Lainee arched both brows and redirected her gaze to her brother. "All I did was cry."

Derek reached out to squeeze his sister's shoulder while Tasha held her close.

"Joey kept checking on me." Lainee wiped a tear from her eye before it had a chance to escape down her cheek. "He would just hold me while I cried, not saying a word. I don't think he knew what to say. I just remember he was there."

Derek breathed out a humorless laugh. "I remember he was going back and forth between your room and finding me downstairs. I mean, it's pretty much a blur when I think about it now. Hell, it was then, too; but, yeah, you're right. He was there taking care of us the whole time."

Derek laughed for real this time and lifted his glass to Kiro. "I think he even channeled Kiro's mom and directed the Tres Widows to do stuff. Those three ladies are a force to be reckoned with when it comes to taking care of people at funerals, but they asked how high whenever Joey said jump."

Kiro raised his glass in acknowledgment.

"He was the big brother we never knew we needed." Derek went quiet for a few long moments. "What do you remember, Dad?"

"Not a damned thing." Abe rested his hands on Derek's shoulders and let out a slow exhale. "I just knew she was gone."

Derek offered his dad a sympathetic nod.

Lainee sniffed and wiped another tear off her face. Abe reached out and gave his daughter a quick rub on her back.

"It took a few days for anything to sink in." Derek shifted his position against the wall. "That's when I started walking."

"And didn't come back," Quinn spoke up. "Your dad was worried sick about you."

Abe reflexively nodded in agreement. "That's true. I was."

Lainee knitted her brow. "I don't remember that."

Derek stared with a blank expression. "I just grabbed a coat and started walking. Ended up over at Storley for a while where I just screamed my head off. Then I walked down to the river." With a nod to Quinn across the room, he continued. "Joey and Quinn found me. God. It all hit me like a ton of bricks."

Chapter 16

─────────

Grant's Crossing - January, 1998

Joey - 16 years old

"I don't know what to say to them, Mom." Joey half-heartedly stirred his food on his dinner plate. "Lainee cries all the time, and Derek doesn't cry at all. I mean, I get it; but I don't know what to do, you know?"

"I know." She set the glasses down on the table and sat down across from him. "But everyone grieves in their own way. They loved their mother, but now that she's gone, they have to face going on without her."

"And they're spending all their time with the Marinovs while their dad drowns himself in booze."

"It's just hard. They lost someone who's as close to them as anyone ever will be, and Derek's father just lost the love of his life. They'll never get over it, and," she hesitated before answering, "it's going to take them all time to learn how to live without her."

"I guess." Joey took a bite of his green beans and washed it down with a gulp of his tea. "I've been thinking about...," he paused to look his mom in the eye, "how I don't have a dad. I know it's not the same, but I can't help it."

She offered a smile of understanding. She reached across the table to squeeze his hand, "I know, baby. And it's okay."

He nodded and returned to pushing his food around on his plate in silence.

A loud knock on the back door pulled them away from their thoughts as they jerked up in surprise. "Renee? Joey?" Quinn's voice sounded urgent.

"Quinn?" Renee jumped up to open the door. "What is it? What's wrong?"

"We can't find Derek." He stepped in and turned his gaze to Joey. "Do you know where he might be? Nobody's seen him since breakfast this morning."

"He's not with Juan?"

"No."

"At the park?"

"No. They said he went out for a walk and never came back."

Joey nodded, and then he perked up. "He could be at Storley. Let me get my coat."

"Be careful," Renee called out as they left.

They rushed out and jumped into Quinn's car. Quinn turned on his police light and siren to make sure they didn't have to bother getting stuck behind another car on the short drive to the large, abandoned Storley Industrial complex that stood across the river from downtown Grant's Crossing. A persistent eye sore, it was where teenagers tended to hang out when they didn't have anywhere else to go despite having a chain-link fence around the majority of the property. It's also where young couples parked to get away from the prying eyes of their parents.

"Over there. Blue Storley." Joey pointed toward the large blue building at the end. This is where they would sometimes stop to rest during their weekend runs. The car had barely stopped when Joey jumped out and ran inside

"DEREK?" He zigzagged his way around the dilapidated office and numerous pieces of large machinery spread throughout the abandoned warehouse that made it impossible for vehicles to enter but ideal for vagrants to remain out of sight. "DEREK?"

"Hold up, Joey." Quinn followed close behind with his flashlight. "Someone's been here recently," he said, pointing to some freshly disturbed dust on an overturned file cabinets.

Joey stopped and looked back toward the Scioto River. "There's not much snow, and the river's not frozen over," he thought out loud. "Maybe..." His voice trailed off as he jogged back out of the building. Each step he took crunched on the frozen ground as he ran across the gravel lot into the overgrown grassy areas by the river.

Joey looked down the river and squinted. In the distance, he saw his friend sitting on their favorite rock, slouched down as if utterly defeated. In the moonlight, Joey could see Derek's shoulders shaking. He took a few steps back toward Quinn, who had just reached the trees. "I found him. Give us a minute, ok?"

"Hold on." Quinn grabbed a blanket from the back of the car and handed it to Joey. "Here. Take this. I'll wait for you by the car."

Joey stopped walking when he was within earshot. "Hey D. You ok?"

Derek jumped at the sound. "Joey?" His breaths were white puffs of smoke in the cold air.

"Yeah."

His gaze darted around as if expecting others to appear from the dark. "What are you doing here?" He rubbed his nose with the back of his hand. "They looking for me?"

"Yeah." Joey took a few steps closer, still clutching a blanket in one hand. He pointed his thumb behind him. "Quinn's back at the car."

"Oh."

Joey unfolded the blanket and dropped it over Derek's shoulders.

Derek then scooted over to make room for Joey to sit down and tossed a rock into the water. The plopping sound echoed in the otherwise dark and quiet evening. "I didn't know what to wish for at the end."

His confession came through a steady stream of tears as he shrugged the blanket closer so it covered him better. His breath shuddered when he inhaled. "I didn't know if I didn't want to let her go, knowing she was in pain and could barely tell we were even there, or if I wanted her to go because then she would no longer be in pain." He sniffed again from the cold. "Is it wrong that I wanted her to go ahead and die?"

"No." Joey swallowed. "I know how you feel." He tilted his head with a shrug. "Kind of. I mean, it sucks either way, right?"

"Yeah."

He shifted on the rock next to Derek. "You know my Dad died when I was a kid, right?"

"Yeah."

"I never told Mom this, but I wanted him gone. I didn't care how it happened."

"Why?" Derek whispered. He leaned over to grab another rock, his fingers turning pink from the cold.

"He beat the shit out of Mom. If he wasn't punching or slapping her around, he always yelled at her, complaining about everything." Joey pressed his lips together. "About me, usually."

"You never told me that." Derek lobbed the rock in the air and watched it hit the water with a loud plunk.

"I know." Joey stared across the river at the trees they could barely see. "He never hit me, but he blamed me for everything. Told me I ruined his life and everything that went wrong or that he didn't have was because of me. As a kid, I didn't understand what it actually meant. I just knew I wanted him dead." Joey's voice cracked on the last sentence.

"I've never said that out loud, but on that last night, I got my wish. He was really drunk and somehow got his hands on a gun. He was beating Mom worse than usual, so I called 9-1-1."

"I knew your dad died, but not how," Derek whispered.

"Yeah. Police had to break the door down to get inside the house. They had their guns pointed at Dad. He had his gun pointed at Mom. I was eight, and even then, I knew it was a total shitshow."

Joey exhaled. "It was storming outside. I remember the lightning and the thunder. It was so loud." He closed his eyes. "Something set him off, and he pointed his gun right at me. That's when the cops fired and killed him."

Joey opened his eyes to stare out at the calm river before them. He tossed a rock into the river, trying to imagine the darkened water rippling out in circles. "Officer Carlos threw himself on top of me as my dad pulled the trigger. The bullet hit him in the back. That Kevlar vest saved both our lives that night." He took a breath and released a slow exhale. "I still hate thunderstorms."

"Shit."

He turned his head toward Derek. "Yeah. Different reasons, D, but I get why you might want to wish for your mom to no longer suffer. I didn't want mine to suffer either." Joey grabbed a rock and lobbed it into the air, waiting for it to hit the water with a plunk before he went on. "Marisol Strager? Quinn's sister-in-law? She's Officer Carlos' sister. That's what brought us here to Grant's Crossing. The Stragers helped us like the Marinovs are helping you." Joey grabbed a handful of cold rocks and threw them into the water, one at a time.

Derek snorted a laugh. "Did you know he started calling me D?"

"Who?"

"Little Kiro Marinov. He's a year behind Lainee. He heard you call me D instead of Derek, so he started calling me that, too." He breathed out a laugh. "He ran to his mom the first time I called him K in return. He was so excited. Thought it was the best thing since sliced bread." He reached down and picked up more rocks. "I think I'll keep calling him that."

They tossed rocks into the water for a few more minutes, sitting in silence broken only by the sound of a lone plop whenever a stone landed in the deep water of the Scioto River.

With a sniff, Derek wiped his nose again with the back of his hand. "I'm cold."

"Me, too."

A shared gaze held an unspoken understanding that it was time to leave.

Quinn stepped out of the vehicle when Joey and Derek emerged from the trees. He opened the back door as Derek reached the car. "I wanna go home."

"I'll take you there."

Outside the Mitchells' home, Joey and Quinn waited in the car until Derek was safely inside. They drove away after they watched Abe pull Derek into a hug.

Chapter 17

Grant's Crossing - present day

"*Little* Kiro Marinov, huh?" Kiro shook his head at Derek's choice of words. Everyone else had worked their way back to the dining and living rooms, where they'd moved the rest of the hors d'oeuvres Kiro's mom had made.

Derek pointed one of the carrots he was chopping in Kiro's direction. "Well, you're not so little anymore, but you'd have been about eleven then." He resumed his work, dropping the chopped veggies into a bowl on the counter.

"Yeah. I was still pretty short my first year of middle school."

Derek flinched when the doorbell rang.

"Logan!" Lainee called out to the tall man as he shrugged off his coat and placed it in Abe's waiting hands. At six feet, three inches tall, Logan was accustomed to being the tallest man in the room. Tonight was no different. He pulled his scarf from around his neck and hung it atop his coat.

"Hi, Lainee." Logan returned her hug and then combed his

black hair back with his fingers while stepping through the entryway. "It's been a long time."

"Too long. I'm so glad you made it."

Lainee's adorable little girl waddled up and stared up at him in wonder. "Is this Catie?" He asked.

"Yes." Pride overtook Lainee's face. "Eighteen months old already. Can you believe it?" She leaned over to Catie. "Can you say hi to Mr. Logan?"

Catie squeezed her hands together in an attempt to wave. Logan waved in return.

"Hi, Catie. They grow up fast. Enjoy it while she's little."

"Hey, Logan." Tasha appeared from the living room and took Catie in her arms with a smile. "Good to see you."

"Hi, Tasha. You, too."

Tank stood up and caught Logan's eye. Tank opened his mouth to speak but ended up nodding instead. Eyes turned, and the general conversation ceased.

"Come on in," Lainee said as she led Logan into the living room, where he exchanged awkward pleasantries with everyone. He forced a smile in exchange for the friendly yet sad expressions everyone gave him now that Joey was no longer a part of his life. Working his way to the fireplace, he stopped dead in his tracks as he glanced at the pictures on the mantel. As if he hit a brick wall, he struggled for a few seconds to catch his breath. A movement to his left drew his gaze. Abe stood back by the couch and gave Logan his space.

Logan's jaw clenched. He swallowed hard and fought back the tears that tried so hard to escape. He'd cried plenty during the last four months since Joey died but hoped to hold himself together enough to get through this evening; his first night seeing everyone since the funeral. He blinked a few times and stepped closer for a few seconds. With shaky fingers, he reached up to touch the picture of Joey and him smiling at each other as if they had the rest of their lives together. The rest of their lives were supposed to last much longer than fifteen years. The rest of their lives were supposed to last well beyond Joey's thirteen years in the Army.

The rest of their lives weren't supposed to be cut short during Joey's final deployment.

"I miss him, too, son." Abe stepped closer and placed a hand on Logan's shoulder. He spoke in a voice low enough so only Logan could hear. "I'd say it gets easier... but I'd be lying. Eventually, you just get better at dealing with it."

Logan fought the tightness in his chest at the loss he constantly tried but failed to push away. He took a few breaths, drawing strength from Abe's words of comfort. "Yeah, but..." His voice trailed off.

"I know." Abe nodded toward the back of the house. "Derek's in the kitchen, Logan. Go on back. Talk to him."

Logan didn't have as much confidence in his ability to talk with Derek as Abe seemed to have, but he knew he had to face the music eventually. With a curt nod, Logan strode in the direction of more voices.

From opposite directions, Logan and Kiro entered the dining room at the same time. Exchanging quick nods, they passed each other; Kiro to join the others and Logan to get away. Pausing a few seconds to collect himself, Logan crossed the threshold into the large kitchen, where he found Derek standing in front of the stove, stirring something in a large pot. The scent of meats, vegetables, and spices filled the air.

Derek added some more spices, stirred them in then picked up a spoon for a quick taste. He bobbed his head back and forth and started stirring again.

Logan remained silent for a minute or two, then took a deep breath. "Derek."

Derek muttered an oath under his breath upon hearing the deep voice behind him. After what seemed like an eternity, he turned to meet Logan's gaze; his eyes slightly wide like a deer caught in headlights. A myriad of emotions passed between them as they made face-to-face contact for the first time since Joey was still alive.

Logan's Adam's apple bobbed up and down as he forced a swallow. He and Joey should be together to bring in the new year.

They should have been married.

They should both be here.

Together.

Alive.

Logan could have sworn he saw guilt flash across Derek's eyes, his own eyes conveying everything from anger to sadness to indescribable grief.

Grief was always the strongest. It was always the first to appear and always the last to leave.

Hell. It never left.

Letting the spoon rest against the side of the pot, Derek schooled his expression and curled his lips up to greet his old friend with a hug. "Logan! It's good to see you, man." He stepped back but kept his hands on Logan's upper arms. "How're you doing? How's your daughter? She's in school now, right?"

Logan forced a smile of his own and hoped the evening would at least go a bit beyond the same awkward small talk everyone always offered while tip toeing on eggshells around him. "Yeah, Allie's really good, thanks. Just started first grade this past fall." He leaned back against the counter and released an exhale as soon as Derek let go to give his food a quick stir.

Logan continued to stare at the floor in uncomfortable silence until he attempted small talk with one of his oldest friends. They'd never had difficulty talking growing up, but now... "Heard you got back in time for Christmas."

While Derek, Joey, and Tank served, they'd always kept in touch, mostly via e-mail. Logan and Joey couldn't always communicate directly for fear that they'd out Joey resulting in a dishonorable discharge for him. Even after 'Don't Ask, Don't Tell' was repealed, the Army wasn't the most accepting place for anyone who wasn't straight. Logan had always hated having to be so careful; but Joey loved serving in the Army, and Logan loved Joey.

Joey's mom forwarded a lot of his e-mails to Logan so he'd know how Joey was doing, but after she passed away two and a half years earlier, that line of communication ended.

Then last August, everything went to shit.

Joey was gone. Their future gutted. And now he and Derek were afraid to even reach out to each other to talk.

As he chopped, Derek dropped his vegetables into a large pan. "Yeah. Christmas Eve."

"Bet your dad loved that."

"Yep."

While he stirred, Derek stared at the pile of unchopped vegetables on the counter.

"Look. I'm...."

"Wash your hands." Derek cut him off.

"What?"

"Wash your hands and help me out."

"Huh?"

"Come on. Just do it."

"Ok?" Logan complied as Derek set another cutting board on the counter.

"Here." Derek pushed some vegetables over as he stirred in more onions and celery, two-thirds of the holy trinity of Cajun cooking. "Slice these. Not too thin."

"More onions, huh?"

"They will give us both cover. They're kinda strong."

"Good idea." Logan started chopping for a few minutes and passed them over to Derek as needed.

"Slice this zucchini while you're at it, too." Derek went back to adding in his bell peppers, the other third of the trinity.

Derek reached into the fridge and opened a bottle of beer for both of them. They worked in companionable silence for what seemed like ages. Derek occasionally gave Logan instructions to help put the finishing touches on dinner.

When the veggies were all chopped, Logan sliced the last of the andouille sausage for Derek to heat up and add to the delicious meal he was cooking. Logan washed up and leaned against the counter again while rubbing his hands dry with a small towel.

"Derek, I'm sorry..."

"You don't need to...."

"No." This time it was Logan who cut Derek off though he held up his hand in a placating gesture to soften the abrupt snap of his voice.

Derek froze for a split second but quickly recovered and started moving the wooden spoon in slow circles.

"Let me say it."

Derek stopped what he was doing and gave Logan his full attention.

"I'm sorry I couldn't make it here after the funeral. I... it... it was too new. It was too much. I...I just couldn't."

"I know." Derek released a slow exhale. "I wasn't in a good place either."

"And are you now?"

Derek turned around and stared at his friend for a long minute. Finally, he tapped the spoon on the edge of the large pot holding the simmering jambalaya and set it down on a small plate sitting on the counter. Still facing the burners, he rested his hands on the counter on either side of the stove and dropped his chin.

Derek stared down at the food cooking in front of him. Or at nothing. Logan couldn't really be sure.

When Derek finally spoke, he rasped out one single word. "No."

"Oh, my god. Look at this," Lainee said from the neighboring room.

As Lainee's voice drew closer, Logan and Derek stared at each other, each man struggling to mask the vulnerability they'd just ripped wide open. They understood the sadness, each coming from their own perspective; Logan losing the love of his life, and Derek being haunted by a misguided sense of guilt.

"Derek," Logan said when the crowd moved into the kitchen. He blinked at the thud that was a high school yearbook landing on the kitchen table.

Lainee, Tasha, and Kiro and the rest of the group crowded into the kitchen ending Derek and Logan's opportunity to say what they both knew needed to be said.

Chapter 18

Grant's Crossing - present day

THE DELICIOUS SCENT OF DINNER WAFTED CLOSER AS KIRO reached for the spoon. "This smells really good, D."

"Yes," Quinn rubbed his hands together. "When's dinner?"

Derek gently held the spoon out of Kiro's reach. "Hey! Main course won't be ready for a while. Hands off. K."

Derek took a deep breath and gave an apologetic look to Logan, who responded with a half-shrug.

Tank pulled out a chair for Araceli, then did the same for Jo. "Logan. Rocio's birthday is coming up in a few weeks, and she wants to have a sleepover with pizza, movies, and a tea party. We'll get Allie's invitation to you after the new year."

"Sounds good."

"Oh, and she wants everyone to wear purple."

"Purple?"

"Have a seat, Logan." Abe insisted as he ensured there were enough chairs around their large kitchen table.

"Thanks."

Tank helped bring in a couple of chairs from the dining room since it looked like the party was moving to the kitchen.

"Yes," Araceli answered. "Everything has to be purple with her. All the decorations. The cake. The candy. The soda. Everything."

Abe chuckled. "Lainee had a party one year where everything was red."

"It's a good color," Lainee said while pouring apple juice into a sippy cup for her daughter.

"It was *my* favorite color," Derek said over his shoulder. "And the mac and cheese is almost ready."

Drew made a face. "We're eating mac and cheese? Quinn and I were promised jambalaya."

"You'll get it. Mac and cheese is the Toddler Special," Derek said as he spooned the cheesy mixture on a small plate with a few slices of zucchini on the side for his niece. "Here you go, Catie Cat." He placed it on the table in front of Lainee, who started cutting them into pieces.

"She eats zucchini?" Marisol's brows shot up.

Lainee blew on the food to cool it off. "Don't know why, but she loves it."

"She still has to have her mac and cheese, though," Tasha's face lit up into a smile. "She is a toddler, after all."

"And now her Uncle Derek spoils her with his homemade mac and cheese rather than just making it out of a box."

"Blasphemy," Derek called out over his shoulder.

Lainee handed her daughter a green kiddie spoon which Catie promptly held in one hand while using her other to pick up the macaroni to stick in her mouth. In typical toddler fashion, Catie did her best to feed herself while sitting on Tasha's lap, getting about one or two pieces of macaroni in her mouth at a time while most pieces landed back on the table.

Kiro snuck closer to the stove for a peek at the slow cooker. "That ready yet?"

"Just about," Derek answered. "Mind ladling the gumbo into the fancy bowls Lainee brought?"

"Hey," she scoffed as Kiro snickered. "I promised Dad I'd do the dishes tonight."

"She's nothing if not smart," Abe bragged about his daughter.

Kiro grabbed the stack of half-pint-sized disposable bowls and started filling them up. "You're going to be very popular at the station with these mad cooking skills." He received an affirming nod from Tank, who passed the filled bowls around the table. "When do you start, anyway?"

"Dig in, everyone." Derek checked the vegetables and cornbread still in the oven. "I start at the end of January. Chief Travis is going to sign me up for some training courses to get up on all the civilian stuff. I'm used to taking care of healthy, adult men in peak physical shape."

Kiro snorted. "Uh, yeah. This'll be different."

"That's what I hear." Derek grabbed a fork out of the drawer and tasted his jambalaya. He bobbed his head a couple of times, indicating he was pleased with the results, and tossed the fork into the kitchen sink, where it landed with a slight clang. Leaning back against the counter, he accepted a bowl of gumbo from Kiro and dug in. "I'll eventually have to take the basic firefighter courses and who knows what else."

"Yeah," Tank spoke between mouthfuls. "You'll be taking classes for a while. And Tiny Tim will be glad he's no longer the newbie on B-shift."

"Tiny Tim?"

"Yeah. He's the candidate who started about a year ago. Tall guy." Tank pointed across the table. "Even taller than Logan here."

The kitchen fell silent for a while except for moans of pleasure at the tasty food they were all enjoying. Occasionally, Jo and Araceli would flip pages of the yearbook Lainee had brought in earlier.

"Look at this, Juan."

"Is this from our senior year?" Tank leaned over Araceli's shoulder to view the pictures on the page. "Ha!"

"Let me see that." Logan rose to peer at the pages.

Tossing his empty soup bowl into the trash, Derek leaned in as well. He tapped his finger on a picture of a young man in a tux with his then-girlfriend in a sleeveless red dress. "You're still gorgeous, Celi. Tank, on the other hand..." Derek shook his head.

"Hey," Tank pushed Derek back with a laugh.

Derek gave Tank a friendly smack on his arm. "Don't know how you ended up with this guy."

"We were so young then, weren't we?" Araceli leaned in against her husband's shoulder.

"We sure were," Tank agreed.

Logan placed his hand on the page to prevent Derek from turning it. He placed his hand over the picture of several couples dancing, including him and his prom date. "That was not who I wanted to dance with that night."

"That's the night that started it all," Derek said.

"Yeah." Logan laughed. "At least I did a good job hiding it."

Derek scoffed. "Hiding what?"

"That I liked Joey."

Derek busted out laughing. "Yeah. Right."

"What? I was subtle."

Derek snorted out a laugh. "You were NOT subtle."

"I was." Hard as he tried, Logan couldn't keep a straight face.

Derek shook his head with a half grin. "Uh... you keep telling yourself that, Shepherd. Come on, if I could figure it out...."

Tasha stood up. "I think I'll take little Catie up for a bath and bedtime."

"Want a hand?" Lainee offered as she wiped Catie's cheese-covered mouth off with a napkin and gave her a loud smooch earning her some giggles.

"Sure."

"Ok. I'll be up in a little bit."

Derek tousled his niece's curls and kissed her cheek. "G'night, Catie Cat."

Logan held up his hands in surrender. "Ok. Ok. That was our first time..." Logan shook his head at the memory. "I didn't know what I was even doing."

"What? After Prom, you mean?"

"Yeah."

Derek returned to the stove and spoke over his shoulder. "Nobody knew what they were doing. That was Kaitlyn's and my first time, too. Shit. That was so awkward."

The men laughed while the women shook their heads and rolled their eyes at the playful banter.

"Maybe I'll go on up now," Lainee stood up. "There are some things about my big brother I never want to hear."

"Don't worry," Derek assured her. "You won't."

Logan laughed as Lainee walked around the table. "Shit. I can't tell you how nervous I was when I kissed him that first time. Hell, I was nervous when I took his hand; I'd crushed on him for so long."

Lainee reached over to pat his arm in support before she left the room.

"I was so scared."

Tank arched a brow at Logan. "You? Scared?"

"Fuck, yeah."

"I've seen you play football; that's hard to imagine."

"Thanks, but uh... I was terrified. That was the first time I'd ever kissed a guy before. And for the longest time, I didn't kiss another. Still haven't, actually." Logan cleared his throat and took a drink from his nearly empty glass. "Looking back, I think I flirted with him for the first time after a track meet a couple of weeks earlier."

Chapter 19

Grant's Crossing - Spring 2000
Joey - 18 years old

"Come on. Come on. Come on." Joey cheered as their second runner closed the distance between him and the next runner on the 4x800 meter relay, the first event of their triangular track meet between the Grant's Crossing Fighting Cannons and two other county high schools, Delaware Hayes and Buckeye Valley.

The Grant's Crossing men's track team was neck and neck with the other two schools' teams as they made the exchange. "YES!"

The team jumped up and down after a textbook handoff as Brent, last year's anchor, took the baton and ran down the track for his two laps before the last handoff.

After five and a half laps for the team, Grant's Crossing was now in a healthy lead. Joey headed out to his spot on the track to prepare for their third and final handoff. While waiting for Brent to round the track, he shook his arms and jumped up and down to loosen himself up. He breathed in a few deep breaths in his nose and out his mouth. The Fighting Cannons had drawn the outside lane, Joey's favorite, for their spot on this relay. He watched the navy blue uniform of his teammate reach the third turn with a comfortable lead over the other schools. "Come on, Brent. Come on. Come on."

In position, he looked back to see how close Brent was,

ready to start running for the handoff. Brent entered the straightaway of the final turn. He was so close. Joey took off, eyes forward with his hand extended behind him, palm straight up.

"Three, two, one." Brent's voice sounded behind him as he felt the baton hit his hand. His fingers clamped around the silver metal cylinder as he took off, shooting down his lane like a rocket toward the first turn.

"RUN, JOEY! GO!" He heard his mom yell from the stands. The other two teams made their handoffs after Joey rounded the first turn. Joey maintained a quick pace as he rounded the final turn of his first of two laps. His teammates yelled his name from the sidelines as he whizzed by them in a blur, his strides long and his pace steady, focusing solely on getting to the finish line before any other runner. He heard the anchor for Buckeye Valley was one hell of a fast runner.

By the time he reached the third turn of the final lap, the cheering grew louder, offering further encouragement to run his heart out. Accustomed to running much longer distances, Joey was just getting warmed up when he rounded the final turn and blasted his way across the finish line. He had plenty of time after his finish to turn around and watch the other runners finish the race behind him.

Brent ran up to him for a chest bump. "You took that baton and made them eat dirt."

"Great job stretching that lead!" Joey said between breaths, mirroring his teammate's enthusiastic grin. "You made it easy for me."

The coach put a quick end to the celebration and shooed them into the infield as the meet was just starting, and the ladies' 4x800 team was next to hit the starting line.

Logan congratulated him as well. "Great job, Joey."

Joey's eyes dipped to a bit of black hair peeking out of Logan's tank top. He reflexively licked his lips and then quickly popped his eyes back up. "Thanks."

Logan smirked, then ran off to prepare for his own events.

"Shit." Joey closed his eyes and winced. "Not now, Joey. Not now."

A congratulatory hand on his shoulder from another teammate pulled Joey from his thoughts, so he turned back to watch the ladies race around the track.

Joey and Brent finished first and second, respectively, in the 1600-meter race, and they won the 4x400 relay much like they did the 4x800. And while they were all but unstoppable for the longer distances, the men's team got their butts kicked in the sprints. The Lady Cannons were the opposite. They won all the sprints but had a tough time with the longer distances, something they knew they'd make up for with the field events.

With the running over, the field events took center stage. Logan took second in the triple jump, a new event for him this year, and first in the long jump.

"You make that look so easy." Joey patted his back as they announced the winners of that event.

"Thanks." Logan's face lit up. "Nice to get a win."

The team crowded around the coach as the people in the stands stood silent. He was busy doing his own calculations as the judges did the same to determine the official winners of the meet. The small crowd erupted into cheers when it was announced that both Grant's Crossing teams, the men and women, won the meet.

With another win in the books, Joey grinned from ear to ear when his mom walked down the stands to wrap him up in a big hug. "I'm so proud of you, baby."

Her longtime boyfriend followed with an enthusiastic handshake. "Great meet today, Joey."

"Thanks, Quinn."

"We'll see you back home."

"Ok." Joey shrugged his bag over his shoulder and waved. "Bye, Mom."

"I love a home meet when almost all our friends and families live within walking distance of the school." Logan mused as they made their way to the locker room to take showers.

The guys laughed as they cleaned up, joked in the locker room, and got dressed. Joey caught some movement near the showers as Logan padded out, fastening his towel as he walked. It didn't hold, and his towel slipped to the floor, giving Joey a full view sans clothes before an unfazed Logan bent down to grab and re-wrap it around his waist on his way to his locker. Joey's eyes widened for a split second before he glanced away and finished pulling his long-sleeved GCHS t-shirt down his torso.

Logan glanced over in time to catch Joey sneaking a peek at him again. Logan's lip curled up on one side for a split second as if he didn't mind being watched.

"Shit." Joey snapped his head around and stared straight into his locker. He released a long exhale out his mouth and counted to ten. When that didn't work, he started reciting the periodic table. He had a test on Monday anyway. Might as well study. "H is for hydrogen. H-e is Helium..." Anything to take his mind off seeing Logan without a towel. "Ugh. Why do my jeans have to be so damned tight?" He muttered into his locker.

"What was that?" Brent called over from down the row.

"Uh... nothing. L-i is lithium..."

"Are you reciting the periodic table?"

"Yeah. Mr. Chambers is giving a test on Monday. Getting a head start."

"Uh-huh." Brent turned back and finished getting dressed.

Joey furrowed his brow and shut his locker. He let his head drop against the cold metal the moment Brent left. "Shit."

He picked up his gym bag, still wondering what just happened. Shrugging it off, he shoved the door open and stepped outside in the cooler air where he'd wait for the ladies' team, which inevitably took longer to get cleaned up after meets.

Still. Logan was handsome. Joey breathed in the cool spring air and let his mind wander to thoughts of what if. What if he and Logan... "No." He shook his head to clear the thought. He paced down the sidewalk outside the gym entrance and paused. He tilted his head to entertain the thoughts of something he'd never really let himself consider. "Why not?" Logan was kind of hot, really.

He paused to stare down at the ground, lost in thought about Logan. Touching Logan. Kissing Logan. A few teammates walked by and waved their goodbyes, snapping him out of his trance. "Shit." Joey untucked his shirt to let it hang out over his jeans so noone could see proof of what he was thinking of. He paced back toward the door just as Lindsey emerged.

"Hey, Joey," She called out with a smile.

"Lindsey. Hey!" One glimpse of her blue eyes and wavy blonde hair she was pulling up into a ponytail, and Joey stepped closer. "Do you have a minute?"

Proud of himself for mustering the courage to ask her out, Joey waved to Lindsey about ten minutes later. She was the winner of two events in today's meet and was now his date to the Senior Prom in a few weeks. Her thick blonde ponytail bounced up and down while she jogged to her parents' car. Just as she closed the door, Joey felt something big bump into his shoulder.

"Lindsey, huh?" Logan asked, turning the corners of his mouth down as if impressed.

"Huh?" Joey was momentarily stunned but quickly recovered. "Oh. Yeah. We're going to prom."

"Nice. Congrats."

"Thanks. She's gonna be beautiful." Joey dreamily raised his hand as she waved through the window.

"Doesn't hurt that she's as nice as she is pretty."

"No kidding." Joey lifted his chin in agreement. "How about you?"

Logan started to walk away but turned around with a grin. Walking backward, he spread his arms out wide. "No idea. I'm sure I'll find someone between now and then." Logan pointed at Joey. "Good job today."

"Yeah. You, too," Joey gave a half-hearted wave after Logan spun around to jog across the lot to his car. Joey stood by until Logan's car disappeared down the street. He shrugged his bag higher on his shoulder and turned for home.

Chapter 20

Grant's Crossing - April 2000

Joey - 18 years old

THE CARNIVAL-THEMED CLASS OF 2000 SENIOR PROM officially came to a close as the DJ queued up the final slow dance. Joey and Lindsey swayed back and forth to the notes of Amazed by Lonestar sounding through the speakers overhead. Derek and Kaitlyn constantly tested the limits of how close two students at a high school dance could get away with, being asked one final time by the teachers to allow for at least a little air between them. Joey and Lindsey weren't too far behind but still had verifiable space between her navy blue dress and his tuxedo. All the couples who were actually dating stole kisses on the dance floor while those who weren't dating just stood around talking and watching.

On the still-crowded dance floor, it was hard to avoid bumping into each other. Joey locked in on Logan's gaze after one such minor collision. Logan gave him a mischievous smile as he and his date rocked back and forth to the music. They both schooled their features when Derek and Kaitlyn danced near them.

Joey wasn't sure why something stirred inside him when he and Logan exchanged glances, but while he was attracted to Lindsey, she was no longer who he wanted to hold on the dance floor.

"Joey?" A voice sounded from the distance as he continued to watch Logan dance, still occasionally making eye contact as they turned.

"Joey?"

The voice was closer this time.

Joey blinked and gazed down at Lindsey. "What?"

A crease formed between her brows. "You're a million miles away."

He pulled her a little closer for the last bit of the song as she rested her head against his shoulder. "Sorry, Linds." He lifted his head again and met Logan's eyes one last time as the song ended. Unlike the last time, it was Joey who tossed out a mischievous grin.

———

Before the night was over, Joey and Lindsey spent a little time alone out on Old Farmer's Road before he took her home, ending the night with the juiciest goodnight kiss he'd ever had. He wasn't ready for the night to end, and a lot of his friends talked of heading out to the Storley Industrial complex to hang out. Sure, the old factory was abandoned and hadn't been used in years, but there were lots of places behind it to just park his car and, with a bit of music, get some thinking in.

Still sporting a smile on his face after dropping Lindsey off, Joey went home to change clothes and leave his mom a note. Once out of the tux and into his favorite pair of comfortable jeans, he drove across the river to continue the night's festivities. Several cars were parked here and there around the largest of buildings, known as Blue Storley, due to the remnants of blue paint on the outside. He wove his way in and around the smaller buildings to a small clearing on the side, not too far from the river but behind a handful of thick fir trees. He passed a car on his way in, probably someone else taking their date home, but the clearing was otherwise empty. Joey was grateful for that. In an out-of-the-way spot where he wouldn't be so easily seen, he killed his rumbling engine.

Amazed by Lonestar started playing on the car's radio. He let out a frustrated groan as his mind wandered to Logan Shepherd.

Logan took a cheerleader to prom.

Typical.

Maybe they weren't actually dating yet since she'd just broken up with her own boyfriend a week or so earlier. He could hope.

Logan never had a girlfriend for long. Then again, neither did Joey, but he'd never wanted to get serious with anyone. Heck, he was only in high school, right? Derek was the relationship guy, having dated Kaitlyn for nearly a year now.

Joey's thoughts stuck on Logan. He'd thought of him a lot lately. Logan was big, full of muscles, and had an enviable amount of actual chest hair; unlike Joey, who had some, too, but it was blond, and he could barely see it. Logan's, on the other hand... Joey sighed.

On top of all that, Logan had the most beautiful smile.

Joey shook his head.

Beautiful smile? What the hell, Joey?

He released a slow exhale while sinking lower in his seat.

Still, Joey couldn't deny that Logan's smile really was gorgeous. Pretty much everything about Logan was really hot. There was nothing the popular girls found unappealing about Logan. Heck, nothing that anyone found unappealing, really. Logan had the looks: dark hair and brown eyes, chiseled jaw, muscular legs...something Joey had noticed in the locker rooms after their meets.

Joey let his hand drop between his legs as he shifted in his seat. His thoughts drifting back to all the times they'd all had to shower at the same time after a meet. He always did his best not to look, but there were a few times he caught a fleeting glimpse of Logan just before he wrapped himself in a towel.

The sound of an engine beside his car pulled him out of his reverie.

"Damn it."

In a knee-jerk reaction, Joey's hands snapped up to the steering wheel. Through his window, a large pickup truck made a tight turn in the small clearing so the driver's side door could match his own. His car was too low to see inside the truck window, but his stomach turned somersaults as soon as the door opened. The tall young man leaned against his truck and folded his arms against his chest. His tight jeans and form fitting henley left nothing to the imagination.

"What the fuck?" Joey muttered to himself. He felt his heart skip a beat, so he closed his eyes and took a deep breath. "Shit." Joey swallowed hard. He climbed out of his own car and leaned back against his own door. He folded his arms against his own chest in a subconscious effort to appear just as calm, cool, and collected as Logan.

"Logan."

His voice didn't crack.

Much.

Logan's eyes made a quick scan of Joey down to his feet and back up again. A confident smirk appeared on his face but was gone as quickly as it appeared.

"Let's talk," was all Logan said before strutting to the back of his truck and lowering the tailgate.

He was so cool. So confident. Everything Joey wanted to be, but thanks to nerves or whatever he was feeling, he knew he couldn't pull off right now.

"I hoped you would come here, but wanted to wait a few minutes after you pulled in." he added as Joey walked around back and put his hands in his pockets.

"Those were your headlights shining in my rearview."

"Yeah." Logan jumped up onto the bed of his truck and dropped a couple of furniture-moving blankets on the bed. Joey noticed a couple more regular blankets folded in the corner by a cooler. "Come on up. I've got some drinks. Just some Gatorade and water."

He shrugged. "We're out of beer at home, and my mom would kill me if I walked off with any of her wine."

He sat down with his back against the cab and reached into the cooler. "We're both old enough to die for our country yet not old enough to buy a case of beer. Sucks."

"Yep." Joey agreed as he climbed all the way in and sat down next to him. Facing the open tailgate, he sat down with his back against the cab. He bent one leg, pulling his foot closer to his body. He attempted to maintain some tangible space between Logan and him but look cool at the same time. Why was he so nervous?

He propped his outstretched arm on his bent knee as Logan handed him an orange Gatorade. "Thanks." He pulled his arm back to twist off the cap and take a swig, then awkwardly placed his arm back on his knee.

"Shit." Logan rummaged through the cooler. "I thought I grabbed two of those."

"Here." Joey offered his drink. "We can share."

Logan reached for it. He froze a moment as his fingers grazed over Joey's, and their eyes met. "Thanks."

"Sure." Joey let go, but his jeans tightened again and his stomach filled with butterflies.

What the hell, Joey. Keep it together, man.

Logan took a drink and handed it back to Joey, who took another swig as Logan started talking. "You ever feel like everything you do is based solely on the expectations of others?"

"What do you mean?"

"My dad played football through college. He didn't make it to the NFL, so he now sells auto parts. Couldn't be more masculine than that, right? My older brother plays hockey. I play football. It's expected of us Shepherd men."

"My dad just blamed me for his lot in life." Joey passed Logan the bottle and stared out the back of the truck. "He died when I was a kid."

"Oh. Sorry."

"I don't talk about him much." Joey found himself fighting the urge to extend his fingers, so they touched the fabric of Logan's jeans. "He wasn't good to my mom." He curled his fingers back.

"I didn't know."

"It's ok, he...," Joey's shoulders tensed when he thought about explaining. "Look. Can we talk about something else?"

"Yeah. Sure."

"Thanks," Joey released a sigh of relief.

"Anyway," Logan returned to his story. "I wanted to go stag to the prom. Or even not at all, but Dad made me go. Said *'a man has to get dressed up and treat a woman right.'*" Logan imitated his dad's boorish low voice. "Especially someone who's going to play in the NFL someday." He took another drink out of the Gatorade bottle and passed it to Joey. "As if nothing else matters. Thing is, I don't want to treat a woman right."

Joey snapped his head around in surprise. "Huh?" He took a drink and passed it back to Logan.

"That sounded bad." Logan paused. "I mean, I don't want to treat a woman at all. I don't even like...." He finished off the bottle and looked down at it. "Shit. It's empty. I'm sorry." He dropped the empty bottle back into the cooler. "Want another?"

"Sure." Joey shrugged and held out his hand. He let it hover a few inches above Logan's leg, ready to receive another bottle.

Logan stared for a moment before grabbing a drink with one hand and holding his other hand directly over Joey's for a few seconds before lowering it just enough for the faintest of touches.

"Joey," Logan stared at their hands, the one almost but not quite touching the other. "Tell me if I'm way off base here, but..."

Chapter 21

Grant's Crossing - Spring 2000

Joey - 18 years old

"I'VE SEEN YOU LOOK OVER AT ME A COUPLE TIMES ... AND...."

"Fuck." Joey squeezed his eyes shut.

The light touch of Logan's hand sent shivers down his spine. He opened his eyes and stared at their hands. Like Logan, he couldn't tear his eyes from their barely-touching hands now even if he wanted to.

His breath shortened.

Still questioning whether this was just his imagination running wild, Joey willed his fingers to curl upward. His movement was slow. Cautious. Subtle. His heart rate shot up the moment Logan curled his own down to meet them, lacing their fingers together.

Logan let out a loud exhale as he rubbed his thumb back and forth across the back of Joey's hand that he now brought to rest on his thigh. He turned his eyes toward Joey with a nervous smile. "I was hoping you would do that," his voice cracked.

"You're not way off base," Joey breathed out at the same time Logan finished his sentence.

"Good. Because I liked it."

Joey's jaw went slack. "You what?"

"I liked it when you looked at me."

Joey's eyes met Logan's as he breathed a nervous laugh. His heart raced. It beat so fast he worried it might explode.

"Look. I don't know if you can tell, but...I've uh...looked at you, too." Logan said.

"Yeah," Joey blurted out as Logan leaned closer, erasing the space that existed between them. Joey's gaze drifted from Logan's eyes to his lips and back. "But I've never..."

"Me neither," Logan said. He tipped his head forward to brush his lips against Joey's.

The moment their lips met, it sent shockwaves of heat through Joey's body, most of which landed right between his legs. He let out a soft moan. Logan's full lips were so soft. They were gentle, unlike the man who brought down opposing players on the football field without a second thought. Still, they conveyed who was in charge, and Joey loved it.

He loved that Logan tasted like orange Gatorade. Sweet and wonderful.

"Whoa," was all Joey could say in return. He licked his lips. He was nervous and turned on all at the same time, trying not to squirm. Shock and disbelief overtook them both. Did he just kiss Logan Shepherd?

Logan touched his forehead to Joey's, his lips barely above his. "I don't... I mean... Ugh." Logan closed his eyes for a second to collect himself. "I mean... I really want to do that again." Logan's thumb traced the outline of Joey's jaw, ghosting his fingers on the pale blond whiskers that had started coming in since he first shaved that morning.

Joey's eyes closed at Logan's soft touch.

"Do you?" Logan asked.

Kissing Lindsey goodnight had been great, but shit. Kissing Logan? So. Much. Hotter.

Joey could barely breathe after a simple touch of his lips, and he had no idea what his heart was doing. Speeding up? Skipping beats?

He didn't know, and he didn't care. Logan's awkward confidence was such a turn-on Joey could barely breathe, much less respond.

"Oh yeah," Joey breathed out and finally opened his eyes, too, breaking into a crooked grin. He gazed at Logan. "Definitely."

Logan didn't even give Joey a chance to take a breath before he crashed his lips into his, tugging his lower lip with his teeth a split second before their tongues invaded each other's mouths.

Dancing.

Tasting.

Exploring.

Joey kissed Logan back. He couldn't get enough. He couldn't even remember how Logan's hand found the back of his neck, but it did, and it was oh so right. Joey knew it was good. And he wanted more.

A lot more.

Out of some previously-untapped visceral need, Joey let Logan ease them both down to the bed of the truck. When Logan leaned over him, Joey was grateful for what little cushion the blankets provided, though any more of this, and he doubted either one would care.

Joey had kissed girls before, but those kisses had never been this needy. He'd never been this hungry. He'd always been the one in control, too, not that he'd ever gone that far in his eighteen, almost nineteen, years; but he had always set the pace. Unlike earlier that evening with Lindsey, this time... Joey was thrilled to let Logan take the lead. It was comfortable and natural and oh-so-good. He just hoped he could keep up because this was entirely new territory. With Logan though, he was up for a grand adventure.

A moan escaped Logan's lips as his hand found its way underneath Joey's t-shirt. Logan had already untucked it and pushed it higher up his chest.

When did that happen?

"Take this off," Logan growled.

"Yours, too, then," Joey demanded in return as they both tossed their jackets and shirts to the side. "Oh, my god."

Joey stared at Logan's chest. He knew Logan had always felt kind of self-conscious about his own chest hair, but Joey couldn't wait to touch it. Joey pulled Logan on top of him, desperate to feel skin-on-skin contact, Logan's coarse hair abrading his own chest.

Joey let out a low groan as Logan's hand rubbed its way down his chest to his stomach. "Fuck," was the only word either of them could get out.

SAT vocabulary lists be damned.

Logan's large and oh-so-strong hand rubbed against the growing bulge in Joey's pants. If Joey weren't already hard, he was now.

"Tell me you want this," Logan's husky voice breathed out between kisses as he set the button on Joey's jeans free.

"Hell, yeah, I do."

"Good."

Logan's deep voice dropped an octave, but his hands still shook. He pulled the zipper down and slipped his fingers underneath the elastic of Joey's boxer briefs.

Joey's eyes rolled to the back of his head. "Fuck me." Joey could get used to this, provided his pounding heart didn't burst out of his chest first like that creature in *Alien*.

Logan started to stroke him, squeezing his hand around him, up and down, while his lips brushed kisses on Joey's neck.

Joey's breath quickened. Aside from doctors, the only hands that had ever touched him between his legs were his own.

Logan's lips moved down Joey's body, brushing kisses on his chest and then all the way down his abs. And then...

"Logan..."

Logan's tongue traced a line further south, down Joey's happy trail, until he paused just shy of the point of no return.

"Yes?" Logan breathed as he lifted his head high enough to

make eye contact. He raised his brows in the unspoken question for Joey. "Keep going?"

Unable to believe his luck, Joey stared back at Logan's dark brown eyes and bit his lower lip. Joey's pupils were already blown. His heart melted a little, knowing Logan wasn't going to go any further without permission. His chest heaved up and down as he fought to catch his breath.

Logan was going to give him his first blow job.

Fuck yeah.

Logan's eyes waited in anticipation, apparently not having heard the frenetic thoughts inside Joey's head when Joey finally nodded his head a few times. "Yeah."

Joey's vocal cords weren't worth much beyond the desperate grunts that exited his throat upon the very first touch of Logan's tongue. His head fell back, and he raised his hips so Logan could rip his pants and boxer briefs down and off one of his legs. Joey bent one knee as Logan pushed it aside to position himself between his legs, anchoring his hand around a thigh. With a mischievous smile, Logan made eye contact one last time before dropping his lips down around him.

Joey let out a low groan, unable to form coherent thoughts, much less speak even the simplest of words. His hand instinctively grabbed a fistful of Logan's hair as his hips arched up the second he felt the back of Logan's throat.

"Oh. My. God. That feels so... ungh..."

The more Logan's hand touched him, the more labored Joey's breathing became. With every pass of his tongue, with every brush of his lips, Joey descended further into all things wonderful and amazing. All things Logan.

If he hadn't already died and gone to heaven, Joey would lose sleep dreaming about Logan's warm touch. Ok, sure. Logan was shaky at first; but once he got going, his confidence clearly grew. The two of them maintained a steady rhythm, growing more and more frantic until Joey's whole body arched upwards toward the sky as if he were levitating above the truck bed.

"Mother fucker..." Joey gasped for air. He gripped the blankets with his fist, letting out one last grunt as he shuddered his release.

Logan dropped soft kisses inside Joey's legs to distract him as his body floated back down to earth. Joey could barely control his hands but frantically needed to drag Logan up to his mouth, where he kissed him with a hunger he didn't know he ever possessed. He could even taste himself on Logan's tongue. Their kiss was sloppy and desperate, but Joey couldn't stop himself. He didn't want to stop himself.

"Shit." Logan pulled back for some air. "Let me breathe, man."

Joey grinned as he closed his eyes and leaned his head back. "I want to do that to you."

"Yeah?" Logan was surprised. "I've never...no one's ever..."

"Oh yeah." Joey's breathing was heavy. "I want to... just... let me... catch my... breath first."

Joey pulled himself back onto his knees and inched his way up Logan's body, kissing as much of him as he possibly could until he reached his lips with what little energy he had left. When that was spent, he rolled off and rested his head on Logan's shoulder, taking advantage of the opportunity to move his fingers up through all that beautiful black chest hair. He closed his eyes, comfortably wrapped in Logan's arms where they lay there without a care in the world.

Logan caught his breath first. "Joey?"

"Yeah." He twirled his fingers in circles on Logan's chest.

"I like you. A lot."

"Yeah?"

"Yeah."

"I like you, too."

"I want to keep doing this, but..."

"But... what?" Joey propped himself up on his elbow as Logan sat up and dropped his chin.

"We can't be open about it."

Joey laughed. "Well, I don't exactly plan to do what we just did in the middle of the square."

Logan's lip curled up into a half smile as he thought of them in the park at the center of downtown. "You're right. That probably wouldn't go over well, but..." His face turned serious. "My dad will think it's a distraction from my football."

"Distraction from football?" Joey leaned up on one elbow and creased his brow. "You're kidding, right?"

"Not kidding." Logan pulled Joey back against his chest and rubbed his back. "I'm not out yet to my parents. They want me to concentrate on my scholarship and getting into the NFL draft. They probably won't care that I'm gay, but they'll want me to stay closeted." Logan breathed out a nervous laugh. "Hell, my uncle is gay, but to my parents, especially my dad, football is the only thing that matters. There are no openly gay football players, so it may hurt my chances. That's why only my uncle knows right now. He's sworn to secrecy because he's never liked my dad, anyway. He said my dad was never good enough for his sister."

"Oh. Wow. Ok."

The wheels started turning in Joey's mind. He sat back up and caressed Logan's stubbly cheeks with the backs of his fingers as if noticing them for the first time. "We'll just have to be careful then. You still go running on Saturdays, right?" Joey pressed his lips to Logan's jaw.

"When we don't have a meet, yeah. Otherwise, I run on Sundays."

"I do, too." Joey kissed his neck just below his ear. "We can run together. I know a good route that takes us around Storley."

Logan grinned, knowing exactly what Joey had in mind. "Storley, huh?"

"Plus, my mom works the late shift a lot, so our place is safe. We could hang out there."

Logan sat up and kissed Joey again. Soft and slow. "You get me."

Joey tilted his head to one side. "Do you still like working on cars?"

"Yeah. I help my uncle out at his shop, but what does that have to do with..."

"Absolutely nothing." Joey nodded toward his car. "But, my car's a piece of shit and could use some work. I don't even know how it made it through tonight."

They both broke out in laughter at the absurdity of Joey's comment.

"I'm sick of having to hide this part of me." Logan turned serious again. "I just... wanna be myself, you know?"

"I'm beginning to," Joey answered honestly as he concentrated on tracing Logan's collarbone with his finger.

"And I have no idea how they'd take it at Ohio State. It's a pretty liberal campus, sure, but there aren't any gay college football players that I know of, either."

"Yeah." Joey nodded as he dropped his fingers down Logan's arm and squeezed his hand. He broke eye contact first to take in his surroundings, his eyes scanning the bed of Logan's pickup truck. After a minute of silence, a laugh escaped his lips.

"What's so funny?" Logan asked.

"We're both buck naked."

Except for their jeans and underwear that were still hooked on the ankle of one leg, Joey's assessment was spot on. Each had one shoe on and one shoe off. Their shirts and jackets were tossed to the side in small, wadded-up piles.

Logan surveyed the truck bed and joined in the laughter. "Maybe next time we can get the jeans all the way off." He looked over at Joey and grabbed his face with both hands, and kissed him on the lips.

Joey broke the kiss first. "Maybe we should put our clothes back on. You know they're going to be out patrolling the area. I'm surprised they haven't already been through."

As fate would have it, a police siren gave a warning sound on the other side of the trees. "Shit. Hurry." Logan said as they rushed to get their clothes back on.

Forget their shirts. They'd barely zipped up their jeans as a police cruiser pulled into the clearing.

They turned to face each other and spoke in unison. "We're dead."

Joey and Logan froze and sat in near silence. Logan swore some more, but he at least had his shirt in his hands when the cruiser pulled up behind the truck bed. Joey was still reaching for his.

Joey swallowed when a young Deputy Drew Strager stepped out of the vehicle, starting with a visual survey of the situation. Logan and Joey knew the deputy was making a mental note of their odd lack of footwear in addition to their conspicuously missing shirts.

"Evening, boys."

Chapter 22

Grant's Crossing - present day

"To his credit," Logan lifted his gaze to Drew, who silently leaned against the counter, failing to hide a proud smirk. "Drew didn't say a word."

Drew stuck his fork in a piece of sausage on the round plate he held. "Nothing to say when you're not breaking the law."

"Yeah, but... you sure took your time walking around my truck... peering over the edges to look inside my cooler." Logan feigned exasperation. "You took your time, drawing it out as if waiting for us to break and blurt out some sort of confession. Those intimidation tactics work pretty well, don't they?"

Derek snorted a laugh and made a quick scan of the room to make sure everyone had what they needed before spooning a healthy portion of jambalaya onto his own plate. Derek placed a piece of cornbread between his teeth and joined the others at the oversized table that filled the center of their large kitchen.

"Yeah. They do." Drew held his palm up. "But in your case, I had to make sure there wasn't any underage drinking going on. Gotta keep you boys safe."

"Yeah, right. Joey and I were scared stiff. Hell. I'm 33 years old, and I still get that nervous feeling in the pit of my stomach whenever I see you, Drew. No offense."

Drew held up a hand, unable to resist some good-natured ribbing at Logan's expense. "None taken. But I'll admit, it was pretty tough keeping a straight face."

Logan narrowed his eyes. "I knew it! We were sure you knew what was going on."

Drew gave an obvious nod with a big grin. "That, I did."

"Yet you've never said anything."

"That was for you to share, Logan. Not me."

"Yeah." Logan responded with a grateful nod. "It was nice. I knew then that Joey and I...." Logan took a few moments to gather his thoughts. "Well, that night after you left, Joey told me I didn't have to pretend around him. I needed to hear that."

Derek pushed his plate away and sat back in his chair. "The day after prom, Joey came over and confessed everything to me."

Abe wiped his mouth and dropped the napkin on his plate, and released a low chuckle. "I remember Joey seemed nervous that day."

Chapter 23

Grant's Crossing - Day after Prom 2000

Joey - 18 years old

Joey grabbed a light jacket and walked over to Derek's house.

He still couldn't believe everything that happened the night before, a great date to prom followed by the most erotic experience of his life. Fine. He was only eighteen and hadn't really had any other erotic experiences, but still.

He knocked on the Mitchells' front door and turned around on the front porch only to jump when Derek's dad opened the door.

"Hi Joey. Come on in."

"Uh. Hi, Mr. M. Thanks."

"Everything ok?"

"Yeah. Fine." Joey panicked. "Wait. Why?"

Abe had an amused expression on his face as he closed the door behind him. He kept Joey in suspense for a moment before answering. "Derek's upstairs in his room. Have you had lunch yet? There's plenty of food, so come back down when you're both hungry."

"What?" Joey's expression froze at hearing the words *come, both,* and *hungry,* as if he'd been caught with his hand in the cookie jar.

Did Derek's dad know? Could he tell?

Abe laughed and pointed to the stairs. "Go on up, Joey."

"Yeah. Ok. Thanks." Joey trotted toward the stairs and ran up. He knocked on the already-open door to Derek's room to announce his arrival. "Hey, D."

Derek glanced up from a graphic novel he was reading. "Hey." He tossed it on his nightstand as Joey plopped down on the end of the bed, closing his eyes as he leaned his back against the wall.

"You ok?"

Joey's eyes popped open. "Yeah. Why?"

Derek gave him a sideways glance and then moved to sit down on his desk chair. Derek used his feet to roll himself back across his room towards his bed, where Joey sat down. "You don't seem like you are."

"I'm fine." Joey blurted out.

"Uh huh."

"Ugh." Joey exhaled, drawing out a long groan.

"Joey. What happened? What's wrong?"

"Nothing."

"Doesn't seem like nothing."

"It really is nothing." Joey closed his eyes and leaned back against the wall again.

"Uh huh." Derek muttered again, knowing otherwise. When Joey didn't say anything more, he grabbed his graphic novel again and opened it up to where he had left off.

Joey finally opened his eyes. "Whatcha reading?"

"Huh?" Derek's eyes jerked up then back down to his book. "Oh. 300. It's about Sparta. Has some epic battle scenes."

"Cool." Joey let out a loud exhale. "So...uh...I didn't... last night. You probably won."

Derek closed his graphic novel again and set it on his desk. "Lindsey wasn't into it, huh?"

Joey inhaled. Slowly. He held the air while he considered his response carefully before letting out his breath just as slowly as he took it in. "Only got to second base."

Derek nodded, somewhat impressed. "Not bad for a first date."

"But she seemed kind of nervous, to be honest."

"What? And you weren't?"

Joey shrugged without answering.

Joey was grateful Derek stood up and closed his bedroom door. He didn't want Lainee to walk by and overhear anything, and he definitely didn't want his dad to walk in.

"So what do you mean?"

"I don't know," Joey mumbled. "I mean, making out with her was definitely fun."

"That's good."

"Honestly? I enjoyed it. Even got a great kiss goodnight. How about you?"

"Me?" Derek grinned and nodded his head up and down. "Home run, baby."

"Yeah?" Joey shared in his excitement. "How was it?"

"How was it? Uh..." Derek stopped nodding, and his grin turned into a vague smile. Then his head fell into his hands. "Oh my god. It was the worst."

Joey creased his brow in concern for his friend. "The worst? What do you mean? What happened? You just said..."

"Shit." Derek faced Joey, his face a little drained of color. After a few beats, Derek held his palms out as if pleading with his friend. "Ok. You've got to promise me you'll not say a word of this to anybody." He stretched out the last word to help press the importance of his request. "Like, ever."

"Yeah. Yeah. Of course," Joey promised, anxious for details.

Derek just stared for a minute until he was convinced of Joey's sincerity. He let out a deep breath. "It was so awkward. I had to use two condoms."

"Whaaa?" Joey's face lit up with excitement. "You did it twice?"

"Shh. No." Derek held out his hands as if to calm them both down. "Oh god. No. I mean, I wish."

Joey scooted forward to the edge of the bed. "Derek. What. Happened?"

Showing every expression imaginable, as if playing a fast-paced, back-and-forth, world championship emotive tennis match, Derek jumped in with both feet. "It was the worst. I mean... it was the best, too, but...." He paused and his face turned bright red as he tried to explain.

"So we were making out, and we both wanted to go on, which I know because I asked and, well... she said yes." Derek paused long enough to grin. "So we got into the back seat, which, in my Chevy, is really small, so we had to keep the door open." He rolled his eyes. "Glad it wasn't too cold out. But... we were just getting started," Derek pointed his fingers toward his chest and made a downward motion. "Her dress was pulled down... and," he grinned even wider this time, waggling his eyebrows up and down as he placed his palms on his thighs and drew them up toward his waist "...and her dress was pushed up...."

Joey rolled his eyes and shook his head, despite hanging on every word.

"Anyway, I couldn't get the condom opened. When I finally did... well... I'd barely gotten it on when I looked over at her pulling down her panties. They were hot pink, by the way." Derek had to take a deep breath, exhaling through his mouth. "I looked down and saw her...without her panties on and... it hit me. I..."

"What?" Joey sat up and scooted to the edge of the bed. "What hit you?"

"I..." He gritted his teeth and dropped his voice to a whisper. Jaw clenched, he was panic-stricken as his eyes darted left and right before he explained. "I came in the condom and my dick wasn't anywhere near her!"

"What?" Joey pulled his head back in confusion until it dawned on him what Derek was admitting. "Oh..." he pursed his lips as he drew out the word. "Oh. Yeah. That's bad."

Derek feigned being insulted. "You're such a dick."

"Yeah, but..." Joey laughed as he asked, "didn't you say you hit a home run? I mean, what did she say? What did you do?"

"Kaitlyn was really cool about it, actually." Derek kicked an imaginary piece of dirt around the carpet with his sock-covered foot. "We laughed."

"Wait. She laughed at you?"

"Not right away." Derek's face snapped up as he shook his head. "What?! No! No. No. No. She didn't laugh at me. She...she's not like that. We just talked and then laughed when we both agreed how awkward it was. Then..."

"Then?"

"She wanted to try again. And well, so did my dick." Derek's fingers pointed down as if Joey didn't know what he was talking about.

Joey was going to strain his eyes with how much he rolled them during Derek recounting of last night's events.

"I'd already flung the used condom out the door." Derek shot Joey another panicked glance. "Wait. Should I have gone back and looked for that?"

Joey closed his eyes and shook his head, trying to suppress a laugh.

"Ugh." Derek groaned before continuing in a rush. "So I grabbed my backup condom and put it on and it went much better. Said she still wanted to do it. And again, I asked, but she said the best thing. She said she wanted it to be with me." He closed his eyes and leaned back in his chair, causing it to roll back toward his desk. "And god did it feel good."

"So it wasn't awkward then?"

"Are you kidding?" Derek scooted his chair back to the bed. "It was totally awkward and I really hope we can do it again. Just not with the seat belt thing digging into her back and her butt not halfway off the seat. But, wow." His grin was back as he exhaled. "Kaitlyn Sutters."

Joey grinned, too. "That's awesome, man."

"Yeah." Derek's thoughts drifted to the night before; his eyes glazed over. "It was."

Joey cleared his throat to pull Derek out of his reverie.

"Sorry." Derek tried to look serious.

He failed.

"So what'd you do after you dropped Lindsey off? Go home?"

"Kind of." Joey shrugged as he retreated back against the wall.

Derek tilted his head, his eyes narrowed. "What do you mean...kind of?"

"Well, it was a Friday, so Mom was working the late shift. Since she wasn't home when I got there, I ditched the tux and headed back out. Figured I'd just listen to music and think."

"Okay," Derek agreed.

"D. I don't..." he hesitated, unsure if he wanted to go there with his best friend. He looked down and picked at something underneath his fingernails.

"You don't what?" Derek looked worried. "What's wrong?"

"Nothing. I just..."

"Nothing?" He pushed. "Something must be up..."

"I..." Joey pulled a face. "I ran into Logan."

"Logan?" Derek arched a brow.

"Yeah. And we started talking."

"About what?"

"Well... about our dads." Joey hesitated.

"What else?"

"What else?" Joey chewed his lower lip.

"Yeah."

"Well...shit." Joey pulled one of Derek's pillows into his lap and let out a loud exhale. Unsure how to go on, he just blurted everything out in the world's nastiest case of word vomit. "We talked and then we shared a drink. But just Gatorade. Orange Gatorade. Then one thing led to another. And his hands and then my hands and... then he kissed me and I kissed him back and we made it to third base and oh my god."

"Whoa." Derek's eyes blinked as he sat up straight. "Wait. What?"

"Shit." Joey's head fell into his hands.

"Um. You... just... threw... an awful... lot... out there, Joey." Derek's words came out as slow as molasses in January.

"Oh my god."

Derek paused a moment before speaking, "Alright. So, how was it? I mean, how do you feel about it?"

Joey's head lifted. "How was it?" His dejected expression did a poor job of masking his regret at the confession he had just made.

"Yeah. Did you both like it?" Derek lifted one shoulder in a halfhearted shrug as if it were the simplest question in the world. "Did you have fun?"

Was Derek serious?

"Did I like it?" Even his words wanted to hesitate as his voice squeaked.

"Yeah." Derek confirmed with another shrug.

"I...I..." Joey's face broke into a smile as if he had just learned that it was okay to smile again. "Yeah. I liked it."

"Okay then. It's all good."

Someone knocked on the door. "Derek? Joey?" Abe's voice sounded through the door.

Joey's eyes went wide; his mouth gaped open. *"SHIT!"* he mouthed.

Derek held out his hand to reassure him everything was okay. "Yeah, Dad?"

Abe opened the door enough to lean his head inside the room. "I have to run out to the Gates Avenue job site for a couple of hours. There's plenty of food downstairs for lunch."

"Is that the one where the owners keep changing their minds about everything?" Derek asked.

"Yep." Abe fought back a few choice words before offering a smug smile. "That's the one."

"Alright. Good luck!"

"Thanks, Mr. M.," Joey responded without meeting Abe's eyes.

Joey let out a sigh of relief as soon as the door clicked shut but jumped when something hit him in the shoulder. "Ow!" A superball had just landed on the bedspread. "Jerk!" Joey tossed it back to Derek who dropped it in a desk drawer.

"It's okay, Joey."

"But...what if he finds out?"

"Who? Dad? Or someone else?"

"Yes?" Joey didn't specify.

Derek shrugged. "Dad'll find out when you want him to find out. And when he does, he'll be fine with it."

Derek dropped his hand off his friend's shoulder and rested his forearms on his own knees. "As for anyone else, same thing. They'll find out when you want them to. For us though, you're family, Joey, no matter what. Nothing's going to change that."

"But...what..." Joey chewed his lower lip. "What... if I liked kissing Logan more than I liked kissing Lindsey?"

Derek shrugged as if it were obvious. "Then you liked kissing Logan more than you liked kissing Lindsey. It's all good either way. He's a great guy. She's a great girl. Just be honest and make sure they both know where you stand."

It seemed simple enough.

Joey nodded his head, still unsure of everything going on in his heart and his mind and between his legs. Well, he was pretty sure of what was going on there. "D?"

"Yeah."

"Do you think it's crazy?"

"Do I think what's crazy?"

"That Logan and I went to third base."

When Derek remained silent, Joey rubbed his hands together. "I mean...I went down on him." He glanced up for a split second, then dropped his head back down. "And... well... he gave me a blow job, too. Am I gay?"

"Well, you said you liked making out with Lindsey, right?"

"Yeah."

"So it sounds more like you're bisexual, really, but you don't actually need a label if you don't want one."

"Uh. Yeah." Joey shrugged. "Right."

"Honestly, I'm happy for you."

"What do you mean?"

"I saw the way you were looking at each other last night at prom."

"You what?" Joey's eyes opened wide. "You saw...?"

"During the last slow dance. I caught you both. You couldn't take your eyes off each other, so, no. I don't think it's crazy at all."

"Oh. Um. It felt good. It was fun. And...it just felt right, you know? Felt comfortable."

"And that's a good thing, Joey. And that's what you want. Of course," Derek laughed, "you kind of one-upped me with the blow job."

"I'm not going to help you with that." Joey's dry response made Derek laugh harder and hold out a palm in surrender.

"I'm good, thanks. Although..."

Joey shot Derek a dirty look.

"Maybe next time I'm with Kaitlyn," Derek grinned as relief washed over Joey's face, "I can ask her if she wants...."

Joey laughed.

"Come on." Derek stood up. "I'm hungry."

"Wait."

Derek looked back with his hand still on the doorknob. "What?"

"Nevermind." Joey stood up to follow. "Let's go."

Chapter 24

Grant's Crossing - present day

DEREK LEANED BACK IN HIS SEAT. "JOEY WAS DISAPPOINTED HE lost the bet."

Logan furrowed his brow. "The bet?"

"Yeah!" Back from giving her daughter a bath, Lainee shimmied in excitement as she returned to her seat at the table. "What bet?"

Abe cleared his throat, keeping his amusement in check.

Derek gave his dad a nervous laugh and shook his head. "Joey, uh, was disappointed he'd only gotten to second base."

Logan guffawed. "That's all he admitted to?"

"With his prom date, yeah."

"Hell. We made it past second base."

Derek snorted. "I know."

"You do? I mean..." Logan quickly schooled his expression and cleared his throat. He glanced up at Drew, who pressed his lips together to suppress his laughter. "Well... we did." His smile was short-lived. "It was pretty great."

"He still had to buy me pizza."

Lainee knitted her brow. "Pizza?"

"Yeah." Derek exhaled. "Whoever went the farthest, the other would buy him pizza.

"Kaitlyn?" Logan asked.

"Uh-huh."

"Who then dumped you in your first deployment," Tank said, his voice dripped with contempt.

"I remember hearing about that. I'm sorry, D."

Tank agreed with Kiro. "Yeah. That was pretty cold, no offense."

"It's all good." Derek waved him off. After a few seconds, his lip curled up on one side. "At least I was stationed on a base with women when it happened."

The room broke out in laughter.

"Joey and I did our best to distract you."

"May not have admitted it then, but I appreciated what you both did. But back to prom night...."

Tank opened his mouth to speak but decided against it.

"What about you, Tank? Celi?" Derek looked at Tank and Araceli, who blushed.

Tank cleared his throat. "I took her straight home and gave her a chaste kiss goodnight." He proceeded to nonchalantly brush off a piece of nonexistent lint from his shoulder.

Araceli's face turned a brighter shade of red.

Derek grinned. "Uh-huh. Sure."

Logan broke in. "At least you weren't interrupted in the middle of anything."

Derek extended his arms. "I thought you said Drew came by after."

Logan folded his arms in front of his chest and let a derisive laugh escape. "Oh, he did. But I'm not talking about Drew."

"What?"

Logan cocked a brow and raised his hand to make his point. "I'm talking about you. Just before July 4th. When you interrupted a perfectly nice evening. As perfectly nice as two almost nineteen-year olds could have, anyway."

Chapter 25

Grant's Crossing - August 2000

Joey - 19 years old

Joey wiped the sweat off his brow with the back of his forearm as he and Logan worked on his car in the gravel lot behind his duplex. They'd already put in a full day at their summer jobs and were now sweating off a few pounds each thanks to the week-long heat wave.

Logan's parents were out of town for the weekend, but he still left his truck parked in the alley behind the house to maintain appearances. Grant's Crossing was too small to believe he couldn't be outed simply because his parents were out of town. His dad's auto parts shop employed a lot of people in town, so he thought it best to keep it low-key whenever possible.

Logan took a step back from under the hood of Joey's car, pressing his hands on his lower back to lean backward for a good stretch. He wiped the sweat off his face with the bottom of his t-shirt as he walked back into the small detached garage they now used as a workshop off the alley behind the house. He reached into his cooler and took a gulp from a cold bottle of water. He grabbed a second bottle and then picked up the wrench he needed.

"Here." Logan tapped Joey's upper arm with the back of his hand to offer the water.

"Thanks." Joey twisted off the lid and chugged half of it down in one long gulp. Logan was already back over the engine, resuming his work under the hood.

They were still working in the late afternoon sun when Joey's mom stepped out of the house wearing her usual all-black pants outfit that she wore to work. "I'm closing tonight, so if all goes well, I'll be back around two," she said as she leaned up on her toes to drop a kiss on Joey's cheek. She waved to Logan as he raised his head up from his work.

As Joey's mom backed out, Logan tightened something underneath the hood. "Ok, Joey. Start it up."

Joey opened the door and slid inside. He left the door open with one foot on the ground outside the vehicle. When he turned the ignition, the car started without its usual sputters. Logan surveyed everything under the hood and broke out into a grin.

He leaned his head around the side of the hood so Joey could hear. "Rev it a few times."

Joey pressed the accelerator pedal a few times with his foot. It sounded good.

"Yeah." Logan lowered the hood and dropped it down the last couple of inches to close it. "Purrs like a kitten." Through the windshield, he shared a grin with Joey, who turned the key to shut off the engine. He clambered out and tossed his keys in the air, catching them with the confidence of a runner who had just won the Boston Marathon.

With a high five, Joey and Logan set to work putting all the tools away. "I think we can call it a day," Joey announced as he closed the toolbox he'd received as a graduation gift from Derek's Dad. Now that he was working for Mitchell's contracting, he was building up his collection of tools.

"I'm hungry." Logan's hand patted his stomach as he pulled the door shut behind him. They toed off their shoes and left them at the back door.

"Me, too, but I need a shower first."

"Want company?"

"Sure." Joey grinned as he looked at Logan's sweaty body from head to toe. "You need one anyway."

Logan gave Joey a friendly shove before picking up his backpack from where he'd left it by the front door. He caught up to Joey upstairs in the loft, both loving the fact that Joey essentially had his own private suite separate from the rest of the house.

Through the bedroom, Joey headed straight for his shower, leaving a trail of dirty clothes in his wake. Flipping on the water, he stepped inside the moment the water turned warm. Logan followed right behind Joey and pulled him close, his front to Joey's back, and let the cleansing water cascade down their bodies. Steam filled the room and clouded up the mirror.

Logan planted kisses on his neck until Joey turned around to face him. Their lips wasted no time meeting as they looped their arms around each other.

Logan's hands worked their way down Joey's back and squeezed below his waist. Dragging his hand around to Joey's stomach, Logan lowered his hand between Joey's legs eliciting the filthiest of moans with every stroke.

Logan eased down to his knees and pulled Joey's thighs closer. "I've been wanting this all day." He took one last look into Joey's eyes before dropping his head.

Joey's hands reflexively reached into Logan's hair to hold him against his body. Letting out a low groan, Joey closed his eyes and tipped his head back. The water splashed his face as his hips pitched forward, rocking back and forth through Logan's hungry lips.

"Oh yeah..." Joey rasped as his motion quickened. "Lo... Logan..." he called out his name again as Logan devoured him. He gasped when one of Logan's hands reached between his legs. Whatever magic his fingers performed on him caused Joey to lose all ability to speak. He groaned and found himself fighting for air. With a loud grunt, he smacked a hand against the wall to support himself. His legs went weak when his body finally gave in to pleasure.

"Unghh." With a groan, he swayed as waves of electricity shot through his entire body, the same electricity that Joey reveled in whenever Logan touched him.

Logan slowed kissed his way back up Joey's body until they were both standing. Joey didn't know how or when his senses came back online, but he knew he felt good. When he opened his eyes, Logan had already risen to his full height directly in front of him.

As the water cascaded down their bodies, Logan reached a hand behind Joey's head and grazed Joey's lips with his own. "Come here." Logan's husky voice was low. "Lean against me. I've got you."

Joey dropped his head on Logan's shoulder and let his body fall against him, his hooded eyes closing and his limp arms hanging by his sides. Logan wrapped his strong arms around Joey and held him steady until Joey's legs regained the ability to stand on their own power.

Joey took a deep breath and raised his eyes. He curled his fingers into Logan's chest and dropped lazy kisses there. He pressed more kisses up Logan's neck and along his scruffy jaw, pausing to lightly caress his cheek with the backs of his fingers. He lifted his gaze enough to meet Logan's eyes before meeting him in a slow, languid kiss. The kind they'd both grown to love. The kind that would always give Joey butterflies. With their foreheads resting against each other, Joey exhaled. "God, I love when you do that."

"I know." Logan kissed him again between smiles. "I think I'm getting better at it, too."

"Uh, you were good our first time."

"That *was* my first time."

"Then you're a prodigy, but anytime you feel like practicing," Joey panted, "I'm here for you."

They laughed and kissed some more. Enjoying the hot water on their bodies, they took their time scrubbing each other down after a hard day working on greasy cars.

When the water turned cold, they shut it off and emerged from the shower to towel off and get into some clean clothes. In the kitchen, they plowed through the rest of the lasagna Joey's mom had left for them; it was, they agreed, probably the best benefit of her working at the new upscale Italian restaurant.

After a short debate while finishing the dishes, they settled on an adventure flick Joey had rented the night before and collapsed on the couch. Lying on his back, Joey let one leg dangle off the couch and rested his head on Logan's thigh. He held Logan's hand against his chest as they watched the movie, sometimes rubbing his thumb back and forth against the back of Logan 's hand. He felt grounded by that simple, skin-on-skin connection.

Sometimes, Logan's other hand strayed to Joey's head, lazily combing through his hair. Joey wasn't sure if Logan even realized he was doing it. It felt so natural. So good. So normal.

So right.

They were most comfortable when they just did nothing. The more time they spent together, the more relaxed they seemed to be in each other's company. They were already friends, but now that friendship had grown into something more. Not just because they were dating, albeit in secret, but because they tended to open up more around each other. They understood each other. At least, that's what they both told themselves.

Joey hoped Logan felt more like himself, too. He certainly did around Logan. Joey wanted their friendship to last and truly believed it would. But he also wanted *them* to last.

Joey still couldn't shake that sinking suspicion that they were just biding their time until the bubble burst. When it would all be snatched away from them one day.

"Hey."

Joey looked up to see Logan's face hovering over him, concern apparent on his face.

"You there?"

"What?" Joey was still in a fog.

"I was calling your name."

"Sorry." Joey blinked and brought himself back to the present, knowing he had no idea what had just happened in the movie they were supposedly watching.

"Get up a second." Logan patted Joey's chest. "I want to get something to drink."

"What? Oh. Yeah. Sorry."

"You ok?" Logan asked as they both sat up.

"Yeah. Was just thinking."

"'Bout what?"

"Nothin'."

"Really?" Logan arched an eyebrow.

Joey exhaled. "About my dad." His lips tightened, and his expression turned grim.

As did Logan's.

"I'm going to get something to drink." Logan stood up. "Want anything?"

"Yeah. I'll take a pop."

"Ok. When I'm back," Logan cupped Joey's face with a mischievous smile, "I'll make you think of something else." Logan kissed Joey and then stood up.

Joey wiped his face with his hands, exhaling again as he tried to clear his thoughts of his dad. He'd been thinking of him a lot more since he had started seeing Logan.

Logan had just turned toward the kitchen when a loud knock at the front door startled them both from the sense of calm they'd been enjoying.

Logan jumped and shared a panicked look with Joey.

Joey perked up as well. "It's ok." He reassured Logan in a whisper. "Just go on."

Joey stood up to answer the knock but waited for Logan to get closer to the kitchen before opening the door to find a pair of desperate green eyes staring back at him.

Chapter 26

Grant's Crossing - present day

Derek shook his head to hide his laughter. "I was not an interruption."

"Yes. You were."

"I needed sanctuary."

Kiro laughed, but Tank choked on his drink. "Sanctuary?"

Lainee leaned into Tasha, who sat down next to her, and grabbed her hand. "Is Catie asleep?"

Tasha kissed Lainee's hand then set the baby monitor on the table. "Out like a light, but she'll probably wake up later."

"Yeah. She's been doing that lately."

"I had to get away from my sister," Derek explained to Tank.

Lainee perked up. "Wait. What? What do you mean you had to get away from me?"

Derek turned to his sister and her girlfriend, then returned to his explanation. "How many times did you watch Titanic the summer after your freshman year?"

"A few times, why?"

"Wrong answer." Derek had a good poker face. "How many? Come on. You can be honest."

Lainee pursed her lips and held her ground for a few seconds until Derek cocked a brow. "Ok. Fine," she huffed. "A lot."

"Exactly." Derek leaned forward, his expression smug. "You and your friends drove me nuts."

"Ha. Yeah, we did." Lainee's amused response wiped the smirk right off her brother's face. "That was so great."

"That was *not* great." Derek appealed to the room. "They would knock on my door and then run away laughing. I *had* to get away."

Split along gender lines, the men in the room all nodded in understanding while the women all laughed.

"Yeah, Lainee," Logan answered in mock exasperation. "Thanks for that. You know what he did?"

Amused, she cleared her throat. "No. What?"

"On a night when Joey's mom was at work until one or two in the morning *and* my parents were finally out of town, this one," Logan pointed across the table at Derek, "*this* one went straight to Joey's house complaining about *Hanson* or *Ricky Martin* or something." Logan lost his battle to keep a straight face.

Lainee laughed. "Hey. Don't knock Ricky Martin. Derek used to dance to him."

Logan slapped his hands on the table and sat up straight. "He what?"

Tank and Kiro each sat up straighter. They exchanged looks, then gave Lainee their full attention.

Tank turned to Derek. "You danced to Ricky Martin?"

Derek tried to wave them off. "No, I didn't."

"Nice try, big brother, but, you did. I caught you. I might even have a picture of it somewhere." She folded her arms across her chest and leaned back in her seat in smug satisfaction.

"I've gotta see that," Tank said as Logan broke out in laughter. He shot a glance at Abe. "Is this true?"

Abe held up his hands. "I'm going to remain neutral."

Derek remained calm and unaffected. "I will deny it to my dying days. You can't break me."

"Deny it all you want, but I saw it." Lainee pointed two of her fingers back at her face and narrowed her eyes. "With my own two eyes."

"Yeah, well," Logan said, his amusement evident, "dancing or not, you interrupted our first night together without any parents in the house."

Chapter 27

Grant's Crossing - August 2000

Joey - 19 years old

"Hey Joey." Derek fist-bumped Joey and let himself inside.

"Huh?" Joey's other hand was still on the doorknob as Derek dropped himself onto the couch and made himself at home. Joey could only watch in disbelief.

Shoes still on, Derek propped his feet up on the ottoman. "What are you watching?"

Joey regained his ability to move and kept his curious eyes on Derek. "Uh...*The Mummy*." He paused the movie.

"Thank god. Something good. Can you restart it?" Derek kept talking as he looked down and noticed the other movie with a Blockbuster label that read *Be Kind, Please Rewind* on the outside. "*The World is Not Enough*. James Bond. Awesome."

He paused just long enough to inhale more air, gesticulating with his arms throughout his entire tirade. "Lainee has her friends over. They keep doing this stupid, girlie door-knocking thing. So annoying. Then, they're taking over the family room, painting their nails and playing with their hair and shit. They're planning to watch chick flicks. Pretty sure they're going to watch Titanic. Again." Derek stood up. "Have any Cokes? I'm thirsty."

He started for the back of the house while continuing his diatribe about how his sister and her friends had taken over his home.

"Uh..."

Joey scrambled to follow Derek into the kitchen.

Best laid plans.

"Anyway, Kaitlyn has a family thing, and I can't stay at home tonight with all that estrogen. I mean, they won't...stop...talking. Oh, hey, Shepherd." Derek extended his fist, which Logan reflexively bumped.

"Hey."

Logan stood frozen, holding the two cans of Coke he'd just pulled out of the fridge. He set one on the table after Derek walked in. He turned to Joey and mouthed, *"What's going on?"* then passed Joey a can of Coke in silence while Derek stuck his head in the pantry.

Joey shrugged, then popped the can open and took a sip.

Derek reached in for a bag of chips, opened it, and tossed a couple in his mouth. He looked at Logan, "Don't you have sisters?"

"Uh...yeah," Logan said. "One. Courtney."

"Does she drive you nuts, too?"

"Sure?"

Derek held his fingers to his head and then spread them wide. "All that talk of makeup and shit? I can't stand it."

Logan and Joey exchanged exasperated glances again, but there was no stopping Derek when he was on a roll.

"And they keep talking about Hanson and Ricky Martin. If I hear MmmBop one more time, I'm gonna lose it. And let's not even talk about Livin' La Vida Loca. I'm already going loca."

"Loco," Joey corrected him without thinking.

Derek creased his brow. "What?"

"Loco. You're masculine. It's loco, not loca."

"Whatever. I took French."

"Only because Kaitlyn was in that class, and it still took you two years to ask her out." Logan joined the fray.

Derek grinned. "Yeah. And she said yes, too!" He dropped his grin and furrowed his brow so he could concentrate. "Had to get a car first. Didn't want Dad to have to drive me around all the time." He grabbed a can of Coke from the fridge and shrugged again. "Can't get lucky with a third wheel." He popped the top to open the can.

"Oh, the irony," Joey muttered under his breath. Logan snorted, then coughed to cover his mirth.

"So, are we going to watch *The Mummy* first? Or do you want to watch Bond?" Coke and chips in hand, Derek didn't bother to wait for an answer. He was already on his way back to the family room. At least he landed in the recliner, this time leaving the couch for his friends.

Logan finally popped the top on his Coke. "What just happened?"

"No idea." Joey held out his hands. "Give me a minute."

Joey returned to the living room and set his Coke on the end table. He then sat down on the couch to face Derek.

Derek had finally stopped talking long enough to let someone else speak. "What's up?"

"Um."

"He knows I know, right?" Derek's voice was nonchalant.

"Uh...about that..."

"He doesn't. Does he?"

"Um...no."

"Jesus, Joey. You gotta tell him."

"It's not that simple."

"Yeah. It is." Derek contradicted him. "I've known since before you've known. Pretty close, anyway. I know about you, *and* I know about him, *and* I've not told anybody about it. Not Lainee. Not Kaitlyn. Not even Dad."

Joey inhaled through gritted teeth.

"Come on, Joey." Derek pleaded before Joey could say anything. "He should know he has friends. You both do. It's..."

A hint of anger flared. "It's what?"

Derek sat forward and rested his forearms on his knees. "Joey, it's gotta be fucking miserable to have to hide all the time. I'm just saying that with me, you don't have to. You can relax around me."

Joey maintained eye contact while considering Derek's words.

"Look," Derek continued. "I really want to get away from Lainee, so I was hoping to escape for a couple of hours. I know being with Logan is more important, but I just needed to get away. If I can't stay, I get it. Just tell me. I can find something else to do to avoid the whole estrogen fest at home. But you should know something." Derek extended his arm toward the kitchen where Logan was waiting. "He and I played football together for four years, and I never remotely suspected he was gay until I saw you two at prom. He hid it so well, but now that I know, he shouldn't feel he has to hide. Not around me."

Joey stayed silent, so Derek kept going. "How often have you been over at our house watching a movie with just Kaitlyn and me?"

"A lot," Joey conceded.

"Yeah. A lot. Because we both like you and like having you around, but we never pretend we're not dating. We still hold hands and," Derek waggled his eyebrows, "go to another room to make out."

Joey rolled his eyes. "And if she didn't like me?"

"That's a no-brainer. We've been best friends since we were ten, Joey. That's not gonna change."

Joey's wheels turned as he debated what to do.

"Which also means that if you want to go ahead and kick me out for tonight, you're still stuck with me. You're my best friend either way."

Joey's eyes didn't stray from Derek's gaze for a moment. "You're right." Joey slapped his hands on his knees. "I'm gonna tell him."

He stood to head back to the kitchen but turned around and pointed as Derek started to follow. "You. Stay."

Without a word, Derek sat back down. Joey knew Derek's eyes followed him as he returned to the kitchen.

"Well?" Logan arched his brows. "What's up?"

Joey hesitated. He made eye contact but dropped his gaze a moment to psych himself up to tell him.

"Joey?"

He stepped to the counter and turned around. He leaned back and decided being direct would be best. "Did you know Derek knows about us?"

"You just told him?" Logan flipped his arms in the air and whisper-yelled, "Jesus, Joey! I can't believe you did that."

"No, Logan. I didn't just tell him." Joey crossed the room and touched his hand to Logan's chest. Logan batted it away.

"He's known the whole time."

"Fuck." Logan was stunned. "Wait." He froze. His eyes turned dark as he glared at Joey. "Wha...whaddya mean the whole time?"

"I mean, he's known the whole time."

"What. The. Fuck." Logan paced a few times, then called out. "MITCHELL!" Logan's tone left no question of his anger.

"Oh shit." Derek choked on his Coke and coughed. "YEAH?"

"GET IN HERE." Logan's gaze never wavered from Joey when he called out to Derek.

Joey shook his head slowly. "Logan. Don't."

Derek trotted to the kitchen, coming to an abrupt halt as he arrived. "Yeah?"

"What did he tell you?" Logan's belligerent tone was unmistakable as he glared at Derek but pointed toward Joey.

"What do you mean? What did he tell me?" Derek's hackles shot up.

Logan spread his arms out, clearly ticked off. "I mean, what the fuck did he tell you? Who have you told?"

"What do you mean, who have I told?" Derek's eyes went back and forth between Logan and his best friend. "Are you sure that's what you want to ask?" Derek snapped back. "Because you might want to ask him instead."

"Oh shit." Joey's eyes darted back and forth from Derek to Logan and back.

"Shut the fuck up, Mitchell." Logan's voice leveled out. "Just tell me what I want to know."

"Uh." Derek snorted out a laugh. "Which is it, Shepherd?" Derek curled his lips back and extended his arms. "Because right now, I can't tell if you want me to shut up or answer you? I mean, does one override the other? Because..."

It took Logan two, maybe three, steps to cross the entire room. He stood right in front of Derek and glared down at him. Any closer, and they'd be touching. Derek was pretty tall, standing steady at just over six feet tall, but Logan still had a good two inches over him. He tilted his head and growled. "Fu..."

Joey could see Logan's fists clenching. "Logan." He kept his voice level in an effort to prevent this from coming to blows.

"Answer me."

"Fine." Derek stood his ground, seemingly happy to be right in Logan's face. "I figured it out for myself."

"What?" Logan snapped as if expecting any other response but that. His glare faltered.

"Come on, Shepherd. You did a great job of hiding it in the locker room after practices and games. You really did. Joey knows I had no idea." Derek's voice remained steady, albeit far less confrontational. "But you did a lousy job of hiding it at prom."

Logan's hands flew back like they'd just touched something hot. As if the wind were knocked out of him, he stumbled back, staring down at the floor for a few seconds.

"What? How?" The fire drained out of Logan's eyes.

"You couldn't take your eyes off him." Derek stretched his arms wide. "You were there, Logan. You saw me." Derek softened his tone and lowered his arms. "You know I caught you looking."

"You..." Blindsided, Logan swallowed; his Adam's apple bobbed up and down. He raised his eyes back up to meet Derek's gaze. "You never said anything. Why...why didn't you say anything?"

Joey's eyes went back and forth between his best friend and his boyfriend as they got on the same page.

His boyfriend.

Joey's heart warmed at the thought. He stepped closer to slip his hand in Logan's. Logan hesitated a second before squeezing Joey's hand in return.

"Why would I?" Derek pulled his head back, his brow creased. "It's not my secret to share. Besides," he said, "and no offense, but your dad's kind of a dick."

Logan breathed out a laugh, tilting his head in agreement as Derek continued.

"I've seen him yell at you at games. Can't be easy. I just never knew this was what you had to hide from him."

"I'm not hiding this from him." Taking another step back, Logan gripped Joey's hand tighter for support. "I'm hiding this from everyone."

"Well." Derek leaned against a counter and crossed his ankles. "For what it's worth, you don't have to hide it from me. I'm not going to say anything to anyone. I have no reason to. Even if I thought I did, there's no point. And... you're welcome to come over to my place for a movie or whatever anytime to mix things up a bit."

"I...I didn't expect...." Logan opened his mouth, unable to voice his thoughts.

"Look, Logan. I didn't come here to fight."

Logan had never appeared anything but sure of himself. It was disconcerting to see him come across as almost afraid. Joey breathed a sigh of relief when Derek extended his hand to Logan.

"Whaddya say? We good?"

Logan hesitated but shook his hand with a nod, visibly relieved. "Yeah." His face curled up into a smile. "We're good."

"Ok, then." Derek put his hands together as if in prayer and pleaded with his friends. "Now, please tell me I can stick around for at least one movie. Help a guy out?"

Logan and Joey laughed, but Logan spoke first. "You are looking rather pathetic there, Mitchell. I guess we can put up with you for a couple of hours."

Relieved, Derek clasped his hands together and exhaled. "Thank you."

"I get it," Logan added as he reached over the table to grab his Coke, never letting go of Joey's hand on the way back to the family room. "My sister is eleven, and everything, I mean *everything*... has to be pink. I let her paint my nails once on her ninth birthday, and it took me forever to get that shit off."

"I remember that, I think." Derek stopped long enough to look back at him as they wandered back to the family room. He furrowed his brows, "Wait. You know there's remover for that, right?"

Logan held up a hand. "I do now, yeah."

Chapter 28

Grant's Crossing - Present day

Lainee could barely breathe from laughing so hard "You didn't know about nail polish remover? That's hilarious."

"I'm a guy." Logan defended himself as if no other explanation were needed. "How would I know that?"

"Pretty sure you were this close to hitting me that night." Derek held his thumb and index finger about a half-inch apart.

"Pretty sure you're right," Logan admitted while mirroring Derek's smirk, "until you told me you'd already figured me out." He rested his arms on the table. "You were the third person to know."

"The third?"

"Yeah, Uncle Aiden, Joey..." he smiled, "and then you." He tilted his head to one side and shrugged. "Then Joey's mom. That was it for the longest time."

"I thought I was the third," Drew laughed.

"Not if Mitchell figured it out at prom." Logan leaned back in his chair at the table and pulled his drink closer to inspect the ice inside the glass. His smile was tinged with sadness. "I felt so at home at Joey's house...probably for the first time ever, to be honest. There was no pressure. No expectations except to treat Joey well and do the dishes."

Everyone smiled.

"I never escaped dishes."

Still staring at his drink, Logan spoke up again when the chuckles died down. "God, I hope he knew how much that meant to me."

"He knew," Derek assured him. "Trust me. He knew."

"I have to admit," Logan finally pulled his eyes away from his drink. "You did give us another place to hang out. My parents never suspected a thing, not that they cared when I came out to them. And Abe," he faced Derek's dad. "you never cared that we were all there, either."

Abe's brow lifted in pleasant surprise. "Not at all. I loved having all of you over. Still do."

Logan's gaze returned to his glass. He used his hands to rotate it in place. "Joey was so nervous about coming out to his mom."

"Yeah, he was," Derek agreed, eyes lifting to catch his dad nodding in agreement.

"He was so afraid she was going to kick him out." Abe said then shook his head at the memory. "I knew she wouldn't."

"No. She wouldn't have," Quinn confirmed. "She knew firsthand what that was like and would never have put Joey through what she went through."

Abe exchanged a glance with Quinn. "I just made sure he knew he had a home here."

Derek started laughing, drawing everyone's attention.

Abe shot his son a sideways glance. "What's so funny?"

"When Joey first came out to Dad, Dad's first question," Derek struggled to stop laughing long enough to tell the story, "...was whether or not he and I were an item."

Logan busted out laughing. "Whaaa?"

"Yeah. Joey was so shocked at the question that he told Dad I was as straight as they come. No pun intended I'm sure."

"Ha! He was right about that," Logan agreed.

Derek continued, "...and that I wasn't his type."

Logan's eyes widened before shooting Derek a wayward glance. "Um... you kind of are."

Derek's laughter subsided, replaced with a sad smile. "I would have been a lucky man if that did it for me." He lifted his eyes in time to see Logan staring back at him.

Abe crossed his arms and leaned back against the counter. "Turns out when Joey told his mom, she didn't even question it."

Logan chuckled as if enjoying an inside joke.

"What?" Abe asked.

"He didn't tell her. She discovered it for herself." His cheeks went pink as he looked up to meet everyone's eyes. "Derek left after the first movie so Joey and I went up to his room after the second." He cleared his throat. "No, she didn't question it. That didn't make it any less terrifying though."

His lips curled up at the memory as he recounted the tale. "We didn't mean to fall asleep. But the next morning, we woke up in total panic to the sound of her calling us down for breakfast." He bit his lower lip when no one reacted. "She called *both* of us. By name."

Comprehension set in as he continued. "And then she made us omelets and... threatened me within an inch of my life if I ever broke her son's heart. Told me she wasn't scared of me."

Logan's face went distant as he thought back to that day.

"And then my dad showed up."

Chapter 29

Grant's Crossing - August 2000
Joey - 19 years old

Logan, Joey, and Renee talked around the kitchen table for close to an hour after they ate, talking about anything and everything, including plans for Joey's belated birthday party and the events from the night before. Well, maybe not *all* the events from the night before. She offered them seconds on their breakfast since their first omelets weren't quite enough to feed the two growing men despite having finished off the rest of the lasagna the night before.

Renee did everything she could to make Logan and all of Joey's friends comfortable and at home when they were over. She had to work long hours to keep a roof over their heads, but even if she couldn't be there all the time, she made damned sure Joey and his friends never once had to worry about saying the wrong thing in front of an iron-fisted patriarch who essentially ruled the household by decree. She had lived with that until her husband died, and based on a few details she could glean from her conversations with Logan, he lived that way now.

Joey's mom had both Logan and Joey in stitches as she relayed a hilarious story about one of her restaurant customers the night before. She was just finishing the tale when a loud knock at the front door caused them to jump out of their seats. "What the..."

She started to stand up when she felt Joey's hand on her shoulder. "I'll get it, Mom."

Joey walked to the front of the house and opened the front door to find a rather large and imposing man filling the opening. "Mr. Shepherd."

"I'm looking for Logan," Ramsey Shepherd's gruff voice demanded. "Is he here?"

Renee's eyes darted to Logan when he visibly stiffened upon hearing his father's voice. Renee recognized the fear in his eyes and patted him on his forearm. "It'll be ok, Logan."

In a flash, she ran into her bedroom off the kitchen. Wearing a big smile, Renee walked out into the living room with the blanket that was usually folded at the foot of her bed. . Joey said nothing, and she had to give him props for keeping a straight face and not showing his surprise.

"You must be Mr. Shepherd. I'm Renee Parker. Joey's mom." She shifted the blanket and extended her hand to Logan's dad, who accepted it.

A tall man, Ramsey Shepherd, dipped his chin as he looked down at her. "Nice to meet you, Mrs. Parker."

Renee could feel the tension that filled the room as Joey and Logan were frozen in place, staring at their respective parents, as if waiting for an inevitable explosion.

"Very nice to meet you, too," she gushed. "Won't you please come in?" She held the door open so he could step inside. She noticed his eyes scanning the room as if he were visually giving it a white glove inspection and finding it lacking.

Then his eyes met his son's.

"Dad." Logan swallowed. "You're home early. Is everything ok?"

"We know you didn't come home last night, Logan." He bellowed. "You know how we don't like you out partying at some place..." He hesitated as he gave the home a disapproving look. "Your mother was worried sick. She..."

"Oh, I'm afraid that's my fault, Mr. Shepherd."

Renee cut him off with her sugary sweet tone. "The boys were up late watching a couple of movies, and I didn't want him to drive home to an empty house after dark, so I made up the couch and insisted Logan stay." Renee held up the blanket as evidence. "He said you and your wife weren't going to be home until later today, so I figured it best for him to stay here where it's safe."

Renee didn't care whether Logans dad were accustomed to being interrupted or not. He opened his mouth as if to start talking again but she never gave him the chance.

"Their friend, Derek, was here as well." Joey had mentioned he was here to watch one of the movies. She glanced down at the coffee table where the Blockbuster cases were laid out. "But he didn't stay up for the James Bond film, which is too bad. It was a good one."

Taken aback, Mr. Shepherd lightened his tone a little bit. "Derek *Mitchell*?" He stressed the last name as if confirming a fine vintage of wine.

Renee nodded in confirmation.

"He comes from a good family. Abe's a good judge of character. Does fine work on older homes. Have you had him out yet for a quote?"

Logan lifted a brow, but Renee ignored the underhanded implication that her home was in need of renovation.

"We were just enjoying our breakfast. I made Western omelets. Would you care for one?" She motioned toward the kitchen, keeping the sweetest smile on her face. "There's plenty of food, and I can brew a fresh pot of coffee."

Logan's face blanched. His dad hesitated long enough to make Renee run a quick mental inventory of the food inside her refrigerator in case he might actually take her up on her offer.

"That's very kind of you, Mrs. Parker, and," he patted his

stomach with a smile, "I do love a good omelet, but we've already had breakfast this morning. Thank you." Ramsey Shepherd changed tactics and turned on that Shepherd family charm he probably used to schmooze his clients.

"Oh, I'm so sorry to hear that." Renee's smile dropped, but just a little bit, for effect. She perked up again. "Another time, then, perhaps when your wife can join us?"

"Yes, perhaps." He looked back inside the duplex, a crease in his brow, "Is your husband not here? He's not working on a Sunday, is he?"

She offered a sad smile. "My husband passed away." She reached out and placed her hand on Joey's arm, looking sadder than she felt. "It's just Joey and me now."

"I'm terribly sorry." Mr. Shepherd's expression seemed genuinely sympathetic. "Was he ill?"

Joey and Logan exchanged questioning glances at such a personal question.

"It was a work accident, actually," she replied with a straight face. When Joey reached his hand up to help mask his cough, she rubbed gentle circles on his back. "That's what brought us here to Grant's Crossing. We, uh... needed to get away. Sort of a fresh start. I'm sure you understand."

Logan's dad nodded in sympathy. "I certainly do. Sometimes a change of scenery is just what the doctor ordered. I'm terribly sorry for your loss and hope you received some sort of compensation. If there's any way my son or I can be of any assistance to you, please don't hesitate to let us know."

"Why, thank you very much. I appreciate that. Truly."

Joey pressed his lips together to suppress a smile, masking it with another cough. Renee patted him on his back a little harder than was necessary, then pasted a charming smile back on her face.

"Well, I best be going so I can get back to my wife." Mr. Shepherd's eyes twinkled as he mentioned his wife but hardened as he locked gazes again with his son. He dropped his voice to a lower, far less pleasant octave. "Time to get home, Logan. You have training this afternoon."

"Yes, sir." Logan's response sounded stiff.

Ramsey Shepherd turned his attention back to Joey's mom. He smiled before speaking. "I thank you for taking care of my son, Mrs. Parker. I appreciate your hospitality."

"It's my pleasure. You've got a wonderful son, Mr. Shepherd. He's welcome here anytime."

"Thank you." He smiled at her, and nodded to Joey, acknowledging him for the first time. Then he turned a glare back to his son. "Logan. I expect you home right away."

Logan swallowed hard but nodded to his father. "Yes, sir."

"Have a wonderful day, Mr. Shepherd," Joey's mom called out with a cheerful wave. "Thank you for stopping by."

After Logan's dad was a few steps past their front steps, she closed and locked the front door. Before she turned around, she could hear both Joey and Logan release a collective sigh of relief.

They gawked at her in disbelief. She returned their gaze, rather unimpressed with Mr. Shepherd's visit. "He doesn't scare me either." She tossed the blanket on the couch and strutted back to the kitchen, leaving Joey and Logan speechless.

"Holy shit," Logan exclaimed. "Your mom is amazing."

"Yeah. She is," Joey agreed, pushing Logan toward the back of the house to get his shoes. "Now you need to get home."

Chapter 30

Grant's Crossing - present day

Quinn let out a hearty laugh. "Renee was never afraid of anyone."

Logan leaned back in his seat. "Nope."

"She told me she always went upstairs and checked on Joey when she got home after work even after he was out of high school."

Logan shook his head with a laugh. "So you were number five then."

"Probably not. I didn't hear about you two until long after, but she told me that she saw the two of you asleep and..." Quinn's eyes softened for a moment. "She said it was obvious you cared about him. It didn't take long for her to realize you two were the real thing."

Logan wiped his hand down his face. "Wow."

"Still," Quinn leaned back in his seat. "I would have paid real money to see her go head-to-head with your father. He would never have stood a chance."

"Oh, he didn't," Logan said, "And it was spectacular."

Lainee closed the refrigerator door after refilling everyone's drinks. "That's cool that your dad didn't care when you came out."

"Mom and Dad didn't care at all," Logan said. "Dad's just never gotten over the fact that I didn't make it big at football despite being a low draft pick."

"The draft?" Tasha questioned Logan who dipped his chin.

"The NFL draft."

"Wow. What happened?"

"Too many injuries in the Shoe…"

Tasha made a face when Logan mentioned the Shoe.

"Ohio Stadium," Lainee whispered to her girlfriend. "Where the Buckeyes play football."

"Ahh." Tasha creased her brow.

Logan continued. "Followed by a really hard hit in Dallas that had me carried out on a stretcher.

"I never did like the Cowboys," Kiro deadpanned.

"That tackle knocked me out and had me seeing stars for a week. I love football and was thrilled to play for the Buckeyes and then the Jaguars, but it was never really my dream to play pro ball as a career. It was Dad's idea but not mine." Logan forced a smile. "I spent too much time icing my body before I was barely old enough to drink. While I put out a good performance at the Combine and then my first few games in Jacksonville, every tackle just hurt worse than the one before. I knew it would take its toll on me, so after two seasons of mostly warming the bench due to injuries, I was released."

"Oh," Lainee said. "But you're doing ok now?"

"Yes," Logan reassured her. "Though Dad still hasn't forgiven me for getting out, not that I had much choice in the matter."

"That stinks," Lainee said

"Yeah. My brother, Dane, plays pro hockey up in Winnipeg, and I'm working a desk job." Logan flipped up his hands as if he were a lost cause.

"What is your desk job these days?" Kiro asked.

"Forensic accountant."

Derek snorted out a laugh. "Who'd have thought you'd grow up to be a bean counter?"

"Don't knock him," Drew said. "His testimony has put criminals behind bars, including some human traffickers."

"Really?" An impressed Derek sat up straighter. "That's really cool. We saw the results of trafficking over in Afghanistan."

Tank's solemn expression and slow nod confirmed Derek's words.

Logan waved them off as if it were no big deal. "I just like crunching numbers."

Drew held up his fork. "Wait a second. You told me earlier that you still get nervous around me. If that's true, how do you handle yourself in court? I've seen how confident you are on the stand. Nobody questions you."

"I think a few defense attorneys would argue that point. When I'm on the stand, I just recite facts. Being an expert witness is easier than being the defendant."

Drew arched a brow with a tilt of his head. "Good point."

"You helped me with math when I was in school. I always struggled with that," Lainee said.

"You just needed the time to figure things out, that's all," Logan assured her.

"Joey helped me figure things out, too," she said softly. "He helped me come to terms with who I am, though I think Mom knew. Somehow, she knew before I did."

Abe stood behind Lainee and placed his hands on her shoulders. "Your mother had a sixth sense about some things. She was always able to piece things together." He eyed Lainee and Derek, then concentrated on Lainee. "You and Joey both came out to me."

Abe smiled at the memory of his kids trusting him, then directed a pointed look at Derek. With a mischievous grin, he gave his son a sideways glance. "Anything you'd like to tell me, son?"

Derek held up his hands as if backing off. "No, no, no. I'm quite happy with women, thanks."

"*All* women, from what I hear," Logan joked.

"Not yet, but now that I'm home...." Derek grinned and wagged his eyebrows.

Lainee covered her face with her hand. "Oh, my god."

"What?" Derek spread his arms wide. "It's good to have goals."

Lainee covered her ears and closed her eyes. "La la la la la."

Derek tilted his head. "What are you? Six?"

Lainee waved him off.

When their laughter died down again, Derek kept his attention on his sister. "You and Joey were always close."

"He was always my favorite, Derek. You know that." She gave Derek a playful punch in the arm. "Joey understood what I was going through. That alone helped me a lot. I mean, you and Dad always accepted me without question, but Joey? He got me."

Derek's eyes twinkled in mischief. "I always question you."

Lainee smacked Derek's arm again. "Not about the important stuff."

"True that."

"I remember the first time you all felt drawn to the Army. It was that be-all-you-can-be commercial."

"I remember. You kept stealing our Hot Pockets."

"I would never...." Lainee drew her hand to her chest in feigned shock. "And it was pizza rolls."

Chapter 31

Grant's Crossing - September 2001

Joey - 20 years old

"Hey! Let me have some."

Derek pulled the plate out of his sister's reach. "No way. Get your own."

"Didn't we just see this same ad last commercial break?" Joey pointed at the TV in the Mitchells' family room.

The *be all that you can be* Army commercial started playing as Derek sat back down in the family room with a plate full of heated pizza rolls. It was part of their efforts to spend a Saturday being lazy and eating Derek's dad out of the house and home as teenagers are wont to do.

Since his mom was working again tonight, Joey, a near-permanent fixture in the Mitchell household, had already spent the day there.

"No. This is the Ranger one." Derek's mouth was full as he pointed to the TV. "We could do that."

"Could do what?" Joey asked as he popped another pizza roll in his mouth. "Be a soldier?"

"Yeah? Why not?" Derek tossed another pizza roll up in the air, barely catching it in his mouth.

"I can't picture you as a soldier."

"I could do it." Derek insisted. "So could you."

"What would you do?

"I don't know."

Joey snorted a laugh.

"Why are you laughing?" Derek asked as his sister snuck in from behind the couch to steal a pizza roll. "Lainee!"

"Save some for the rest of us, you jerk."

Derek rolled his eyes. "Don't you have swim practice or something?"

"School just started this week, and swimming season doesn't start 'til October, big brother. You know that."

"You gonna be captain of the team this year, right?" Joey asked.

"Hope so."

"Seriously though," Joey picked up another pizza roll and held up the plate for Lainee to grab another. "What would you do?"

"I don't know. I... I like science." Derek looked annoyed as she plopped down next to Joey. "I could be a doctor."

Joey nearly spit out his food. "A doctor?"

Lainee shot a smile toward her brother.

"I was studying biology, remember?" Derek exhaled, thinking back to the one year of classes he completed at Ohio State, last spring. "I could be... a medic or something."

"A medic, huh?" Joey debated. "Ok. That's actually kind of cool. I could be a soldier defending your medic ass. Or maybe work in construction."

"And they'd pay for the rest of college when we get back," Derek added.

"Whoa! Look at that." Derek sat up and pointed to the soldiers parachuting out of a plane. "That would be so cool."

"Yeah. It would." Joey leaned forward for a closer look.

"Why would you want to jump out of a perfectly good airplane?" Lainee took advantage of a momentarily stunned Derek and Joey to grab the last pizza roll.

Derek stared at the plate when his hand came up empty. "You just let her have the last pizza roll."

"I did." Joey's eyes remained on the TV.

"What the hell?"

Lainee laughed at her brother. "Now you know why Joey's my favorite."

Joey wrapped an arm around her shoulders and dropped a brotherly kiss on the top of her head. "It's true. I'm her favorite."

"No respect." Derek joked, still pondering the Army commercial that just played.

———

The sun shone brightly on a beautiful September morning. The sound of hammers and saws filled the air. Wearing jeans and a long-sleeved t-shirt rolled up to his elbows, Derek walked up to an old Victorian home currently undergoing major renovations and filled his lungs with the smell of sawdust. Out front, a member of his dad's crew held up a piece of lumber as Joey hammered nails into the end to secure it against a support beam for the front porch.

"Hey, Joey. Hey Dan." Derek approached the two men working on the front porch.

"Morning, D." Joey looked over at him. "You looking for your dad?"

"Yeah."

"Should be upstairs."

"Thanks."

Derek made his way to the top level, where they were framing the roof.

Abe finished talking to his foreman then pulled keys out of his pocket. "Son, I need you and Joey to take the truck and head over to the shop to pick up some supplies for the Mason Ave job site. Ben should have them all ready to load. I'll hitch a ride with Glenn in a bit once we finish up here."

Derek grabbed the keys from his dad. "Ok. See you there."

"Thanks, and be careful."

"Will do."

Trotting back downstairs, Derek waved goodbye to everyone he saw on his way up before stopping on the porch. "Hey, Joey - Dad needs us to head to the shop. Come on."

Joey looked up at the supports they just put in. "You ok here, Dan?"

"Yeah. All good, thanks."

They drove to the main workshop of Mitchell Contracting, where they were met by an older, scruffy, salt-and-pepper-haired man who had helped Derek's dad open Mitchell's Contracting nearly twenty years earlier.

"Hey, Uncle Ben!"

"Derek! Good to see you!" He turned the TV down in the background. "Hi, Joey."

"Hi, Ben."

"Did you see the Bengals on Sunday?" Derek asked.

"I did! Always a good day when we can beat the Patriots!"

Derek laughed. "Dad sent me over here for some supplies for the job on Mason."

"Yes, he did. Got 'em right over here."

Joey's phone rang. Grabbing it off his belt, he flipped it open. "Hey, Tank. What's up? You working later today?" He asked, knowing he was probably going to work his usual evening shift.

"No, I'm off. Have plans with Araceli later. Are you near a TV?"

"I'm at the shop with D. What's up?"

"Something's happening in New York. A bomb or something."

Joey caught a breaking news flash across the bottom of the TV screen behind the counter. The live feed showed smoke coming out of the World Trade Center.

Joey held his phone away from his ear and called out to Derek's uncle. "Hey, Ben. Mind if I turn up the TV?"

"I thought you two were supposed to be working."

"Yeah, but Tank says something is going on in New York."

"New York?" Ben shared the same confusion as Derek as they walked over to the TV and turned it up just in time to hear the announcers talking about a plane hitting the World Trade Center. A few seconds later, they watched in horror as another plane hit the second tower.

"My God," Ben exclaimed as they all stood there, watching in disbelief.

Bringing his phone back up to his ear, Joey said, "Tank, are you seeing this?"

"Yeah," the voice on the other end cracked.

The sun was just starting to set as Derek walked down toward the Square. He saw Joey, hands in his jacket pockets, waiting for him on the steps to the town hall.

"Hey, D." Joey stood up and walked over to his friend.

"Hi, Joey."

"Tank said he'd meet us at Corner Tavern." Joey said as they crossed the street together before passing Town Hall. Walking through the park inside the square in the center of town, they crossed the street to where they saw Tank.

Heading toward an open booth in the back of the tavern, they nodded to a few folks they knew before slumping down in the seats.

They ordered burgers and sodas. From time to time, they glanced up at the TVs, which showed closed-captioned news programs since no baseball games were being played out of respect for those lost on 9/11. For a Friday night, the tavern was full of customers but hosted a rather subdued crowd considering what had happened three days earlier.

Joey finished a bite of his burger and spoke first. "President said today that he heard us and that the people who knocked down the World Trade Center will hear us soon." He looked over at Derek and Tank, getting a nod from Derek. "Derek and I are going back to talk to the Army recruiter again tomorrow. I don't want to just sit here and watch TV when I can do something."

"I know we've all been thinking about enlisting for a while now." Derek looked over at Tank and Joey, who both nodded in agreement. "I say we go ahead and do it. We've already taken the ASVAB. And there's no question we're all in good shape even if we have been out of school for a year."

Tank spoke up. "Yeah. They have something called the Option 40 contract that lets us train to be Rangers. It's a more elite force, not just regular infantry."

"Joey and I were looking at that, too."

"Derek wants to be a combat medic," Joey laughed.

"Don't laugh." Tank gave Joey a stern look. "Who do you think got us both through science classes? He'd be good at that."

"Right." Joey conceded. "Good point."

Derek breathed out a humorless laugh as he looked at his friends. "Seriously though, I'd be able to get a job as an EMT when my enlistment is up."

"If you don't reenlist."

Joey looked at Derek, who tilted his head and agreed. "True that."

"You don't want to keep working for your dad?" Tank asked Derek.

"I can always help him out on weekends or on leave."

"Have you talked to him?"

"Yeah. Kind of. He knows I've been considering this for a while. That's why I'm taking a year off school."

"Joey?" Tank asked.

"Mom knows," Joey admitted. "Honestly, she's struggled for as long as I can remember, so my enlisting will probably make things easier for her."

"My parents know, too. Not sure Mom likes it, but Dad seems cool with it." Tank told them. "What time are you going tomorrow?"

"Before lunch." Joey responded.

"Ok. Let's all go together."

Chapter 32

Fort Benning, Georgia - January 2002
Joey - 20 years old

Dear L -

Started basic training today. I have no hair, but neither do Derek & Tank. Derek's probably traumatized the most by it. Nothing but yelling so far. Yes, Drill Sergeant. No, Drill Sergeant. It sucks, but otherwise, it's pretty easy. Glad we ran back in high school since so much is about physical training. Of course, pit stops at Fort Benning aren't nearly as fun as they were at Storley.

- Love J

"MOM!" Joey jogged over to his Mom after their Basic Training Graduation Ceremony to greet her with a big bear hug. Quinn reached down and shook his hand with a hearty congratulations and a pat on his back.

"Congratulations, Joey." Quinn beamed a big smile at his girlfriend's son.

"Thanks, Quinn."

"I'm so proud of you, baby," Joey's mom gushed as she looked him up and down. "Look at you! So handsome in your uniform."

With smiles all around, Abe and Lainee joined in greeting Derek, Joey, and Tank with hugs. Naturally, every parent had to take lots of pictures, including one of the three of them hamming it up for the cameras. Then the parents all rebelled and asked for a few serious pictures. Lainee even joined in getting a picture with all three before Tank and his family left for dinner. She couldn't resist getting pictures with each and then one of her with Joey and Derek. At 6' and 6'1, respectively, she was still only four and five inches shorter than the two. Joey's mom convinced Abe to get in there for a picture as well. Just as tall as Joey, he fit right in. Derek, Joey and their families all ended up at the same restaurant together.

Joey's mom stuck close to him as they stepped out of the car. The sound of laughter pulled their eyes in the direction of two young military couples exiting the restaurant, arm in arm. Quinn was a few steps behind them when Joey's mom spoke. "I'm so sorry Logan couldn't be here. That could be you."

Joey froze as he gently grabbed his mom and pulled her aside before they walked into the restaurant. "Mom," he whispered as he looked around at the other people in uniform walking through the parking lot. He looked up to see Quinn waiting. "Quinn, would you give us a minute, please?"

Quinn leaned in to kiss his mom on her cheek. "Of course. I'll wait for you inside."

"Thanks." Joey waited for Quinn to be out of earshot as he pulled his mom a little closer to the side of the building.

"Joey? What's wrong, baby?"

Joey pressed his lips together as he thought about how to explain himself. "Mom. Please don't mention Logan. I wish he were here, too, but he can't be."

"Why not? I don't understand."

He took a deep breath and held it before exhaling slowly. He kept his voice low. "If they find out I have a boyfriend or that I like men at all, they'll give me what they call an Other Than Honorable discharge if not an outright Dishonorable Discharge. If anyone outs me, I could get kicked out of the Army. I could also lose some or all of my GI benefits."

"That makes no sense."

"I know, but as much as I hate it, I have to hide it."

"But Derek knows."

"Yeah, but Tank doesn't."

She pulled him into a hug. "Joey, I'm so sorry."

"Yeah. Me, too." He hugged her back. "I'm so glad you're here, though." He pulled back and looked her right in the eye. "When you see him, tell him I miss him, ok?"

"I promise." She gave him another hug and then followed him inside to where Quinn and the Mitchells were already seated.

Joey placed his hand on Quinn's shoulder. "Thanks, Quinn."

"Love the new hairstyle, Joey." Lainee joked as Joey walked behind her chair and wrapped his arms around her shoulders in a brotherly hug. He gave her long, blonde pigtail a tug as he sat down and removed his own black beret.

"You should try it. Might cut an hour off your morning routine." He said as he sat down next to her. His mom sat on the end of the rectangular table between him and Quinn. "How are you even here, Lainee?"

"Dad pulled me out of school this week so I could be here."

"What?"

"Well, when my father tells me I have to do something, I do it."

Abe threw his hands in the air. "*Now* she listens to me!"

They were still laughing when the server dropped off their drinks and took orders. Abe raised his glass in a toast. "To Derek and Joey. Congratulations, men."

They all held up their glasses as Lainee joked, "You're both still jerks, of course."

"Of course," Derek mused. "What are big brothers for?"

Abe laughed, "So what's next now that basic is done?"

"Training."

"Then RIP."

"Huh?"

"Ranger Indoctrination Program," Joey and Derek answered at the same time.

"The way it's been described to us," Derek continued, "it'll be four weeks of pure hell in an attempt to get us used to what it's like to be a Ranger."

"And what happens after that?" Lainee looked back and forth between her brother and Joey.

"After that, Ranger school."

"And then," Joey interjected, "Tank and I would have some more training, which," he hesitated as he looked around the table, "would open us up to deployments."

The table went silent. Troops were already being deployed to fight in Afghanistan, and they were beginning to hear murmurs about Iraq.

"What about you, son?" Abe directed his question to Derek.

"Assuming I make it through everything, I'd go to SOCM in Fort Bragg."

Quinn spoke up first. "What's that?"

"Special Operations Combat Medic course." Derek responded, his face serious. "But I'd have a lot more training before I'd be open for deployment."

"Can't believe you're going to be a medic," Lainee laughed, breaking the tension at the table. "Please tell me they'll teach you to use something other than duct tape."

Joey and Derek both snorted out laughs.

"Clearly, we missed something." Renee's confused expression mirrored Quinn's.

They both turned to Abe, whose palm covered his shaking head. "No. You didn't."

"When Lainee was little," Joey gave her a sideways glance,

"well… she's still little," he flinched as she poked her elbow into his ribs. "She fell off the slide at the park. Derek and I got her home without drawing too much attention because she was crying the whole way. But, we were lucky because their mom and Abe were out running errands."

Derek tried to contain his laughter as Lainee tried, but failed, to look as if she were pouting.

"Anyway, her leg was bleeding, and we tried to cover it up. Derek ran upstairs for some Band-Aids but couldn't find them. So, he wiped off her leg with some paper towels and fastened it all with duct tape. He was convinced his parents wouldn't notice."

"We noticed." Abe assured everyone at the table.

"Yeah." Derek shrugged while he took a sip from his glass. "Stopped the bleeding, though."

"Yep," Joey laughed.

"Yeah, thanks! It hurt like the devil to pull off." Lainee added, unable to truly be mad for something her brother did nearly ten years earlier.

"Ahh. Those were the days." Abe laughed.

"Yeah, they were," Renee agreed out of parental solidarity.

Lainee folded her arms against her chest. "I'm not that little."

Chapter 33

Grant's Crossing - present day

Breaking through the laughter, Lainee said, "All that training jargon was confusing. What's with all the acronyms, anyway?"

Tank's face turned dry. "It's the government. They like to confuse everyone. Even RIP is now called RASP. Ranger Assessment and Selection Program," Tank explained. "It's a few weeks longer now, too."

"I always thought basic was going to be a lot harder. We had no idea how easy it would be, did we?" Derek laughed.

"Right. It really wasn't that bad, but that's probably because we were all in good shape to begin with."

"True. It was still an adjustment, though," Derek smirked up at his father. "Dad was definitely a lot more lenient."

Abe shook his head with a laugh. "I knew I should have made you iron your underwear as a kid."

Tank snorted. "And having to sleep with all those men in the barracks. Hey!" Excited, Tank sat up straighter and snapped his fingers a few times. "Who was that guy who snored so loud?"

"At Benning?"

"Yeah."

"Baker?"

"No."

"Bear-something."

Tank scrunched his face. "No..."

Derek pointed at Tank. "Behrens!"

"Yes! Behrens!"

"Ha! I swear it was quieter at Bagram."

Tank snorted. "Yeah. For sure."

"At least we can have all-we-can-eat Italian food."

"What?" Tank took a few seconds before he caught Derek's reference. "Oh yeah! Galliano?"

"Galliano?" Abe perked up and knitted his brow. "Isn't that in a Harvey Wallbanger?"

Lainee looked confused. "What's a Harvey Wallbanger?"

Tasha leaned over and whispered, "It's a cocktail."

"Oh."

Derek piped up. "Gallo!"

"Gallo." Tank nodded his head. "That's right. He was a good guy."

"Who was that?" Araceli asked her husband.

"He's a guy from New York. Queens, I think. Was in our class at basic but he was *not* a runner."

Derek shook his head and laughed. "Definitely not."

"He fell behind on a run one morning, and Joey, who was easily the fastest of all of us...." Tank looked across the table to see Derek nodding in agreement. "... stayed back and made sure he finished. Derek and I were up front and didn't realize they'd fallen back until the end. When we saw them, we ran back to help. All the other guys were already heading toward the barracks for a shower."

Derek laughed. "Joey got smoked by the drill sergeant for not opting to take care of himself and stick with the main group. Joey was so serious when he responded with," Derek cleared his throat to recite his next words in a deep and formal voice, "Rangers never leave a man behind, Drill Sergeant!"

They both laughed at the memory.

Derek sighed. "He wanted so badly to be a Ranger. We hadn't even finished basic, and he was already living the creed."

"Yeah, he was." Tank's smile turned sad as he thought back to their time in basic. "We found out at dinner that night that Gallo had washed out. A week or two later, Joey received a letter from him saying the three of us should stop by his family restaurant called..." he grinned and invited Derek to say it with him. "Gallo's," they said in unison with a laugh. "Dinner would be on the house. 'Best Italian food in Queens,' he always bragged."

"Yeah, if we're ever in New York."

Derek sat back in his seat. "I think Joey made it out there. I remember he spent a few days up in NYC a time or two. They still keep in touch," he pulled a face when he caught himself. "*Kept* in touch." Derek cleared his throat again. "You know...it was all a blur, but I think I remember seeing flowers from the Gallos at Joey's funeral. No idea how he even knew."

"I called him."

Everyone turned their attention to Abe.

"Joey gave me a list of people to call or visit. Just in case." Abe dropped his hand on Logan's shoulder.

Tank squeezed his wife's shoulders as he spoke. "Joey was always going out of his way to help the other guys, you know? He might have had it tough as a young kid, but he really didn't want anyone to be left behind - literally or figuratively."

Chapter 34

Iraq - Autumn 2004

Joey - 23 years old

Dear L,

We just arrived in Iraq. Nothing but shit, dust, and camels. Some guys call it the dust bowl from hell. I don't even know what to call it myself, though sandbox is thrown around a lot. I remember sandboxes being a lot more fun when we were kids.

We're in a country we invaded, and for what? Oil? Goodwill? So far, I've not seen either. They called us liberators, but I'm not holding my breath for a big ticker-tape parade or anything. Do people even still have those? Over here, we go out on missions and try not to get shot, while at the same time, we shoot back at total strangers. Kill or be killed.

Love, J

Double-checking their gear, Joey and Tank completed their final preparations for the night's mission. "Heard from Derek lately?" Tank asked as they approached the staging area.

"Yeah," Joey answered as he slung his pack over his shoulders. "He's halfway through SOCM, living it up in the air conditioning at Bragg."

Joey laughed. "He was whining about having to study all evening and all weekend long just to keep up. Claimed his year at OSU was much easier."

Tank grunted while securing his weapons. "It probably was."

Placing their helmets on their heads, they grabbed their night vision equipment and waited for the mission to go ahead to board the helicopters.

Joey stepped back to make space for the other Rangers heading out with them. "He's got another four months to go, but said about a third of the original class has already washed out."

"Damn." Tank stood at the ready. "If anyone is going to make it through, it'll be Derek."

They climbed inside as soon as their sergeant gave the signal, sitting next to a newly-arrived Ranger that had just reported for duty that week. Tank and Joey were both three months into their first deployment in Iraq, but they were probably as nervous when they first arrived as Specialist Thompson seemed to be today. By now, they both had a good idea of what to expect. Muscle memory gained in their training had gotten them through every mission so far, and it would again tonight.

About ten minutes into the mission, the helicopter's miniguns started firing, and Thompson's head popped up. "What's that?"

"They're just firing back," Joey said, his expression nonchalant.

"At what?"

"Whoever just fired at us."

"What are we supposed to do?"

"Nothing we can do while we're in the air." Joey exchanged a shrug with Tank. They both hated it, but while in the air, they had no choice but to trust the pilots, even when they couldn't see the enemy.

It was the only time they ever felt remotely helpless.

On the ground, any helpless feeling would vanish in a flash, and their training would take over.

Insurgents fired as soon as the Rangers breached the door of an isolated, concrete house a few hundred yards outside a small village. Two insurgents immediately dropped to the ground the moment the Rangers entered the room and fired their weapons.

In the back of the house, a Ranger took a bullet just above the knee before two more Rangers fired back, putting the insurgents on the ground. Tank and another Ranger took up position in the back to cover both the exit and the medic who had already dropped his weapon to take care of the injury. While using the wall to support his weight, the wounded Ranger kept his own weapon at the ready while he was being treated, occasionally firing shots as needed.

With two other men, Joey and Thompson entered through the front to clear the rooms on the ground floor, one by one, hearing more shots fired on the floors above where the Special Forces were apprehending their target. Joey and Rakes entered the first room while Thompson and Seavers entered the second. A wardrobe door flew open, and a man inside fired, putting a bullet into Seavers' shoulder. With no hesitation, Thompson pointed his rifle and fired two shots in the man's chest and one in the head, sending the shooter crumbling to the ground. Weapon still aimed, Thompson backed up until his back hit the wall. His eyes remained fixed on the man he just killed. The dead man's cold, lifeless eye stared right back at him.

From the next room, Joey appeared in the doorway, weapon up and ready to shoot. Rakes was right behind him. A quick glance at the unmoving man on the floor confirmed his suspicions that he was dead. "Shit, Thompson," Joey said. "Right through the eye. Nice shot."

Rakes kicked the weapon out of reach to be safe and approached the wardrobe. With the tip of his rifle, he inched the other half of the wardrobe door open just to make sure there were no more surprises inside.

Once they confirmed there were none, Joey turned back to Thompson, whose gaze was still locked on the blood oozing out of the dead man's body, creating a pool of thick red liquid around his head and shoulders on what had probably once been a nice carpet. Joey slowly pointed Thompon's weapon in a safer direction. "Better him than you."

The all-clear came over their coms as the Special Forces captured and removed the men they'd come to apprehend.

Through the open doorway, Joey caught Tank in the next room, working his way toward the front where two more Rangers detained some non-combatants, women, and children. The medic finished patching up Seavers' shoulder and helped him up.

Joey gave Thompson a friendly squeeze on the shoulder to snap him into the present. "Let's go, Thompson."

He and Tank had similar reactions the first time they'd aimed their weapons at another person, but they snapped out of it much quicker. Just like Thompson, their training did its job.

Thompson's gaze didn't break away from the body.

"Come on." Joey pushed at his back and urged him out of the room, getting a curious look from Tank as they exited.

With a nod toward the room, Joey explained to Tank. "Took out a man hiding in a closet."

"Good," was all Tank said in response, his eyes watching everything in an effort to secure their exit.

Joey and Tank were ready for dinner the next day when Joey tapped Tank on the arm and tilted his head in Thompson's direction. The newest Ranger sat on his bunk, staring out into the distance.

Knowing he'd already skipped both breakfast and lunch, Joey approached him. "Come on, Thompson. Let's get some food."

His eyes looked up as if just now realizing other people were in the room. "Not hungry," he said, more to himself than to Joey.

Joey grabbed his arm and dragged him up to his feet. "Come with us anyway."

They arrived at the Rangers' dining facility, or DFAC, with Thompson, whose body moved as if on auto-pilot. Joey handed him a tray and took one for himself.

The guy behind the counter asked if Thompson wanted the chicken or the roast beef. Thompson stared into space. He still didn't answer when asked again so Joey answered for him. "Give him the chicken."

This continued down the line, with Joey making sure the whole way that whatever food they put on his tray was put on Thompson's tray, too.

Joey and Tank sat down and took a few bites of their food. Thompson sat and stared at nothing. Joey leaned over and spoke softly so only Thompson could hear. "Come on, man. Ya gotta eat."

Joey grabbed the fork and knife and wrapped Thompson's fingers around them. Thompson fumbled as if his brain didn't quite register how to use them. Without a word, Joey leaned over and cut Thompson's food for him. He took the knife out of Thompson's hand and placed it next to his plate. Then, he stabbed a piece of chicken and placed the fork back in Thompson's right hand.

Resting a hand on his shoulder, Joey kept his voice low. "You're ok. Just put it in your mouth and chew, ok? One bite at a time."

Tank watched them in silence while eating his own meal.

Without acknowledging what Joey said, Thompson slowly lifted his fork to his mouth and chewed. Joey returned to his own meal but kept a watchful eye on the other man to make sure he kept putting food in his mouth.

The other Rangers recognized the glassy look in Thompson's eyes. A few nodded to Joey when they saw him helping every step of the way.

They'd all been there, to some degree at least, and from one side or the other, they could all relate.

Chapter 35

—————

Grant's Crossing - present day

"Joey kept having to encourage him to take another bite," Tank explained. "It's the man next to us who gets us through a mission, but on or off the battlefield, we had each other's backs."

"Yeah." Derek's eyes went distant, a million miles away from where he sat. "He never told me about Thompson."

"Don't know if he ever talked about it much, but yeah. The first time you have to squeeze the trigger is the hardest, but the instinct to stay alive takes over. That guy, Thompson, did what he had to do then froze like a deer in headlights." Tank took a pull of his beer. "I wonder what became of him."

After a long moment, he grinned. "Then you joined us. What was your first mission?"

"That would be covering for that guy, Markham, I think, who sprained his ankle trying to imitate LeBron James during a pick-up game that morning. He was out for a couple of weeks. What an ass." Derek's head snapped up, "Sorry, Araceli."

Tank's wife waved him off with a smile, but Lainee was incensed. "Sorry, Araceli?" She held up her hands in frustration. "What about me? What about Jo?"

"Yeah," Jo agreed. "What about me? Or Marisol?"

Derek looked at his sister. "You're my sister. You don't count. As for Jo?" He met Jo's gaze. "You can handle it."

Araceli joined in the fray. "And I can't? You'd be surprised at how strong women in a soldier's family can be."

"You're right about that," Lainee quipped as she, Jo, and Araceli all exchanged knowing looks.

"Same with having law enforcement officers in your family, too," Marisol added, referring to her brothers-in-law.

Conceding, Derek held up his hands in surrender. "Yeah. Ok. You're definitely right about that."

The ladies at the table offered reassuring nods as Tank snickered. "You left yourself wide open for that."

"Anyway, I'd barely checked in when they first sent me out. Was quick and easy though. No major injuries."

"Where were you over there?" Jo asked.

"Bagram mostly," Derek and Tank responded in unison.

Derek arched a brow. "We could tell you other places, but then we'd have to kill you."

Tank shook his head and laughed.

"But yeah. Mostly we were out of Bagram which was a good thing."

"Why was that a good thing?" Jo eyed Derek with suspicion.

"Yeah, Doc," a smug Tank prompted Derek. "Tell us. Why was that a good thing?"

Derek's grin turned mischievous. "Women. It was much better than the other *bases*." He used his fingers for air quotes, "if you could call 'em that. There were never any women."

"No women?"

"No, Lainee. Not in the Rangers. Although, as of this year, they can now at least go for it. They weren't even allowed to try before."

Tank leaned forward. "I wonder how many we'll see in there?"

"Don't know. Half the men wash out as it is. But, women in the Army are tough, so they'll get in. I'm sure of it."

Tank laughed.

"What?" Derek asked, amused by his friend's laughter.

"If I never have to carry another log again, it'll be too soon."

Derek dropped back against his chair. "No kidding. Still, Cardiac Hill was probably good training for you now that you're a firefighter."

"Oh, man. Don't remind me."

Lainee asked. "Remind you about what?"

Derek turned to his sister. "During RIP, we had to be able to carry each other up and down this steep hill."

"Affectionately known as Cardiac Hill."

"We used it though."

Tank nodded. "Yes, we did."

Chapter 36

Afghanistan - 2005
Joey - 24 years old

DEAR L,

We're in Afghanistan now - Bagram - so we see more than just Army personnel here. It's pretty desolate. I mean, there are villages nearby, and in the distance, there are mountains. We have to march in and around those mountains when we go on missions. Not march, so much as trek. In another time or place, I'd think of them as pretty, but here, it's different. I look at them but instead of beauty, I see danger lurking behind every tree. I can imagine Taliban fighters hiding underneath a rocky outcropping, ready to ambush us. I see valleys where we'd be lambs to the slaughter to anyone on higher ground. Were it not for the fact that someone really is trying to kill us around every corner, it would make for some great hiking. But from a distance, I can let my imagination wander to nicer, friendlier possibilities. It's so different from the flat cornfields in central Ohio.

Sometimes, we see children playing in the villages. They seem so out of place, so...off. They just laugh and play as if the world isn't actually falling apart around them.

- Love, J

The truck careened down the hill toward what was once a cafe until bullets went through the front grill and took out the engine. Still rolling forward, the truck exploded as soon as it hit a small grouping of vendor stalls right next to the building wall sending shards of glass and weathered plaster in all directions.

"MEDIC!"

They were taking heavy fire in a small courtyard off the cafe next to an old municipal building where a local Taliban leader was said to have taken refuge. Deltas were inside, extracting their target as the Rangers secured the perimeter.

In his first combat deployment after spending a week at a base in Germany, Derek had only arrived at Bagram that morning. He barely had time to check in and report for duty when he was pulled into this operation.

Hearing the call for a medic, Derek dropped his weapon and rushed toward a man with gunshot wounds in his leg and upper arm. Derek pulled him back behind an abandoned vehicle and out of the line of fire to assess and treat his injuries. Bullets flew overhead as others stepped up to cover them.

Derek patched him up well enough to hold him since the injuries weren't life-threatening. The injured Ranger hobbled up to take a defensive position, then switched arms to fire his weapon with his other hand until they could return to base.

Next, a few minor injuries needed to be treated, thanks to a collapsed wall. Derek continued to take care of those who were hurt even after the targets were extracted and on the return trip to Bagram.

Once back, Derek helped a limping Ranger inside to the doctor. Fortunately, he would be fine and could probably just recuperate on base. Derek grabbed his duffle bag left in the admin building and headed toward the barracks when a familiar voice caught his attention.

"HEY, D!"

Derek turned and grinned as Joey ran up and greeted him with a big hug, slapping each other on the back.

"When did you get here?"

"Just got in this morning and was sent out on a mission. Some guy sprained an ankle or something, and I got pulled in."

"Yeah. I heard." Joey tried to look serious. "Markham. He's shit at playing hoops. You never want him on your team."

———

Two days later, Joey and Derek walked along the inside perimeter of the base, catching up. Derek froze when he heard what he thought were children's voices. He sniffed the cool air and narrowed his eyes, scanning the area for the source. After a few moments, he shook it off and kept going until he heard them again. He came to an abrupt stop.

Joey stopped and turned back. "What's wrong?"

"Nothing. I thought I heard..." Derek turned his head toward the outside wall. "Nevermind. It's nothing."

He heard it again and stopped.

"What?" Joey reached out and grabbed his arm.

"I could have sworn I heard children's voices." He looked at Joey. "It was nothing."

"You're not hearing things. Children are always playing just outside the base."

"Children?"

"Yes, children." Joey confirmed. "You can't always see them, but you can usually hear them just outside the walls."

"Wow. That's..."

"People live here, D."

Derek nodded as they kept walking. "We're helping them, right?"

"Yeah. We're helping them."

On their return to the barracks, they found letters waiting on their bunks.

"Yes!" Joey snapped up his weekly letter from his mom, pulling out the latest Sunday comics from inside.

"Looks like the mail has already found you." Tank walked up to Derek with a big grin and greeted him with a hug filled with laughter and back slaps.

"Tank! Great to see you, man." Derek's entire face lit up. "I hear you've been holding down the fort out here. Thanks for fixing the place up for me."

"Yeah," Tank joked as Joey walked over to them. "You've been holding down the cushy assignments back at Bragg while the rest of us have been out here doing the real work."

"Yeah, well. You knew I'd eventually have to come out here and check up on you." He laughed and exchanged another hug as they all landed on their respective bunks. "Joey said you were gonna be outside the wire for a couple days."

Tank grunted then opened a package from home. "Hey! It's another care package from Mrs. Strager's class."

"Awesome!" Joey sat down next to Tank, peeking his head over for a better view. "What's inside?"

Tank laughed as he opened a big envelope. "They wrote us letters in Spanish." He handed some to Joey to translate for Derek."

"And some toothbrushes, toothpaste, razors, and shaving cream. Clearly, they think we need help with our hygiene." He dug inside and pulled something out that raised eyebrows. "And summer sausage. I love this stuff." He reached in his pocket for a knife to open it. He handed chunks to both Derek and Joey. Still chewing, he pulled out packs of gum and boxes of candy. "This is great!" He tossed some gum to a couple of other guys walking by. "And some spy novels."

Derek perked up. "Which ones?"

"Um... something by Vince Flynn and some other guy." He handed them across to Derek.

"May I borrow these? Haven't read them yet."

"Don't worry. They'll get passed around."

Joey gave a friendly smack to Derek's arm, "So, who are they from?"

"What?" Derek asked.

"Your letters."

"Oh." Derek stood back up and grabbed the letters he'd inadvertently sat on. He took a look and sat back down. "One is from Dad, and this one," He broke out into a grin, "is from Kaitlyn."

"You just saw her, right?"

"Yeah, I did." He examined the envelopes before opening his dad's letter first. "Dad had to leave for Louisiana before I went back to Benning, but it looks like she sent hers while I was still home. They both took a little while to get out here."

"That's normal with deployments," Joey explained as he read the letter from his mom. "Mail sometimes takes a while to catch up to you."

Derek sniffed the letters and debated which one to read first. He tossed Kaitlyn's letter on the bed beside him and started reading his Dad's. "Dad's in New Orleans with one of his work crews rebuilding some houses."

"Your family all ok?" Joey asked as Tank looked up.

"Mom's family is fine, but their house took a fair amount of damage from Katrina. It's almost livable again. They were living in an RV for awhile; they drove up to a cousin's farm outside of Baton Rouge before it hit." Derek explained. "Dad and his crew are finishing the work on Uncle Mick's house, including a new wheelchair ramp for him. They're also working on some other houses in Uncle Mick's neighborhood." He laughed. "Sounds like some of the guys aren't used to all the spicy food my grandmother has been making for them."

Tank joined his laughter. "How people live without hot sauce is mind-boggling."

"You got that right." Derek moved on to Kaitlyn's letter. Within a few lines, his smile disappeared. He crushed the letter until it was a tight ball of paper in his palm.

"Fucking..." He pursed his lips together on the verge of unleashing a whole string of expletives when an officer walked through. He held his tongue while getting concerned looks from Joey and Tank.

"What's wrong, D?"

Derek three the wadded-up letter on the ground. "Nothing." He leaned over, resting his forearms on his knees, and stared down at the floor.

Joey leaned down and picked it up off the floor. He worked it open and scanned over the few lines written over the pink paper. "Shit. She broke up with you? After what, six years? That sucks, man. I'm sorry."

Tank leaned toward Joey and tapped him on the knee. He nodded toward the letter. Joey handed it to him. "Wait. The date on this.... Weren't you still home when she wrote this?"

"Yeah." Derek said sharply as he snatched the letter out of Tank's hands. His friend lifted his hands in a show of surrender. "We were still together. At least, I thought we were. Guess she wanted a few more fucks out of the deal before I left."

"I wonder how long she was with the other guy...." Joey said before Derek cut him off with a fierce look.

"Sorry."

"Shit. That's cold." Tank empathized. They sat in silence for a minute until he looked over at Joey. "What time is it?"

Joey checked his watch. "Almost 1730. Why?"

"Dinner time." Tank arched his eyebrows toward Joey as he sat down on Derek's bunk and placed a tight hold around his shoulders. Derek struggled to free himself from the hold, but Tank wasn't having it. His grip was too strong. "He's been on base a few days now, so I think it's time we start taking our man Derek here on a tour of the other DFACs."

While Derek sat there with an annoyed expression on his face, Joey started smiling. He was already trying to determine which dining facilities had the most women to help get Derek's mind off his breakup. The Ranger camp only had men going in and out, but the other camps, with regular Army, Air Force, and Marines...all... had...women.

And the possibilities were endless.

Chapter 37

Grant's Crossing - present day

"Yeah. Bagram had its upside," Derek insisted. "I won't lie about that."

"Doc, you're such a man-who..." Tank quickly cleared his throat after Araceli gave him a friendly smack on the back of his head. "Uh... player."

Abe cleared his throat to suppress a laugh.

Tank caught Drew, Quinn, and Kiro doing the same. Logan just shook his head.

Abe knew his son well enough to know exactly what Tank was about to call him. He had his thoughts on that, but that was a conversation for another day.

"Still," Tank added as he pulled Araceli a little closer. "Going on leave was something we all lived for. I got to come home and see my girl."

"Seriously, Araceli," Derek extended his hand in Tank's direction. "What do you even see in this guy?"

"Well, he's smart. He's funny. He loves his family. He's really hot. He can..."

Tank waved her off while clearing his throat. "They don't need to know that, Celi."

Araceli giggled while her cheeks turned pink, but she continued on. "Well, because he's a good man. Like you are, Derek Mitchell." She smiled across the table at Derek.

"I have my moments, but not when I came home after my first deployment. Seeing Kaitlyn for the first time after she dumped me wasn't easy. She was married and pregnant. Not easy."

"I'll bet," Tank agreed.

Derek turned his smile over to Jo. "Jo always made it good for us though."

"Agreed," Tank raised his glass. "To Jo. Your welcome home parties were the best."

"To Jo," Derek said as he clinked his glass with Tank's.

Jo tilted her head with a smile. "You boys are worth the effort. Back when he was still active, every time Mike came home on leave, we just wanted to get together so he could see as many people as possible when he first arrived. Then he could relax the rest of the time he was home."

"I remember Joey's twenty-ninth birthday a few years back." Logan paused before continuing on. "We all celebrated early since you'd be back over there for his actual birthday. You had all just come home and... well, I know his mom was plotting all sorts of ways to bring about my demise."

"You broke his heart," Derek responded.

"Yes, I did."

"But he forgave you."

"Yes, he did."

"He loved you too much not to."

"I'm a lucky man."

"Yes, you are." Derek lifted his eyes and met Logan's. "But then again, so was he."

Logan's appreciative smile spoke volumes.

Chapter 38

Grant's Crossing - July 2010

Joey - 28 years old

Dear L,

We're coming home soon. It's only for three weeks, but I can't wait to see you. Will you be at the big party at Jo's? Tell me you'll be there. I need to hold you.

Love, J

"WELCOME HOME!"

Dozens of voices yelled out as soon as Joey, Derek, and Tank, all beaming excited smiles, appeared through the front entrance of Jo's Bar & Grille, formerly known as the Corner Tavern, on the square in downtown Grant's Crossing. A large sign with the words: "WELCOME HOME" echoed the crowd's greeting and hung on the back wall above the old jukebox.

Directly below was an added sign: "HAPPY BIRTHDAY, JOEY!"

The three men were treated like celebrities. Everyone greeted them with hugs, handshakes, and occasional kisses on the cheek by some of the single ladies at the bar. Tank fended them off in favor of kissing Araceli, who arrived early after dropping their kids off with their grandparents. She was waiting for him at the bar with open arms and a big, sexy grin. Joey played along and happily hugged and accepted kisses from anyone who offered, but it was Derek who took full advantage of all the attention lavished on him by the ladies. He happily timed swift turns of his head to receive those kisses on the lips. He occasionally dipped a pretty woman backward, reminiscent of the WWII sailor who kissed a woman in Times Square, for a full-blown kiss that drew wolf whistles and cheers.

Not a single one of them paid for drinks the entire night. Jo's husband, Mike, a veteran of Desert Storm, started them off with a round on the house. This was followed by a round from Abe. Kiro Marinov, or K, as both Joey and Derek now called him, bought the next set of drinks. He was fresh out of college and well on his way to becoming a paramedic firefighter with the nearby city of Delaware.

After that, they had no idea who bought them which drinks, or when. They just held out their hands, and drinks appeared.

Joey lived it up the entire night, finally giving Tank a handshake with a man hug along with a kiss on the cheek to Araceli when they called it a night shortly after eleven. Abe was already gone by that time. Derek left with a blonde he knew from high school but never actually dated, not that he was the dating type anymore.

Joey sat at the bar drinking and talking to Mike Porter for another hour before Drew, still just a deputy at the time, stopped in during his shift to check on his sister and brother-in-law behind the bar. After Jo and Mike assured him all was well, Drew offered to take Joey home. Joey accepted as there was no way he could have walked in a straight line, much less gotten home on his own.

Two days after their welcome home party at Jo's and mere hours after Joey safely felt he'd survived his hangover, he knocked on the front door of Logan's new house a short distance from Grant's Crossing. He checked out the wraparound porch imagining the two of them sitting outside, talking about their days or even just reading a book, just happy to be together.

He returned from his thoughts when he heard the door open. A petite young woman in a pair of jeans and an Ohio State sweatshirt with dark brown hair pulled back in a high ponytail answered the door with a smile. "Hi. May I help you?"

Not expecting anyone but Logan to answer the door, Joey glanced back up at the numbers beside the door to confirm he was at the correct address. "Yes. I, uh, was looking for Logan Shepherd."

"And you are?"

"Joey Parker," he said before adding, "We went to high school together."

"Sure, Joey." Her smile widened. "Come on inside. I'll go get him."

"Thank you."

Joey stepped inside and took in the interior of the house with its hardwood floors and wood trim around the doors and entryways. Figuring the home was well over 100 years old, he touched the wood trim, marveling at how well the original details had been preserved. His head popped up as footsteps drew near. Logan rounded the corner with a guarded smile on his face as Joey's mouth opened into a grin.

"Joey."

"Logan." Joey took a step toward Logan, but before he could reach for a hug and a kiss and before he could even say anything more, a small child, still in diapers, waddled up to Logan's leg. "DADDY!"

Joey stopped dead in his tracks. His heart sank, feeling like a heavy weight deep in the pit of his stomach. "Daddy?" Joey coughed out.

Logan leaned down and effortlessly picked up the little girl and rested her on his hip as if he'd done the same thing a million times before.

Stunned, Joey's eyes drifted down to Logan's hand, making note of the gold band on his ring finger. He glanced at the toddler he held and then looked back at Logan. Moments later, his eyes were pulled over to the woman who reappeared in the entryway.

"Joey... I can explain."

Joey coughed out a breath like he had just received a punch to his stomach. "You... can... explain," Joey repeated, his voice low and steady. Anger was brewing just below the surface, causing it to shake a little bit. Joey couldn't breathe. "Explain what...exactly?"

"Maddie, can you take Allie, please?" Logan asked his voice calm, presumably for the sake of the child. Her arm rested on his back, but her smile seemed forced.

Joey was fuming, sure. He was heartbroken, too, but part of her smile almost conveyed something he couldn't quite define. Understanding, perhaps? He couldn't quite explain it since his emotions were all jumbled with anger, jealousy, and heartbreak. With all three emotions in the ring vying for top honors at the moment, he dismissed the thought.

"Sure." She held her hands out for the little girl and smiled. "Come on, Allie. Let's finish our snack."

She spoke to Logan but included Joey with a quick glance in his direction, "We'll be in the kitchen if you two need anything."

Logan paused long enough for her to disappear down the hallway, then turned his gaze back to Joey. "It's not what you think."

Joey forced out an exhale mixed with something that sounded like a laugh. "Not what I think? Do you have any idea how patronizing you sound right now? Because I'm thinking I just heard a little girl call you daddy."

"In here." Logan's voice was terse as he tilted his head toward a room off the foyer.

Reluctantly, Joey followed him. "And I'm also thinking that's a wedding ring on your finger, you asshole."

Logan's eyes widened as he shushed Joey through his teeth. He held up his hand. "Keep it down," he whisper-yelled as he led Joey to an office and shut the door behind them.

"And I'm guessing that *woman....*" He stressed the word, "Is your *wife!*"

"I said I could explain."

"Explain that you're married, Logan? Joey's heart raced a million beats per minute and had already sunk to the pit of his stomach.

"Yeah."

"How long?"

"For about six months now."

His eyes widened. "SIX MONTHS? And you never thought it important enough to tell me?"

"It was the only way. I wanted to... Allie needed..." he started.

"Only way?"

"You haven't been home in over a year, Joey."

"What? And that makes this my fault? What the fuck, Logan?"

"Calm down," Logan whispered as he held out his hands.

"Calm down?" Joey held up his hands and took a few steps backward to create distance between them. Then, he immediately stepped forward again to get right in Logan's face. The smell of Logan's aftershave nearly brought tears to his eyes. "You've got to be fucking kidding me. You. Got. Married." He shoved Logan back. "And... you married a WOMAN. What. The. Fuck!"

"It's not like that. We don't...."

"How is it not like that? YOU HAVE A KID!" Joey dropped his arms and backed up a few steps again. He felt like he just had the wind knocked out of his sails. "How could you do this to me?" His voice dropped to a whisper. "To us?"

"I'm not her biological father. Yeah, I'm her..."

Logan began to explain, but Joey held up his hand.

"No. I...I can't, Logan." He pressed his lips together and stared at the floor, unable to even look up to meet Logan's gaze. When he did, he held up his hand again, shaking this time, and shook his head on a loud exhale. "I thought we were…" Joey struggled for his words as his chin trembled. His breath shuddered as he inhaled, his eyes watering, "Logan. I…I love you," Joey took one last look at him, "but I wasn't enough, was I?"

"Joey…I love–"

"No. Just…don't." Joey turned his back on Logan and walked out the door and out of the house.

"…you, too," Logan muttered to Joey's back.

Joey made it to his car before the tears began to fall.

Dear L,

I'm breaking here. I can't hold myself together without you. The thought of your hands touching me. Your lips pressed against my skin…pressed against my lips. Your hands between my legs and your tongue… the things you do to me make me lose myself in you. And knowing I'll never touch you again and that we can never share our bodies again tears me apart. It makes me lose myself. Not in you, not in bliss, but lose myself… as if I'm wandering through an endless maze with no end in sight where the walls keep moving, trapping me in forever. The thought of a life without you makes me question everything we had together.

You said you'd always be here for me. You said you'd wait for me. You said you'd be here when I got back.

We promised each other, L.

You just didn't keep yours. And now you're breaking us. You're breaking me. And my god, it hurts. It hurts so much, L, and I can't take it.

Love, J

"I came as soon as I heard." Derek greeted Renee with a hug. "How is he?"

"He's heartbroken, Derek." She explained as she welcomed him inside. "I didn't even know they were married. Joey said he even has a little girl, too."

"Son of a bitch," Derek muttered under his breath, earning him an understanding look from Joey's mom. "Sorry."

"Don't be." Anger was etched on every feature of her face. "I said far worse when I heard the news." She tilted her head toward the loft. "Go on up. He needs you."

Derek gave her shoulder a quick squeeze before jogging upstairs to Joey's old room. The lights were out, and the blinds were drawn, so it took a minute for his eyes to adjust. He found Joey sitting on the floor on the other side of the bed.

His friend had clipped a small reading light to the bottom drawer of his nightstand and was looking at pictures of him and Logan from as far back as high school as well as from every leave during the last few years.

Derek dropped to the floor and sat back against the wall a few feet across from him, noticing the pen on top of the notebook Joey always had with him. He thought he kept it as a journal since he was always writing in it inside the barracks. It was currently serving as a coaster for a half-empty bottle of beer.

"I can't throw any of these away," Joey said as he wiped his nose with the back of his hand as his eyes maintained their focus on the pictures. "I can't do it. I just... I thought we had something real, D." He lifted his head, and even in the near darkness, Derek could tell his eyes were bloodshot. "I was wrong."

"I'm sorry, Joey. I don't... even know what to say. It sucks. I thought Kaitlyn and I had something, too. Now she's married with two kids." The sound of the front door opening turned Derek's head for a moment as Renee greeted Quinn downstairs. Their voices grew softer as they made their way to the kitchen in the back of the house.

He returned his attention to Joey but hesitated, "Maybe they can't handle the military life. Deployments are hard enough on our own families."

"Yeah, but," he sniffed again and splayed his hands out, letting the pictures fall back down to the floor as the backs of his hands landed on his legs. "I love him, D."

Derek whispered his response. "I know you do."

After dropping her daughter off at daycare, Maddie Shepherd swore at herself for leaving her gym bag at the house. Pulling her car into the driveway, she clicked the remote on her car's visor to open the garage door.

Logan's car was inside. "What's he doing home?"

The engine was still running."Oh shit!"

She shoved the car into the park and jumped out of her car to find him passed out inside the front seat. "No, no, no, no, no. Logan. No."

She pulled the handle, but the door was locked. Panicking, she scanned the garage and ran to the shelf with his power tools to grab a large drill. As hard as she could, she pounded it against the passenger side window until the glass shattered. She reached inside, but didn't even notice the sharp point of the glass scraping her arm. Blood dripped down her arm as she opened the door from the inside handle. With shaking fingers, she ripped the key out of the ignition to stop the engine. She pulled her phone out of her pocket and dialed 9-1-1 as she ran around to the driver's side and yanked the door open. She had to get some clean air into his lungs. Maddie knew she was too small to pull his limp body out of the car, but she tried her damndest anyway.

She practically screamed at the 9-1-1 operator who dispatched an ambulance. A sheriff's deputy was only a block away at the time of her call. Out of the corner of her eye, she saw lights flashing. Deputy Drew Strager ran toward her.

"Help me!" Maddie coughed out as she struggled to pull Logan from the vehicle. Drew took over and pulled Logan out of the car and into the yard as the paramedics arrived.

Renee poured two glasses of iced tea and placed one in front of Quinn before taking her own seat at the table.

Quinn's phone pinged with a text message. Several more texts arrived as he read the first.

"Everything okay?" Renee asked, her brow furrowed in concern.

"Logan Shepherd. Didn't Joey go to school with him?"

"Yes. Why?"

"Just heard from Drew. Logan's just been taken to the hospital. Looks like carbon monoxide poisoning from an apparent suicide attempt."

"WHAT?" Renee shot out of her chair and bolted upstairs.

Chapter 39

Grant's Crossing - present day

"YOU SAVED MY LIFE THAT DAY, DREW." LOGAN TOOK A FEW seconds to make eye contact. "Thank you."

"It's a life worth saving," Drew responded, earning a proud look from his sister, Jo.

"I don't know that I ever thanked you before now."

"Renee knew Joey needed to know," Quinn added. "He and Derek ran out of the house so fast."

"He had to get to you," Derek explained. "He had to see for himself if you were okay."

"Joey showed up at the hospital knowing my family would be there but not caring if they saw him or not," Logan muttered, thinking back to his lowest days when he couldn't go on because he'd shattered the hopes of the man he truly loved. "If nothing else, he figured they'd think he was just a friend from school showing his support. Maddie told me later that she explained to him why we got married."

"It was all for Allie." Logan knitted his brow. "Maddie had a rough pregnancy and struggled to keep a job as a result. Her boyfriend ran off to Seattle, not wanting anything to do with his own kid. Being the asshole that he is, he even signed away his parental rights."

"Allie was diagnosed with a congenital heart defect shortly after she was born. She was ok with medication for a while, but after her first birthday, the medication wasn't enough. She was going to need surgery. Maddie didn't have the ability to pay for what was needed, and her family wasn't able to help either. They wanted to; it's just that it's so expensive. I had just started a great job with the state of Ohio, which gave me terrific benefits. We did what we thought was best and got married. Doing so allowed Allie to get the care she needed. Maddie and I talked it over, and eventually, I adopted her." Logan shook his head. "When the time comes, I don't know how we're going to explain all of this to Allie."

"You'll figure it out," Abe assured him. "You always do as parents."

Logan cleared his throat. "Mom and Dad originally insisted we have a ceremony, but we stuck with a courthouse ceremony with a Justice of the peace. I think Mom just wanted the big day, but she understood. Financially and logistically, though, it made sense. Definitely made things easier for Maddie. We'd been good friends since college, and when she was having such a tough time, well... working together made it better for everyone. Besides, Allie needed the amazing doctors at Children's Hospital. She's doing so much better, too. Just down to her regular checkups now."

"So she's doing okay then?" Abe held his sleepy granddaughter on his lap.

Logan's face lit up. "Oh, she's great. Better than great. She's in first grade and already reading way above her grade level." Logan couldn't resist bragging. "Never thought I'd actually be a dad." Knowing smiles from Abe, Tank and Drew met him as he scanned the room.

"Best thing in the world," Tank's eyes shone with fatherly pride.

"Absolutely," Drew chimed in.

Logan nodded. "Still, breaking Joey's heart was the worst."

"But you got through it." Derek encouraged him. "You worked it out."

"Maddie spent a few days with her parents to give Joey and me time to talk and, well, just be with each other. She's remarried now, which means Allie has a mom, two dads, and a little brother on the way."

"Do you get to see her much?" Derek asked.

"Oh, yeah. All the time." Logan patted his chest. "Look. I'm her dad. That's never going to change. Plus, we have shared custody. The best part is that we all get along great." Logan laughed. "Oh, man. Allie was hilarious in the school play last month. She kept running to the side of the stage to wave to us. She doesn't have a shy bone in her body."

"I remember that." Tank shared a knowing look with Araceli.

"She's like Rocio!" Araceli said. "I love energetic young girls."

"Rocio takes after her mom," Tank said.

"Lainee was like that," Abe shared a smile with his daughter. "Catie is going to be just like her. Girls definitely keep you on your toes, that's for sure."

Everyone sat back, content in the moment and also with having finished a delicious and filling meal.

Kiro scanned the table and stood up. He tapped Lainee on the shoulder. "Help me out. You said you were going to do the dishes."

Lainee joined him at the sink as others helped clear off the table to make quick work of the cleaning while Abe led the Stragers to the living room to sit and chat, leaving the younger generation in the kitchen.

"Joey and I both re-upped the last time just before we came back for his birthday." Derek turned to Tank. "You were just finishing up, ready to get home to your kids."

"Right. Rocio was just about potty trained and Daniel was

already walking." Tank paused a few moments and gazed into his wife's eyes. "I missed their first steps."

Araceli rubbed his arm to comfort him. Tank covered her hand with his then continued. "Dios mio. The stuff we saw over there," Tank shook his head. "I don't know how you did it, Doc. I don't know how you could stay so calm in the middle of a firefight without aiming your weapon. I mean, bullets would fly over our heads, or ... more likely right at us, and you would just drop your weapon like it was nothing."

Derek shrugged. "I was trained for that. Just like you were trained to cover me. I wasn't worried."

"Joey and I used to talk about how amazing you medics were."

"We had a lot of training." Derek waved him off, clearly uncomfortable with the compliment. "We all had our jobs to do. You know that."

"That's true."

"Wait," Lainee held up her hand and stared at her brother, tears welling in her eyes. "They were shooting at you, and you dropped your weapon? I'm glad I didn't know that while you were still over there."

As Tasha rubbed circles on her back, Lainee visibly relaxed.

"Yeah." Derek shrugged. "If someone got hurt, that's the first thing I did. The other men covered me while I took care of injuries."

"But...how were you never shot?"

"Because of the men next to me," Derek answered as if it were obvious. "The men serving with me were so well-trained. I didn't even have to look to see if I was being covered. I just knew I was. They're that good, Lainee. The best there are."

Every eye in the room turned toward Tank, who didn't flinch at the compliment. He just took it as fact because Derek was right. Their training made everything automatic.

"He's right. Situational awareness was key. Communication was key. But Derek's ability to stay calm under fire helped save lives."

Tank admitted, his eyes taking a few seconds to meet Derek's. "When I was injured...."

Araceli squeezed her husband's hand. Her reassuring touch initially startled him, but eventually calmed him and drew a smile in return.

"I won't lie. I was scared." Tank released a long, slow exhale. "I mean, scared shitless. And Derek," Tank pointed to his friend. "never once panicked. I mean, if you did, you didn't let on." He rubbed his thumb over the back of Araceli's hand. "Whatever you said to me made me think I'd actually make it home."

Derek reached across the table and held out his hand, which Tank took. "Anything for you, brother."

"I honestly don't remember much except that it was so frigging cold that day." Tank released Derek's hand and leaned back in his seat, wrapping his arm around Araceli's shoulders to pull her closer to him.

"Yeah, it was," Derek agreed. "That cold helped you."

Chapter 40

Afghanistan - January 2011

Joey - 29 years old

"WE NEED A MEDIC!" RASS' VOICE YELLED OUT AS HE AND Joey carried a severely wounded soldier covered in blood into the makeshift casualty collection point during a nighttime operation. The man was writhing in pain; his whole body was shaking.

"D, IT'S TANK!"

Derek barely heard Joey's voice over the wounded man's screams, but he grabbed his pack and ran in their direction. He already recognized Tank's cries. There were a couple of rugs on the ground not far from where they walked in.

"Down there," Derek directed them toward the rugs just inside the door. They gently set Tank on the ground. Tank's arms shot to his groin, and he curled up into a ball, moaning in pain. Blood spilled out from everywhere.

Derek conducted a visual examination to determine which wound was the most serious. "Stay with me, Tank." Derek's calm voice carried over his cries of pain. "Help me hold him down. Joey, get his shoulders. Careful with his left arm." Derek instructed, seeing it was bleeding from what were probably gunshots or shrapnel wounds. "Rass, get his legs."

Tank was all muscle, but he was in pain. His instinct to protect the damaged parts of his body, combined with his strength, kept him wriggling on the ground.

"I said hold him!" Derek barked out.

Tank stared at Derek, nothing but fear in his eyes. "Doc, don't let me die." His voice shook. "I don't wanna die."

Moaning in pain, Tank's hands were still covering the wound by his groin, blood seeping through his fingers. Derek put his hands over Tank's hands and gazed directly into his terrified eyes, "I'm not gonna let you die." Derek slowly worked his own fingers under Tank's to loosen them up. "I've gotta take a look, so let me help you. Trust me to help you, okay?"

Tank's hands didn't move. "I don't wanna...." Blood dripped out his nose past his mouth as he cried out.

"I know you don't, Juan." Derek cut him off by using his given name and keeping his voice low and calm. "I'm gonna take care of you." Derek felt Tank's fingers loosen, allowing him to get a look at the gaping wound right next to his groin near the top of his leg. Another wound right next to it was deep and had nicked his femoral artery.

"There it is," Derek thought.

"So c...cold." Tank struggled to get the words out.

"I know it is. You'll be warm soon enough," Derek assured him. It was the cold that was saving him; slowing his body down, so it didn't bleed out as quickly.

Blood spilled out as Derek pressed a QuikClot bandage against the wound to help stem the bleeding. He just needed a little time to set up an IV to keep what blood he still had moving.

"Talk to him, Joey." Derek's voice remained unflappable while he worked to remove what shrapnel he could get away with to make sure he could pack off everything that was bleeding. He didn't want Tank to bleed out from something he couldn't find.

Joey spoke softly to Tank to help keep him calm. "Look at me,

Juan. Derek's got this. I know it sucks right now, but you're gonna be okay, alright?"

Derek grabbed the scissors and cut the top of Tank's pants open so he could clearly see the entire wounded area. *"Fuck,"* he thought. His heart raced upon realizing the severity of the wound, but Tank was finally beginning to calm down. Not wanting to cause additional panic, He continued packing the injured areas and smirked. "Not that I ever wanted to see your junk, Tank, but I'm happy to inform you that it's all still there."

Tank's shaking was just beginning to lessen as he breathed out a panicked laugh that quickly turned to coughs. His eyes followed Derek's hand as it reached behind him for something and applied pressure right where his leg met his torso.

"Araceli would never let me hear the end of it if it weren't, so," Derek joked as he worked, but his face was dead serious. "Speak well of me the next time you're together, okay?"

He leaned over so only Rass could hear him. "Get Sgt. Gales and have him call in a medivac. Do it now, or he won't make it." Tank's shaking had slowed enough for the soldier to let go of his legs.

Rass shot up and sprinted away. Derek appeared calm except for his clenched jaw which showed that Tank's injuries were a lot more serious than he was letting on. "Keep talking to him, Joey." Derek glanced up in time to see Tank's eyes beginning to close. "Keep him awake."

Joey leaned down. "You're gonna be alright, Tank; you know that, right?" Tank didn't answer.

Joey kept talking and received an occasional grunt from time to time, each one weaker than the last.

Rass returned. "Medivac on the way. ETA four minutes. Southeast courtyard."

"Roger that." Derek kept packing up Tank's leg and groin

injuries, securing the leg with a tourniquet. He looked up and noticed Tank's eyes starting to close again. "Stay with us, Tank."

Tank's eyes fluttered back open.

"We're getting you and your balls out of here, okay?" Derek looked across the room when he heard the chopper in the distance.

He tilted his head across the room. "Joey, grab that stretcher off Mik's pack over there." Derek wrapped Tank's shoulder, then enlisted Joey and Rass' help to move him onto the stretcher.

"Ok, let's go. Hurry."

They picked him up and rushed him to the opposite corner where the chopper landed. The in-flight medic jumped out long enough to listen to Derek relay all the pertinent details as they placed Tank inside.

Derek ducked down and backed away as it took off again.

"He's gonna be okay, right, Doc?" Rass asked Derek.

"He is now," Derek confirmed as they rushed back inside.

Joey followed him. "How is he, D? Really."

"It'll take them six minutes to get back to the closest base with doctors, and he'll be in surgery a few minutes after. Assuming no other delays, his chances are good."

"His chances?"

"I don't have the tools or the knowledge to perform surgery, Sergeant." Derek turned to his friend with a glare, addressing him by rank to drive home just how serious he was. "We won't get back for another few hours at the earliest. Without a medivac, he wouldn't make it. He needs a lot more help than I can give." Derek dropped down next to a soldier who called out for Doc and rechecked his bandages as Joey returned back outside.

Hours later, upon their return to base, Derek went to check in on Tank. He found him in recovery, awaiting the next chopper out to

Bagram, then probably to Germany for follow-up treatment. Tank slipped in and out of consciousness, still groggy from the anesthesia.

The doctors told him that Tank almost bled out internally on the trip back. Derek had stopped a lot of it, but the IVs would have only delayed the inevitable had he not been medivacked when he was.

Tank's eyes slowly blinked open. "Hey, Doc." His voice was breathy, barely audible. He struggled to lift his hand, but Derek offered an encouraging smile and clasped it with his own.

"Good to see you, Juan."

"Am I alive?" He spoke in a whisper, but sounded as well as expected under the circumstances.

"Yes. You're alive."

"Thought so. Everything hurts."

"Doctors say you're going to be okay. You'll need more surgery, but you'll be okay." Derek grinned. "You're flying out of this shit show first thing in the morning. Sounds like you'll even end up stateside."

"Don't mean to leave you guys."

"That's alright. Party isn't big enough for all three of us."

"I still can't believe you and Joey are sticking with it for another four years."

"Gluttons for punishment." Derek shrugged. "I like it, though. I like helping. Besides, now that I saved your ass, you'll have to buy me drinks for the rest of your life."

His laugh was more of a grimace. "You got it." Tank winced in pain.

"Hey, hey. Sorry. Be careful. No more joking until you've had a chance to heal."

Tank nodded, his brow furrowing. "I thought I was gonna die out there."

"I would never let that happen to you. You know that. But," Derek's grin turned mischievous, "you'll have to let Araceli know that when she's ready for a real man, she can call me."

Tank may have been injured, but his dirty look at Derek left no room for misinterpretation. "That's my wife you're talking about, Doc."

"I know, I know." This time Derek's smile turned genuine. "She'd have been a fool not to marry you. You're a lucky man, Tank. Just be sure to send us updates."

"Promise."

"Good." Derek patted Tank's hand and set it back on his stomach. "Now get some rest, alright?" He stood up and started to walk out when Tank spoke up again.

"Hey, Doc?"

Derek turned. "Yeah?"

"Will you call her for me? Tell her I'm not burned. She's afraid I'll get burned."

Derek knew some of the worst injuries were when a soldier was burned in an explosion and had obvious scars that drew stares for the rest of their lives, no matter how well they healed.

"I'll call her," he promised.

"Gracias, mi hermano."

Derek nodded and walked away.

Dear L,

Tank took a bullet today. A few bullets, actually. It was pretty serious and scared the shit out of all of us since he lost so much blood. Derek was there and took care of him like it was nothing. He had to be medivacked, so I think it was a lot more serious than Derek let on. Derek's usually pretty unflappable; but I've known him for too long, I could tell it wasn't as superficial as he made it out to be. I don't know how he stays as calm as he does. It's like nothing ever seems to faze him. They say that if a Ranger gets back to base with a heartbeat, his chance of survival is pretty good. I hope that's true. Tank and Derek were the first two friends I made in Grant's Crossing. I don't know what I'd do if something happened to either one of them. We've lost men before, but I can't lose them. I can't.

The doctors are working on Tank as I write this. If he makes it, they'll probably send him to Germany, maybe even Walter Reed. Derek's with him now. Some of the medics are assisting since a lot of the medical staff are down with the flu that's going around. We've all had it recently. Right now, we're all on pins and needles waiting to hear about Tank.

I think of you all the time, L. Sometimes, when there's a quiet moment, not that it's ever actually quiet, but when the shooting is at least in the distance, I let my thoughts wander. When I'm back in the barracks, and the lights are out, I think of you. I can dream of happier times. I can dream that we're together.

I love you, J

Joey slammed his notebook closed when the door shot open. Derek walked in, his body barely upright; he was so exhausted. He tugged off his sweat-stained shirt as he trudged over to his bunk. Reaching for his shaving kit and a towel, he lifted his eyes only to be met with the expectant gaze of every man there. They'd gathered around him, eager for news on Tank.

"Tank's gonna be okay," Derek announced.

Those words alone breathed a collective sigh of relief into all the men in the room.

"He lost a lot of blood, but he's stable and will be flown out tomorrow morning for more surgery. Doctors are optimistic about his recovery."

Derek sat down on his bunk and scrubbed his face with his hands, dropping his forearms on his knees. With an exhale, he lifted his head to look up at Joey. "He asked me to call Araceli. Joey, if you and Rass hadn't brought him in when you did...." His voice trailed off as Joey's hand landed on his shoulder.

Neither one wanted to finish that sentence.

Chapter 41

Grant's Crossing - present day

"Yeah." Tank said. "There I was thinking I was gonna die, and Derek did nothing but joke to me about how I uh... was uh... still intact, as it were." His cheeks reddened.

Derek chuckled. "I was just trying to help you out. And with six kids now..."

Araceli's eyes widened. "Just three, thank you."

"With one on the way." Tank added.

Lainee shared in the excitement. "When are you due, anyway?"

Araceli placed her hand on her stomach. "April."

"And it's not twins or anything?" Derek inquired.

"Bite your tongue, Derek Mitchell!"

Tank leaned in to kiss his wife as they all laughed.

"You know, Tank, my offer still stands."

Tank tossed a friendly glare toward his friend.

Now it was Araceli's turn to sit up straight. "What offer?"

Tank cleared his throat. "Uh, nothing, babe. Nothing." His response earned him a look that promised she'd bring it up again.

"Fine. I'll tell you later."

With a satisfied smile, Araceli leaned in to receive another kiss from her husband.

Lainee's expression changed to worry as she knitted her brow. "So... what would have happened had you not been medivacked out? How close was it?" Her eyes bounced back and forth between her brother and Tank.

Uncomfortable looks were exchanged across the table as Tank and Derek both acknowledged what would have happened had they not called for the chopper.

"Really...close." Derek stretched the words out, almost afraid for them to escape his lips.

Tank exhaled, then looked Derek in the eye. His face paled, and worry creased his brow. "I wouldn't be here, would I?"

Derek's solemn expression confirmed his suspicion.

One look at his pained expression, and his wife was suddenly on the verge of tears. She glanced over at Derek when Tank spoke up.

"Personally, I think it was just Doc's way of ensuring I'd always buy him drinks."

And just like that, the tension in the room fell away.

Derek chuckled quietly and shook his head. He looked up enough to tip his bottle toward his friend. "Yep. And for the record, it's been a while."

"Next time at Jo's," Tank promised.

"You're on."

Never dropping his eyes from Tank's, Derek's smile faded. His eyes went distant as his voice softened. "I just wish I could have done that twice." A sense of defeat saturated his tone, which had no breath behind it. He spoke softly as if the words were meant for him and him alone, but he was heard by those closest to him, and in an instant, the mood turned somber again.

The guilt oozed off him. Thick as tar and weighing him down like a boulder that he couldn't push off his chest. Derek would never rid himself of it. Of that, he was certain. With what took as much effort as he could muster, he lifted his eyes just enough to see the sadness in Logan's eyes, all the while receiving a sympathetic glance from Tank.

Speaking in a whisper as if the words were sacred, Tank spoke first. "You're not God, Doc. You don't get to decide who lives or dies."

"Aren't I?" Derek tilted his head to one side. "Aren't you? When we're out there, Tank, we decide who dies. Why can't I decide who lives?"

"You saved a lot of lives over there, Doc," Tank added. "A lot of lives. Delivered a few babies, too, if memory serves."

Derek released a loud exhale and nodded, though more in acquiescence rather than agreement. "Four," he confirmed, holding up the requisite number of fingers. "But that includes one set of twins. And in really shitty conditions, too."

"During the clinics, right?"

Derek nodded.

"That's why you asked about twins." Araceli's upper octave voice broke through the chatter.

"Yeah. So when you both are ready for your next few kids," he mustered up a warm smile for her, "I'm here for you."

Araceli's breath hitched in her throat as a tear escaped her eye. She raised her hand and wiped it off her cheek, smiling as if it were no big deal. Tank wrapped his arm around her shoulder and pulled her close, giving her the strength to continue.

"I was so scared when you called." She looked up at the ceiling and blinked her eyes to try and stop another tear but gave in and let it slide down her cheek. "What a roller coaster. I was excited." She smiled at Tank. "I thought I was hearing from Juan, and then it was Derek's voice on the phone telling me he'd been hurt, that he'd been medivacked, and was on his way to Germany for more surgery. Medivacked." She swallowed, taking a moment to collect herself. "I never thought I'd hear that word about my husband. Derek called again when Juan was on his way to Walter Reed. Said I could at least meet him there, but I was just terrified." She sniffed and reached across the table to squeeze Derek's hand, who squeezed hers in return. "You told me as much as you could. I was scared, but you helped make it a little more bearable."

Derek looked her directly in the eyes. "All he could think of was you, Araceli. All he wanted was to get back to you."

Quinn, who had been quiet for a long while, spoke up next. "Those calls are the worst."

Araceli wiped another tear away. "What?"

"Getting a call just to let you know someone you love has been hurt."

Jo's eyes started to water. Drew dropped his head and released a slow exhale.

"Renee." Quinn breathed out a laugh with a nostalgic glint in his eye. "She turned me down at least twice before finally agreeing to marry me. Said she wanted to make sure Joey was always first. And when she said yes, I was thrilled." He smiled, still staring at the floor. "She was gone way too early."

"They both were," Jo confirmed.

Quinn continued. "I just remember getting that phone call from her coworker. I knew that if she couldn't call me herself, it had to be bad. But we just had no idea..." he trailed off.

"I've received some alarming calls in my time, but that was awful," Drew said.

"When you stopped in the bar that night, Drew, I knew it was bad." Jo's voice grew softer. "We were busy, but my husband had to go with you. I could handle the bar. He had to take care of our family."

Abe met Drew's gaze. "And then you showed up on my doorstep late that night. I just knew something had happened to one of my kids." Abe nodded toward Jo. "I'm just glad Mike was able to help us get an emergency call through."

Chapter 42

Delaware, Ohio - Autumn 2012

Joey - 31 years old

QUINN PICKED RENEE UP AND CARRIED HER PAST THE swooshing doors into the Grady Hospital emergency department. "Need some help, here!"

A nurse and doctor rushed over to him.

"My fiancée. She's been experiencing bad headaches," Quinn explained. "She has extreme sensitivity to light and can't stand up or maintain her balance."

"In here." The doctor directed them into the closest trauma bay, where Quinn laid her down on the gurney. As they started examining her, the doctor spouted off a bunch of acronyms while the nurse put it all into action. Renee moaned out a few answers when the doctor checked her eyes and asked a few questions.

"Is she on any medication? Any allergies?"

"She usually takes Ibuprofen or something for the headache. No allergies." Quinn answered, standing back just far enough to be out of their way.

"Usually?" the doctor perked up. "How long has she been having these headaches?"

"Forever, but they've been worse the last few months. Never so bad that she couldn't stand on her own."

"What has she eaten today?"

"I don't know. I was on duty until a couple of hours ago. Haven't seen her all day until about fifteen minutes ago."

"On duty?"

"Delaware Police."

"Heart rate is through the roof." The doctor issued more orders to the nurse. "We're going to take her back to run some tests. You can wait outside, officer."

"Detective," Quinn's face cringed as he corrected him without thinking.

"Whatever. Wait outside."

Rendered helpless, his chest tightened as he watched them roll her away. He thought he heard CT scan among the myriad of acronyms the doctor had rattled off.

"Detective?" Another nurse walked up to him. "Can you please help me with her name and other info? And is there a family member we can contact?"

Quinn lost sight of Renee as they disappeared around the corner. "I'm sorry, what?" He directed his attention toward the diminutive nurse.

"Is there a family member we can contact for her?"

"I'm her fiancé," he replied as if reciting something from rote memorization. "Her son is currently deployed."

Quinn gave the nurse all the pertinent info. They said it would be a while before she was brought back out. It was a busy night in the ER, so he stepped outside to call his brother.

"Drew, I need you to do something for me."

Abe had just set his book on the end table. Ready to call it a day, he scrubbed his face with his hand as he turned his wrist to check the time on his watch. At 9:45 pm, he jolted upright at a sharp knock at the front door. "Who is knocking at this hour," he muttered as he wandered toward the front of the house to answer. He hadn't yet gotten to the door when someone knocked again.

"I'm coming already," he grumbled. Unlocking the door, he flipped on the outside light and pulled it open. "Drew," he said, surprised to see the sheriff on his doorstep, in full uniform and holding his hat in his hands; Abe stumbled back a step. "Is it Lainee? Is she ok?"

Drew held up a hand. "I'm sure Lainee's fine. I'm not here about her."

Abe's eyes scanned the street behind him for any sign of a military chaplain or officer. "Derek?"

"I'm sure he's fine, too," Drew assured him, though it didn't really rid Abe of the pit in his stomach. "Abe, I need your help."

Dear L,

It was fucking awesome to hear your voice today. I'm sorry you and Maddie are separating. Wow. I still can't believe you were married for two years. But I'm happy she's found someone who wants to give her more children.

I won't lie. I'm happy we can be together now. I would love to have seen her new man's face when you told him he was more your type than she was. Tell me, is he good to Allie? When are you going to start teaching her how to play football? You're lucky, L; you'll always have her as your daughter. She's adorable. I just hope she becomes a runner. Nothing better than the open air first thing in the morning.

When we're back from Afghanistan, and when things are finalized with you, you should plan a trip down to Atlanta. Maybe I can use part of my leave to come up there for a few days or even a week. When I think of all the things I want to do to your body, I can't even see straight!

I miss you.
Love, J

It was just after six in the morning at Bagram Air Base; the Rangers were eating breakfast. Joey let out a big yawn before shoving a bite of eggs in his mouth. Some of the men were still talking about President Obama's visit a couple of days earlier. They were due to head home in another few weeks, just in time for Memorial Day.

"My kids are going to stay with their grandparents while I bang my wife for at least three days straight," Jonesy grinned. "She already told me she has new lingerie, just waiting for me to rip it off her."

Everyone at the table laughed.

"Why bother?" Rass wondered aloud, his virtuosic Texas twang singing out. "My wife already plans to meet me at the door buck naked. We won't even make it up the stairs."

"What about your kids?" Jonesy asked. "You aren't worried about them seeing you fuck their mom?"

"Nah," Rass waved his hand. "It's natural. Part o' life. Why hide it?"

"That's messed up, man," Masters said. "I'm all for taking my girl away from her parents' place where she's staying and setting her up in a nice hotel room with room service to feed us so we only have to pause long enough to catch our breath and go at it again. She's already told me she misses my BBC."

Rass furrowed his brow. "She likes your cable news package?"

"Nah, man. My big, black... Hey!"

Jonesy cut Masters off with a sharp elbow to the ribs. "Different package, Rass."

Masters laughed. "Maybe she'll even be pregnant before our next deployment."

Derek laughed at that one. "I thought you usually want to avoid getting them pregnant."

"Not this one, Sarge," he waggled his brows with a big smile. "She's the one."

Derek shook his head. "You're so whipped."

"Yeah." His eyes lit up. "Speaking of which, I wonder if she's into that?"

The men at the table let out a collective groan.

"Really, Masters?" Joey laughed and shook his head, all while failing to stifle another big yawn.

"You just ran five miles," Derek mirrored Joey's yawn as he brought his coffee up for a sip. "How are you not awake?"

"I can run five miles in my sleep, D. You know that." He chewed another bite. "And you just ran it, too."

"Yeah, good point, but...." Derek trailed off as he glanced up at some women who sat down at the table across from them. "Hey." He nodded at them with a suggestive smirk.

Jonesy dispensed more advice to Masters. "Just make sure you're the one getting her pregnant. Remember what happened to Sanders?"

"Nah." Masters shook his head. "What happened?"

"He got home, and his wife was three months' pregnant," Jonesy said.

Masters shrugged, still confused. "Yeah? So?"

"He'd just gotten back from a seven-month deployment." Jonesy clarified. "Do the math."

Masters looked up in the air as he held up his fingers one at a time. Finally, his eyes went wide as comprehension took hold. "Oh... that sucks."

"Yeah. He took it hard." Jonesy filled his mouth with a large bite of food. "And I can't believe you just used your fingers to count that."

"I have no problem getting up to twenty-one." Masters laughed as he gnawed on a piece of bacon.

The men continued their banter over their breakfast as Derek checked out every woman who passed by their table.

"God, I love Bagram." Despite their backs being to him, Derek didn't take his eyes off the two blonde women at the next table. "I may have to introduce myself and see what they look like with their hair down."

Joey rolled his eyes as Jonesy and Rass turned their heads to glance at the girls. "How about you, Parker?" Jonesy nodded in the direction of the women.

Derek cut in just as Joey opened his mouth to answer. "Nah. Not his type. He goes for brunettes."

Joey shrugged. "He's right. Blondes don't really do it for me, though Lindsay looked pretty hot at prom."

"Prom?" Masters laughed. "It's... uh...been a while since high school, don't you think?"

Joey smiled while shoving another piece of bacon in his mouth.

Derek's eyes moved to some more women who joined the first two at the next table. He nodded again as one turned around and smiled at him. "And they're enlisted, too. Perfect."

"What?" Jonesy laughed. "No good-looking officers for you?"

"Oh, plenty," Derek said. "Have you seen those Navy nurses? I just don't want them to risk a conduct unbecoming, which is too bad because that new blonde in there?" He used his hand to make a circling motion at Jonesy, Rass, and Masters. "Since you men are all off the market, that leaves more for me." He grinned again as his eyes followed a few women from the Air Force as they walked by. "And we're not even limited to the Army."

Joey gulped down some orange juice. "You're such a man-whore, D."

"Yeah." Derek joined in the laughter. "And I have two more weeks here to see how many of these soldiers...oof." He exhaled sharply and let his eyes follow a group of female Marines walking by. "And Marines... I can get to know."

His mouth full of food, Masters pointed his fork at Derek. "You own stock in Trojans yet, Sarge?"

"No, but it's probably worth looking into. I can get some of my money back." Checking out the next table, he grinned. "I think I'm going to say hello."

He stood up to head toward the woman who had smiled back at him, but he was cock blocked by a Lieutenant. "Sergeant Mitchell. Sergeant Parker."

"Ma'am," they both responded in unison.

"Come with me."

"Yes, ma'am." Derek set his tray back on the table and shrugged when Jonesy, Rass, and Masters gave them both questioning looks.

Derek and Joey were led to a big room commonly reserved for service men and women to talk to their families back home. Neither one was expecting a call today. They were usually planned in advance for weekends, at least on weekends when they thought they might be there.

They were taken to a cubicle with a computer setup for video communication. Derek rushed to a chair as soon as he saw his dad and Drew on the camera. It was still late at night the day before back home in Ohio.

"Dad! What's wrong? Where's Lainee? Is she okay?"

Abe held up his hand. "Lainee's fine, son. I just spoke to her. Are you doing okay?"

Derek exhaled in relief. "Yeah. I'm good. I'm good." He furrowed his brow, "What's Drew doing there?"

"Hi, Derek." Drew nodded.

"Is Joey with you?" Abe asked.

Joey sat down next to Derek, confused at the question. "Yes, Mr. M., I'm here." Derek made room for him to get in front of the monitor.

"It's your mother, son."

"Mom? Is she okay? Where is she?" Joey started rattling off questions.

Drew leaned forward. "She's in the hospital."

"What happened?"

"She collapsed at work. They're running tests on her now."

"Collapsed? What?"

Derek dropped a calming hand on Joey's shoulder.

Joey continued with his questions. "Is she going to be okay? Is Quinn with her?"

"Quinn took her and is with her now." Drew relayed the details as Quinn had described them.

As Drew talked, Mike Porter walked into Abe's house without bothering to knock. "I got through to my contact in DC." He glanced up when he realized he was in view of the camera. "Sergeants." He called them by their ranks before turning his shoulder while he spoke to Drew.

"What's Mike doing there?" Derek asked his Dad just as the Lieutenant returned to their cubicle.

"Sergeant Parker?"

Joey popped up. "Yes, ma'am."

"Go pack your duffle. You're flying out. Wheels up in thirty minutes."

"Yes, ma'am." As the lieutenant walked out. Joey gave Derek a confused look.

"Go." Derek nodded his head toward the lieutenant, and Joey jogged after her.

Derek waited until Joey rounded the corner before turning back to his dad, who was still watching him on the screen. "What aren't you telling us, Dad?" He pointed his thumb over his shoulder in the direction where Joey had just headed out. "Lieutenant just told Joey he's flying out."

Drew and Mike turned around to face the camera, but Abe's grim expression spoke volumes. "They don't expect her to make it, son."

Derek collapsed back in his chair like he'd had his med kit taken away from him in the middle of combat with six wounded soldiers to triage. "No," was all he could get out.

Joey spoke to Quinn on his layover in Atlanta, having been booked on a commercial flight the rest of the way home after he connected in Germany. The news wasn't good. They'd discovered a brain aneurysm that hadn't yet ruptured but that they couldn't reach. The doctors said it was only a matter of time. Joey's nerves were shot by the time he arrived in Columbus. Traveling in uniform had its advantages since someone traded him their first-class seat assignment so he could be the first off the plane. It had its disadvantages, too, when people wanted to shake his hand when all he could think about was getting to his mom.

Drew was already waiting for Joey when he arrived at baggage claim. He greeted him with a worried handshake. "How is she, Drew?"

Knowing Joey was accustomed to combat situations, he didn't bother mincing words. "Not well, I'm afraid."

Drew's blunt answer sucked the air right out of him. "Is she...?"

"She's hanging on. Let's get your bag, and I'll take you straight there. I'm parked right outside." Drew nodded toward his marked

SUV at the curb. Being friends with a deputy sheriff had its advantages.

Joey swore under his breath when another person came up behind him to pat him on the back to thank him for his service. He forced a smile and nodded as he shook their hand.

Turning back to Drew, his voice cracked, "Is she really...."

"I'll get you there, Joey. I'll get you there." Drew answered as the light flashed and the conveyor belt started moving. Joey watched the first few pieces of luggage appear in front of his own standard-issue duffle bag. Reaching down, he picked it up and slung it over his shoulder. Within a minute, it was tossed in the back seat, and he climbed in the front seat of Drew's marked SUV. As soon as he fastened his seatbelt, Drew turned on the flashing lights and drove away, adding the siren once they were out from under the cover of the passenger pickup.

Making it to the hospital in record time, Drew led Joey straight to the ICU, where Abe was waiting for him. He extended his arms and pulled Joey into a hug. "She's awake, son." He led him into her room, where Quinn was sitting next to her bed, her hand gently wrapped in his.

Joey paused the second he passed through the doorway. His stomach fell. His mom was hooked up to a bank of machines, an IV needle stuck in the back of her hand, and an oxygen tube was in her nose. Machines were beeping with lines going up and down in different colors. After a split second to take it all in, he rushed to her bedside and grabbed her hand.

His voice cracked when he spoke. "Mom."

Her eyes narrowed, taking a couple of seconds to recognize her son leaning over her. When she did, she smiled weakly and whispered, "Hey, baby."

"Hey, Mom." Joey tried to smile.

"You're so handsome." She turned her head to get a better view of him. He pushed her hair off her face like she'd always done when he was sick.

He finally looked across the bed to Quinn, whose face could no longer mask the worry he was trying to hide.

"I love you, baby." Her smile weakened. "More than anything."

Joey forced a smile and whispered, "...and no matter what." He held her hand while she drifted off to sleep.

Those were the last words his mom ever spoke to him.

After three hours, she lost consciousness.

After eleven hours, she suffered a hemorrhagic stroke and had to be resuscitated but returned with decreased brain activity.

After fourteen hours, brain activity ceased altogether, and her body was kept alive only with the help of life support.

Abe stood with his hands on Joey's shoulders as the doctor spoke to him about organ donation. Joey agreed and signed the necessary papers. He stood up to kiss his mom's forehead. "I love you, Mom," he whispered. "More than anything and no matter what."

He broke down and cried into Abe's shoulder just after she was wheeled out of the room by the transplant team.

Chapter 43

Grant's Crossing - present day

"THAT WAS WHEN HE TALKED TO ME ABOUT BECOMING HIS emergency contact." Abe reminisced as Logan nodded. "He gave me a power of attorney to be able to take care of his finances and anything else while he was gone. Said he didn't want to burden you with all that if anything happened while you were going through your divorce."

"I know. He told me. That was all so hard for him," Logan explained. "He came home to clear out the only stable home he'd ever had, knowing he could never return to it."

"Rod and Marisol offered to hold the place for him," Jo said.

"We did," Marisol confirmed. "We just wanted them to have a good home."

Logan nodded. "I don't think he could have stayed there. All his memories of the place were tied to his mother." He pressed his lips together and then broke into a smile. "That's when we started talking about marriage. It's still not legal here in Ohio. I thought we should go to Niagara Falls. I was going to propose so we could get married in New York." He swallowed. "I picked up our rings the day Abe told me...." Logan's words caught in his throat as he fought to keep himself together.

Derek put his hand on his friend's shoulder as Lainee spoke up.

"The Supreme Court will hear the case in the new year," she said, hope filling her voice.

"What?" Logan perked up and sniffed.

"Yeah," Lainee said. "Obergefell v. Hodges. It started here in Ohio and the governor fought it all the way to the Supreme Court." She glanced over to Tasha, who grabbed her hand. "I mean, we'll see what happens. Tasha and I want to get married, too, but we can't. Not here, anyway."

Derek shook his head. "So ridiculous. That needs to be allowed."

"Agreed." Abe leaned down, wrapped his arm around his daughter's shoulders, and dropped a kiss on the top of her head. "Yes, it does."

Logan wandered away from the kitchen table to look through the window to the backyard, illuminated only by a single light over the deck. After a long minute, he turned back toward Marisol.

"You were so good to us."

Chapter 44

Grant's Crossing - Autumn 2012

Joey - 31 years old

Dear L,

I can't believe she's gone. She's done everything for me. She faced my dad's fists just so she could make sure I stayed fed as a kid. She literally put her body in between him and me to protect me. She uprooted herself to bring me here so we'd have a better life. Shit, that means she brought me to you. She's always been there, offering hugs when I needed them, good advice and support; the kind she never received from her own family that kicked her out at sixteen. Somehow... she instinctively knew how to love me. And you, too.

It's just me now. I'm alone.

Thank you for being with me while I was home. There's no way I could have gotten through this without you. There's something I have to do, and I hope it doesn't anger you. The Mitchells aren't related by blood, but they've always been there for me. Abe's the only father I've ever known. I'm so scared because of what I have to ask him, but Mom once said it was okay. I just never thought I'd need it.

She'll know I'll always love her, right? I can't believe she's gone. Why is she gone?

Love, J

. . .

Tank and Araceli Palacios, pregnant at the time with their third baby, sat behind Joey, Logan, and Quinn at the funeral. Next to them were Abe, a pregnant Lainee, and Tasha. The entire Strager family was there, complete with spouses, children, and extended family.

Joey wasn't alone in his grief since Logan's divorce was now final. It meant he could be open about his feelings toward Logan, something he didn't fear making known on this day.

With the repeal of Don't Ask, Don't Tell a year earlier, Joey no longer had to hide who he was, so they were able to be themselves in public as well as in private. While on duty, Joey didn't actively advertise, but he didn't have to deny it, either. It was as if a weight had been lifted off his shoulders. Logan's parents weren't happy about his divorce and what it seemed to say about their family; but they offered unexpected understanding when Logan came out to them, and were happy their granddaughter would still be a big part of their lives.

Logan stayed by Joey's side the entire day, from before the funeral service started through the wake that followed.

Marisol had offered her and Rod's home for family and friends to gather after the funeral. It also left Joey and Quinn the opportunity to return to their own homes when they needed to grieve on their own.

Knowing the Stragers were hurting along with Joey, a trio of older ladies, affectionately known in town as the Tres Widows, pitched in to help with all the food and cleanup. They were always there to help clean a house or cook food in someone's time of need. They also ended up with dates after each funeral as well, shameless flirts that they were.

Joey walked through the front door of his house, heartbroken at how empty it felt now, even though everything was still inside. Standing behind him, Logan closed the front door while Joey paused to scan the living room. Wandering back toward the kitchen,

Joey's eyes caught sight of his mom's favorite jacket hanging on a hook on the wall. He stepped closer to run his fingers down the length of the sleeve.

Walking into her bedroom, his breath caught in his throat at the sight of the picture on her nightstand. It was of him and his mom at his graduation from basic training. He eased himself down on her bed and picked it up, his fingers touching her smiling face. "She told me she was so proud of me," he sniffed. "I can't believe it's been eleven years since this was taken."

Logan leaned against the door frame while Joey slowly registered the reality of his mom's death. Joey opened the drawer on the nightstand and found all his letters. He started to reach inside, his hand hovering just above them but snapped back as if fearing it would burn him like a hot stove. Pressing his lips together, he closed the drawer and raised his eyes toward the ceiling. He blinked a few times to stave off inevitable tears.

A knock on the back door snapped his head forward. "I'll get it," Logan said.

Joey heard Marisol's voice greet Logan. "So much food was dropped off. I wanted to make sure you both had plenty, so you didn't have to worry about meals for the next few days. I've got more in my car."

The door closed then reopened a couple of minutes later. The casseroles, soups, and salads made by friends and neighbors were loaded into the fridge. If nothing else, they wouldn't go hungry.

Still holding the picture, Joey rose off the bed and wandered to the kitchen, prompting sympathetic looks from both Marisol and Logan. Marisol stopped what she was doing and wrapped him in a warm hug. For a while, she didn't say a single word, just hugged him as she would have held any one of her own children.

She cupped his cheeks as she pulled back. "She loved you so much," she said, her own eyes watering as a tear slid down Joey's face. With a nod, she stepped away. "I'll be back tomorrow to take care of whatever dishes you both used, so don't give a second thought about that."

She hugged Logan. "Take good care of him, Logan."

"I will," he promised.

"...and call me if you need anything."

Joey was already walking upstairs by the time Marisol left. He took off the dress uniform he wore for the funeral, letting each piece of clothing fall to the floor of his bedroom before stepping into the shower.

Logan was waiting in Joey's bedroom by the time he stepped out of the shower. Joey wrapped a towel that hung low around his waist. His shoulders sagged, and his eyes scanned the room as if he were looking for something he knew he wouldn't find.

Logan had hung up his uniform while he was in the shower and there was a plate of food and two bottles of water on the desk. Joey hadn't eaten all day, but didn't have an appetite. Seeing Logan, he walked right up to him and dropped his head on Logan's shoulder. Logan wrapped his arms around him and held him tight.

Joey sniffed. "I miss her so much."

"I know you do, sweetheart," Logan said softly. "I know you do."

After trying to get him to eat a little something, Logan led him to bed. "Come on. Just get under the covers."

It took Joey a good minute or two before he was able to muster enough will to move away from Logan. Once he did, he dropped the towel and crawled under the covers. Logan hung the wet towel over a doorknob, then undressed. The mattress dipped a bit as he climbed in and pulled Joey to his chest, resting a hand on his head and rubbing his back with the other, hoping it would help calm him. Joey's tears fell on Logan's chest until his breathing evened out, signaling he'd fallen to sleep.

"I love you, Joey." Logan kissed the top of Joey's head and wrapped his arms around him to keep him close.

"Joey?" Logan took in a long inhale and sat up when he noticed Joey wasn't in bed. Trying to get his bearings, he checked his phone and saw it was after midnight. They'd come up here before six p.m. and had fallen asleep.

"Hey." Joey entered the room and sat down on the bed, dropping a kiss on Logan's lips. "You're up. I hope I didn't wake you." He popped a grape in his mouth.

Logan sat up behind him, wrapping his arm around Joey's waist and resting his head on his shoulder.

"I was hungry. Want one?" Joey held up a grape.

"Mm... hmm," Logan replied as Joey dropped one in his mouth. "Thanks," he chewed it. "Mmm. It's sweet."

"Yeah. They're good."

"We both crashed pretty hard."

"Yeah." Joey handed the plate off to Logan as he took a drink of water. "My body's still on Afghanistan time. I have a feeling my schedule is going to be off for a while."

"Probably." Logan wrapped his other arm around Joey's waist and gave him a gentle squeeze. "How are you doing?" He kissed Joey's shoulder.

"Okay? I guess? It's hard. It really sucks." Joey broke a piece of cheddar cheese in two and fed one to Logan, then took the other for himself. "It's not like I remember with Dad."

"Neither one of us fared so well in the dad lottery."

"I kind of did." Joey caught himself. "I mean, he's not my real dad, but he treated me well."

"You mean Abe, right?"

"Yep." Joey leaned his head against Logan's. "Did I ever tell you he was the first person I told?" Joey's lip curled up on one side. "After Derek, of course."

"Of course," Logan chuckled. "No. You didn't tell me. How was it?"

"I was terrified. I'd barely figured out I was bisexual, but I was so scared of my mom kicking me out like her parents did to her." Joey's breath caught in his throat. He took a moment to find his voice again. "I practiced by telling him first."

"How'd he take it?"

Joey took a deep breath and held it for a few seconds before exhaling. "I cried on his shoulder when he told me I was part of his family no matter what. He said my mom wouldn't kick me out, but if I ever needed to, I could move in with them. It was such an obvious solution to him." He swallowed down another drink of water. "And then, as you know, when Mom found out, she just made us omelets like it was nothing." He sniffed. His breath shuddered when he took his next breath.

Logan laughed again. "She was only afraid of me breaking your heart."

"She wasn't afraid of anyone after my dad." Joey coughed out a laugh as he wiped tears off his face with the palm of his hand. "Don't mess with my mom."

Logan rested his hand on the side of Joey's head and held him close. "It's okay. I've got you."

Joey sniffed again and wiped a couple more tears. "I love you so much. I couldn't get through this without you."

"Yeah, you would." Logan cupped Joey's face. "I'm just glad you don't have to." He pressed another kiss to his shoulder. "And I love you, too." He reached out for a bottle of water and took a couple of drinks. He took the plate from Joey and placed it on the nightstand. "Come on. Let's lay back down."

Logan backed up underneath the covers and held them up for Joey. They faced each other as he extended his hand over Joey's waist.

Joey rested a hand on Logan's chest and ran his fingers through his chest hair. He raised his eyes to meet Logan's. "I wish we could be married."

Logan lifted a shoulder in a shrug. "We can be."

"No, we can't. It's not legal here."

"Not in Ohio, but it is in other places. New York. Chicago. Even Iowa, I think."

"Iowa?" Joey narrowed his eyes. "You're kidding."

"No. I'm not. When you get back, we should get married."

"That sounds great, but," Joey pulled back, "it wouldn't be recognized by anyone. The Army won't recognize it...unless Secretary Panetta wants to make some changes. DOMA prevents people from having to care about us."

"But you and I would recognize it." Logan paused for a few seconds, "And you'd be a stepdad."

Joey breathed a laugh. "Allie."

"Yeah." Logan smiled, thinking of his daughter. "She's terrific. Plus, maybe someday, the laws will change."

"Fucking homophobic assholes," Joey spit out.

Logan pulled him closer. "I know."

"Logan?"

"Yes."

"Will you help me pack up the house?" Joey made an abrupt change of subject. "I can't stay here."

"Of course I will."

Joey stilled his fingers and pressed his palm against Logan's chest. "And I need to tell you something. I..."

"What is it?"

"It's...something I need to ask Abe." Joey took a deep breath, "But I'm afraid it'll sound like I'm betraying my mom. Like I'm betraying you."

"I don't think there's anything you can do that would betray your mom. And there's nothing you can do to betray me, certainly not worse than what I did to you."

Joey's fingers curled into Logan's chest. "You know that's long forgiven, right?"

"Yeah. Whatever it is, Joey. I'll be here for you." Logan pulled him closer and tipped Joey's chin up to look into his eyes. He dropped a soft kiss on Joey's lips. "We have another couple weeks here. Yes, it'll be busy. It'll be hard. It'll be awful, but I'll be with you every step of the way."

"I have to pack everything up and…" Joey stopped when Logan pressed his fingers to his lips.

"Let's tackle that tomorrow. Way back when, after I was in the hospital for…well… you remember." Logan couldn't get the words out when thinking back to his suicide attempt a couple of years earlier. "You took care of me. Let me take care of you, alright?" He leaned in and pressed another kiss to Joey's lips.

"It's not all awful," Joey whispered just before he fell asleep in Logan's arms.

Joey opened the front door. "Thanks for coming over, Abe."

They shook hands and slapped each other on the back in a warm hug as Abe walked inside. Abe nodded to Logan, who set another packed box down on the floor. "Sure. You said you wanted to talk."

"Yes, I did." Joey closed the door behind them. "I mean, I do."

"I see you're packing up the house." Abe made a sweeping gesture with his arm, "What are you going to do with everything?"

"Stick it in storage, I guess." Joey took in a deep breath as he considered. "I don't know. There's not really a lot. Donate some of it, maybe? Mom helps out at the women's shelter." He swallowed as he corrected himself. "Helped at the women's shelter. Maybe I can take some there."

"Well, if you're moving out of here, then you'll need a place to stay when you're on leave and when you move back home. I've got a room already set up at home. We should be able to fit everything you don't donate into our house."

"Abe, I can't...."

"Yes, you can. You're family, Joey. Always have been." Abe placed his hand on Joey's shoulder. "It's done. We can move everything over this weekend. I've already got some folks who would be happy to help. I'm sure Logan can be talked into helping, too."

Logan agreed. "Of course I will." He walked up and greeted Abe with a handshake. "Good to see you, Abe."

"You, too, Logan." He turned back to Joey. "You don't have to worry about a thing."

Visibly moved, Joey nodded. "Thanks."

"Now, son. What did you want to talk about?"

Chapter 45

Grant's Crossing - Present day

"You treated us well, too Abe," Logan said. "We couldn't have gotten through that without you."

Abe nodded slowly. His eyes went distant.

"Dad?" Lainee asked. She exchanged glances with Derek. "Dad? Are you alright?"

"I was just thinking back to the day we found out he'd been killed." He blinked a couple of times and refocused on the family and friends in the room. He met Lainee's gaze. "I couldn't have made it through without you and Mick."

Logan creased his brow. "Mick?"

Abe clarified. "My brother-in-law. Katherine's half-brother."

"That was the worst day." Lainee wiped a tear off her face as she described that hot August evening. "We'd just finished dinner and were having the best time. Then they knocked on the door."

Lainee took her time, breathing in and out a few times before she continued. "The moment I answered the door, I knew it was going to be the worst possible news. A captain and a chaplain stood on our doorstep. They were almost cold in the way they asked for you. And they asked for you using your full name. I could hardly speak, but somehow managed to let them inside."

Lainee's next breath shuddered, and Tasha wrapped her arms around her. "It's okay."

"And for the minute it took me to get you and come back, I didn't know if they were there for Derek or Joey..." Lainee broke down. Her sniffles filled the quiet room. Everyone patiently waited in silence for her to continue. Collecting herself, Lainee sniffed and went on. "I know Uncle Mick was heartbroken, too, but I'm so glad he was there. Except for when Mom died, I'd never seen you that sad before, Dad. And with mom, I only really remember it as a big blur of feelings."

"I know." Abe wrapped his arm around his daughter's shoulders and hugged her tight. "We knew it was going to happen with your mom. With Derek and Joey, we could only hope it wouldn't."

Chapter 46

Grant's Crossing - August 2014

"AND THEN DEREK CAME RUNNING AROUND THE CORNER LIKE a bat out of hell..." Abe could barely speak through his laughter while regaling Lainee and Mick with the story of one of Derek's exploits.

They had just finished dinner outside on the deck when the doorbell sounded.

"I'll get it." Still laughing, Lainee jumped up and disappeared inside the house. Mick was in town visiting for a long weekend and Abe thoroughly enjoyed telling him about his kids' grade school days when Lainee came back out on the deck after answering the front door.

Abe's laughter cut off the instant his daughter reappeared. Her face was as white as a ghost. "Lainee, honey? What's wrong?"

Her hands shook, and she tried to catch her breath. Tears streamed down her face, and she seemed on the verge of hyperventilating. "Da...Dad."

Abe jumped up and pulled her into his arms. "What's wrong, Lainee?"

Mick grabbed his cane and stood up. He recognized that

expression; he'd seen it plenty in the days leading up to his own service in Vietnam.

She was barely able to speak. "Dad. There...there's an Army captain and a chaplain in our living room. They're asking for you."

Abe's stomach sank as he turned his head back toward Mick. They both knew exactly what that meant. The only question was, for which son were they here?

Abe looked up at the sky, closed his eyes, and swallowed hard. He squeezed Lainee and kissed the top of her head. Without a word, he turned back to Mick, who placed a hand on Abe's shoulder with an understanding nod. "We'll be right there with you."

Abe steeled himself for the inevitable, devastating news and strode into the living room at the front of the house, where the captain and chaplain were patiently waiting.

"Mr. Abraham Elias Mitchell?" The somber captain confirmed Abe's identity as Mick and Lainee joined him in the living room. Lainee grabbed his right hand as Mick stood by him on his left.

Abe swallowed. "Yes." His voice was stiff as he tried to brace himself for the captain's words.

Addressing him directly, the captain spoke the words no family ever wanted to hear. "The Secretary of the Army has asked me to express his deep regret that Joseph Miles Parker was killed during combat operations in Afghanistan early this morning."

Abe's knees buckled. Mick let his cane fall to the floor as he jerked forward to help ease his brother-in-law to the couch. He sat down beside him, keeping his arm on his shoulder to hold him upright. Lainee collapsed back against her dad's other shoulder, her hand covering her mouth as she cried.

Abe closed his eyes for a minute, biding a little time to collect himself enough to speak. He took a few deep breaths trying to lessen the tightening of his chest. "What about my other son?" He swallowed hard, thinking of Joey as his own son like he always did. "What about Derek? Is he alright?"

"I don't know anything about that, sir."

"Was he on the same mission? Does he even know?"

This was to be Derek and Joey's final deployment. Neither one planned to re-up when their enlistments ended in December. Abe knew Derek would be devastated.

"He'll be notified directly, sir."

That didn't answer his question, but the Army probably had its own way of handling notifications.

The rest of the conversation was a blur. Unless they needed a verbal response from Abe, Mick answered their question as best he could. The captain said something about making another visit to discuss funeral arrangements, including honors at the ceremony itself.

After Abe signed a document confirming his contact information, the captain stood up. "The Secretary of the Army extends his condolences to you and your family for your loss."

Chapter 47

Grant's Crossing - present day

Derek, Logan, and Tank returned to the kitchen after the Stragers said their goodbyes. Jo offered to take Araceli home so Tank could stay with Derek a bit later.

Wishing them all goodnight, Tasha and Lainee headed upstairs to bed.

In the kitchen, Derek stared at the wall drinking another bottle of beer.

Logan and Tank sat across the table from him, sharing the same concerned look when Abe returned to the kitchen.

"It was a meeting with tribal elders," Derek spoke to no one in particular. He stared at nothing in particular. "Like all the others. We were on our way back when they ambushed us. They just came out of nowhere."

Derek stood up and wandered out of the room, stopping when he reached the fireplace. He picked up the picture of Tank, Joey, and him in their combat gear. "They were so fucking well-armed."

Derek turned his head to find they'd all followed him into the living room. His eyes glistened with a hint of unshed tears. "Why was it Joey?"

Abe lowered himself to the couch. Logan took up a spot

standing behind Abe, his eyes drawn to the picture of Joey and him on the mantel. Tank leaned against the archway separating the living room from the dining room behind him.

"It could have been anyone else." Derek fought the pain that filled his chest, but his voice began to shake. "Why was it him? Why wasn't it me?"

Derek had seen death before, but never got used to losing men in the field. He lost two men that day. Yes. That was part of combat. Men and women got injured. Men and women died.

"Nearly every other man I ever treated... if they were alive when I got to them, they made it. Why didn't Joey?"

Logan, Tank, and Abe remained silent.

"What did I do wrong?" Derek asked, his tone almost helpless.

"Doc," Tank said. His voice was barely above a whisper. "Don't do this to yourself."

"I wasn't needed back here." Derek's voice cracked as he spoke, staring at an undetermined spot across the room.

"That's not true, son."

"I wasn't," Derek's eyes focused on his father, his voice unsteady. "Joey wanted to get married. He had somebody waiting for him." He waved a hand through the air toward Logan and then Tank. "Same as you, Tank. You had to make it back to Araceli."

He let out a humorless laugh. "Kaitlyn dumped me as soon as I left for my first deployment. I didn't have anyone here who cared."

"Son–" Abe protested, but Derek quickly cut him off.

"No, Dad. Joey was the one who made sure people were ok. Don't you see?" Derek swallowed, his face grimacing, finally showing the pain of his loss. "He took care of Gallo, and Tank told us how he took care of Thompson. He was the one who got Tank to me in time to save his life. He took care of his mom. Hell," he pointed his fingers back to his chest as his voice steadily rose in volume. "He took care of me when everything went to shit with mom. He was the only one who knew where to find me."

Derek turned back toward the fireplace, resting one hand on the mantel while he took another pull from his beer bottle. "It's so... fucking unfair. Of all people, why Joey?"

When he turned around again, he had tears in his eyes. "Tell me. Why did they take the good one? It makes no sense." He sniffed and took another drink.

Tank pushed away from the wall. "It's not supposed to make sense, Doc. It's war."

Derek pursed his lips and shook his head. His eyes were red with anger. "Easy for you to say," he lashed out. "You're not the one who let him die."

Abe smacked his hands against the coffee table and bolted to his feet. "Damn it, son. You did *not* let him die." Abe's voice shook with a rage Derek didn't know he possessed. "I'll be damned if you let yourself take the blame for that."

Logan remained silent as he took a slow step back from the couch.

"He's right, Doc," Tank urged. "It's not your fault. You didn't *let* him do anything, least of all die."

"Well, he did die," Derek growled, "and I didn't save him."

"You're so good at your job. So many men are alive thanks to you." Tank took a step toward Derek. "You're good at your job," he repeated.

"Not when it counted," Derek spat out. He slammed his beer bottle on the mantel, barely catching it before it tipped over.

"Yes, when it counted." Tank now stood right in front of him.

"It. Wasn't. Enough. I wasn't good enough, Tank." Without warning, Derek shoved Tank back. "Don't you see?"

Tank got right back into Derek's face. His voice was angry as Abe stood at the ready. "DAMMIT, DOC! Jonesy told me what happened. Joey had already been shot in the shoulder and had rejoined the fight before the RPG hit. He had lacerations on his head." Tank proceeded to list out all the injuries Joey had suffered.

"He had mortar wounds in his other shoulder. He had mortar wounds - plural - on his torso. His legs were literally cut out from under him. He. Bled. Out. Jonesy said that even if you had surgeons right there, he wouldn't have made it."

Logan paled at the description and backed against the opposite wall with a groan.

Derek and Tank both turned their attention to the sound Logan made. Logan leaned forward with his hands on his knees, trying to catch his breath.

Tank's face dropped, his expression contrite. "Shit, Logan. I'm sorry. I thought..."

Logan held up his hand as if it were okay. "I... didn't know how... he..." he gasped for air, breathing in with short bursts.

Abe rushed over to Logan and placed his hands on his back and upper arm and whispered a few words only Logan could hear. Logan nodded then visibly swallowed. Logan's eyes closed as he gulped in air.

With a long exhale, Abe helped him stand back up and disappeared with him down the hall toward the back of the house.

Turning back to Derek, Tank's voice didn't hold the same heat it did moments before, but it carried no less bite. "I don't know what ridiculously high expectations you've set, Doc, but you need to get over yourself."

Tank took a step back, but continued on, anger combined with tough love in his eyes. "You were still two klicks out from the rendezvous point, already having to carry the lieutenant's body back, not to mention Rass and Conrad's injuries. And while we're at it, let's talk about your own, Doc. You had a possible concussion along with shrapnel you literally pulled out of your own arm."

Derek huffed out a breath. "It was my job to keep the men alive."

"Your job."

"YEAH! MY JOB." Derek yelled, his face red with anger. His chest lifted and fell while he took a few breaths. "And I didn't do it."

"*Ay coño.*" Tank closed his eyes and shook his head. "We don't get to choose who lives and who dies, Doc. It's fucking war. People die. It sucks. We've both seen it. So yes, you did your job. You got your men through it, and you got them back to the base."

"I didn't get them all."

"You left no one behind."

Derek's eyes flashed anger as he sneered. "FUCK YOU."

Unfazed, Tank continued. "You brought them all home to their families."

He patted his hand against his chest, which heaved as his breathing grew heavier. "I WAS HIS FAMILY, JUAN. HE WAS A BROTHER TO ME. MY BROTHER. ALL I BROUGHT BACK WAS A BODY... IN FUCKING PIECES."

"Jesus, Doc," Tank furrowed his brow and lowered his voice. "What sort of miracle were you expecting to pull off?"

Derek shuddered a few breaths and rasped his response. "The same one I pulled off for you." Derek's sudden intake of breath at his admission came with the realization that he never had as much control as he once thought he had. His face fell as he fought back tears. He opened his mouth as if to say something more but swallowed instead to gather his thoughts. As if his hope were completely washed away, he made his confession. "You shouldn't be here. So why isn't he?"

A single tear finally escaped down Derek's cheek.

Tank was taken aback; his face reflected the hurt Derek's words caused. He dropped his voice to a whisper. "Don't go there, Doc." Tank shook his head back and forth. "You didn't kill Joey. It was the Taliban. They killed him. Not you."

Tank asked, but Derek denied him a response. They both knew the truth of what happened, but the silence stretched, yielding no resolution.

Waving off his friend, Tank muttered something in Spanish and stomped into the foyer. He pulled his coat off one of the pegs by the door. He shrugged it on and straightened his collar. Tank grabbed the doorknob and paused. "It was never because of you."

Derek looked over at the front door as Tank closed it behind him. Through the bay window, he watched Tank walk down the sidewalk. The colorful glow of the Christmas tree reflected off the glass as Tank got into his car and sped off. Derek took another swig of his warming beer, his outstretched hand still gripping the mantel.

Footsteps sounded behind him in the hallway. Abe handed Logan his coat.

For a moment, Derek and Logan made eye contact; the devastation of the loss of Joey was mirrored in their gaze. Logan brought his scarf up around his neck and thanked Abe. He gave Derek an almost imperceptible nod and walked out the door.

With a sigh, Abe shuffled over to Derek and placed his hand on his shoulder. Derek shrugged it off.

"Tank's right, son."

"I can't, Dad. I just can't," he turned back toward the glow of the fire. "Not tonight. Please."

Abe nodded and took a few steps back. "Goodnight." He turned the light out on his way upstairs.

Derek stared at the fire, burning and crackling in the fireplace, moving only to take a final pull from the beer bottle he still held. He stared back at the picture of Joey, Tank, and himself, taken at Bagram.

Chapter 48

Afghanistan - August 2014
Joey - 33 years old

"Fuck, it's hot out here," Masters wiped his forehead with the back of his hand while trekking along the rocky terrain.

"Quit your whining, Masters." Jonesy kicked a rock on the side off the trail if they could even call it a trail.

Captain Evans and his men took point on the return trip. At the same time, Lieutenant Stevens led the rear after a pre-dawn meeting with some tribal elders in a small village about two or three kilometers away from this morning's designated rendezvous point. They were about halfway through the return trip when the sun started to rise in the east.

"No," Rass said in his usual Texas twang. "He's right. It's hotter than a billy goat with a blow torch out here."

Joey laughed, "Hotter than a what?"

"It's true," Rass maintained. He nodded toward the sky. "Look. The sun's barely even up, and I'm already drippin' with sweat."

"You're always dripping with sweat," Jonesy laughed.

"I have active glands," Rass said matter-of-factly.

"As long as you take a shower when we get back to base, I'll be happy." Derek chuckled but never stopped scanning the terrain in the distance. "You stink."

Rass stuck his nose in his pits for a strong whiff. "I don't smell anything."

"You're not downwind."

"Cut the chatter, men," Lt. Stevens called from behind them. "Let's concentrate on getting back. I'm starving."

"You're always starvin'," Rass called back.

"Hold up!" The captain gave the signal to stop.

The men immediately fell silent, eyeing the area around them.

"Keep your eyes open," Lt. Stevens commanded, "and watch as we round this next bend."

"Still hearing chatter about ambushes?"

"When do we not hear about ambushes, Jonesy?" Lt. Stevens replied in a low voice, pointing his weapon out as if expecting indigenous fighters to rise up and fire at them at any moment.

The captain signaled the okay for them to continue. They remained vigilant. There were reports of roaming bands of fighters near some of the villages. As the men rounded a bend in the trail, shots rang out. They started taking heavy fire.

"TAKE COVER," the captain ordered.

The men hit the ground and returned fire. Taking cover where they could against the craggy slope of the mountain, they were pinned under a slight overhang leading to a shallow cave tucked behind a few short trees.

Rass cried out and clutched his right arm. Derek immediately dropped his weapon and scurried over to him. Without hesitation, Joey, freshly promoted two weeks earlier to Sergeant First Class, stepped up and took Derek's spot to ensure they were covered.

"It's nothing, Rass," Derek said while wrapping a bandage over his wound. "It's not even your trigger arm. You'll be fine." He taped it off and pulled Rass' uniform back over to protect the injury.

Rass laughed. "Thanks, Doc."

"We'll stitch it up right when we get back." Derek patted Rass's other shoulder to reassure him.

Patched up, Rass returned to his defensive position as Joey cried out.

"Joey!" Derek's eyes focused on the blood dripping out of Joey's right shoulder and tore the shirt to inspect the wound. "Hey. You're okay. You're okay," he assured him as the weapons fire continued. "It's just your shoulder. Nothing vital."

Joey winced in pain. "Hurts like a son of a bitch."

"I bet," Derek looked at Joey's back to see where the bullet exited. "Looks like it went straight through. You're going to be fine."

Joey winced in pain as Derek applied pressure to his shoulder. "I can still fight."

"Roger that." Derek finished taping it down. "You're good."

Joey returned to his position and fired off a few shots when someone yelled, "RPG!"

With no time to dive away, the men in front were all forced back by the explosion, momentarily stunned by the blast. The men in the wings closed in to make sure they were protected until they could rejoin the fight.

Derek heard shots ringing out in the distance, the sounds muffled, as if being projected through a thick pillow. He had the wind knocked out of him since he landed on his back. He gasped for breath, struggling to suck air into his lungs. Looking straight up, he saw the bright light of the sun trying to shine through clouds of orange and brown dust-filled smoke.

After a near-Herculean effort, he finally drew in enough air to catch his breath, but a searing pain demanded his attention. Still on his back, he turned to see something sticking out of his left arm. He slowly secured his weapon against his chest and reached over with his right hand to pull it out of his left bicep; blood, fortunately not too much, trickled down his arm.

"Shit." He coughed and examined the jagged piece of metal he'd just pulled out of his arm and dropped it on the ground as the gunfire continued all around him.

Derek took a deep breath and flipped onto his stomach to regain his bearings and take in the situation. He winced in pain when he rolled over his injured arm. He squeezed it again with his right hand then determined he could go on. He wiped the sweat off his forehead, leaving it blood-covered instead.

Blinking a few times to focus, he turned his attention to the men to see who had been hit.

Crawling over to Jonesy, Derek could see he was stunned as well. "You okay, Jonesy?" Derek patted him on the chest and helped him up.

"Yeah, Doc." Jonesy coughed a few times as he steadied himself.

"Stevens?" Derek felt for a pulse on the lieutenant, who seemed to have taken the brunt of the blast. After a few seconds, he dropped his hand. The man was dead.

"Doc!" Rass yelled. "It's Parker!"

Derek spun to see Joey was on his back and his legs gone below the knees. Blood leaked out of multiple spots on his body and Joey was gasping, desperately fighting for air. Derek fought back his initial panic of seeing his best friend so severely injured and turned to his training that had served him so reliably over the years.

"SHIT!" Derek rushed over and, without hesitation, he tied tourniquets around Joey's legs to stop the filthy ground from turning even redder before methodically examining his other injuries.

"He pushed me out of the way. I would have been right there when it hit," Rass choked out. "What can I do?"

Derek set up an IV with TXA to curb the bleeding as the shooting died down "Hold this up," he commanded Rass as he shoved the saline bag into his hands. There was a new shoulder wound, this time to the left shoulder. Derek packed it off, knowing some shrapnel was still inside.

"Hold on, Joey," he spoke softly as he worked.

"Logan." Joey coughed. Blood dripped from the corner of his mouth.

"You'll see Logan soon. Stay with us." Derek ripped Joey's uniform open to find wounds on his torso.

"D? You there, D?"

"I'm here." Derek grabbed Joey's shaking hand. "You're okay, Joey."

Joey gasped for air, "D? Help me."

"Look at me, Joey. I've got you."

He was still losing blood but Derek couldn't find it. He rolled him on his side and found yet another wound in his torso. The blood was quickly turning the ground a deep red.

"Shit. Shit. Shit."

Derek couldn't lose his best friend. He couldn't lose Joey. "Training, Derek. Use your training. You know what to do." He whispered to himself.

He reached into his pack for another QuikClot bandage to stop the bleeding, but it was too severe a wound to repair in the field.

"Tell Logan I love him, D."

"You can tell him yourself when we get back," Derek's voice shook as he pressed the bandages to the gaping wound in Joey's chest. If he could just get the bleeding stopped....

The shooting ceased, and the acrid smoke drifted away. The chirping of birds in the distance filled the sudden silence. Their captain called out orders as the enemy either fled or was dead.

"I wasn't there for him, D," Joey grunted, his pain obvious. "He tried...to kill himself because of me."

"You were there, Joey. It's not your fault. It was never because of you." Derek filled a syringe and injected pain meds into Joey's arm. He then returned to pack the shoulder wounds as best he could. There was too much blood loss already, but Derek would never give up trying.

His friend's eyes darted around as if he were looking for something or someone, not really seeing the men who were there with him. "Mom. Where are you, Mom?"

"Don't go there, Joey. Stay with us. You've got to get home to Logan, remember? I'm not supposed to tell you, so you have to act surprised, but he's going to propose. You're gonna get married." Derek's voice shook as he pressed harder on the wound on Joey's chest.

The other rangers gathered nearby to maintain a silent vigil for the fallen soldier. "Mom...Mom..."

Working like hell to pack his wounds, Derek put another bandage over his torso.

"Hold this down," He barked at Jonesy.

"Doc," Jonesy started to say.

"DO IT!" Derek ordered.

Jonesy released an exasperated sigh as pressed down on the bandage covering Joey's chest.

"Mom," Joey called out again.

Derek grabbed Joey's hand. "No, no, no. Joey, don't do this. You stay with me. Look at me."

"D..." Joey's voice sounded weaker as he called out. His voice slurred. His eyes flitted back and forth without ever landing on anything around him. "Mom...Mom..."

Derek's throat tightened. "Come on, Joey."

"Mmm..." Joey's eyes glazed over.

Derek leaned down. There were no breath sounds. "FUCK!" Derek called out as he shoved Jonesy away and started chest compressions.

Joey wasn't moving.

"Don't leave me, Joey," Derek's voice cracked as he yelled, no commanded, his friend to stay alive. Desperation drove him.

Joey's lifeless eyes stared up at him, but Derek didn't stop. "Don't go, Joey." He begged. "Please," his last word came out as a raspy whisper.

"Doc." Jonesy reached out to stop him from continuing the chest compressions. "He's gone."

"No!" Derek shoved him backward and continued pressing on his chest to make his heart start beating again. "Come on, Joey," he pleaded, "Come back."

"SERGEANT!" Jonesy yelled.

Stunned, Derek's wide eyes met the other soldier's gaze. His blood-covered hands were still planted on Joey's chest as his grief-stricken eyes alternated between Rass and Jonesy. His own chest rose and fell as if he'd just finished their daily run three times over.

Derek couldn't move. His eyes scanned the area in the hopes that he'd wake up somewhere else and discover this wasn't real. It had never occurred to him that Joey might not make it back with him.

They were both going to make it home. They had to make it home.

He looked at the other Rangers in disbelief. This wasn't supposed to happen. Derek was their medic. They relied on him to get them home. Failure wasn't in his job description. Derek closed his eyes for a minute and swallowed down the bile rising in his throat. "Fuck," he said mostly to himself.

He took a deep breath to force himself back into the present. They had work to do and they still had to get to the rendezvous point. He wiped his forehead again with the back of his hand, leaving behind a new trail of blood.

They were still on a mission.

Derek looked around, eyes moving from face to face. "Anyone else hurt?"

No one spoke.

"I SAID, IS ANYONE ELSE HURT?" He barked out.

"No."

"Rass?"

"No, Sarge."

"Jonesy?"

"All good, Sarge."

He took inventory of his fellow rangers, catching head shakes and hearing muffled 'nos'. A movement to his left caught his eye. Masters helped Conrad hobble toward him.

"I just rolled it," Conrad explained as he eased down to the ground.

Derek examined the injured ankle and put a splint on it. His training continued to function even though his heart was shattered. "That'll keep it from rolling again. Can you walk? Rendezvous point isn't far."

"Yeah. I'm good." Conrad grimaced as he stood back up.

"Masters," Derek called to him. "We need your stretcher. And find Anderson. We need his stretcher for the Lieutenant."

Masters immediately removed his pack and grabbed the stretcher and popped it open.

They could hear Captain Evans barking out more orders as they regrouped.

Anderson came over with his stretcher so they could transport Lt. Stevens' body. Derek, Rass, and Jonesy took care of Joey. Derek paused long enough to close his eyes and make the sign of the cross, prompting a few raised brows of concern. He wasn't a practicing Catholic but figured now was as good a time as any for a quick prayer.

Not that it would do any good.

He placed the saline pack that was still hooked up to Joey's arm on his chest before carefully placing him onto the stretcher.

"Wait." Derek turned and searched the ground. He swallowed hard to keep his stomach from emptying on the spot, but he had to find the rest of his friend. With a clenched jaw, Derek found what he was looking for. He walked over and recovered Joey's severed legs.

The other men watched in silence as he placed them in a bag and secured them on the stretcher. Joey's body may have been torn apart, but Derek would be damned if he left any piece of him behind in this god-forsaken place.

Someone else grabbed Joey's weapon while holding his own weapon at the ready. Derek handed Joey's pack to another Ranger to carry back. He didn't say a word as he grabbed one end of the stretcher to take his best friend home.

Derek 1 signaled to the captain that the injured were ready to go.

"All right. Let's move out," the captain called.

The men started walking with two of the fallen in tow. All their eyes dissected the landscape around them with their weapons held at the ready should another ambush be waiting for them.

Derek risked a final glance back to where he'd last seen his best friend alive. He squinted as his gaze followed a trio of snow finches fluttering up from the blood-soaked ground toward the light of the rising sun. Their brown and white feathers glistened in the morning light.

"Come on, Sarge."

Jonesy nudged Derek on the shoulder, startling him from his thoughts. Adjusting his grip, Derek didn't say a word to anyone. The nausea he felt at losing Joey accompanied him the entire march back.

His best friend was gone, and there wasn't a damned thing he could do to bring him back.

Chapter 49

Grant's Crossing - January 2015
Five months after Joey Parker's death

Logan turned down the hallway of his modest apartment to adjust the thermostat. It was an unusually cold January, and he couldn't seem to shake the chill he'd been fighting all day long. In the kitchen, he retrieved his dinner from the oven and set it on the stove. Opening a cabinet, he set out a single plate and glanced at the pamphlet about grief counseling they offered at the LGBTQ-friendly community center in Delaware. He hadn't attended any meetings since just after Thanksgiving. He grabbed the pamphlet and wadded it up with one hand, tossing it into the open trash can in the corner. Then he dished out a serving of chicken and rice to take to his small kitchen table.

He ate alone.

Again.

In the five months since Joey's funeral, he thought of Joey every minute of every day. Joey was supposed to have been discharged right before Christmas. The two of them were supposed to have brought in the new year together.

They were supposed to be happy.

They *were* happy.

But for Logan, the grieving didn't end. He would never be able to get past the loss of the man he loved. The huge, gaping hole inside his heart would never close.

Logan would never get over Joey, but he thought he might be able to start living without him by now. Instead, it was one torturous day after another. One massive effort to breathe, to get out of bed every morning, to go to work, and to pretend he was okay. When in reality, he was falling apart at the seams.

Logan mourned not only his love but also the life they were going to make together.

The life they never even had a chance to start.

Aside from work and familial obligations, Logan had hardly been out in months. He couldn't bear the sight of seeing other couples together, laughing and holding hands. Sharing knowing looks. Stealing kisses when they thought no one else was looking or even when they were. He never begrudged them their happiness, but seeing a happy couple, whether it was a man and a woman, two men, or two women together, his mind would wander to what could have been.

What should have been.

Logan pushed the food around on his plate. He often berated himself for being unable to gather enough courage after the funeral to talk to Derek to learn how Joey died. Overhearing Tank and Derek argue during what should have been a celebration of Joey's life was like a punch to the gut. Now Logan wondered if it had been quick. His heart broke every time he thought of Joey suffering, even for a moment.

A knock at Logan's front door released him from the thoughts that held him captive after he came home each night and made him shut out the world. Flipping on the outside light, he opened the door and sucked in a quick gulp of air.

Derek Mitchell stood before him, his face stoic. His wavy hair had grown out from the military cut he'd had when they last saw each other before New Year's, and a thick beard now covered his face. A backpack was slung over his right shoulder, and his nose was red from the cold.

How long had he stood there before knocking?

"Logan," Derek choked out. "May I come in?"

He blinked a couple of times and then pulled the door open wider. "Sorry. Yes. Come in."

"Thanks." Derek took a few steps inside and turned while Logan shut the door. "Your uncle gave me your new address. I hope that's okay."

"It's fine. I was just having dinner. You want anything?" Derek declined as Logan walked back into the kitchen. "Glass of wine? I don't have any beer."

"Sure." Derek teetered back and forth on his heels as Logan grabbed a wine glass.

"Have a seat," Logan called over his shoulder as he poured a glass of merlot. Logan caught Derek scanning the sparsely decorated yet tidy apartment, filled with warm colors on the walls and inviting furniture. A small cabinet full of colorful books and toys and a small table for Allie took up residence in one living room corner.

Derek took off his coat and sat down. He set his backpack on the floor by his feet. Logan handed Derek the glass of wine, and sat back down.

Derek stared at the red liquid in the glass for a few seconds and took a sip. He set it down on the table, his eyes fixed on his hand wrapped around the stem of the glass.

"I didn't mean to leave things the way I did." Derek lifted the glass again for another sip of the wine as Logan picked up a fork and returned to pushing his food around on his dinner plate.

"I know you didn't." Logan had always hated small talk, and this was especially uncomfortable. "It was hard to hear, that's all."

The awkward silence stretched between them. Logan dropped his fork on the plate and pushed it away, slouching back against his chair. He lifted his chin and peered at Derek.

"I miss him so much." His voice cracked. Logan pressed his lips together to keep the trembling under control.

Derek blinked and swallowed as Logan picked up and emptied his own wine glass. "I know. Me, too."

With a sniff, Logan stood up and poured himself another glass of wine, setting the bottle on the table this time as he sat down again and took a long drink. Holding his glass with both hands, Logan stared at it as he spoke. "So you were with him?"

"What?"

"When he died? You were with him?" It took every ounce of effort he had, but Logan managed to hold himself together as he spoke.

"Yes."

"Was it quick?"

Derek knitted his brow.

"I mean," Logan licked his lips as his mouth went dry. "Did he suffer?"

"It was quick."

Logan stared at the man and maintained eye contact for a few seconds. Even if Derek were lying, it was the answer he wanted to hear. Logan sipped his wine as he stared across the table, not quite at Derek, not quite at anything. "Good."

"His last thoughts were of you. He wanted me to tell you he loved you."

Logan inhaled sharply. His lungs didn't seem to work, as if he'd just had the wind knocked out of him.

Derek took a deep breath and let out a loud exhale that sounded more like a cough. "I told him he could tell you himself." Derek reached down and pulled his backpack into his lap. Unzipping it, he pulled out a stack of spiral notebooks.

Logan glanced at the top of the notebooks. "What are those?"

"Journals that Joey kept while he served. He was always writing in them, but I didn't know what he wrote until..."

"Journals?"

Derek's voice was thick with emotion. "More like letters, really." He pushed them across the table toward Logan. Derek's hands were still on them, his white knuckles pressing them against the table as if he were preventing them from floating away. "To you."

Logan tilted his head, unable to pull his eyes away from the stack of notebooks. He lifted his hand and let it hover directly above them. He noticed Derek's hands didn't move as if he didn't want to let go of this piece of Joey. "And you've read them?"

Derek cleared his throat. "Yes."

Logan nodded as he lowered his hands to the notebooks and eased them closer. With another quick glance, Logan could see Derek's teeth clench as he let go. Logan steeled himself as he flipped through the pages of the first notebook, recognizing Joey's handwriting that filled the space between the light blue lines.

Logan placed his palm on top of the paper and closed his eyes. Then, he opened them and read the words the man he loved wrote. This passage was written just after Joey's first jump during airborne training. He'd been so excited to be serving and was so optimistic.

Pulling his brows together in concentration, Logan tried his best to blink back the tears burning at the back of his eyes. He didn't want to let them fall while Derek was still here.

Logan grabbed another notebook and opened it to a random page. On this page, Joey wrote about the possibility of the repeal of Don't Ask, Don't Tell, the very policy that could have gotten him dishonorably discharged simply because Joey and Logan loved each other.

Logan whispered. "Oh, Joey." His fingers brushed across the words on the page as if it were a precious relic.

Derek zipped the backpack closed as Logan continued reading. After a few minutes, Logan lifted his gaze, not caring that tears filled his eyes.

"I know." Derek said. "It took me a while to get through them."

Logan closed the notebook and slowly exhaled. "Yeah."

"Um, is there anything of his that you wanted?" Derek blurted out. "We've been keeping everything for him since his mom died."

"No." Logan could barely find the breath to form words. "I don't want anything."

"He, uh," Derek went on, "designated me as his beneficiary but, it should go to you."

Logan looked confused. "What?"

Derek closed his eyes for a moment before answering. "The... the payout the Army sent when he died...in combat. It should go to you."

"I don't need it, no." Logan sat up a little straighter. "I don't want it. Besides, you're his family, and you went through," his voice cracked again, "what he went through. It should stay with you."

"But you were going to get married," Derek pushed.

"That life is gone now." Logan half whispered, half spoke as if talking to the air... as if no one else were there to hear him. "I didn't even get to propose."

The silence was just as painfully awkward as the rest of their conversation.

"Are you still driving that old Chevy you drove in high school?"

Derek smiled, welcoming the change of subject. "Yeah. Just drove it here, actually."

"Can't believe it still runs."

"It does. Barely."

"Buy yourself a new truck. With his money." Logan forced a laugh. "I mean, you're going to need it if you're working for your dad when you're not at the fire station, right?"

"Yeah."

"Then do something good with whatever's leftover."

"I can do that."

Derek stood up and grabbed his coat. He shrugged his backpack over one shoulder and turned back to Logan, still seated at the table, clutching the notebooks in his hands. Derek reached into his jeans pocket and pulled something out. With a clinking sound that drew Logan's gaze, Derek set it on the table.

Logan stretched his arm across the table to pick up Joey's dog tags. He pressed his fingers around them and closed his eyes.

Derek walked to the door and grabbed the handle just as Logan spoke. "Tank was right."

"What?" Derek breathed out without turning around.

"Joey's gone, and it fucking sucks. More than anything; but, it's not your fault. You didn't kill him."

"I didn't save him, either."

Derek's eyes stared down at the doorknob he held in his hand.

"I know what it's like to feel like you have no options. For the love of…" Logan's voice caught in his throat, "Whatever you do, just stop blaming yourself."

"I should have brought him back to you," Derek choked out in reply.

"Don't," Logan snapped. "We both know he would never have wanted you to think like that."

"It's too late." Derek turned around and held Logan's gaze for an instant before opening the door and disappearing outside.

Clutching Joey's dog tags, Logan gave up the fight and let the tears fall.

Leaving his barely-touched dinner on the table, Logan poured himself another glass of wine and moved to the couch with the notebooks. He switched on a lamp, giving the room an eerie glow as the wind blew outside his fogged-up windows. With a shiver, he took a sip and set down the glass as he stared at Joey's last letter that he kept on the end table by the couch.

As he jostled the stack of notebooks, one fell to the floor. A picture slid out. Hands shaking, he picked it up. It was of him and Joey smiling at each other without a care in the world. He wiped his tear-soaked eyes with the back of his hand and tried to smile, but the tears put up too good of a fight.

Logan gently placed the picture of them on the arm of the couch and picked up the letter. He'd received it last August, a week or so after the funeral. It was the last one he ever received from Joey. He took care opening the envelope, setting it on the end table after he withdrew the letter. It was folded into thirds, so he pulled down the bottom third with one hand and flipped up the top third with the other.

It was dated two days before Joey died.

With a deep breath, he started reading it again.

Dear Logan,

God, I miss you! You're all I ever think about and the only thing getting me through each day. Another few weeks in this place, and we're back to Fort Benning. I'm ready to get back home and hear nothing but languages I understand. I want to go back to bad radio stations and sleeping in my own bed with a real mattress. In a few months, I'll be back home for good, where I can hold you in my arms. God, I miss that. So much. Remember that first night way back when, when we fell asleep by accident and woke up in each other's arms the next morning to the smell of bacon frying downstairs? I slept so well with your body against mine. I want that every day for us, L. Every fucking day.

I have plans for us, just like we talked about. I can't wait for us to go to Niagara Falls. Maybe we can even get married. Sure, our state won't acknowledge us yet, but until then, I can't wait to go to New York with you. Ha! We can make it a destination wedding. And yeah, it's not like flying off to the Caribbean, but it's perfect for what we need. It's perfect for us. Wait! I think I just proposed to you. Not very romantic, but I love you and want to be with you forever. I just turned 33. I'm already getting old. Do you think you can live with an old man like me?

Logan chuckled at that part since he was only two months younger.

Speaking of getting old, I'm a Sergeant First Class now. An E-7. Just got promoted the week before last. Talk about a great early birthday present. I wish Mom were still here to see this. She would have been so proud. Of course, Derek no longer outranks me. He always gave me dirty looks whenever I called him sir. He never ordered me not to, but I did it because I knew it annoyed him.

You'll be happy to know I'm not going to reenlist in December. I promise you; I'm done. I'm ready to get out into the real world, whatever that is these days. Sometimes I wonder. Do you think what we see over here really is the real world, and back home is just an escape? I don't know. Maybe that's crazy.

I already have a job lined up. Abe said he'll happily hire us back if we want, though Derek'll probably get a job as a paramedic instead of working for his dad full-time. He's far too good at helping people not to put his training to use back home. As for me, I miss pounding nails and building things, so I look forward to working for him again.

God, I miss you, Logan. So much. All we do here is destroy. I want to create something again. I want to create a life with you. When I get back, let's buy an old house, get naked and christen each room as we fix it up. Or before we fix it up, I don't care! As long as you're with me, I'll be happy. I can only hope that I make you happy, too. That's all I want in this world, L, for us to be happy and grow old together. We can do that, right?

I can't wait to be home. I promise we'll be together soon. Being with you at Niagara Falls will be incredible. Starting our new life will be the best thing in the world.

In the meantime, Logan, don't ever forget how much I fucking love you. More than anything and no matter what.

- Joey

Logan carefully refolded the letter and slipped it back into the envelope. He left the wine glass on the end table but picked up the journals. He drifted back to his bedroom, where he undressed and sat on the side of the bed. He opened the nightstand drawer and placed the letter inside, safely nestled next to a small box that contained the matching wedding rings he'd picked up the day Abe told him Joey was gone. He didn't know what else to do with Joey's dog tags, so he slid them over his head and let them hang on his chest that would never again feel his lover's touch.

As he did every night before he went to sleep, he spent a few moments memorizing Joey's picture before he turned out the light and crawled underneath the covers.

"I love you, too, Joey." Logan whispered into his pillow. "More than anything and no matter what."

Epilogue

Grant's Crossing - Six months later

DEREK SET UP IN HIS BED WITH A START. THE ROOM WAS PITCH black. A gentle breeze flowed through an open window carrying with it the sounds of crickets chirping.

He ran his hands through his damp hair as he tried to catch his breath. He tore off his sweat-soaked t-shirt and tossed it on the floor.

The dreams were so real - as if he were back there in Afghanistan, reliving that last ambush night after night.

After night.

And every night, he held his best friend's hand as Joey called for his dead mother while he breathed his last breaths.

Derek flipped on the lamp on the unpacked box he was using as a bedside table and made his way to the bathroom to splash some water on his face. Lifting his head, he stared into the same bloodshot eyes he saw each time he woke up like this.

And, like each time before, he dealt with it the same way.

Ignoring the piles of clothes and books filling his bedroom, Derek padded out to the kitchen and opened the fridge to grab a bottle of beer. A few of these, and he could get back to sleep. It usually worked, anyway. Forgetting was his preferred alternative to remembering. He sat down on his couch; Joey's couch. Derek decided to put it to good use since he didn't have any of his own furniture beyond his new bed and what was in his old bedroom at his dad's place.

Derek grabbed the remote and hit the power button. The glow of the TV lit up the room. Flipping through the channels, he settled on a baseball game playing on the west coast. The time on his clock above the counter in the galley kitchen read well after midnight. He wasn't on shift tomorrow, so maybe he could call Sarah. She was usually willing to stop by on short notice.

He finished off the bottle and got up for another, opening one and grabbing another to keep on deck.

Nearly five months into his new job as a paramedic, Derek was grateful for the distraction of a workplace where people no longer fired bullets at him. Regulations required him to shave off his beard, but at least he could let his hair grow out beyond what he'd worn while on active duty.

Kiro was proving to be good for Derek, even fun at times, though he still had a lot of adjusting to do. They worked well together and Kiro was incredibly good at his job; not to mention patient when it came to teaching him the civilian ropes. The competent, yet snarky man, was a big change from the little kid who once got so excited when Derek first called him K.

Tank also helped him get through rougher days which, at this stage, accounted for nearly every day. Tank understood what Derek was going through since he'd already made the transition to civilian life himself. Tank constantly assured him that it would get easier, something Derek often questioned but could only assume might be true.

Eventually.

He tipped the bottle back and emptied it..

Derek grabbed the previous day's Columbus Dispatch newspaper from the table and smiled at the headline.

He popped the top off another beer and took a healthy swig as he zigzagged his way through unpacked boxes and sat back down on the couch and opened up the laptop sitting on the coffee table.

With a quick glance around his sparsely furnished new apartment, he opened a new email and started typing.

Logan,

I followed your advice and used some of the money from Joey's payout to make a donation in his name to an organization that helps wounded veterans. He would have liked that, I think. They do a lot of work helping amputees get help with the prosthetics they need, along with additional physical therapy. Like Joey and my uncle, so many of our soldiers lost limbs in combat.

I also made a donation to a national organization that helps LGBTQ youth figure out their identities and provides them with safe havens. They have a suicide prevention hotline as well as shelters for kids and young adults whose families aren't as supportive as they should be. I hope you're okay with that. Maybe things will be easier for the next generation. I stuck the rest in savings, so when you're ready to get your youth center off the ground, count on me for help.

In the meantime, I just moved into a new carriage house apartment at a property being renovated by a homeowner who lives out east somewhere. Apparently, this house was his childhood home, and in the process of fixing it up, he wanted someone to live on-site, offering cheap rent in exchange for keeping the lawn mowed. Seems easy enough, but in all honesty, it's nice to have my own space for a change. I don't think I'll be good around people for a while.

Speaking of distractions, I'm cooking again, like my mom taught me. If you ever need, you always have a place to crash. It may just be a couch and a blanket, but I can at least provide you with some New Orleans-style cooking. Don't worry, I'm trying out the recipes on the guys at the station first. Bring your own wine. I'll only have beer.

I hope you're doing alright. It's been tough, but I'm trying my best for Joey's sake. Working with Tank helps. He's been a great friend and has done a lot for me now that I'm back home. It's just been so much harder without my brother and best friend.

I know you know how I feel.

- Derek

P.S. Bought a new truck.

With a smile, Derek attached a picture of his brand-new blue Silverado sitting in the driveway and hit send. He finished off his third beer while he closed the laptop. Maybe it was his fourth. He never bothered to count.

After a while, he stood up and dropped his empty bottles into the trash, the glass banging into the other empty bottle he knew was still cold. He reached into the refrigerator and popped the top off another and took a long pull. He was perfectly happy to drink himself into oblivion tonight.

Again.

He reread the headline of the morning Columbus Dispatch and smiled, thinking of how happy Joey and Logan would have been.

Gay Marriage Now Legal in Ohio

He walked over to the table and reached into one of his many unpacked boxes and pulled out a framed picture. He set down his beer bottle long enough to press his hands against the glass. Beneath it was a picture of three men: Derek, Joey, and Tank on the day of their graduation from basic training. With care, he set it on the empty shelves he'd assembled after he got off shift the day before.

The next picture from the box was a picture of his family. They were all in the backyard. Lainee was on their father's back while Derek's mom had her arms around both him and Joey. He and Joey must have been ten or eleven at the time. Lainee couldn't have been more than seven or eight.

They all looked so young and happy.

He placed that on the shelf, too. His hand reached for the last item in the box but hesitated long enough to take another drink of beer, something he needed more and more just to get through each day, though he never drank on the job. Setting the bottle back down, he steeled himself and reached inside.

He pulled out a simple, triangular-shaped frame, inside of which rested the flag his father received at Joey's funeral. He took great care as he held it with both hands and, reverently, placed it in the center of the shelf, right between the two pictures.

Derek finished off the bottle.

"I'm trying, brother. I'm just not good at this yet."

Two mornings later, at the Grant's Crossing Fire Station, Derek changed into his paramedic uniform and tossed his duffle into his locker. He paused to stare at the picture he taped inside It was of him, Joey, and Tank from one of their deployments to Afghanistan.

Tank opened his locker further down the row, dropping his own duffle inside. "Morning, Doc."

"Hey, Tank."

"We've got a new guy starting in a few weeks."

Derek arched an inquisitive brow. "Oh yeah?"

"Yeah." Tank shut his locker door with a loud clang that echoed in the otherwise empty locker room. "Chief said he served in the Marines. Needed a fresh start or something, so he's transferring down here from, uh... Michigan, I think."

Derek grunted.

Tank peered over Derek's shoulder at the picture of the two of them with Joey Parker and set a hand on Derek's shoulder. "I promise it'll get easier."

"I know," Derek acknowledged. "And it is, but...how do you get through it?"

"You don't really. You just get by. One day at a time." He forced out a small laugh, but his smile was genuine. "Sounds cliché, but we have to keep going."

"I know. And I will. It's just...."

"Hard?"

"Yeah. Next month." Derek's Adam's apple bobbed up and down. "He'll have been gone a year. We never planned for this, you know? We were all supposed to come back."

"Yeah. We were. He'd want you to keep going–"

The overhead alarm sounded, announcing a car accident.

"Come on, Doc." Tank offered an encouraging smile. "That's us."

"Right." Derek took one last look at the picture of his best friend and slammed his locker door shut.

"For Joey," Tank said.

Derek forced a smile. "For Joey."

The End

Your favorite Grant's Crossing characters return in Safe Now, Heroes of Grant's Crossing Book 2, a companion novel to Wayward Guilt. Available for pre-order at your favorite booksellers now.

Safe Now: Heroes of Grant's Crossing Book 2

Excerpt from Safe Now - Heroes of Grant's Crossing Book 2

Detroit, MI - Spring 2015

HILL STREET WAS THE WORST PART OF THE WORST neighborhood. Its glory days came and went before the first rock 'n roll tunes ever played at school dances. Once the war production slowed and came to a sudden halt, people sought out other options. In the late 1940s, families moved to the suburbs. One by one, businesses began to shutter, and soon after, schools started consolidating and bussing students farther and farther away. Pawn shops and bail bondsmen moved in where grocery stores, salons, and dressmakers once sold their wares. What were once family homes became tattoo or massage parlors. Storefront churches popped up on one end of the street, only to close and reopen on the other end under a new name with the hope of rebuilding their meager congregations. Much to the dismay of hotel management, the churches did their best mission work next to the places that rented rooms by the hour.

Street cleaners came in from time to time, but newspapers, cigarette butts, and empty bottles decorated the streets and uneven sidewalks. A police car drove by at least once per shift. Sadly, everyone knew they couldn't do much to curb the petty thievery and prostitution running rampant on these blocks. The boarded-up windows and paint peeling off the siding of foreclosed houses offered the perfect locations for squatters and drug pushers who would move in for a month or two until the police ran them out. But once the cops drove away, they would set up again in a neighboring house, occasionally renting space to the working girls and boys who walked the streets after the sun went down.

Dressed in blue jeans, a black leather jacket, and black boots, Steve Cook pulled his Harley up to the curb next to a woman wearing a short skirt and torn fishnet stockings. He rested a boot on the ground to anchor himself and pulled out a phone. He held it up to her as he took off his helmet, revealing a hard, scruffy face framed in dark blond, messy hair.

"Hey, baby." A long-haired brunette wobbled up to him on her way-too-high heels while chomping a big wad of gum. Her thick red lipstick provided a marked contrast to her chipped, yellow teeth. "Ya wanna take me on a date?"

He held up his phone and showed her a picture. "Have you seen this man?" He asked in a deep baritone voice.

She never fully closed her mouth while chewing. The smacking sounds grated on his nerves like nails on a chalkboard. Her eyes skimmed the picture. "Or are you into boys?"

Unfazed, he held it back up to the woman.

"Look again. He'd be older now. In his mid-20s."

The photo Steve showed her was of a man in his late teens or early 20s. He popped the stand of his motorcycle and rested both feet on the ground.

In front of the flickering neon lights of a payday loan store, the young woman took a better look at the picture. Leaning forward to showcase her wares on display behind a sheer, low-cut tank top and flipping her long, straight hair over to one side, she shook her head. Her caked-on makeup made her look ten years older than she probably was. She popped her gum and repeated her answer. "Nah. I ain't seen 'im."

She put her hand on his chest, and her bright red lips broke into a smile. She nodded toward the open door of the seedy motel behind her. "But if you want, baby, I can pretend I have."

Without changing his expression, he gently pushed her wrist away. "No, thanks."

"Another time then."

She turned and strutted her way to a car that had just pulled up, propositioning the driver as if Steve never existed.

"I don't think so," he muttered to himself. He secured his helmet to his motorcycle, unzipped his leather jacket, and stepped up to the curb. A small piece of trash blew down the street in the late-night breeze the moment he lifted his boot.

Steve asked the next woman and got the same answer. "Nope. Don't know him."

He repeated the question to everyone working the street that night, turning down several offers along the way.

After about a half hour, Steve spoke to a short, round man who suggested he try the next block over at the all-night diner. "Ask for Lenny. He's a skinny guy. Kind of skeevy, but he knows people. He may know him." The man walked down an alley to a parked car with a woman sitting in the passenger seat. Her head disappeared below the steering wheel the second he closed the driver's side door.

Sliding his phone into his pocket, Steve made the short walk to the aptly named Buster's Diner. He was grateful for his military training on nights like tonight. His ever-vigilant gaze scanned the area, seeing anyone and everyone who lurked inside recessed doorways or behind windows.

The neon sign was partially burned-out, making it read as Bust rather than Buster's Diner. He released a humorless laugh since it seemed par for the course in this neighborhood. Hell. The whole area was a bust. A flickering streetlamp caught his eye. It caused the shadows on this side of the street to dance around like demons ready to strike.

Nearing two am, the all-night diner kept its lights on for anyone looking for a cup of coffee or a piece of leftover pie. The last customer, who fit Lenny's description, was pulling his wallet out of his back pocket to pay his bill.

Finding a spot outside the entrance without chewed pieces of gum stuck to it, Steve leaned back and waited for the lone customer to walk out.

After a few minutes, a middle-aged man slinked out of the diner's double doors. With greasy, slicked-back hair and two-day-old stubble, he pulled a pack of cigarettes out of his jacket pocket. His shifty eyes darted around as if he were being followed.

Steve leaned back against the door frame with his hands in his pockets, and one knee kicked up against the weather-stained wall.

The other man tensed and gave him a suspicious sideways glance that didn't go unnoticed despite the fact he was trying to play it cool. Tapping the pack against his palm a few times, he stuck a cigarette between his lips and returned the box to his pocket. He brought a lighter up to his face. Cupping his other hand in front to block the light breeze, he tried to light it. No matter how many times he flicked it with his thumb, he couldn't get it to spark a flame.

Moving slowly so as not to spook him, Steve pulled a box of matches out of his jacket pocket and held it up for the man to see. He lit one and held it out to his cigarette. After taking a few quick puffs, the man narrowed his eyes while taking a long drag. "Thanks," he muttered while holding the cigarette in his mouth.

"Nice night. Isn't it?" Steve uttered as he slipped the matches back into his pocket.

The lanky man grunted, releasing tendrils of smoke from between his narrow lips.

"Lenny." Steve added.

The man stiffened.

Steve was close enough to grab him if he tried to bolt, but neither man moved.

Lenny's breathing quickened but his shifty eyes didn't make eye contact. "Do I know you?"

"No," Steve admitted with narrowed eyes. He surveyed each corner of the intersection and turned to face Lenny. "But I'm told you might help me find somebody."

"I don't know anybody."

Steve stuck his phone in front of the man's face. "This man."

Lenny's eyes looked everywhere but at the phone. Steve gently placed his hand on the man's shoulder and gave it a slight squeeze. It wasn't enough to hurt but it was enough to convey it could.

Lenny looked at a smiling young man in the photo wearing a St. Louis Cardinals T-shirt. His wavy, blond hair stuck out from underneath the red ball cap.

Steve had cropped himself out of the picture he showed, though he kept a copy of the original in his wallet.

"He's a kid," Lenny exclaimed.

Steve dropped his voice. "Look again. He'd be a little older now."

Lenny spent a few seconds studying the photo before recognition flickered in Lenny's eyes.

"Yeah. I know him."

Steve's heart raced, but he kept his cool.

"That's RC," Lenny whispered.

"RC?"

"Yeah."

Where is he?"

"Not here. They moved out last night."

"Moved out? Where are they going?"

"Columbus."

"Ohio?"

"Yeah."

"Where in Columbus?" Steve squeezed tighter.

Lenny shrugged.

"Who's he with?"

He looked away. The end of his cigarette glowed bright orange as he took another long drag. He didn't answer.

"Who?" Steve tightened his fingers.

"Some of Jett's people." He cringed and tried to free himself from under Steve's tightening grip. "They took him a while back when Mac wasn't looking, but you didn't hear it from me."

Steve dropped his hand off the man's shoulders and dropped his chin to his chest. He released a long breath and turned to face the wall. With no warning, he smacked it. Hard. "FUCK!"

He didn't care that he made Lenny jump and scamper down the street. He stalked down to his motorcycle without another word, glaring at anyone who dared look in his direction. He was as close as he'd been to his brother in months.

And he missed him.

Pre-order your copy of Safe Now, Heroes of Grant's Crossing Book 2, at your favorite booksellers.

Safe Now: Heroes of Grant's Crossing Book 2

Acknowledgments

Thanks so much to my family and friends for supporting and encouraging me throughout my writing journey!

Joey Parker got his start when I wrote my initial draft for *End of a New Life*, what will be book 3 or 4 in the Heroes of Grant's Crossing series. In that book, Derek opens up to his eventual love interest enough to say his best friend, Joey Parker, didn't make it back from Afghanistan. It was only a sentence or two, but it spoke volumes to me. That one event completely changed the trajectory of Derek Mitchell's life and turned him into the broken man he becomes.

I didn't know Joey then but felt he needed his own story. He needed his own family, his own background, his own life, his own friends, and his own love, his own loss. I'm thrilled to have given it all to him, even though I knew from the start that I would take it all away.

Derek and Joey were best friends, and this book shows the beginnings of a man dealing with an unspeakable trauma from a hellish situation when Joey was lost on the battlefield. Derek has a long, arduous road ahead of him. I hope you'll all want to travel alongside him.

So without further adieu, I want to thank my mom who told me to write my own book after I complained about a bad romance novel I'd read. My parents have read through so many excerpts and so many iterations of this story with the response of: "Might have a few too many f-bombs in this chapter...", or "So, when are you publishing?", and "When's the next book coming out?". And folks wonder why I have no patience!

Thanks to Kai for inspiring me to accept my mom's challenge.

Thanks to the world's best alpha readers: Dan Dakoning, Liberty Jasnoch, and Andrea Ard; and some absolutely fabulous beta readers: Michael Robert, Yvonne Long, Laura Hagerty, and Mom & Dad (obviously!).

To my editor, Amy Lehman of Sagewood Publishing: Thank you for helping to ensure that the book I release into the wild is the absolute best quality story it can be. I appreciate your letting me pay you to judge me - especially my punctuation skills, or lack thereof, which are oh - so - judgeable!

Thanks, Kylie, for the beautiful cover that draws readers' eyes to my book.

Thanks to Jeremy Eldred for my first-ever pre-order!

There's no way I could have ever written this book without the generosity of both time and knowledge of two awesome U.S. Army Rangers - including one combat medic-turned-paramedic, the real-life version of my character, Derek Mitchell (job-wise, anyway)! They declined to have me include their names, but jokingly agreed that "Awesome Army Rangers" was a more-than-sufficient descriptor for them both. Personally, I don't think it does them justice - neither for what they've done to help me personally nor for the service they provided our nation. From the bottom of my heart, gentlemen: THANK YOU!

To Amy, Deb, Kristy, and Rachel - a.k.a. Keira Collins, Emme Grange, Krissyann Granger, and Maquel A. Jacob, four fabulous Indie authors and friends. Thank you so much for putting up with my myriad of questions since our 20BooksVegas trip. I will be forever grateful to all of you for all the help you've provided and patience you've shown throughout my publishing journey. Everyone needs Vegas friends and we definitely need to go out to Gordon Ramsay's Burger again.

About the Author

Wayward Guilt is H.M.S. Brown's debut novel and Book 1 of her Heroes of Grant's Crossing series. She is an avid knitter, crocheter and voracious reader who stumbled into writing during lockdown in 2020 after complaining to her mom about a book she didn't like. When her mom challenged her to write her own, Grant's Crossing was born.

Though hired to do the bidding of her evil, yet adorable cat, Michonne, she keeps her day job in order to maintain a roof over her library and yarn stash.

In the meantime, you can find H.M.S. Brown online at the following locations.

Official Website www.hmsbrown.com
Instagram https://www.instagram.com/grantscrossing/